Fic LANDERS
Landers, Scott, 1952-
Coswell's guide to
Tambralinga : a novel

WITHDRAWN

P9-CJF-963

Coswell's Guide to

Tambralinga

Coswell's Guide to

Tambralinga

A novel by

Scott Landers

Farrar, Straus and Giroux / New York

Farrar, Straus and Giroux
19 Union Square West, New York 10003

Distributed in Canada by Douglas & McIntyre Ltd.
Printed in the United States of America
First edition, 2004

An earlier version of chapter 6 of this novel appeared in the Fall 2003 issue of
Cimarron Review under the title "Loved Thing."

Library of Congress Cataloging-in-Publication Data
Landers, Scott, 1952–
    Coswell's guide to Tambralinga : a novel / Scott Landers.
        p.   cm.
    ISBN 0-374-13021-3 (hardcover : alk. paper)
    1. Americans—Asia, Southeastern—Fiction.   2. Asia, Southeastern—
Fiction.   3. Culture conflict—Fiction.   4. Married people—Fiction.
5. Travelers—Fiction.   6. Islands—Fiction.   I. Title.

PS3612.A5478C67 2004
813'.6—dc22

                                                           2003021116

EAN: 978-0-374-13021-3

Designed by Jonathan D. Lippincott

www.fsgbooks.com

10   9   8   7   6   5   4   3   2   1

For Leah

Frédéric's ideal was to furnish a Moorish palace for himself, and spend his life reclining on cashmere divans, beside a murmuring fountain, attended by native servants. And the things in these daydreams became so real that in the end they made him feel as miserable as if he had lost them.

—Gustave Flaubert, *L'Éducation sentimentale*

Contents

Part One

Brothel

1

That morning a certain phrase lodged itself in Conrad's head, a quote from the guidebook that began playing itself over and over like a refrain from a French rondeau. The phrase concerned Ko Neak Pean, the island just adjacent to the one he and his wife were visiting, the second of seven from the mainland, whose dark profile Conrad had glimpsed on the afternoon of their third day, just a hairsbreadth above the horizon. The guidebook had said something like, "Recent years have seen an increase in ferry traffic to the island, mostly from mainlanders visiting the infamous Princess Daha Hotel. Single male travelers invariably tell us that when things get slow on Ko Banteay or Ko Prasat, one can always take the boat over to the brothel." This last part—about taking the boat over to the brothel—was what stuck.

Conrad liked the sound of the words. It was a phrase he might drop while describing his vacation to one of the engineers in the office: "And of course, you can always take the boat over to the brothel." It was a phrase greased with the insinuation of tropical delights, yet at the same time suggesting the smug indifference of an enlightened traveler. Conrad classed the phrase with others he'd come across in travel memoirs ("we arrived in Carcassonne without so much as a *sou*"), phrases that alluded to an enviable sophistication. At least Conrad envied it. He'd never been farther from the U.S. than Canada before this, never taken a vacation longer than ten days, let alone a sabbatical.

"On sabbatical"—here was another phrase you could swish about your palate like pricey cabernet. Of course it wasn't a sabbatical in the traditional sense, just a long vacation his company compelled upper-level employees to take every five years. But if he could repeat, without blushing, the revised mission statements that came down from the CEO's office nearly every quarter, statements that included phrases like "creating wisdom infrastructure" and "information empowering," then perhaps "sabbatical" might not be such a stretch.

Conrad adjusted the pillow in his hammock and looked across the porch of his teak bungalow, past sand and sea to a hazy white patch along the horizon. He regretted losing the guidebook. He would have enjoyed rereading the section on Ko Neak Pean, for gradually the refrain in his head was beginning to represent an entitlement, a compensation he was owed for agreeing to take his wife to an obscure and preposterous vacation destination.

"I was on sabbatical, you see," he heard himself reminisce at a hypothetical party (at his stage of life, parties were becoming increasingly hypothetical), "when I found myself on this boat going to the brothel." He pictured his lanky form being swept up in a general rush from the ferry dock and down a narrow, winding street, throngs of young men pressing him forward.

The brothel itself he could not quite picture. The term "brothel" was deliberately vague, he felt, unlike "whorehouse" or "hookshop," for instance, and suggested wholesome and invigorating sport. Perhaps it was because its first syllable was "broth," which Conrad associated with heartiness and health; and because the entire word sounded like "brawl," thus suggesting rigorous activity.

He opened a distressed paperback and tried to find his place, but none of the paragraph starts looked familiar. He went back page by page to the middle of the previous chapter before anything clicked. This backward scanning left him with the beginnings of a headache. For a moment he was lost in the rows of faded letters, his gaze following the white spaces between the lines as if trying to penetrate the gaps in a picket fence.

He closed his eyes, meaning to rest them for just a moment. The wind nudged the leaves of the shading banana tree, so that sunlight fell across his closed lids. Against the flickering orange screen that suddenly filled his field of vision, he pictured his wife's silhouette, the mass of wavy hair hanging just above the shoulders, the slim, taut torso, the pouting lower lip. It was a familiar form, one that had once been the entire world, but was now just one of its regular features, like fog and traffic lights. There was in fact something menacing about the habitual tilt of the head.

Lucy had arisen early that morning and gone down to the restaurant without him, still angry with him for losing the guidebook. It was just as well. Since their arrival on the island, Conrad had all but given up breakfast. Dishes at the bungalow restaurant were invariably fried, and Conrad's stomach couldn't handle oily foods before noon. Lucy had returned while he was shaving and announced her plan for the day's outing. "A trek in the jungle," she'd called it, and he'd seen right away that she meant to discourage him from joining her. There was no forest to speak of on Ko Banteay, just groves of banana and coconut trees. And she knew his dislike of strenuous hiking. If she'd used the word "stroll," he'd have taken it as an invitation.

She'd become moody and withdrawn the last few days, the way she'd been at home for months until she'd received the inspiration for this trip. In a bookstore one rainy evening just before Thanksgiving, she'd been transfixed by the calendar images of white sand and green corals, and temple ruins swarming with monkeys. At first Conrad was taken aback by this unprecedented spasm of romanticism, but was later grateful for it when Lucy's dismal spells vanished and she began planning and organizing the trip with something like her old cheerfulness. "Cheerfulness" was not quite the word. She'd done a lot of smiling, but always there was an edge to it, like sunshine on a clear winter's day.

And Conrad had humored her, not believing she would ultimately go through with it. While he and Lucy had often talked about taking an extended trip, their speculations had always centered on the Mediterranean. No thought was given to Southeast Asia, to tiny nations he'd never heard of, in the middle of seas he couldn't find on a map.

The silhouette faded. Conrad found himself mentally composing the note he would leave:

Gone to the mainland to change money. Back by morning.
Or the next day at the latest. We'll see how it goes.

Gone to the mainland. Possibly it was not a lie. Possibly he
would make it to the mainland, where they had electricity on a
grid, and therefore banks, and change his traveler's checks into rials. But there really was no urgency. He might not make it past
the next island, if anything there caught his fancy.

Back by morning. Or the next day at the latest. A lot could be
accomplished in a single afternoon. On the other hand, a night or
two apart might not be a bad thing for them. He sat up in the
hammock and rubbed the purple splotches from his eyes. It was
such a simple proposition: get a moto-taxi into town and then
walk to the ferry. The ferry schedule was posted on the restaurant
wall, right next to the counter and the little window where he ordered food and paid bills. He'd scanned it a dozen times while
waiting for his change.

Now came a familiar surge in his nether regions, a feeling unwilling to declare itself as either anxiety or excitement. He stared
at a group of sunburned German children trooping down to the
water's edge, resplendent with fluorescent snorkeling gear. As
they donned their pink flippers and adjusted their sparkling green
masks, Conrad realized the children intended to swim along the
reef before the sun got too high. By noon it would be too hot to
do anything but sit under the thatched roof of the open-air
restaurant and write postcards or play chess with the island's lone
Japanese tourist. Lucy, back from her walk, would huddle in the
bungalow, tired and sweaty and peeved for no reason. It might be
useful just to see what a brothel looked like. He was certainly old
enough to have been in one or two, but regrettably he hadn't.
He'd entered a bar maybe a dozen times since leaving graduate
school, and the last time was to ask for directions.

He spent little time packing, spurred by the thought that Lucy
might return early from her walk and start asking a lot of annoying questions about the purpose of his trip. Or worse, decide she
wanted to come along. He stuffed some T-shirts and a pair of

khaki slacks into the large nylon duffel bag, a bag he'd meant to fill with souvenirs. The guidebook had insisted such a bag was a necessity on this kind of trip, but the handicrafts available on the island were a huge disappointment: tremendously ugly silk paintings of palm trees and sunsets, crude clay statues of reclining Buddha or sitting Buddha, top-heavy figurines of Hindu gods carved from sandalwood, penis-shaped amulets to be worn around the neck or attached to key chains, exotic insects encased in clear, hard plastic. It was as if the idea of handicrafts had not occurred to the locals before the arrival of tourists. Around the restaurant he'd heard it said that Ko Banteay had already been spoiled by surfers and scuba divers, that if you wanted an "authentic" experience of the country, you had to visit the undeveloped parts of the bigger islands or go up into the mountains on the mainland. This struck Conrad as a dubious proposition, authenticity in his mind being closely aligned with parasitic worms and an absence of indoor plumbing. Still, a search for the real Tambralinga was as good an excuse as any for wanting to get off the island. He started out the door and then, as an afterthought, returned to fetch his sleeping bag—a light nylon job that took up hardly any room in the duffel.

Past the restaurant, a steep path led up to the road. There, under the shade of a huge tree, three motor scooters stood. Reclining on each, feet on the handlebars, heads pillowed on the rear fenders, were the drivers, gracile young men with slick black hair and sunglasses, dressed in batik shirts and immaculate white trousers. At the sight of Conrad, they all sat up and took hold of their handlebars. One of them patted the seat behind him and beckoned to Conrad. Another started his motor and smiled.

A price was negotiated—that is, the driver reduced it by two rials when Conrad hesitated—and Conrad climbed aboard the biggest of the three bikes. As they pulled away the two other drivers resumed their reclining positions on their scooters. At no time had their feet actually touched the ground.

"Tambralinga," Lucy had announced one night over a cornish hen stuffed with morels and red grapes, and a salad of watercress

and blue cheese. "Tam-bra-ling-ga." It might have been the name
of the featured instrument on an album of world music, a bowed
instrument of polished horn and oxhide favored by the nomads
along the Silk Road. "Tambralinga." Possibly a chapter in the
Kama Sutra.

"It's like Shangri-La," she assured Conrad. The country was
guarded by steep mountains on the west, by dense mangroves to
the south. But the islands in the gulf were the big draw. The *New
York Times* said they compared favorably to Bora-Bora, and yet
no one seemed to have heard of them until just last year.

"I thought we were going to the Aegean," Conrad said, but
was made to feel timid and conventional for this protest. Greece
was overrun, and expensive. Too close to Germany.

"If you want a real getaway, you have to travel to the frontiers
of our despoiling civilization."

Conrad recalled these words as the motorcycle bounced along
the dirt road, winding its way through hills strewn with precari-
ously placed boulders. Lucy had been quoting something of
course. She was always quoting, could not engage in a discussion
unarmed with references of some sort. As they descended toward
the town and the harbor, gaps appeared in their path, places
where the monsoon rains had washed away the road. The driver
slowed the bike and coasted around the inside rim of an enormous hole, sounding his scabrous buzzer as another moto-taxi
charged up the hill. There was really only one way around the
hole, and both motorbikes had reached its perimeter at the same
time. Conrad looked the other way as his driver cried out, felt the
rush of air as metal and flesh brushed past. In this country there
was no such thing as a margin of error; the compromises drivers
made when vying for space on the narrow roads were always
worked out at the last possible moment. On their way from the
airport Conrad had felt what he'd imagined was his life starting
to flash before his eyes, as their bus driver attempted to pass a
row of cars on a blind curve and discovered a truck coming the
other way. The situation had been resolved miraculously, mysteri-

ously, on the other side of Conrad's splayed fingers, while Lucy sat impassively, leafing through a magazine.

He remembered being surprised that she could read on the bus. Just glancing at a page while the bus was in motion would make Conrad ill. During the fifteen years they'd been together, they'd never ridden a bus together. Nor a boat, unless one counted the ferry ride from San Francisco to Sausalito.

They hit a rock. Conrad felt himself sliding off the back of the bike. He grabbed the driver's shoulders for balance and then noticed the outlandish size of his thumb and fingers against the man's back. In a country of bantamweights, of fine-boned, delicate frames, his own body felt grotesque: a stomach that required three normal portions before it began to feel satisfied, legs that invariably hung over the edge of hotel beds, feet that could not be squeezed into locally made sandals. Should he choose to enter the brothel, he would undoubtedly have to stoop. The birdlike women would laugh and banter in their unintelligible language about who would tow this lurching juggernaut up the narrow staircase.

Or perhaps not. Perhaps there was no staircase. Perhaps the girls would barely look up, exhausted from a recent boatload of German tourists. (The Gulf of Siam, as it turned out, was swarming with them.) Most likely he would experience no embarrassment, no feeling at all, and the whole affair would boil down to nothing, an empty day in another empty week.

The terrain leveled off. There was pavement. Huts offering cold drinks and souvenirs appeared. Signs nailed to the trunks of coconut trees announced hotels, restaurants, and scuba-diving schools. They passed building sites where bare-chested workmen in short sarongs wielded picks. Then a row of buildings sprang up on either side of the road, with shops selling T-shirts and snorkeling gear and used paperbacks in English, German, French, and Dutch, and open-air bars where big-bellied white men in baseball caps sipped drinks from green coconuts. Music blared from the shops and the bars, rock and roll from Thailand, folk tunes from Malaysia, disco from Hong Kong.

At the pier a group of touts—young men with a few words of English or German—had gathered to meet the next boatload of tourists from the capital, whom they would drag off to hotels in town or bungalows on the other side of the island or steer into nearby fabric stores for a hefty commission. The boat was just unloading as they arrived, bursting like a milkweed pod with the billowing white forms of the budget tourists, who almost without exception were dressed in loose-fitting cotton pajamas that Tambralingan tailors seemed to have created just for them. The guidebook had stressed the importance of covering the body, especially the legs, to avoid offending the sizable Muslim population. The heat and humidity rendered blue jeans too uncomfortable, and tying a sarong so that it didn't fall off at an inopportune moment was too tricky for the average visitor. But already Conrad had begun to question the way things were laid out in the guidebook. As he saw it, entering this country was like being admitted to a hospital. They issued you a uniform, a simple garment that identified you as recipient of services offered. Maybe it helped the people cope with this influx of foreigners, to be able to think of them as patients. His own uniform was of nylon and rayon and polyester, was mostly khaki and light green, featured large pockets with zippers and trousers that converted to shorts. It had about it vague intimations of safari, or at least the fantasy of jungle adventure, and marked him glaringly, he realized, as a middle-aged, middle-class American.

As he purchased his ticket at the little office at the foot of the pier, Conrad felt the first flicker of doubt. Was he perhaps doing exactly what Lucy wanted him to do? Was it possible that her moodiness had been subtly engineered to produce just such an outcome? For her spells never dissipated until he did something reckless, something out of character. Once, he had left her in a restaurant, in the middle of the soup course, and walked the three miles back home. Another time he'd shattered a vase by throwing it on the floor when her back was turned, explaining afterward that it had "just slipped." And both times he'd detected relief, even sly rejoicing on her part. It was his equanimity that made her crazy.

He slipped the ticket into his pocket and slung the duffel over his shoulder. During this outburst, anyway, he would maintain his equanimity. As he walked down the wooden pier, the expedition took on a symbolic importance. A visit to the brothel now revealed itself as the main purpose of his trip to Tambralinga, just as a visit to the Wailing Wall or the Church of the Holy Sepulcher might be his purpose in traveling to Jerusalem.

The boat was not the one he'd pictured. True, it was larger and slower than the one he and Lucy had taken from the capital. It sat lower in the water and had a pleasant weather-beaten look about it. But instead of natives, the boat was filled with young tourists in their white pajama outfits. He moved carefully down the steel ladder to the deck below and picked his way through the travelers who sat cross-legged next to their rucksacks and bedrolls, smoking cigarettes and chattering in languages that could have been Dutch or Danish or German dialect. Seating was available in the air-conditioned cabin for an additional eighty rials. But Conrad now kindled vague notions of being an outdoorsman, someone who drank healthy broth and engaged in vigorous brawling, and so he sought a space on the open deck big enough to park his large frame. The rear deck was packed. At the very back of the boat, a thin young man with longish blond hair had set up a video camera on a tripod and hovered anxiously over some bit of equipment, adjusting knobs, pressing an earphone against his ear. And when he moved the tripod, he failed to notice how the legs jostled the passengers seated nearby.

Conditions on the forward deck looked more promising. Two young women made space for Conrad and motioned for him to sit down. He nodded his thanks and one of them, big-boned and blond, with those full Scandinavian lips so familiar from cigarette ads, smiled at him. She looked a little like Liv Ullmann and Con-

rad wondered if she might be Swedish. As he settled down next to
her, she said something indistinct to her friend, a petite woman
with long hair on the cusp between light brown and dishwater
blond. The smaller woman laughed and covered her face, and
replied in hushed tones. Conrad straightened up and looked out
to sea. They were undoubtedly regretting their invitation to him,
had miscalculated the amount of space he required. He felt his
ears and forehead flush.

The blond woman laughed in a husky, sensuous way, then
turned to Conrad and smiled again. She really did look like Liv
Ullmann, he thought, the young Liv Ullmann he'd seen in a movie
many years before. It had been a black-and-white movie about an
invasion of a small seaside town. He recalled Liv being forced to
say something to the invader's movie camera and later seeing herself on TV, mouthing army propaganda—the slogans having been
flagrantly overdubbed onto her grimacing lips.

The smaller woman said something and her eyes momentarily
met Conrad's. He could tell that she didn't mean to catch his eye;
apparently she only wanted to avoid looking in the opposite direction. Conrad remembered how at the movie's end Liv Ullmann
sat in a lifeboat floating in a sea of corpses, speaking slowly at the
camera. Liv was Norwegian and so must have been speaking
Swedish with an accent, probably the equivalent of a Canadian
accent if the whole situation was somehow transported to North
America. North America was where he'd seen the movie. It had
been his first date with Lucy, a rainy Wednesday in Berkeley, an
evening at the Pacific Film Archive, and even then the film had
seemed ancient.

Conrad identified the source of the women's amusement. Farther up the deck, toward the prow, stood a Westerner dressed
only in a sarong. While this form of dress was approved for
workmen and farmers, it was deemed inappropriate for men of a
higher station, especially Europeans. The guidebook had been
very clear on this point, filling half a page in bold type. It was not
just that the foreigner had bared his heavily muscled torso, but
that his sarong was unbelievably short, little more than a

miniskirt that left his pole-vaulter's legs exposed to mid-thigh. He stood, arms folded, looking out to sea, his blond hair, streaked here and there with hints of gray, falling nearly to his shoulders. He had to know he'd become a figure of fun, Conrad noted, and that his pose made him look even more absurd. He was certainly old enough to know that.

As this thought arrived, Conrad again felt himself flush. He pretended for a moment that the heat in his face was the result of the sun emerging from behind a cloud. He noted the sweat that was pouring from his hands where they touched the deck. But then it occurred to Conrad that he and this fellow in the miniskirt were probably the only two on deck over thirty years of age. He was drawing down the spotlight on both of them, making them both ridiculous. By his stance he seemed to mock everything Conrad was trying to do. There was no longer any pretense of being "swept along"; the whole business had become appallingly deliberate. The visit to the other island suddenly seemed a rickety proposition. Perhaps he would go on to the mainland and spend the day exploring the city or the town or whatever there was to explore. Perhaps he would just get off the boat now.

The blond one spoke distinctly in her Scandinavian tongue. Each word contained a nugget of something familiar, something tantalizingly close to English, but the meaning remained out of reach, enclosed by a hedge of Norse consonants. The other woman replied and Conrad sensed a latticework going up around him, a construction of concepts and perceptions too subtle to be rendered into English. And he felt the familiar fear that he was missing it, that better half of existence, the throbbing center of what it meant to be alive, that everything was slipping past.

He stood up, intent on leaving the boat. A young man at the stern, a Tambralingan dressed in baggy blue pants, blew twice on his silver whistle. A boy on the pier untied the rope and threw it to him. The engines surged. The boat lurched forward. Conrad sat back down. Okay, so he was going to the island. And then maybe the mainland. Lucy wanted to be alone, that was just fine. She could be alone all goddamn week.

2

The breeze picked up as they headed out to sea. A lock of Scandinavian hair blew across Conrad's face. Its owner, the smaller woman, apologized in English as she recaptured it and tied it back, and this led somehow to introductions. Her name was Birgit. The tall blond woman's name was Eva. They were both from Stockholm.

"Are you going to Ko Neak Pean or on to the Sri Kala?" Birgit asked.

"The island," Conrad murmured, embarrassed to admit that he didn't know what she was talking about. "Then maybe the—the other, if there is time."

"There's always the time," Eva replied. "In this place always. That's why we come." She produced a cigarette from her woven purse and put a match to it, which the wind immediately blew out. She tried again with the same result. The third time Conrad tried to shelter the flame with his hands, but instead knocked the cigarette out of the girl's mouth. Birgit convulsed with laughter. One of those moments, Conrad consoled himself, that appear funny when witnessed from a certain angle.

"Here," Eva said, handing Conrad the matches. "You light, okay? And I'll cup my hands around." She produced another cigarette and everything went as she proposed.

"Everyone in the States is trying to stop smoking," Conrad said and then immediately felt foolish for having done so. It wasn't true, for one thing. Women and teens were lighting up more than ever, and cigars had suddenly come out of hiding. Conrad tried to qualify his statement: in some states smoking was banned in the workplace, in restaurants, and even bars.

"Ah yes," Eva smiled, pushing a strand of blond hair behind her ear. "The Puritans." Conrad cleared his throat. He hoped she wasn't lumping him under that category. He'd been warned that foreigners often had extraordinary ideas about Americans and that there was no point in trying to argue with them.

"Everyone in this country smokes," Conrad forged ahead. Eva nodded.

"American cigarettes, yeah?"

"Hey," Birgit said. "You think that Tarzan guy up there, you think he is smoking?" Conrad looked at the deck in front of him.

"I don't know."

"He's American, yeah?" There was an unpleasant edge to her voice.

"I don't know."

"Yes! Obvious. He is so extreme. America is a big country and so has the many extremists."

"I don't follow you. Why does that mean he smokes?"

"Yes, I think so," Birgit said.

"No," Conrad replied. "I'm asking you. What does being an extremist have to do with smoking?"

"Because," Birgit answered. "Extremists have always the contradiction inside. So I say he is pushing—making the push-ups with the heavy things—"

"Weights? Lifting weights?"

"Yeah. And after that, lighting his cigarette. I can see it, yeah?" She exchanged a slightly ironic smile with Eva and then they were quiet for a while, apparently mesmerized with the deep blue of the sea and the jagged silhouettes of small islands rising along the eastern horizon.

Eva pursed her full, Swedish lips and Conrad found himself wondering if her legs were also like Liv Ullmann's—the young Liv Ullmann, that is. What was the name of that film? Lucy would remember the name. She had a good memory for details.

Conrad started as the lips fired off a question in his direction. Was he traveling alone, they wanted to know. Was he married? Before he knew what he was saying, he confessed that he and his wife were considering a separation. Birgit didn't seem to grasp what he meant by "separation," so he said "divorce" and she took that to mean that he was recently divorced. And as these words tumbled out, he realized that everything had just ratcheted up a notch. Had they separated? he wondered. *We'll see how it goes.*

If he didn't come back tonight, surely Lucy would take it as a sign. Would she feel relieved that one of them had finally made a decision, that now she was finally free? No, the relief would be only momentary. Weeks of blind rage would surely follow. "How dare he?" she would repeat to herself, to her friends on the phone. Then, playing the part of the jilted spouse to the max, she would run home to clean out the bank accounts, sell off the portfolio, hire a lawyer, report to their friends what would turn out to be the defining moment of their marriage: how she had struggled to save it with a second honeymoon (did people still use that expression?), and how he'd destroyed it with his belligerence. Or, better still, how he'd ripped up her picture-postcard paradise and thrown the pieces back in her face.

She had a way of knitting a verbal cocoon around herself, of recounting events even as they occurred, realigning them along the axis of her peculiar logic. The trip was because of him, for his sake. He'd forced her hand, yes, because somebody had to do something. Never mind that he'd expressed not the slightest interest in exotic vacation destinations, that he couldn't keep his eyes open at any of Dave and Linda's slide shows. Never mind that since they arrived on the island she couldn't stand being in the same room with him for more than twenty minutes. No matter what happened, it was always his fault.

He looked out at the water. An unnatural blue, he noted, a color produced by the toilet-bowl cleaners his mother used to buy. Flying fish appeared off the starboard bow and everybody stood up to see them. He remained seated, looking instead at his open palm. One of the lines represented his life, another his heart, but the vast majority were just wrinkles.

When Lucy returned from one of her walks or from an hour

or two of snorkeling along the edge of the reef, she would at first seem flushed and exhilarated. She would look at him with a shy eagerness, a look he remembered from years ago, her mouth poised for a smile. The smile never arrived, however. Invariably, he would miss some allusion in her conversation, some reference to the island's geography, or the strange history of the country, or the magical atmosphere they were supposedly soaking up. And when his remarks betrayed his ignorance, she would squint at him as though he were a stranger who'd stumbled into the frame of a picture she was trying to compose. He'd feel himself growing translucent, insubstantial, as his every attempt to regain substance brought on a scathing response.

"Did you say the big mosque was just over on the mainland here?"

"Page five in the guidebook. Right where I showed you yesterday."

"Right."

"I thought you'd have gotten past page five by now."

"Okay!"

So he'd set about studying the guidebook—and not just to please her. To tell the truth, he'd begun to covet her enthusiasm, as well as her command of local place names and the bits of historical gossip she could recite. But then he'd lost the guidebook—and after going to such lengths to protect it! He covered the book with a towel while he ate his lunch, locked it inside the bungalow when they went swimming, washed and dried his hands before sitting down with it that afternoon. But somehow after his nap it was missing, and although he searched the room and the porch and even the sand underneath their little stilt house, he failed to find it. Lucy was livid. Getting a new copy in all likelihood meant a long trip by boat back to the capital, to one of the few English-language bookstores in the country that might have it in stock. The used editions for sale in the little bookstores along the waterfront in Ko Banteay were too old to be any use. And the government publications, little blue books printed on pulp paper, were so full of misinformation that experienced travelers claimed they were dangerous. There was really only one guidebook for Tambralinga, written by a New Zealander and a German, printed in Australia, available everywhere, it seemed, outside the country itself.

"On purpose," Lucy had hissed. "You did it on purpose. You don't think I can see that? And not only my book, but my lists, all of my lists are gone."

She was a great one for making lists, long lists of sites to visit and of transport schedules, all laser-printed and highlighted in different colors to correspond to sections of the guidebook that she'd blocked out in the same colors. Without her lists, the structure, momentum, the whole point of the trip was thrown into jeopardy.

"Well, you're mistaken," Conrad said, trying to sound unruffled.

"Well," Lucy mimicked, and then stalked off.

The need to defend himself, to justify himself, evaporated at that moment. He watched her stomp off—he could admit this now—with a certain amount of satisfaction. Protesting his innocence would have been pointless. Obviously she'd made up her mind that he was the root of all evil, and if he could do no right, then why not enjoy the fruits of his alleged wrongdoing? He summoned the beginnings of what he felt would be an ironic smile— he hadn't enough bile for an outright sneer—and hoped that she would turn and see it. She kept going, however, without looking back.

He gave up on his hopes for Eva's legs. Pointless, he decided: he might have had a daughter her age, if he'd met Lucy earlier, and married her right off the bat—and if she'd been able to conceive. He only meant to have a look at the brothel and now he wouldn't even do that, not with Tarzan in the picture. Yet it seemed that he was already divorced, at least when the whole business was translated into Swedish.

"You will visit the ancient city?" Birgit asked, leaning forward to intercept Conrad's gaze. It came to Conrad that she had asked the question twice.

"On the island, you mean? I didn't know there was one." He explained about the guidebook.

The ruins of Tambralinga, the ancient city, were on the mainland, Birgit explained, near Sri Kala. Temples made of sandstone and granite, covered for centuries with jungle, uncovered only twenty years before. If he wanted to see it, he had better go quickly. A dam, financed by the IMF and lots of Malaysian money, was scheduled to inundate the small valley where the ruins were situated. The dam would generate badly needed electricity but would wipe out most of the rain forest in the new national park. It would also destroy the fisheries on one of Tambralinga's major rivers.

"And when the dam is finished, there is so much debt, they must sell the electric power out from the country, yeah? To Kuala Lumpur," Birgit concluded. The Swedes looked at him with one face, a sardonic expression meant to suggest a wisdom beyond their collective years. Conrad remembered such wise faces from his college days at Berkeley, as well as from Lucy's college days (which, admittedly, came much later). Particularly vivid in his memory was the insufferable smugness of Lucy's friends, the ones who'd been too young for the Free Speech Movement or even the Black Panther period, but who nonetheless finessed the impression of having seen it all.

Conrad shook his head, as if to express solidarity with the Swedes' wonder at human stupidity. Yet it was hard for him to see how a country could get along without electricity. Did they really expect the Tambralingans to stay in the dark forever?

"Politics is always a slippery business," he said.

And what was his business, they wanted to know. The term "systems architecture specialist" was out of his mouth before he knew what was happening and this led to an overly long explanation of computer systems and business-to-business transactions and the problems of integrating client-server and Web technologies with older mainframe systems.

Eva bit her luscious lower lip and frowned slightly. It was hard enough getting this stuff across to native English speakers, and Conrad could see how the women chafed under the assault of acronyms, but he couldn't stop himself. Clearly, they lacked a basic understanding of the infrastructure that was the future of world commerce, of civilization itself. His own role in this long march, in this great leap forward, was a modest one: once he'd been on an engineering team that was creating new products; now he was more of a consultant, helping companies build their information systems. But it was bracing to be involved in breakthrough after breakthrough, a revolution that was going to utterly transform the globe.

"That's very interesting," Birgit said when he'd finished. She turned to Eva again and said something indistinct. Eva dug in her purse and produced another cigarette, which she helped Birgit light.

"Don't worry," Conrad smiled. "End of lecture."

"No, it was very interesting. Really."

"But I still don't know—" Eva confessed. "You're an engineer?"

"Sure, if you like. It's more about—" He stopped himself. He could go on all day about the implications, but instead asked the girls about themselves. They were both still in school, Eva in chemistry, which she hated, and Birgit in psychology.

They were quiet for a while. Flying fish appeared off the left side of the boat and Eva decided to go over for a better look. Conrad stayed put. Ahead, the vague intimations of a land mass lying low along the horizon was evolving into something mountainous and green, looming with possibilities. For the first time since leaving home, Conrad felt a twinge of excitement. For a single mad moment, he let himself wander on jungle paths and sleep naked on deserted beaches, staring up at the stars through coconut palms. Of course there was no reason to think that the island ahead would be radically different from the one he'd left behind, yet it seemed to possess a hopeful radiance.

His gaze fell on the Tarzan character, who was lighting a ciga-

rette. As he watched, Conrad noted (with some irritation) a growing envy in himself. The man wasn't just smoking; he was in-
dulging in a vice, visibly relishing every articulated sensation.
This was obvious from the way he rolled the thick, probably
French cigarette between thumb and forefinger and the sensuous
way he pursed his lips. No sign of the casual grimace chain-
smokers employ when exhaling, only the plume snaking about in
the breeze.

Birgit's voice broke into his thoughts: another question about
computers. Conrad was surprised and then a little excited. Perhaps his talk had opened some doors for her. But the question itself proved sadly remedial: Why was email so much cheaper than
long-distance calls, if both ways of messaging used the same
wires? He explained that sending email did not involve a direct
connection between one computer and another; instead, the email
message went through a string of networked computers bundled
with other messages.

"Oh. I see." Birgit smiled. Conrad had the unpleasant feeling
of being diagnosed.

"The path a message follows is recorded in the header of the
email message," he explained. "When email comes back undeliv-
ered, you can sometimes tell, by reading the header, where along
the route the message got lost." Conrad was suddenly pensive.
The idea of returned messages, their fruitless journey from server
to server, rang a distant and sad bell.

Just a few months earlier, he'd discovered a returned email
marked "user unknown" in the home mailbox he shared with
Lucy:

Antoine—At the very LEAST you could return my voice-
mail, if just to say NO. Have I been that much of a bore?
This kind of treatment makes me seethe. —L

Conrad had given the matter little thought at the time. Lucy
was a real estate agent and had hundreds of contacts in the field.
Deals were always being proposed, set up, ruined. Squabbles over

commissions were common. Yet as the week went by, he found his thoughts returning to the message. A couple of things bothered him about the name Antoine:

(1) It belonged to no one he'd ever heard of.
(2) It possessed a disturbingly romantic resonance.

Later, when cleaning out the file cabinet, he went through the folder of phone statements and found a record listing seven toll calls, each over thirty minutes, to a mysterious number in San Rafael, which, when dialed, connected him to a recording of a deep male voice with a slight French accent. "Sorry, I am not available," the voice said, without bothering to name itself. Conrad quickly shelved his suspicions, however. It seemed inconceivable that Lucy would be carrying on an affair while they were in their eleventh-hour struggle to conceive—a project almost entirely her own idea. The whole scenario seemed fantastic. And so he continued applying the usual business-related explanations.

Still, the dates on the phone bill recalled for Conrad one of Lucy's happiest periods. Frequently, she became giddy over dinner, with plenty of wine still left in her glass. And about that time words like "paramour" and "liaison" began seeping into her speech, oblique references perhaps that paved the way for more blunt terms like "boyfriend" and "motel."

"Paramour," he mouthed silently. It was a word that stank of cologne, a word illuminated by a halo of vanity lights. It gave the event an aura of tradition and refinement. You could not say it angrily or even in a loud voice. The most you could manage was a derisive snort: "Paramour!"

In the waiting room of the fertility clinic Lucy had once joked about trysting with a Frenchman earlier in the day. They had both laughed—at the quaintness of the notion, he supposed, the obsolete pairing of "French" with sexual sophistication. Now the very real possibility that she had been with someone earlier that day occurred to him. Perhaps she had been laughing at him, Conrad, and the quaintness of their own pairing.

He drew his knees up to his chest and hugged them. The mountains on the approaching island were not really big enough to be called mountains, yet in places they behaved like mountains, thrusting their white cliffs straight up out of the jungle. Conrad looked back at Ko Banteay, where Lucy hiked alone, presumably, along the palm-fringed ridges. The island ahead looked decidedly different—bigger, wilder.

Conrad tilted his head back and let the sunlight play upon his closed eyes. A vast field of light opened up before him, first red, then light blue. Abruptly the image of Lucy's labia appeared before him. This surprised him. He could see in close detail the sprawling thicket of her pubic hair, the wispy tendrils spiraling up across her abdomen. And then a massive glans, beet red, slowly worked its way into the picture. Many feelings arrived at once, against a background of general alarm: excitement, foreboding, revulsion, anger, surprise. There was surprise that Lucy's genitalia could still excite him, that just the idea of her genitalia could excite him; there was the sense of doom as her labia swallowed up the intruding glans, then surged and puckered around the shaft. There was something like the thrill of watching a touchdown pass in the final seconds of the Super Bowl, of being the delirious spectator cheering the big screen from a teetering bar stool, the happy confusion that allowed him momentarily to see the shaft as his own. Then came the sudden fear that the wrong team had scored, that he was the one being penetrated; and finally the deflating realization that it was neither, that the picture didn't include him, was complete without him. The image faded. His fist closed around something small and hard, the certainty that he had been swindled.

"Cheated," he heard himself say. And while this word in no way captured the kaleidoscopic range of emotions of the previous moment, it grew shrill and insistent, and cried out for redress. Wasn't that what this little jaunt was all about? He unclasped his knees and took a breath.

"What did you say?" Birgit asked. "Cheated?"

"Oh," Conrad said, coming awake. "What you were saying about the dam? It seems so unfair."

Birgit squinted at him.

"Yes, it is that. But there is now this—moving—to stop it, to change the—politics."

"Student movement?" Conrad suggested.

"He was a student in Sweden. I know his cousin in fact. I mean the leader, Usen Tatoh. You have heard of this man?"

"I'm sorry." Conrad shook his head.

"He is this man with much *karisma*—how do you say it in English?"

"Like that: charisma."

"He is bringing together many different groups," Eva put in. "Different ethnic groups." Birgit enumerated these on her fingers: Paktai, Mon, Yawi, Chinese.

"So there is hope," Conrad said quickly. "That's good."

The air smelled of fish. They were passing a fishing boat, a red and blue wooden vessel where shirtless men were casting dark nets into the water. Ahead, the harbor and the only town on Ko Neak Pean appeared as a white strip along the shoreline. Some tourists yelled to the fishermen and waved. The fishermen waved back. All around Conrad cameras clicked, telephoto lenses and camcorders appeared. The blond kid from the rear deck moved past him carrying a large camera on his shoulder. Conrad opened his eyes wide, feeling a sudden urgency to pay close attention to everything going on around him. Some sort of line had been crossed. The scope of possibilities had widened in a way he was only beginning to comprehend, and for the first time he truly realized that he was far away from home, moving into parts unknown.

3

Pak Sai, the sole town and harbor on Ko Neak Pean, feels in many ways as exotic today as when the British first arrived in the late nineteenth century. Many of the ramshackle buildings along the waterfront date from the Portuguese period. A casual stroll down crooked streets will take you past a Chinese temple, two dilapidated mosques, innumerable Buddhist shrines, and boisterous open-air markets. Squint and you can see what it was like at the turn of the century.

—*Coswell's Guide to Tambralinga* (1997 ed.)

The first glimpse of Pak Sai proved disappointing. A string of low-slung concrete buildings had replaced the old colonial façade described in Eva's guidebook. The buzz on the deck was that a fire had nearly gutted the old buildings the previous year, and the group of investors from Singapore who had taken over the waterfront decided that repairing them would not be cost-effective. On a tiny spit of land just south of the harbor the same group of aesthetically challenged investors were constructing a five-star hotel, with as many floors. As the ferry approached the pier, the hotel's somber gray shell peeked out from behind a screen of bamboo scaffolding.

An air of momentary defeat hung over the Swedes as they stood up and prepared to disembark. The Tarzan figure was the first one off the boat. The women watched with obvious annoyance as the man strolled up the pier. His bare-legged swagger seemed to mock their own conscientiousness, their prescribed pajamas. Being the first ashore, Greystoke seemed to lay claim to the island; and the looming form of the new hotel seemed to confirm this.

Conrad remained on the boat until most of the other passengers had disembarked, a rejuvenated sense of dread holding him fast. It struck him how cautiously, up to this point, he'd proceeded through life. He'd treated his life as a precious liquid, something to be poured carefully from one container into another. In the morning he poured himself out of bed and into the bathroom, then out of the bathroom and into the kitchen, from the kitchen into the garage and car, from the car into the office. And so on, the whole of his life structured around this sequence of containers. Only now he was truly outside, a jellied approximation of a man, waiting to take his first steps.

These first steps were inauspicious: the planks in the dock seemed to shift beneath his feet as he climbed out of the boat. It was some perceptual thing having to do with the motion of the boat and the glittering waves, but the effect refused to be explained away, and Conrad was forced for a moment to squat on the pier and press thumb and forefinger gently against his closed eyelids. His first day of kindergarten, his first attempt at the highdive, the first time he'd launched himself, lips parted, in the direction of a female face—the terror of these moments came back in glaring detail, together with the humiliation that in each case had followed: the urine pooling around his five-year-old self as he sat cross-legged on the floor, the windmill of arms and legs his tumbling form had assumed by the time it hit the water, the astonished laughter issuing from the mouth he had meant to kiss.

I'm a grown-up, he protested, but none of the other voices in his head came forward to second the motion. There was only the wobbliness of the pier, the seesawing of green hills and ocean horizon.

At the end of the dock, a ragtag group of touts encircled him, each boy shouting out the name of a different hotel or beach resort, waving smudged photos and crumpled business cards.

"Golden Lily Bungalow!" one of them said, taking hold of Conrad's duffel bag. "Have best swim."

"No! Wisnu House best swim!" another boy countered, taking hold of Conrad's free arm.

"No, thanks." Conrad looked from one anxious face to the other and yanked himself free. "I want to stay in town."

"Princess Daha Guesthouse in town best price!" the first tout shouted, reestablishing his hold on Conrad's bag. "Close by! Come!" The other tout responded in kind and a tug-of-war ensued.

Conrad let himself be dragged a few steps until a policeman appeared and dispersed the boys with a blast of his whistle. Conrad watched dumbly as the policeman pursued the boys up the street, and then took a few steps in the same direction. The street was mostly dirt, with a few paving stones jutting up at oblique angles here and there. He wondered vaguely why the policeman was giving chase and then noticed with some irritation that he was following them, the boys and the policeman, around a corner and up the street toward the central marketplace.

The policeman stopped to tear something from a wall, a handbill with the picture of a dark, moon-faced man wearing a white cap. Conrad bent over to examine the poster. It was covered with strange writing, like Arabic.

Up the street he passed an old woman in white robes crouching near the base of a large statue, a god of some sort, with four heads, each looking in a different direction. A metal fence enclosed the shrine; Conrad paused, steadied himself against the bars. The statue was surrounded by flowers and miniature wooden elephants and sticks of incense stuck in small flowerpots full of sand. The old woman held a brass cup in one hand and small garlands of white and yellow flowers in the other. She looked up at the statue and muttered something, an incantation perhaps. Conrad's seasickness returned; the scene smacked of voodoo, of obscure perversions.

The still air offered a bouquet of preposterously matched scents: charcoal and urine, fried banana and garlic. He pushed on toward the central market, a covered area open on all four sides, where vendors sold food and other items from little stalls. Here and there the concrete floor seethed with live eels and gasping fish. Merchant women constructed resplendent pyramids of bright green and yellow vegetables or red and purple fruits, displaying an abundance of foods unknown to Conrad.

Vendors beckoned him with free samples. Conrad allowed an old woman to feed him fried chunks of a mysterious fruit. The flavor was strange and complex, at turns intoxicating and nauseating, and the neighboring vendors—old women every one of them—watched carefully for his reactions, laughing uproariously whenever he stopped chewing. He persevered, convinced that he was being tested and determined to pass. As he chewed his way through the sample, the wretched sweet flavor of the fruit filled his consciousness and for a moment it seemed that he had entered another universe in which all sensation was like this taste: intriguing, revolting, excessive.

An hour later Conrad was sitting at a table in an outdoor café, gazing at a crumbling brick wall covered with creeping vines. The café was situated in a courtyard off a narrow lane. Entry was through a small doorway beneath a carved stone lintel. The carving featured the stylized head of some sort of grinning demon, but it was impossible to be sure because the stone was so weathered and the face so tightly woven into the patterns of rosettes and lotus petals. A smooth stone curb, nearly half a foot high, marked the threshold of the doorway. And in the space framed by the doorway now and then a bicycle appeared, or women with baskets of produce balanced on their heads, or small men bearing heavy loads on either end of poles balanced across their shoulders.

Seated all around him at white plastic tables identical to his own were thin young men, Westerners, in batik shirts, and their anxious, frail-looking girlfriends, poised over iced drinks and cigarettes. Conrad felt conspicuously alone, physically tenuous.

A waiter approached his table, but then glided past without a glance. Conrad called after him, but to no avail. Why were they avoiding him? Another waiter materialized from inside the small house at the back of the courtyard, carrying a tray loaded with iced drinks in plastic tumblers.

"You lack sums sing?" he smiled at Conrad.

"Yes, I'd like a café au lait."

"Coffee okay," the waiter said. "Okay, okay." Conrad noticed he was slightly cross-eyed. But after he'd delivered his tray of drinks, he came back to Conrad's table and gestured with his head at the large spiny fruit lying on the ground next to Conrad's feet.

"No, please," he pronounced carefully. "Durian no allow inside. Make bad smell."

Conrad looked at the fruit by his feet. So it was called "durian." In the market, he'd thought it a sort of pineapple. He was not certain how the old woman had persuaded him to purchase it, but there it was. And the smell was awful.

"Yes, sir!" the waiter went on, as if meaning to take both parts of the dialogue. "I can please leave outside." He bowed slightly—more like a robust nod—and gestured with his right hand toward the courtyard entrance.

Conrad picked up the fruit obediently, but then paused.

"But everything in this country smells," he protested meekly. Not understanding, the waiter gestured again at the doorway and smiled. Conrad complied, propping his trophy against the stone threshold just outside the doorway. But now the waiter grew agitated.

"No! No! Sir—other side, please." Conrad looked at him for a moment, puzzled, and then realized he wanted the fruit stashed on the other side of the lane, away from the entrance. He looked both ways as he crossed the lane, but this was really unnecessary, as the passage was too narrow to permit cars. He propped the durian up against the wall of a building and then hurried back.

As he reentered the courtyard, he sensed a young couple at a nearby table scrutinizing him through dark sunglasses. When he sat down again, he was pleased to find that he could still see his prize, framed by the doorway.

The waiter brought him what appeared to be a glass of warm milk with one or two teaspoons of Nescafé stirred into it.

"I ordered a café au lait," he protested.

"Coffee okay," the waiter said, smiling, and made a stirring motion with his hand. Conrad picked up the spoon, which was of light aluminum and bent in several places, and stirred the mixture carefully, then tapped the spoon gently against the side of the glass. He tasted the drink, found it tepid and nauseatingly sweet.

"Coffee okay?" the waiter asked.

Conrad stared at him. The young man smiled and, bowing slightly, departed.

Conrad toyed with the idea of sending the drink back, of walking out without paying. He'd be well within his rights, he figured, and might even be doing the next customer a favor. But in the U.S. he'd never sent a dish back, not even the rubberized veal that was to have been the centerpiece of his fifteenth wedding anniversary dinner. Why should he pick on an obsequious waiter in the smallest goddamn country in Asia, someone who had probably never seen real coffee, let alone steamed milk?

He took another swallow. It wasn't as bad as the rubberized veal, and he'd swallowed every bit of that. (Fortunately Lucy had ordered the sea bass.) He'd been unwilling to say or do anything that might jeopardize her good mood, instead blaming himself for not making a better selection. He'd certainly had enough time to study the menu—Lucy had come directly from work and had been over an hour late. When she did finally arrive, flushed and radiant and giggling like a teenager, everything she tasted delighted her, and she ate with rare appetite.

Conrad stirred his glass of Nescafé. He picked it up for a moment, then put it down. He stared out at the street. Of course she'd been with her lover that evening. He could see that now.

Later a woman, a Westerner, came into the café, dragging a small, whining boy. She was a small, dark Mediterranean type, dressed in the prescribed pajamas, and at first glance Conrad thought she might be Arabic. She and the boy were in the midst of an argument, in whispered French, as they took a table next to Conrad's. He listened for a while, finding himself intrigued by the conspiratorial quality of their conversation. The boy, who couldn't have been more than five years old, showed all the signs of age-appropriate restlessness, repeatedly leaving his seat to wander among the tables in the courtyard, staring now and then in the direction of Conrad's durian.

The woman called her son back and then ordered a café au lait and a hot chocolate, and when the waiter brought their drinks a predictable discussion ensued, the woman insisting the drink was not "au lait," the waiter with obsequious persistence assuring her it was in fact "okay." The boy, whose drink Conrad guessed was equally unpalatable, grew irritable and once again left the table. He began playing by the doorway, now and then jumping up on the threshold. Another waiter, an older man, came running out from the little house, hissing and fluttering his hands at the boy. The boy stopped jumping and looked at him quizzically, with the expression of a cat confronted by a moth.

"Oh, missus! He should not stand there," the young waiter explained in halting phrases. "Bad luck. Berry bad—*phii* live inside. Come out, make sick."

"*He* live inside?" the woman asked in heavily accented English. "I don't understand."

The old man moved toward the boy with outstretched hand. The young waiter put himself between the old man and the boy, then gently guided the boy outside, away from the entrance.

"*Maman!*" the boy cried. His mother shushed him and pointed to the waiter. The waiter gestured in a way that announced his intention to demonstrate something. The waiter adjusted and expanded his smile—he'd been smiling throughout the entire interaction—and then turned toward the threshold and, placing his palms together against his chest, bowed slightly. He muttered something that might have been a prayer and bowed again. Then he reentered the courtyard, taking a big, deliberate step over the threshold. The young man sitting nearby removed his sunglasses and tried to explain:

"He's saying not to step on the—oh, what do you call it? The step thing there," he said in a Dutch accent. "There is a ghost—*revenant*—inside. They say *phii* in Tambralinga. If ghost gets offended, it comes out and makes the people sick. All sickness is caused by ghosts, you know?"

The mother rolled her eyes.

"I think they are dreaming this," she said.

"Sure," the Dutch man said. "You disturb their house and the spirits will give you nightmares. Come flying into your head at night like bats into a cave."

"Philippe!" the mother called sharply to her son, who was in the process of climbing back onto the threshold. The boy replied in a plaintive voice. He seemed to be arguing the point. Some back and forth between mother and son ensued, and then he stepped over the threshold and disappeared down the narrow lane.

"And if they don't come out of your head in the morning, you go mad," the young man concluded. The mother didn't seem to be listening.

A tree with large white blossoms grew in the center of the courtyard. Conrad looked up at an overhanging branch and contemplated the humid, aromatic atmosphere of the place. There was a palpable languor in the air, a sensuality being emitted by the earth and the stones and vegetation as they slowly decayed. Maybe that was what made the tropics seductive, that feeling of everything rotting away.

He looked over at the mother, who he decided could be described as "handsome." She was without a doubt long past thirty, and perhaps beyond forty, her movements tinged with an uneasy mixture of sensuality and midlife weariness. He wondered vaguely where her husband was.

"Philippe—" she called in a singsong voice. The boy put his head around the corner of the doorway and smiled. She said something to him in French and he answered. Then she called the waiter over and attempted to order lunch for the boy. But the waiter was unable to understand her pronunciations.

"Fry noodle with chicken," Conrad translated for her. "And one lemonade."

The mother looked over at him with surprise.

"Oh, hello," she said. "I didn't see you before."

Conrad nodded, flushing slightly. He hesitated for a moment, afraid he was intruding. And then abruptly he found himself telling her everything, his name, his nationality, how long he'd been in the country, how long he was planning to stay, the fact that he'd left his wife on Ko Banteay and that he'd purchased a large stinking fruit for no apparent reason.

She looked at him blankly for a long moment, then glanced in the direction of the entrance.

"You buy this thing?" she asked, pointing at the durian. "You eat? You are very brave man."

"I've only eaten it cooked," he said hastily. "It's a—very sophisticated flavor."

"Pardon me, but it smells like shit." She held her nose.

"Well it doesn't taste like that. More like onion-flavored ice cream."

"Yes?" She looked at him again for another long, blank moment.

"I'm just kidding," he said.

"I see."

He looked down in his lap. Somebody had warned him about trying to joke with the French.

"What else will you buy here, I wonder," she went on.

"Oh, the guidebook, I think," Conrad stammered. "I need a guidebook."

"Book?" she asked. "No. I think it better not to know too much. I think, you know—better for discover yourself." She tossed a book of matches on the table and then rummaged in her purse for a cigarette. By the time she had the cigarette in her mouth, Conrad managed to get one of the matches lit. She accepted the light without comment, as if she'd been expecting it.

"We—I'd planned on going to the Aegean originally," Conrad confided.

"Very lovely, the islands," she agreed. "But so crowded now."

"Well, right. That's why we, that is, I—"

"Philippe!" she called abruptly; the waiter had arrived with a plate of noodles. The boy came out of nowhere and took his place at the table. His mother admonished him for a moment and then he slumped forward in a sulk. When Conrad had lit the woman's cigarette, he'd scooted his chair closer, and now he occupied an uncomfortable zone halfway between their table and his. Under the boy's tense stare, he began to feel exposed. Conrad glanced over his shoulder at his cup of tepid Nescafé and considered a retreat.

"You have this face of someone," she said, squinting at Conrad. "You looking like this—guy—I used to know. A bit."

The boy began to eat. This seemed a good omen. Conrad turned his back on his Nescafé.

"How long in Tambralinga?" she asked. Her eyes were large and lit with a peculiar intensity. Conrad told her again that he'd only been in the country for five days, but planned to spend five weeks.

"Five week? Good. Same for me," she said. "It's the best place left, yes? Not so developed."

She squinted at her son and made a face. He had become difficult since his father left for Ko Banteay, she explained. His father wanted to get certified to scuba dive and then to take a three-day trip along the reef. All the best reefs were at Ko Banteay. Of course Philippe had wanted to go. She tossed up a hand and let it fall back in her lap. Her hands and feet were small, and Conrad allowed himself a moment's speculation on what she looked like beneath her billowing shirt.

Philippe's spoon fell to the ground. He conferred with his mother in whispered French, and then folded his arms over his chest. Apparently he'd had enough of the noodles. His mother produced a pencil and a spiral-bound sketchbook from her bag and put it in front of him. Philippe turned his head away, nose slightly elevated. But his movement put Conrad directly in his line of sight and that startled him.

"Hi there," Conrad said. His voice was tense. And he quickly realized how his greeting must sound to a little boy who knew no English: like a threat. Indeed, the boy seemed momentarily paralyzed. Conrad remembered then that he had in his duffel a few candy bars—not actual candy, but energy snacks that Lucy always took to the gym with her.

"Wait!" he commanded the boy. He scooted his chair back to his table and dug a bar out of his bag: chocolate almond fudge. When Conrad put the bar in front of him, the boy hesitated a moment, but then snatched it up and ran out into the lane.

"Philippe!" the mother called in a scolding voice.

"Please excuse him," she called over to Conrad. Conrad picked up his coffee and pretended to taste it. She turned her chair so that she was facing him, her left arm extended, resting on the table. She beckoned with her right hand for Conrad to come and sit with her.

Did he and his wife fight about money, she asked as he joined her. She and her husband fought about money all of the time. They could never have afforded this trip on their own. It had been a present, an anniversary gift, from her father, who was well connected with the airlines. The idea was that they could take a break from their constant bickering. But on the island it was worse.

"In our case, money wasn't the problem," Conrad confessed.

"No? And what was the problem?"

"I'm not sure." He looked down at his coffee, which he had inexplicably brought with him. He felt suddenly hot and awkward. She patted his hand.

"I was thinking," she said. "When I was young, you know, I spend this whole summer on a Greek island—Ios. I live on the beach. We all live on the beach the whole summer, I and my friends. Young kids from all over, Holland, Germany, France, Sweden, States, Australia. We—hang out, you know. Getting high, listening to little radios. All the time swimming. And the water so blue and nobody wearing any clothes. My entire body was brown. People see me first time saying 'She is Egyptian!' I roll in the sand and it is like sugar on my body and my skin all brown like—I don't know."

Like a dessert, Conrad thought. It was easy to see how she

might have been a beauty. The woman looked at him for a moment, as if sensing his thoughts.

"Sounds wonderful," Conrad said, trying to restart the conversation.

"Oh. Ios. Wonderful," she said, extinguishing her cigarette and shaking a new one out of the pack. "Wonderful to be young also. But here is better, I think."

"Yes, of course," Conrad said. He lit her cigarette. Her features were nicely proportioned, he thought, almost doll-like.

"You remind me of this guy I met that summer." She leaned back in her chair and blew a plume of smoke at the overhanging branch. "I have three boyfriends that summer," she said, smiling.

"And I remind you of one of them?"

"No. Somebody else. This German guy who drowned."

"Drowned?"

"Yes. Too much retsina. Jump off a big rock into the sea and hit his head on another big rock."

She laughed. She had a hoarse laugh that squeaked when it reached its apex.

"It was awful," she said, suddenly sober. "But I didn't worry so much then. Life goes on. I just let the days go by, you know. Going anywhere you feel like, any time of night or day, with whoever you want . . ."

Conrad lost the thread of her words, momentarily overwhelmed by the vastness of all that had passed him by. He remembered hearing of places like Ios and of similar scenes along the California coast, back before he'd met Lucy. Of course it had been fashionable to dismiss hedonistic excess in those days (there are always fashionable ways to dismiss anything fashionable) and he had availed himself of those rhetorical devices. But the rumors had scared him a little, had seemed to mock his modest aspirations in the realm of *amour*.

The woman continued:

"There was this guy, you know, at the *taverna*, this Greek guy, with a big belly and white hair. And when I go there with my girlfriends in the evenings, he always singing for us and with the guitar, you know, sitting on the big stool. Looking at us, you know, like this—"

She made her eyes narrow and sultry.

"—and then, you know, making his head go back."

She tossed her head back in a way that suggested haughtiness.

"And he says to my friend—he really likes her—says to her in English: 'What's up, pussy cat?' "

She squeezed her eyes shut and laughed.

"Like he is some kind of sexual object, you know?"

"Yes," Conrad said, smiling uneasily. "I know." He suspected that she was comparing him to this middle-aged Greek fellow. Did he, Conrad, seem that much older than she? He reminded himself that he'd made no decision to pursue this woman, even with all of this business about moving chairs back and forth.

While they were talking, Philippe had returned to the table and had begun drawing in his sketchbook. The waiter, passing by, stopped to look.

"Oh, naga!" he said approvingly. When Philippe held up his drawing, Conrad saw that he'd drawn a large serpentine dragon.

"Naga, naga," the other waiter, the old man, said as he approached the table.

"The naga is some kind of snake, I think," the mother said. "More of their—spirits, yes?"

"Sure." Conrad wanted to be agreeable. The picture was uncommonly ugly. The body's curves were lost in a confusion of slashing lines, the red gash of a mouth overflowed with crude black triangles meant to be teeth.

"Very good," Conrad said, turning to Philippe and mustering what he hoped was a fond, paternal tone. The boy said nothing— probably he hadn't understood—and left the table abruptly. Out in the lane he discovered Conrad's durian, which he crouched over and began prodding with a stick.

"And your wife is where?" the woman asked.

"On Ko Banteay," Conrad replied quickly. "We're separated."

The symmetry of the situation—their respective spouses each being one island removed—was suddenly unbearable.

"You divorce?"

"Not yet."

"No babies?"

"No."

She touched his hand again.

"It is still difficult, yes? You want a cigarette?" She shook the pack at him. He drew one out slowly, but instead of putting it to his lips, began tapping it against the tabletop. Was he staying here in town, she wanted to know. He should consider the bungalows out at Ligor Bay a little ways up the coast. She'd heard they were very nice. Conrad picked up his coffee and then put it down again. Was she inviting him to visit her at the bungalows?

"But my husband," she said, "doesn't like."

"No," Conrad agreed.

She stood up, called to the waiter, and paid her bill.

"I must go now," she said to Conrad. "I am sure we will see you again."

"Sure."

"My name is Rosanette."

Conrad introduced himself again.

Rosanette stepped carefully over the threshold and called to Philippe, who was nudging the durian along the ground with his foot. Conrad called out to him that the durian was his if he wanted. At a word from his mother, Philippe picked up the durian, whose spiky brown shell was now cracked in several places, and turned solemnly toward Conrad.

"Thank you very much," he said in English.

"You're very welcome," Conrad answered, a little dazed from the abruptness of their departure.

The boy raised the durian over his head and hurled it onto the threshold. The fruit splattered across the courtyard.

"Philippe!" Rosanette said, slapping him lightly on the head. Philippe answered sharply and gave his mother a push. Meanwhile, the tourists sitting at the tables closest to where the fruit had landed got up, waving their hands in front of their faces, and departed. A pair of goats appeared and went to work on the mess, but it was too late. The smell, like a renegade djinn, had broken free and begun working its vengeful magic on the remaining patrons. When the smell reached Conrad, he too decided to flee.

4

With the stench of the shattered durian burning in his nostrils, Conrad reawakened to the raison d'être for his expedition, for this whole lousy trip. To the brothel! Or perhaps simply "To brothel," like a nursery rhyme. The dank, cloying atmosphere of the courtyard café had disappeared before the onslaught of a dry wind, bearing the faint scent of charcoal and banana. The afternoon sun burned with an undeniable enthusiasm, with almost personal regard as he followed the narrow street around the hill.

To brothel, to brothel, he hummed to himself. Perhaps it would be a quick trip after all. He might not bother with a hotel, but simply take the night ferry back to Ko Banteay.

Then home again, home again, jiggle-de-jig.

The question was: Where was the brothel? He had only vague ideas of what one might look like. He paused under a shop awning and studied the crumbling building across the street. In place of a front door was a gaping, arched entrance, nearly the width of the building itself. Swaths of accumulated dirt streaked what had once apparently been cream-colored walls. Weeds grew from the cracked masonry above the two second-story windows—the green eyebrows on this dirty child's face. The inside looked dark as a cave. It was impossible to tell what kind of business was housed inside. A brothel? But he discovered that he wanted the brothel to be housed in something wooden and French colonial, a House of the Rising Sun sort of thing.

To brothel, to brothel, he hummed to himself as he slung the duffel over to his other shoulder and pushed off again. The sentimental mood that had victimized him back in the café had been routed; the task before him now appeared as a small business matter, a shopping expedition. He supposed if things went well, he might become a repeat customer. But already he was looking forward to the ferry ride back to Ko Banteay, the sea wind in his face, a newfound steadiness percolating through his body. This last sensation he imagined would be like the flush that follows a swallow of hot brandy, a pleasure with a slight medicinal quality. And lying down next to Lucy with the scent of a strange woman still on him might very well do him some good.

At the top of the hill the street ended in a sort of square, a wide, open area of bare, compacted earth. Looming up on his left, there it was: a decrepit wooden structure whose grand entrance and broad veranda spoke of former glories. A faded, hand-painted sign hung over the door: PRINCESS DAHA. Conrad remembered the name from the guidebook.

That's it, Conrad thought. I'm here.

The building stood alone, with no others touching its walls. A bicycle rickshaw stood in the shade of the eastern wall, the driver asleep in the passenger seat. Sleeping dogs were scattered around, their bodies inert, like dusty sacks of flour. Conrad regretted that he hadn't brought a camera. Solemnly he climbed the few wooden steps, long planks that sagged in the middle, up to the veranda. He paused at the threshold.

A voice called to him. He turned around. Eva and Birgit waved to him from the street.

"Hey, we are lost," Eva confessed. "Do you happen to know where is the mosque?"

Conrad stared at her, feeling a hot surge come into his face.

"I didn't see it," he said finally. "I don't even know what a mosque looks like exactly." He came down the steps and strode over to them quickly, as if helping them find the mosque was of the utmost urgency.

"I came from down there," he said. He pointed down the hill and in doing so managed to get them to turn their backs on the Princess Daha. "So probably the mosque would be down that way," he said, pointing in another direction. Eva cocked her head to the side and looked at him.

"It's really not so important," she said, eyeing him uneasily. "I didn't mean to—agitate—you."

"It's no—I just—I hate being lost myself." His voice quavered and then grew stiff as he spoke.

"There is a map here," Birgit said, opening the guidebook. "If you are lost."

"I'm not lost, it's—"

" 'Princess Daha,' " Eva read out loud over Birgit's shoulder. "That's it." They all turned back around to face the sagging structure.

"Daha," Birgit mumbled as she peered into the guidebook. Conrad felt his face flush again as he listened to the silence that surely meant that she was reading the passage describing the establishment. Birgit looked up from the page. Conrad found himself searching for an excuse.

"The touts at the pier," he started to say.

"Look! There is the mosque!" Eva interrupted. "See the dome?"

Conrad's gaze followed her finger toward a golden sliver visible just above the roof of the west wing of the old building, like a harvest moon about to rise.

"It's on *that* side of the hill!" Eva said. "Didn't I say so?"

Birgit said something in Swedish and Eva replied quickly, laughing. They both looked at Conrad and then at the Princess Daha.

"There's better places to stay, I think," Birgit said to Conrad as she waved goodbye. "We stay at the Cozy Comfort down by the water."

"That sounds good. Maybe I'll—" Conrad called after them. "I hear the bungalows out on Ligor Bay are nice, too."

"Yes, yes. See you."

He watched them go.

Then he turned his eyes back toward the Princess.

5

The lobby of the Princess Daha was dark, cavernous, with two ceiling fans slowly stirring the overarching gloom. The air from inside felt cooler, but more humid. A clamminess came over Conrad as he stepped inside. Again the entire project felt ridiculous.

"*Willkommen!* Yes, come in! *Bon jour!*" the man at the front desk called out. He seemed a long way off. As Conrad moved inside, bits of furniture emerged from the shadows, rattan chairs, sofas covered in leather or imitation leather, tables of carved teak, inlaid with ivory or mother-of-pearl. Here and there an ottoman appeared, or an ancient sitting chair with faded plush upholstery. The far wall seemed to be hung with weapons: muskets and spears and blow guns perhaps, but it was too dark to make them out. Except for the man at the front desk, the place seemed to be empty.

A dim fluorescent bulb hanging from the ceiling above the desk clerk illuminated his lean, elongated face. He was a young man, small, with dark hair, neatly coifed. Conrad supposed he was Chinese; the Chinese were meant to run the economy in Tambralinga. His gaze was fixed on something outside, something he seemed reluctant to look away from even while talking to Conrad. He held a cigarette in his left hand, which he had propped up on an elbow so the smoke drifted up and away from his face. On a high shelf just above him was some sort of shrine, a statue of the Buddha, or somebody else, strung with tiny Christmas lights. Conrad found his heart pounding as he approached the desk. Probably he'd come too early. Probably they would ask him to wait for an hour or two and buy a lot of expensive drinks. Probably the girls were indolent and sacklike, like the dogs lying about outside. Where were the girls, anyway?

"*Deutsch? Anglais?*"

"English," Conrad said slowly.

"You want a room?"

Room? Is that the euphemism they employed here?

"Uh—how much?" Conrad asked.

"Twenty-seven rials single, fifty double."

"Oh."

Do they even need euphemisms? he wondered. Wasn't the whole business supposed to be legal here? It made sense to be cautious.

"What comes with a double?" he asked.

The young man looked at him.

"I mean," Conrad went on. "What kind of—service—goes with that?"

The man put his cigarette to his lips and slowly inhaled, giving Conrad a leisurely once-over.

"Do you want a room?" he asked again. Smoke poured from his nostrils and then drifted up to the shrine.

"I think so. I'd like to look at one. We'll—we'll just see how it goes."

The hallway was lit with tiny bulbs, about the size of the appliance bulbs Conrad used in his refrigerator. The fixtures were positioned along the wall every ten feet or so just above the doorframes. The wiring was external, held up here and there with a nail or a piece of black tape, and the sight of it chafed Conrad. There was no waiting room ahead, he feared. No one-way glass overlooking a lounge where the girls awaited his call, nothing like the Bangkok massage parlors his cousin, an ex–air force pilot, had described to him many years ago. At best there would be a girl and a massage table, maybe an attached shower.

The clerk showed him to a small room with dingy yellow walls and an ancient ceiling fan that seemed to be hanging by its wiring. It contained neither girl nor massage table but did feature an attached bathroom. When the clerk opened the bathroom door, a bug the size of his palm scuttled across the floor and disappeared down the shower drain, which was little more than a hole in the tiled floor. Conrad sat down on the bed and breathed out heavily, extinguishing the last remaining spark of his enthusiasm. He'd wanted something boisterous and bawdy, something overflowing with good cheer. He'd wanted a *brothel*, for Christ's sake.

"You want anything, soft drink, whiskey soda, dinner, breakfast, anything, can get," the clerk said. "You ask front desk." Conrad looked at the ancient window frame next to the bed, at the flecks of old paint that studded the wood. "You need anything," the clerk had said. Perhaps "massage" was the operative word. But the prospect of a sordid transaction with a desk clerk in a hotel big enough and dark enough to qualify as a basilica depressed him. The sex he knew would be nothing special. The thrill would be to have it out there in plain view, served up matter-of-factly, cafeteria style. Everything casual, everyone laughing.

He thanked the clerk for his trouble and left.

So the Princess Daha was just a hotel. Funny that the only bit of information he'd retained from the guidebook turned out to be wrong. He took a last look at the forlorn building as he set off down the hill. He laughed quietly, but it seemed a cruel sort of joke.

A fly bobbed against the ceiling, amid a herd of tiny geckos. The geckos were well spaced, each guarding its territory with a ferocious single-mindedness. For any one of them, pursuing the fly meant trespassing in another's territory, which meant being attacked and driven off. So each lizard stayed where it was, snapping at the fly when it came close, but not giving chase. The fly seemed to be aware of these boundaries. Even though it couldn't distinguish the white ceiling from the open air, each time it collided with the ceiling, it hit a midpoint between two geckos.

At first Conrad's sympathies were with the geckos, especially

the smaller ones who hovered around the small circle of light
stemming from his bedside lamp. Then he found himself rooting
for the fly to come to its senses and fly off in a new direction. But
the fly could no more overcome its stupidity than the lizards
could overcome their timidity. The same scene repeated itself
again and again, the fly bumbling, the geckos lunging and missing, until Conrad, in disgust, wadded up the note he'd been writing to Lucy and hurled it at them.

He looked at his watch. It had stopped at a quarter to one. He
tapped it and the second hand started moving again. Roosters
had crowed an hour ago, but it was still pitch-black outside. Why
was sleep necessary, anyway? It struck him that he rarely went to
sleep because of being tired. Usually he went to sleep as the result
of certain rituals and because of associations with certain pieces
of furniture—the bed, for instance, and the nightstand that held
the glass of water. Certain noises had to be made, swishing and
spitting noises in the bathroom, grunts and sighs when climbing
into bed. Sleeping was just protocol. It was the way the days were
organized.

He got off the bed and picked up the crumpled note and
smoothed it out.

Lucy—I might be gone a few more days. We both need
time off, I'm sure you'll agree. I'll meet you at the airport
in Nagasari on the 20th if I don't make it back before then.
Sorry to be so vague. —C

"Lucy," he read out loud. It was an unsatisfactory sound. The
whole note was unsatisfactory. He closed his eyes and pictured
her at the beach in swimsuit and sun hat, leaning over him for a
kiss, her smile reconfiguring her face with childlike openness.

He picked up another wad of paper from the floor and un-
crumpled it.

Lucy—I might be gone a few more days. We both need
time off, I'm sure you'll agree. For some time now, I'm sure

you'll agree, we have been drifting apart. I feel like we have been, anyway. ~~I know you've been~~ *I guess it wouldn't surprise me if you have been seeing someone else. There was that time—*

He wadded the note back up again. Where was his evidence? In the last analysis he had only a frail web of suppositions shored up by the suspicious sounds of certain words: paramour, liaison. Yet these words, once uttered, had created a sense of certainty. If he wrote them down now, whether true or not, they would become the defining features in their relationship.

He recalled again Lucy's embrace, the nervous tremors of her slender body, her giddiness during their first full day on the island.

He tore a fresh piece of paper from his writing tablet and began again:

I know you've been unhappy.

Okay, that was a fair statement. Just a few months earlier, she'd accused him of abducting her in her youth, stealing the best years of her life. According to her, he'd "coerced" her into marriage, taken advantage of her youth and inexperience, and had since kept her inside a bauble. Actually she'd used the word "bubble," but Conrad had at first heard "bauble" and now was stuck with the image. He'd sealed her off in a tiny world of car, apartment, office. She felt stifled, cheated. (Again that word!) Conrad pictured car, apartment, and office miniaturized inside a plastic pendant, with a tiny version of himself included as well. No doubt that was how she saw him, as a hapless bug trapped in amber, trapped in his work.

But he liked his work. He enjoyed its intricacies, its problem-solving aspects and the unambiguous way he proceeded step-by-step from problem to solution. He liked to think that in small ways he was dispensing logic into other people's lives. Creating order. And how could she suggest the apartment was stifling? It

was an entire third floor of a San Francisco Victorian, where
guests often marveled at the thirteen-foot ceilings and command-
ing views, the original details of the dining room and parlor.

*No matter what I do, you act annoyed and angry. Every-
thing I do annoys you, it seems like.*

This sounded too much like an accusation. He crossed it out.
He had to move cautiously here.

*Something has been bothering you for a while and I don't
seem to be much help.*

He reread the words and felt himself getting angry. How can
you help someone who's hell-bent on making your life miserable?

*I've decided some time apart might be a good thing. It
would give you the space you seem to need and give me
some time to think things over. I guess I've been pretty restless myself.*

He became aware that he was gnashing his teeth.

*This is exactly what you wanted, isn't it? I hope you enjoy
being on your own. I certainly intend to. Enjoy myself, I
mean.*

He wrote in hard, slashing strokes. It made his hand tingle.
He folded the note carefully and wrote the address on the
blank side: Lucy's name, the name of the bungalows, the name of
the island. If he posted it in the morning, she would have it by the
next day.
As he stared at the address, he realized he'd neglected to state
what he was doing on the island and when, if ever, he planned to
meet up with her. How much simpler things would be if the

brothel had been a brothel and not a hotel. He would be on his way back to Ko Banteay by now.

He put on his shoes and went downstairs. In the dark lobby an old man, a sort of night watchman, unlocked the gate at the hotel's main entrance. He looked at Conrad strangely as he pushed the gate open for him. Was it safe to walk around at night here? Conrad wondered. No doubt the old man would have issued some sort of warning if he'd known enough English. But Conrad was surprised to find himself indifferent to possible danger. He just had to get out of the Cozy Comfort.

He skirted the open area in front of the hotel and found a street that seemed to lead out of town. He followed it to where the pavement ended. The air smelled like rain, yet the moonless sky blazed with stars. He could make out ahead of him the silhouettes of coconut palms against the Milky Way. Carefully he went along the road, now little more than a dirt track, and climbed a short hill and passed through the coconut grove. There the road petered out into a narrow path that zigzagged through some rice paddies. He had no idea where he was going. The path ascended steeply, and now when he turned to look behind him, he could see the dark line that must be the ocean, with the stars rising out of it, but nothing else.

He spotted some lights along a ridge above him. Strains of gamelan music arrived on the wind, barely audible over the drone of the night insects. It was a village, he decided, a bunch of thatch houses set up on stilts. He shivered with the sensation of being far from home, in someplace strange and real.

"Hello! Who's there?" a woman's voice called out.

Conrad started.

The voice seemed to be floating somewhere above his left shoulder. A flashlight beam skittered around his ankles, then settled on his face. Conrad put his hand up.

"Good evening," he managed. As the beam moved away, it illuminated a stone wall. Conrad realized that he'd been traveling along the edge of a rice field on a steep, terraced hillside. A group of tourists were sitting on one of the terraces. Conrad had come within inches of bumping into their dangling feet.

"Dark tonight," Conrad said.

"Yes," the woman's voice answered. "They just turned off the electricity from the town. We have watched." A familiar accent, Conrad noted.

"Can see this where you are?" It was a man's voice, with soft, East Asian pronunciation. Conrad was invited to join them and managed, with the help of the flashlight beam, to climb up to where they were. The paddies here were dry and strewn with rice straw.

By the time Conrad was settled, it was clear who he was dealing with: Eva, Birgit, and a young Tambralingan man. Conrad found himself seated next to Birgit, with the young man on her other side and then, farthest away, Eva. Eva explained that they had been up at the village, watching a shadow puppet performance. Boon, the young man, had been trying to explain the story to them, but the performance had gone on too long and they had decided to take a walk.

"The shadow plays go all night sometimes," Eva said.

"Right," Conrad agreed, although he didn't have a clear idea of what a shadow play was. He assumed it had something to do with the music.

"Boon was saying that many of the puppet masters don't use the leather from the water buffalo anymore to make their puppets. They are using plastic! Milk jugs and things like that. I think it's bad."

Conrad hummed his agreement.

"Not so bad, I think," Birgit put in. "You can't see the puppets. Only the shadows on the screen. They make the same shadow as before, I think."

"It's not the same," Eva said. "Like having the fake sapphire in a ring. You don't feel the same about it. I'm sorry, but you just don't."

"Wan' more drink?" Boon asked. Birgit's arms moved in the

darkness and there was the sound of liquid sloshing inside a bottle. Then she pressed the bottle into Conrad's hand.

"Rice whiskey," she said.

It was sickly sweet, rather like caramel, but went down smoothly. Birgit stuck her legs out and then let them swing back against the terrace.

"I like this," she said. She seemed to be looking up at the sky. "It's like a seat in the Coliseum, or—or—"

"Like bleachers," Conrad said. "In a football stadium."

"No football," Birgit said. "Fighting—gladiators, yes? Here is Orion, the great hunter. And coming up over there is Scorpio— coming to sting him to death!" She shuddered and made small thrashing motions with her arms and fists. Eva laughed.

"Poor Orion," she said. "Wanted so much to be a star, yeah?" Conrad laughed at the allusion, but tried in vain to remember Orion's story. All he knew was that the three stars formed some kind of logo at the start of certain films he and Lucy rented occasionally. They chased each other in a circle that eventually became the "O" in "Orion." The appearance of this logo was a good indication that the film would have subtitles.

"What do they call the constellation here in Tambralinga?" Conrad asked.

"Al-Jabbar," Boon replied softly. "He is a—guide. Guide for the sails."

"For the sails? Sailors?"

"Yes. When you debt, sail goes into sky. Flying. After debt."

"Sailors after debts? You mean they owe a *debt* to the guide for helping them navigate?"

"He means 'death,' not 'debt.' Death and souls," Eva put in.

"Yes!" Boon replied. "Souls. Guide souls."

"Well, in the West he is Orion, the hunter," Eva said. "The most beautiful man in the world. And the strongest. He kills all of the wild beasts on the island of Chios, so he can marry the king's daughter. But the wicked king puts out his eyes afterward and throws him into the sea."

Birgit laughed and took another swallow of rice whiskey.

"How do you know all that?" Conrad asked.

"Her father the engineer says she must study chemistry," Birgit said. "But this is what she loves, these stories and ancient things."

"An oracle tells Orion," Eva went on, "that only Helios—the sun, you know—can restore his sight. So he travels far to the east, across the ocean to where the sun rises, and he gets Eos, the sister of Helios, to help him. She is in love with him, you know, because he is so handsome."

"She goes to bed with him, yeah?" Birgit laughed.

"Everybody goes to bed with him," Eva said. "That is the problem." She paused and took a swig from the bottle. "He turns his eye sockets toward the sun just as it's rising and he catches the very *first* rays of the rising sun and—wow! He can see again!"

Boon laughed. "Nice story," he said. "Happy story."

Although it was too dark to see, Conrad detected some rustling of arms and legs in Eva's area. Boon laughed again and then yelped.

"I haven't finished the story," Eva said firmly.

"Oh," said Boon.

"And it doesn't end happily," Birgit said as she passed the bottle to Conrad.

"Nobody who ends up as a constellation is happy," Eva said. "When Orion gets his sight back, what is the first thing he thinks of?"

"Revenge?" Conrad said, taking another swig of whiskey.

"Right. He goes back to Chios and looks for the king, but the king is hiding underground in a cave Hephaestus has made for him. Orion thinks, 'I bet this asshole is off on another island.' So off he goes to Crete looking for this king, who is the grandson of King Minos—the ruler of Crete, yeah? But when he gets there, he meets Artemis, the goddess of the hunt. She is really, really good-looking, yeah?"

"Uh-oh!" Birgit said as she took the bottle from Conrad.

"Not only is she good-looking, but she likes to hunt. She is as good a hunter as Orion, and maybe better. She is a goddess, you see. And Orion thinks that this is everything he's ever wanted in a girlfriend!"

Birgit, choking with laughter, sprayed a mouthful of whiskey onto the dry paddy below.

"But Artemis has a big brother: Apollo. And he has heard from Helios many bad things—gossip—about Eos and Orion. And Eos says to her brother, Helios, 'Well, I just couldn't help myself. He just looks too fucking good, yeah?'

"So Apollo goes to Mother Earth, who is a good mother but for some reason can only give birth to monsters; and he tells her that Orion, this hunter, this man, this—"

"Mother-fucker," Birgit added.

"He tells her that Orion will kill all the wild animals in the whole world. So Mother Earth sends one of her babies, a big scorpion, out to kill Orion. Orion is out hunting and this scorpion the size of the Taj Mahal comes after him. And he shoots his arrows and he throws his spear and he stabs at it with his sword, but it can't be killed because it is immortal. So he runs down to the ocean and jumps in and starts swimming back to the East, back to Eos, his old girlfriend, hoping she is going to protect him.

"Apollo then goes to Artemis and tells her, 'See that thing bobbing out on the waves, way over there in the East? That mother-fucker just seduced your high priestess and he's been chasing your best girlfriends, the Pleiades, all over Boeotia.'

"The Pleiades were supposed to be virgins, but everyone knew they'd slept around rather a lot—with Zeus, Poseidon, Ares, yeah? But for Artemis, that is really beside the point. She doesn't want to see her girlfriends pushed around. So she fits an arrow in her bow and lets fly. And the arrow hits Orion right between the eyes."

Birgit slapped her thigh.

"I like that story," she said after a minute. "But I thought the scorpion got him."

"In some versions."

"That is a—big story," Boon said slowly, badly slurring the word "story."

"I think not so big as the shadow play," Eva replied. "Not so long as the 'Princess of Daha.' The *prologue* was ninety minutes."

Everybody laughed.

"Princess Daha?" Conrad said, grateful for a change of topic. "Isn't that the local brothel?"

"Yeah?" Birgit said. "Where we were today when we meet you?"

Conrad tried to explain, but Boon interrupted him with loud laughter.

"Princess Daha!" he cried with obvious delight. "Oh, very funny." The women laughed too, exchanging remarks in Swedish as Conrad tried to resume his explanation.

"No! Don't say any more," Birgit nudged him. "We know all about *your* type."

Conrad stopped talking. The darkness grew constricted, as though he had been stuffed into a small box. An uncomfortable silence fell over the others and for a moment there was only the droning of insects and the starry swatch of sky.

Eva began talking about their plans for the next day. She and Birgit were going up to Wat Tara Sek, the Buddhist temple up in the hills. Boon was coming along as a guide. He was going to show them the rituals and explain the customs and perhaps get them an interview with the head monk. It was going to be a wonderful day. Conrad, she insisted, should think about joining them. They could hire a taxi together. It would be almost as cheap as taking the bemo—one of those little pickup trucks with a canvas awning and benches in the back. And the taxi would be a lot more comfortable.

"Oh, well—yes," said Conrad, recovering his mood. "Let's be comfortable, by all means."

6

The fabled kingdom of Tambralinga, Keats' "resplendent queen of Siamesian dawn," is now just a crescent-shaped swath of territory along the Gulf of Siam. Ethnic rivalries pitting the predominantly Buddhist Paktai (southern Thai) against the Muslim Yawi (ethnic Malay) have colored local politics since the end of World War II. (Other minorities, such as Mon, Chinese, and Indians are also in the mix.) Low-level insurgencies kept Tambralinga virtually closed to tourism for over two decades, but in recent years the country has stabilized. In 1995 the Sultan of Tambralinga extended the olive branch to non-Muslims in what some call an historic speech before the new Parliament. The Sultan hoped for much-needed foreign capital, but the most immediate result was a surge of Western tourists.

The big draw so far has been the islands—arguably the last unspoiled ones in the region. But the mainland offers unique opportunities for both the "culture" and the "eco" tourist. However, travelers should be prepared to deal with very basic accommodations and relatively primitive amenities.

—Introduction, *Coswell's Guide to Tambralinga* (1997 ed.)

Lucy spread her long arms out in a morning stretch and tilted her head back, taking in the breadth of the cloudless sky. The blue sky here seemed to lack the crystalline depth of the skies back home, perhaps because the wind off the sea was balmy instead of frigid, and the air thick with moisture. She let her breath out slowly. Lucy had awakened that morning gripped with the feeling that this day would be different, would yield great changes. The previous night was the first night in almost five years she'd spent apart from her husband.

She'd been in poor spirits at first, still angry over the loss of her guidebook. Conrad's blinkered, plodding mannerisms had driven her over the edge and she'd blown up over some trifle, some bit of sarcasm she thought she'd detected in his voice. The truth was, she never knew with Conrad, was never absolutely sure if his aggravating qualities were congenital or the result of years of hard practice. The way he'd dragged his feet when they were preparing for this trip—that was almost understandable. Left to his own devices, the idea of traveling to exotic countries would never have occurred to him. (It had come to *her* from out of the blue.) She could hardly expect him to get excited by it. But losing the guidebook—that bore all the earmarks of outright sabotage. He'd known how hard she'd worked on their itinerary and how hard it was for her to move forward without a game plan. Losing that book had effectively marooned her on this damn island. And if she had to be shipwrecked on an island with somebody, let's face it, she'd rather it not be Conrad.

Yesterday, when she'd returned to the bungalow after her morning walk, she'd discovered Conrad had gone. There was just a note on the bed. She'd felt a pang of guilt—she had been treating him harshly—but in the end, it was only a pang. The note on the bed, the romantic starkness of it, brought a rush of relief. It was, she realized, what she'd been working toward all along. Perhaps that was a cold way to put it, but it was colder still not to admit what she was really doing.

She'd been ready for him to go away for a year now, if she had to be honest. But she'd put off telling him. Could not simply come out and say it. For how can you tell him you want a divorce when he's looking at you with that trusting and somewhat mournful expression? It would be easier to shoot a basset hound. And so you put it off for another week or two; the situation does not, after all, demand immediate action. The fling with Antoine had fizzled some time before; he'd come to resemble the transitional figure he was. But transitional to what? That was the question.

She took another deep breath, attempted to exhale her annoyance, her guilt, and the chorus of argumentative voices filling her head. It seemed to work.

She resumed her walk in a radiance of unprecedented delight. The palm trees leaning out toward the water, the gaily painted fishing boats drawn up on the sand, the sound of the breaking waves—all this seemed to have been arranged for her pleasure, as if constructed from answers given on a marketing questionnaire.

In general, I prefer tropical breezes that:
(a) come off the ocean at 5–10 mph and have a slight cooling effect.
(b) come from the land at 3–5 mph and have a slight warming effect.
(c) gently move the tops of trees but don't actually touch me.

Yet all moods, she knew, were fleeting.

She came to the middle of a deserted beach walled in on either side by granite ridges. She bent down to pick up a shell, a tiger cowrie, and studied for a moment the pattern of spots on the top side. The top was suffused with a faint orange, and against this backdrop were black spots, each with a dark red rim. Upon closer inspection, each of these spots became the image of a total eclipse, the lunar silhouette haloed by the sun's red corona. That movements of the sun and moon could be mirrored in a bit of calcium seized Lucy's imagination. Was this what magical thinking was like? Certainly she was incapable of thinking this way back home. For one thing, the beaches back home were hopelessly bland, offering only gray sand dollars and mussel shells. The sand also had a grayness to it, was merely small gravel. Here it was powdered sugar.

A small bird swooped close overhead and was gone before she realized it was upon her. Lucy moved a little inland, where the sand was softer, and resumed her walk. It was odd to be on a beach with no other people on it. Almost all of the beaches on the island had a small hotel and restaurant. Probably every beach on every island in the Gulf of Siam had at least one hotel on it. The Thai islands, she'd heard, were wall-to-wall with hotel and bungalow operations. Rumors of this sort dismayed her adventurous side, but now she discovered a different sort of dismay creeping into her thoughts, the old North American fear of venturing unescorted into lonely areas.

The islands were supposed to be safe for women traveling alone. That's what everyone at Dak's Bungalows said. The Buddhist men were said to be mellow, not sex-obsessed like their puritanical Islamic brethren on the mainland. Certainly Lucy wanted to believe these pleasant generalizations, but lately it was hard for her to picture men who were not preoccupied with sex. Unless they were somnambulists, like Conrad.

She studied the ridge ahead for signs of movement. The route she'd chosen was supposed to take her to a narrow path that climbed the ridge and then led over to another beach, where the snorkeling was said to be exceptional. Vegetation covered the ridge; here and there jungly-looking patches were squeezed in between coconut groves. Nothing moved. Along the water's edge far ahead of her, birds were flocking. Conrad hated hiking, generally hated being out-of-doors. He worked out religiously on the Stairmaster, would go on indefinitely as long as he had something to read. But put him on an actual trail, place him among some trees and flowing water and throw a few logs in his path, and he'd be exhausted by the time he'd gone a hundred yards. No curiosity. No need to see what was around the next bend. Just some vague anxiety because there was no way of telling exactly how far he'd gone, how many calories he'd burned up.

She thought she saw something moving along the base of the ridge, an orange dot with a gait that suggested a person walking. She stopped and tried to focus on it, but then lost it. Funny how the prospect of another's presence made her heart palpitate. It felt like an invasion of her privacy. My beach, she thought. And this made her wonder about who actually owned the land she walked on, for everything was owned by someone, and she'd heard disturbing rumors about whole villages being plowed under to make room for hotels and shops, the people awakened in the middle of the night and scattered like so many earwigs.

The place where the birds were flocking now emerged as a lump of something that had washed up on the shore. Lucy picked up her pace a little. She'd heard about porpoises washing ashore in these islands. But if the birds were eating it, the thing was probably already dead. Why hurry to see a corpse, she asked herself. One became a corpse soon enough.

A boat appeared around the rocky promontory in front of her. It looked at first like a *kolek*, an old-fashioned fishing boat, painted bright red, with a long prow that curved up out of the water and a stern built much the same way, so that the boat's profile resembled the horns of a cow, or a crescent moon half-submerged. It was not a *kolek*, however, but a water taxi taking tourists from one beach resort to another. Lucy planned to take a boat like that back to her bungalow at day's end. Passengers could ride all the way around the island if they wanted to. She had suggested that as a day's outing for Conrad several times. It was just his style, a slow boat puttering close to shore, a gentle unfolding of ocean and island vistas. He could have stopped in town for lunch, chatted with other travelers in a bar. Instead he had insisted, with cordial stubbornness, on staying in the bungalow, in the hammock, reading. He'd seemed determined to strut his indifference, to punish her with it. His idea of revenge? No, he hadn't a clue about the thing with Antoine. He was just doing what came naturally. That is, mechanically. She wondered if he'd taken the water taxi to the harbor to make his escape. That would be in character. He'd probably been planning the whole deal for days. In any case, when he returned, they would make up and then go on with whatever could be resurrected from their itinerary. A visit to the old Portuguese fort in Lingga Baharu on the mainland. Maybe a half-day tour of the mangrove swamps. There was a famous mosque somewhere, and a Buddhist temple known for its frescoes and gold leaf. And a festival dedicated to a sea god in some little town down south, the name of which she could not recall.

But the thought of the lost guidebook suddenly irked her. The bastard had done it on purpose, though he would never admit it, even to himself. If she had dared to call him on it, his eyes would have gotten all rabbity and tender and his voice would have grown soft and concerned and he would have made her feel in an instant that she was to blame, that her selfishness was always to blame. Just picturing the scene made her hot. And his note! He'd offered only the flimsiest pretext for leaving, a sudden need to go to the mainland to change money. Not a word about being angry. And he was deliberately vague about when he would return. "We'll see how it goes," he'd concluded.

How dare he waste her precious vacation time with some stupid jaunt? Was she supposed to wait around while he made up his mind as to whether or not he would enjoy himself?

The thing at the water's edge was surrounded by vultures, which grew restless and then flew off as Lucy approached. It was a corpse all right, but of what she could not tell. It was about the size of a large dog, but had no legs and no head and no hide. Obviously it had been floating around in the sea for some time. It seemed to be just a sac of muscle and organs, white and purplish and bilious yellow in spots, encased in a translucent skin that reminded her of the membrane enclosing a leg of lamb. Here and there the vultures had bitten through the membrane to harvest a liver or kidney.

It might have been a calf at one time. Or a goat. Maybe a pregnant whale had miscarried and this was the result. Did whales miscarry? She supposed it was possible. Maybe they knew instinctively when they were going to miscarry and came here to do it—an elephant's graveyard sort of thing. That would explain why there was no bungalow operation here.

As she passed, the stench overwhelmed her for a moment, but then it was behind her with all of the flies resettled and the vultures patiently regrouping. Life goes on. Now she could let herself feel sick. She stopped for a moment and picked up another shell, a delphinula, the best one she'd ever found. Also a corpse, in a way, she couldn't help thinking, as she studied its delicate stripes.

The last part of the body to dissolve away, like the teeth in a human. She tossed the shell toward the water and picked up her pace. The place was giving her the creeps.

She came to the end of the beach more quickly than she'd expected. The ridge was not as high as she'd first thought and not nearly as steep as it had looked from the midpoint. She found a path and noted with some relief that it had a well-used look about it.

The trail proved longer than she'd hoped, however, winding through coconut groves and plots of peanuts and vegetables and then, where the slope became very steep, into a scrub forest. Here the path grew indecisive, branching off in different directions. She chose one and soon found herself in a stand of small trees, which became denser as she went on. The path narrowed; she began feeling crowded by the polelike trunks. She considered the possibility that she had been on the wrong path from the start and cursed, briefly, out loud. By the time she made it to the other beach, the sun would be overhead, and she couldn't afford more burning to her shoulders. She'd neglected to bring a T-shirt to wear over her bathing suit, had worn only her long-sleeved denim shirt. It wasn't something she felt safe swimming in. She remembered too clearly *Hamlet*'s Ophelia being dragged to the river's bottom by her waterlogged garments. Though now that she thought of it, she supposed that the lack of adequate safety instruction was as much to blame. The poor dear had been born before the buddy system was established. On the other hand, because she, Lucy, had no buddy for this outing, all the more weight should have been given to proper attire.

In the midst of these thoughts, the path took a sudden turn and she almost poked her eye on a dead branch. Startled, she yanked her head away and stumbled backward. As the branch came into focus, she could see that it had eyes of its own, was in fact a snake that had wrapped itself around the trunk and extended its neck and upper body outwards, holding them rigid so as to mimic a branch.

"Jesus!" she said, putting her hand on her throat. The prospect of being bitten by a venomous snake in a remote portion of a remote island in a country nobody had ever heard of now seemed an imminent possibility.

"Jesus!" she said again. She looked around her. A few trees away another snake had struck a similar pose. Or was that an actual branch? The trees ahead had twigs and branches sticking out all over. She'd probably have to go to the capital, or farther, to Bangkok, before she could find competent doctors, reliable serums. By then she could be dead. King cobras abounded in Asian jungles. Everyone knew that. A bite meant death in seconds. This was also well known.

She was growing dizzy. Had she already been bitten? No, she was hyperventilating. She crouched down and put her head between her knees and tried hard not to picture herself as a headless torso, rotting away in the bush. This was no way to proceed. She had to clear her head. But, Jesus, she hated snakes!

Okay, was this in fact a king cobra she was looking at? Was this a jungle she was in? A "no" answer for the second question increased the likelihood of a "no" answer for the first question. She decided to look at the forest first. The trees were all the same, almost looked as though they'd been planted. Maybe they had been planted, planted and forgotten. Her arms began to tingle. She was holding her breath, for Christ's sake. This was not the thing to do after hyperventilating. She concentrated on her breathing: in and out, in and out. What a chore breathing would be if you had to think about it all day. And forget about ever getting a decent night's sleep. In and out. In and out. That was better. It was getting better . . .

She glanced up at the snake and then down at her feet. It couldn't be more than three feet in length. Cobras were meant to be big, like boa constrictors, weren't they? (Conrad would know, of course. He was full of all sorts of irrelevant facts.) Of course its not being a cobra didn't necessarily mean it was harmless. Still, if this was not a jungle and the snake was not a cobra, there were grounds for optimism.

She stood up slowly, reminding herself again to breathe. The snake stared out at her in the all-encompassing, expressionless way of reptiles. If the thing was trying to look like a branch, maybe it would let her duck underneath as if it actually were a branch, maybe if she approached slowly, with her head bowed sufficiently low. She could try to go around the tree, but the other trees were particularly crowded at that spot and probably contained more snakes, hidden away. This one was at least out in the open.

She inched forward, then quickly bowed her head. As she came close again, her nerve failed her—she was certain the thing was going to drop on her head—and she backed up hurriedly. When she looked again, the snake was gone. No sign of it on the ground or up in the tree.

"Jesus," she murmured, "it's fast."

Now was the time to proceed slowly and deliberately, but again her nerve left her and she ran ahead along the narrow path, swatting at twigs and brushy things and anything that moved, until she was out of the trees.

She found herself on somebody's homestead, on a muddy path that zigzagged around plots planted with corn and melons and squash. The path petered out around a row of banana trees, on the other side of which stood a typical Tambralingan house, built on posts with walls made of woven split bamboo and a peaked thatch roof. One side of the house opened onto a raised wooden platform that seemed to be a sort of patio. From the eaves of the house hung two birdcages made of wood and bamboo. Inside each was a white dove. Lucy circled the house, looking, without success, for a continuation of the path, her spirits sinking as she began to estimate the time it would take to retrace her steps and then find the right path. A large bantam rooster came out of nowhere and darted between her legs before taking cover under the house. A strange cry, strangled and high-pitched, that seemed to belong to somebody else, erupted from the back of Lucy's throat. She stopped and looked around. The house looked empty, spooky.

"*Sawatdee!*" A voice called faintly from inside the house. As

Lucy came around to the front again, a monk dressed in a saffron robe emerged from the doorway.

Christ, she thought, is this a monastery? Probably she'd busted up their midday meditation session.

"*Sawatdee! Selamat pagi,*" she ventured. As an afterthought, she put her palms together and then raised her hands up to her forehead in a Buddhist *wai*. The monk nodded curtly.

"*Khun sàbaay dii máy?*" he asked. He sat down on the platform, legs crossed underneath him. His voice was soft.

"Sorry to bother you. I'm lost. Do you know how to get to Kutan Beach? The sea?"

"Ah! I see!" the monk said.

"Yes, the sea. Do you know the way?" and here it occurred to her that she was talking too fast. She took a breath and began again.

"You go sea?" she asked, carefully enunciating each word.

The monk grunted.

"Was that a 'yes'?" Lucy asked. "Which way Kutan Beach?" She pointed in different directions. The monk followed the movements of her finger with a look of puzzled anticipation, rather like that of a small dog. And just when Lucy labeled the situation hopeless, the monk's expression changed, as though some internal mechanism that processed English utterances had been switched on and was now warming up.

"Heh-witch. Hway. Oh! Which way. Which way Kutan Beach. Yes. Are you *anglais*?"

"I speak English. I'm American."

"Oh—'merica," he smiled briefly. "Numba one, yeah?"

"Yes. And I'm going to Kutan Beach," Lucy persisted, pronouncing each word with exaggerated precision. "Do you know the way?"

"Sore-ree," the monk replied. "Not from here. I am Thailand monk."

"You're not from this island—from Ko Neak Pean?"

"No. From Thailand. Surin. Near Surin. Near Kampuchea.

But many Thai peoples in Tambralinga, so have many friends. I visit." It took a while to get this all out.

The monk unfolded his crossed legs and let them dangle off the edge of the platform and rest on a short railing that seemed to have been constructed for that purpose. Lucy took a half-step backward. The schoolgirl part of her worried about the proper etiquette one was supposed to display when talking to a monk. There had been a long passage about it in the guidebook. Another part of her worried about just how much of a monk this monk actually was. Monks were supposed to live at the *wat*, on the temple grounds. They weren't supposed to be roaming about visiting friends' houses when nobody was home. Perhaps he was one of those guys who played at being a monk for a couple of years. In Thailand, taking temporary vows was sometimes an alternative to military service, or at least it used to be. But this guy looked too old to be a draft dodger.

"So you travel around a lot?" Lucy asked. She folded her arms for a moment, then remembered that the gesture was considered rude, a sign of anger in fact, and quickly dropped them to her sides.

"Travel many. Much travel. Visit different *wats*. Stay in Tambralinga when rain."

"The rainy season? You mean, when it's rainy in Thailand, you come down here for a few months?"

He nodded.

"But now you're all alone?"

"Yes."

The doves in the hanging cages began cooing and hopping around. For a moment, Lucy could think of nothing to say.

"Missus, please. What you have in bag?"

"This? Just snorkeling gear. You know, mask, fins, snorkel."

"Snuggle?"

"Snorkel. Snore Cull."

"Ah! Snore Cull."

"Are there other monks staying here?" Lucy asked uneasily.

"Sore-ree. No uddah monk here."

Lucy took a half-step backward. There was no need to get too close.

"I am—I help sick peoples. Give cure. Med'cines."

"You mean herbal remedies?"

He grunted. He hadn't understood the question. Lucy rephrased it:

"You go into the jungle, you find medicines from plants—in the forest?"

The monk looked at her for a moment, as if waiting for her words to settle into some kind of sensible pattern. But Lucy's thoughts rushed ahead: there were thousands of medicinal herbs and plants in the rain forests, a treasure trove of genetic engineering. This according to the article she'd read in the in-flight magazine. And across the globe, in small pockets and enclaves, there were still traditional healers, albeit fewer and fewer every year, whose collective wisdom held the key to these treasures. She touched her throat where her jugular throbbed with apparent enthusiasm.

"I learn from Muslim man in Tambralinga," the monk went on. "He know many things. I take back to Thailand. To help the peoples there."

"You take back herbs from here? Plants, I mean. From the rain forest?" The monk smiled, a broad, dazzling smile. And for a moment Lucy wondered if she hadn't stumbled onto an international network of native healers. She remembered then that standing in front of a monk was considered bad manners. One must always keep one's head lower than the monk's. She sat down slowly on the ground, tucking her legs under her so that her feet pointed away from the monk. It was not comfortable, but nonetheless somehow urgently necessary.

"I help peoples in Thailand," the monk repeated. "If sick, I help. If they want some baby or wife want husband to come back, I help. I help with people lose things."

"You help people lose things? No—you help people find *lost* things."

The monk grunted. From a small woven bag he produced a package of cigarettes and shook one out.

"I don't understand," Lucy asked as the monk continued to rummage through his bag. "How does a plant—medicine—help you find a lost thing?"

The monk grunted again and then, putting his bag down, looked back at Lucy.

"Please, missus," he said. "Have matches?"

"Oh, sure—" She opened her daypack and, pushing the rubber fins and snorkel aside, uncovered a box of matches. As she stood up, arm extended, she remembered it was taboo for a woman to touch a monk. She pulled her hand back and tossed the matches into his lap.

"Okay?" she asked as she sat back down. The monk laughed.

"Okay—okay. No problem." His eyes all but disappeared when he laughed.

Timidly, Lucy asked for a cigarette. The monk tossed one to her and then followed up with the matches. Lucy laughed as she caught them. She hadn't smoked a cigarette in years. She felt suddenly like she was doing something very naughty. She lit up, then casually tossed the box of matches on the ground next to her bag.

"So what kind of plant—do you use to find lost things?"

"No plants, missus." He made a motion around his neck, seemed to be groping for a word. "Like necklace—gem."

"Oh," Lucy said, confused. Suddenly it hit her: "You mean an amulet?"

"Omelette," the monk nodded.

So he did some sort of magic to retrieve lost items. That could be handy.

"Well," Lucy went on. "I've lost the guidebook. And now my husband is missing."

The monk pulled on his cigarette and considered her with a cool eye.

"Which more important?"

He blew a smoke ring with his last syllable. It hung in the dead air between them for a moment, rotating around an invisible center. Lucy stiffened. Was this guy flirting with her? Why had she let it slip about Conrad being out of the picture? That couldn't have been smart.

"Many wife come to me for help," the monk said. "They say, 'Husband have gull friend. Help me get him back.' In Thailand many men have gull friend—number two wife—so much business for me. In Tambralinga, Muslim man have number two, tree, four wife sometime. So Muslim *pawang* have much business."

"So you come here to learn from the Muslim healers," Lucy said slowly, "because they have more experience in—love?"

The monk smiled. His smile made him look goofy, like a little boy. Lucy found it disarming.

"In Thailand peoples think Muslim man have best magic for love. They say I am best monk, because I come to Tambralinga and learn. But in Tambralinga, Muslim peoples come to me for love magic. They say Thai monk have best magic. Because I am from far away. Very funny."

Lucy smiled with some effort. It seemed to be time to be on her way, only she'd lost her way and was no closer to finding it.

"So how long before you go back to your—your *wat*?" she said as she snubbed out her cigarette in the ground. Were monks actually allowed to smoke? She supposed it would make fasting easier.

"Six week I go back. Nine week maybe."

"So you're on sabbatical sort of, huh?" she said, slowly getting to her feet.

"Sah-bah-i-clah," the monk pronounced slowly, smiling. He seemed to like the word, as if it had a taste.

"A long vacation. Look, I have to be going now. I want to thank you for—you know."

The monk's smile went away. He had a small mouth when he wasn't smiling.

"But, missus, I help you find you loved thing." He drew an amulet from his bag. It dangled on the end of a chain, small and triangular, the color of dirty bronze.

"Find my what? Oh, the guidebook."

The monk held the chain out with his right hand. She could see now that the amulet was part of a necklace, that he meant her to come forward to receive it.

"Omelette have Buddha image," he said. "Can't throw at you. Bad disrespect. I put round you neck, no touching."

Lucy felt her urban instincts kicking in. The shaved head and brown skin took on a menacing cast. She took a step backward. The smile returned. She took another step backward. He didn't look insulted. But who could tell, she thought, with the way they smile at you all the time.

The birds in the surrounding trees grew still as somewhere above a large dark form swept past, honking queerly, like an asthmatic Canada goose. The sound filled Lucy with a sad yearning, and she discovered a magnetism in the monk's smile, in its obliviousness, its crazy insistence. She found herself moving toward him again, recovering the ground she'd lost. When Antoine had asked her that first time to ride with him to the ocean-view property, it had felt exactly the same. Something about the play of light on the eyes and the way the lips parted in anticipation of her answer had made his face radiant.

She moved closer to the monk. He will kill you after he rapes you, a familiar voice in the back of her head nagged. She hated that voice, which she now associated with her husband, or at least that part of her that had once argued for marrying him. But abruptly the voice was quieted. Lucy lowered her head to receive the necklace, felt a trembling seize her limbs as she stared at the rough-hewn posts that supported the house. She sensed the monk extending his arm over her left shoulder as he casually looped the necklace over her head; then stared at the amulet as it dangled down over her bathing suit top. It seemed to her that the monk was breathing on her face. His head was very close to hers and he had not yet released the necklace. The monk inhaled audibly. Flyaway strands on the top of her head brushed the tip of his nose, or so she supposed. Her heart began to race. The monk murmured something in a deep voice, then inhaled again. He was smelling her, for Christ's sake!

She pulled back; for a moment it seemed she would faint. The monk looked down at her with the face of a dreamer freshly awakened.

"Missus," he said. "I don't finished prayer yet."

"It's okay. No problem." She was breathing hard; it occurred to her that she'd been holding her breath. If this was Buddhist foreplay, she wanted no more of it. The monk looked down at her blankly, like a cat perched on a windowsill.

"Missus, I must finish prayer. Make omelette find you loved thing."

"I'm sure it'll work just fine," she said, backing up. She bent down to pick up her bag. "Like a charm. I mean, it is a charm, right?"

She brought her palms together and bowed hastily. She noticed the matchbox still lying on the ground where she'd tossed it, but decided to leave it there. The monk nodded slightly, and returned her *wai* using only one hand.

"Thank you very much," she said, as she continued backing away. "I'll tell all of my friends at the bungalows about you."

Meaning what exactly? she wondered. That the tourist dollars would come his way? She realized she was babbling, something she did when she was really scared. But she wasn't scared, not really, and the monk was smiling at her as if at an indulged child. Perhaps they had struck some kind of bargain.

She turned and walked quickly back the way she'd come. A yellow cur sleeping in the shade of the house opened one eye and followed her footfalls. Maybe the guy had been praying. Wasn't that what religious types were supposed to do? But young men became monks for a whole host of reasons that had nothing to do with religious calling. She'd been wise to get the hell out of there. He could have had a knife—or anything—hidden in those robes. Probably thought nothing about handling corpses. Hadn't she read somewhere that Buddhist cremations were all handled by monks? She thought of the carcass on the beach and then decided to put aside further speculation.

She found herself on a wide path that took her inland along

the crest of the ridge, where it met another well-worn path. A crude, hand-painted sign pointed the way to Kutan Beach, but she decided to go in the opposite direction, down through a grove of coconut trees to the other beach and back to the bungalows. On the way down, she noticed the amulet on the metal chain bouncing against her chest and suddenly felt giddy, as if she'd gotten away with a bit of shoplifting. She stopped to examine it: a tiny sitting Buddha encased in a clear plastic shell. The bronze image was old and worn, perhaps even a little dirty.

As she crossed the beach, she stayed away from the water's edge, afraid of encountering the carcass again. Happily, she saw no sign of it. The tide had come in.

The first glimpse of the peaked roof of her bungalow filled Lucy with relief; she resigned herself to waiting a few days for Conrad's return. She told herself she would ignore Conrad's subtle hostilities and instead marshal all of her energies toward making the remainder of the trip relaxing and interesting for both of them. Later, however, while straightening up the room, she found the guidebook. It was in Conrad's pillowcase, underneath the pillow itself, most likely stashed in a hurried moment and then forgotten. Inside, like so many pressed flowers, she found her lists, her itinerary, with the locations, dates, prices, and travel times rendered in unblemished, laser-printed letters. And these things, the essential building blocks of her much-planned trip, now seemed endowed with magical luminescence. She no longer needed to wait for Conrad.

Again she examined the amulet still hanging around her neck. Besides the Buddha image, something else was encased in the plastic, a bit of grayish smut. When she shook the amulet, the stuff moved around. "Ashes," she thought, picturing cremations. She replaced this image with that of a cigarette, and then found herself craving one.

7

The taxi was a tight fit for Conrad. He was assigned the front passenger seat, in which he rode with head bowed and knees pressed against the dash. The inside of the cab was too small to allow him to sit up straight, and he had pulled his seat as far forward as it could go to give the women and Boon as much room as possible in the back. The road was little more than a gash in the mountain, an unyielding series of steep switchbacks. Conrad's head repeatedly hit the ceiling, but he answered all inquiries about his comfort cheerfully, and made a point of laughing when they hit a particularly deep rut. Boon, meanwhile, seated between the two women, would shift his body around, apologizing for the inevitable rubbing of knees and thighs. He was a handsome young man with a compact, muscular frame. There was a smoothness about him, an ease of manner that matched the plasticine sheen of his skin and the wide planes of forehead and cheek. He reacted to everything the same way, with a soft, creeping smile, a smile that suggested profound insight.

And yet what insight Boon did possess, Conrad felt sure, did not apply to women. He was trying too hard with Eva, making flimsy excuses to touch her and talking first very loudly, then very softly, as if unsure how to approach her. He seemed to lack a sense of timing and any aptitude for gauging from moment to moment another's receptiveness. But then again, Conrad reflected, maybe the women found this clumsiness amusing. Maybe it made them feel safe.

Halfway up a steep stretch, the taxi began to overheat. The driver pulled the cab over into a shady spot. They all got out and stretched. After a short while, a bemo, overloaded with tourists and locals, came grinding up the hill.

"Ha!" Birgit said. "I think they will win over us."

The taxi driver leaned against the front fender and smoked a cigarette. Deeper in the shade, Eva and Boon were in a huddle, talking. Conrad detected an edge to Eva's voice. Reading Boon the riot act, he supposed. He asked Birgit for a cigarette.

"Ha!" she said, exultant. "I thought you were so *clean* about this, this smoking."

"When in Rome," he said. She took out her pack and handed it to him. He glanced at the label.

" 'Willow Leaf,' " he read. "Is that a local brand?"

"Not so good as your American cigarettes, you think?"

"I didn't mean it that way."

She glanced over her shoulder at Eva and Boon, then looked back at Conrad. The sun was directly in her face and this made everything tighten up.

"Everything in America is the best, isn't it?" she said. "Everything is the world's greatest or the world's biggest. Maybe you need a really *big* cigarette."

Conrad stammered a reply: She'd misunderstood him.

"I'm only joking," she said, touching his arm. She struck a match and came in close for a moment so he could light his cigarette. The cigarette was short and smelled strongly of cloves. He managed to inhale a little of the harsh smoke. Did they call it Willow Leaf because they used willow leaves instead of tobacco, he wanted to know.

"Willow Leaf is this legendary figure," Birgit said. "Like Eva, you know, the first woman. I don't remember exactly." She looked over her shoulder again.

"I don't know why she lets this guy hang around," Birgit said quickly. She lit her own cigarette and then walked away. When she'd gone a little way up the road, she turned and gestured for Conrad to follow. Perhaps they would find a view up ahead, she suggested. But in fact, they were on a forested hillside and the

trees were dense along either side of the road. Birgit's movements
were brisk and hard.

"I don't know what we are doing up here," she said, stopping
to take a drag on her cigarette. "Too many tourists. I want to see
the real country. On Kuala Vimaya, on the mainland. My friend
Rahman is there. We met at university." She looked back the way
they'd come. Conrad looked back too. Everything was around
the bend, hidden from view.

"Good friends?" Conrad asked.

"Friend. At university," Birgit replied, still looking back. "He
explains to me of the troubles here, the politics. I am more interested in this, in the protests. I want to see this—movement."

"What are they protesting against?" Conrad asked carefully.
Birgit's face contorted with disbelief.

"Everything! Everything here is so corrupt—it's—it's—everything. Most people are Yawi—Muslim, you know. But all the
land, the businesses, is owned by a few rich families, mostly Chinese or Paktai. They pretend this is a sultanate, they even have a
parliament; but the Paktai run the police and the army. The Sultan does whatever they tell him, the parliament has no power.
They destroy the forest, they—destroy the fishes, they stealing
land from the poor, they—they tax everything, but the money gets
taken away."

"Embezzled?"

"Yes. The Sultan's family. The police. Army. No money for
schools or university. No medicine. And everywhere the rickets—
the prostitution, the extortion, the stealing."

She was pacing back and forth in the road as she spoke, gesturing with her cigarette.

"If you are protest leader, they put you in jail. They make up
big stories about how they are drug dealings or stealing children
out of the country, to China or Marseilles, to sell them for prostitution or for the organ trains."

"Organ transplants?" Conrad asked. "Who's doing this?"

"No one! It's the government *saying* that they do this thing so
they can put the mens—the leaders of the opposition—in jail."

Birgit began to cry. She pressed the heel of her palm against her eyebrow and squeezed her eyes shut. Conrad looked at her, confused. After a moment, he decided to apologize, although he was not sure what for. He raised his hands up, meaning to place them lightly on her shoulders, then hesitated.

"Hey," he said. "It's going to be okay."

She knocked his hands away and slapped him across the face.

"Nothing is going to be 'okay,' you idiot!"

A moment passed before he understood what had happened. Inside himself was something like a wind, a fierce corkscrew tunneling through him. And it was this force and not the blow that was making his face burn. Birgit turned her back to him and held her face momentarily in her hands.

"I am sorry," she said into her hands.

"It's okay," Conrad said again, with less conviction. He touched his nose, discovered a droplet of blood on his fingertip. A hot, numbing silence descended upon them. He perceived himself trying to fill it with half-formed statements: Didn't mean to upset, It seemed rather like, Couldn't tell whether—

"It was a misunderstood," Birgit said, turning around.

"Yes, that's the word," Conrad said. "Thank you. I meant to say that. But I couldn't think of it."

"I get overexcited, sometimes. This political business."

"I understand. I'm the same way."

"I'm not really mean, you know. It is just I have—so much inside."

"Emotional," Conrad said.

"Yes, too emotional. Here—" She produced a tissue from her woven purse and handed it to Conrad.

"But you're caring too," Conrad said after a moment. "That's important."

"Yes, I agree," Birgit said. "Not good to be all shut up inside, but still—"

"Yes," said Conrad.

"I'm sorry about your nose."

"It's always been like this. Sometimes it bleeds for no reason." Conrad blew some air between his lips to emphasize how prosaic this was.

"I am so stupid sometimes," Birgit said.

"I guess we all got carried away." Conrad noticed faint circles under her eyes. Looking her directly in the eyes became difficult. He let his gaze wander across the road.

"Sometimes you just can't express emotion so neatly," he went on, suddenly aware of the stiff way he was standing, hunched over with his shoulders nearly touching his ears. "Sometimes it just spills out spontaneously."

"I'm sorry, but I don't believe it is right to—to be acting that way."

"But sometimes it's good, don't you think? It clears the air." Conrad began what he intended as a grand sweeping motion of his arm, but only managed to execute the opening of his palm.

"You are being too graceful," Birgit said, extending her hand. Conrad took it and they shook.

"No, really. I understand. I get that way about politics all the time."

Why had he said that? He wasn't in any way political. Not since way back when, since before personal computers, since before Watergate. But now she was looking at him strangely, as if seeing him in a new light.

"I went to school in Berkeley in the sixties," he added quickly, as if that explained everything. This seemed to spark something in Birgit.

"You were of the antiwar movement?"

Conrad paused. He'd been dragged to a couple of rallies and breathed some tear gas, but that had been nothing special, almost unavoidable in those days.

"I—I worked with the Committee," he said solemnly. Another lie! The sheer audacity of it took his breath away. What committee could he be referring to? He had no idea. No matter, the ambiguity of the word was working wonders, if Birgit's expression was any indication.

" 'Ho! Ho! Ho Chi Minh! The NLF is sure to win!' " he recited. Where had he heard that one? On the TV probably. Or from his roommate, who had enjoyed parodying the political fashions of the day. Birgit laughed, covering her mouth with her hand. It must have sounded silly. She obviously felt embarrassed for him.

Conrad looked up at the clouds and the sun. He hadn't the slightest idea what to do next.

8

On the polished wooden floor in the main hall, a handful of Tambralingan women prostrated before the altar. Following Boon's example, Eva and Birgit slipped off their sandals and stepped carefully over the threshold. Conrad hung back. His face still tingled where Birgit had struck him. He watched the women sit down on the wooden floor, tucking their feet underneath them Japanese-style, and cautiously salute the Buddha image by pressing their palms together and raising them to their foreheads. He found himself repelled by the incense and the flowers and by the gold leaf that seemed to be peeling off one of the statues like dead skin. Conrad drifted out into the big courtyard with the beginnings of a headache, past odd, pyramid-like shrines that had what looked like knobby flagpoles rising out of their centers.

What was all this for, he wondered. He began studying the faded murals along the compound walls, as if they might offer clues to what had happened between him and Birgit. Here was the Buddha preaching to mendicants in the forest, here was the Buddha as a young prince being carried around in a litter, and farther along were pictures of clashing armies and hilltop fortresses set ablaze. Were these all part of the same story, Conrad wondered, or scenes from different stories all jumbled up? There were no borders separating one scene from the next. They all seemed to be happening at the same time, spread out across the same landscape. The warriors in the battle scenes wore golden helmets with long, pointed peaks. Some had tusks and huge bulging eyes and held short bows with exaggerated, sensuous curves; probably these were the bad guys. On closer inspection, however, it seemed that both sides had their fair share of demonic warriors.

A few yards from Conrad, a young man in dark glasses approached the mural. There was a quiet, purposeful air about his movements that suggested knowledge, perhaps even intimacy with the paintings. Conrad heard himself ask a question. The young man answered casually, without turning his head away from the mural, as if he were continuing a conversation begun sometime before.

"Scenes from the *Ramayana*, I think," he said. "Here is the demon king abducting Sita, Rama's wife. And there is Rama's army led by Hanuman, the monkey god." He spoke softly, but because of the clear timbre of his voice, still loudly enough to be understood.

"I guess I don't see the sequence."

"Well, you see, these painters didn't portray events linearly. This scene here actually comes before that scene over there; and in between is the birth of Rama right there. Makes no sense timewise. It's more how these events might appear if you were standing outside space and time. You might say."

He spoke with an accent that sounded vaguely of England, but also of Southern California. Conrad wondered for a moment what the monkey-headed god had to do with the story of the Buddha, but hesitated to raise the question. Something about the murals began to disturb him, their similarity to the Stations of the Cross he knew from his childhood. These had been painted in the cathedral near his grandmother's house, in an old Chicago neighborhood. Until his grandmother's death, Conrad's parents had forced him once a year to sit through a long and excruciating ceremony, during which the priest and his accomplice swung censers around each picture and detailed in harsh voices the various humiliations Jesus suffered on his way up the hill. There had been something chilling in the way the painter had portrayed the passion of Christ. And Conrad now sensed that same chill in the muralist's rendition of burning fortresses and battle-crazed demons. Conrad regarded the young man carefully.

"You seem to have given all of this a good deal of thought."

"I'm sort of a student of the culture." The young man turned his head toward Conrad. "In a small way.

"I used to wonder why the battles of a Hindu god were plastered on the walls of Buddhist monasteries," the young man went on. "Why these scenes of war and bloodshed—over a woman, no less—in a place that is ostensibly dedicated to monasticism? To celibacy?"

He took off his sunglasses, revealing an oddly intent expression around the eyes.

"While on the one hand, you have the king of the Nagas—that seven-headed cobra over there—shielding the meditating Buddha from the rain with his spreading hood, over here you see his daughter, Willow Leaf, sailing out to meet Prince Kaundinya's boat with a ship full of warriors—they marry, you see, and found the first lineage of kings of Tambralinga. But there is a sensuousness in these moving figures," he said, brushing a bit of hair behind his ear, "a sense of the body that you otherwise wouldn't see much of in Buddhist art."

Conrad looked, but failed to see what he was talking about. The figures looked weirdly stiff and unnatural, crooked swastikas with faces and hands. He assured the young man that it was a "fascinating question," and then quietly excused himself.

Conrad wandered across the temple grounds toward one of the side entrances, where a man dressed in ragged clothing sold small birds in wicker cages. Worshipers coming through the gate stopped to purchase the birds for a few coins. Then, just as they were about to enter the compound, they opened the cage door and let the bird fly free. For a moment Conrad was smitten with the idea. It made a wonderful picture: the cage door swinging open, the bird rising toward the heavens. But to achieve this moment, all of those birds had to be captured and put through the panic and suffering of being caged. In the end, it seemed merely another sort of business.

Conrad drifted back to the main hall just as Birgit and the others were emerging. He found his heart thumping erratically as he came face-to-face with Birgit again.

Eva gushed about how elegant the ritual had been, with its simple offerings of flowers, incense, and candles. A monk, brandishing a lotus flower, had sprinkled them with holy water as they bowed before the altar. The space was light and airy and saturated with a feeling of peace.

Birgit remained unmoved.

"We bow down to the gold statues, yes," she said. "We burn incense to the emperor. So they let us keep our heads."

Boon smiled faintly and clasped his hands behind his back. Eva replied sharply in Swedish.

"It's a state religion, yeah?" Birgit answered in English. She looked to Conrad for confirmation. "Set up to make the king powerful and to protect the rich."

Eva objected. Tambralinga had an Islamic Sultan, not a Buddhist king. Birgit answered that for all practical purposes it made not the slightest difference. Eva turned away from her and walked slowly across the courtyard, wondering aloud in English when

the dancers would start their rehearsal. Boon immediately fell
into step, and Conrad, after a hesitant appraisal of Birgit, decided
to follow.

"When *does* the rehearsal start?" he echoed Eva.

Nobody seemed to know. Boon smiled when Eva suggested he
ask somebody. It was an inward sort of smile; the notion amused
him apparently. Eva then demanded that Boon at least tell everyone the story that the dancers would be enacting, but could get
little out of him besides the fact that the story was about Manora
and that she was some sort of bird.

Manora is not in fact a bird, but a bird-woman, Eva explained
when it was clear that Boon lacked the English vocabulary to get
this across. She is captured by a great hunter when she makes the
mistake of removing her wings to bathe in a lake. The hunter is
forced to sell her to the king and the king makes her marry his
son. Later, after many adventures and plot twists, she escapes her
earthly prison by performing a beautiful dance that has all who
watch it completely hypnotized. Before anyone can move, she
puts her wings back on and flies away.

"Happy story," Boon said.

"Yes, happy story for a change," Conrad said. He looked back
at Birgit. She seemed to be studying him. He wondered if there
would be a bruise on his face in the morning. No matter, he decided to force a smile.

Birgit smiled back. It seemed to Conrad that an implicit understanding was growing between them.

The Manora dancers began assembling in the courtyard. It was
an arresting sight: a patchwork of woven mats were laid out on
the dirt as a sort of stage. A small orchestra, made up of gamelan
and drums, set up a little way behind the staging area. The
women dancers, each wearing an elaborate gold and silver head-
dress that came to an impossibly delicate point and wrapped in a
long silk skirt, green or orange or red, with a narrow apron of
gold brocade, stood with arms folded, along the back of the

stage. The male dancers, their otherwise bare chests crisscrossed with strips of embroidered cloth, wore silver bands along the length of their arms. The women dancers wore sleeveless tops that shimmered with iridescent greens and blues and reds and large silver pendants fringed with silver tassels.

At the sound of a gong, a small woman standing next to the orchestra began to sing. Her voice seemed strange at first, something inhuman, extraterrestrial. She seemed to be crying out to heaven in pain. But then two of the dancers stepped toward the center of the stage and spread their arms in a way that suggested a bird in flight, and Conrad understood that the singer was meant to sound like a bird. An older man, probably the dancing master, stepped between the birds and made his way with careful but fluid movements to the front of the stage. The master seemed to be well past forty, yet he was able to push his body through the series of difficult poses with ease, bending his hands back at the wrist, turning his arms into rippling snakes, moving his head from side to side with quick, precise birdlike motions. Another dancer, wearing a carved wooden mask, fell in step behind the old man. The singer narrated the story of Manora in her plaintive, birdlike voice. The orchestra droned quietly in the background.

For the first fifteen minutes, it seemed a fascinating spectacle, but at twenty, Conrad was surprised to find that an hour had not yet passed. After thirty minutes, he found himself slipping in and out of consciousness, his crossed legs going numb. Periodically the singing was interrupted with an interlude of instrumental music. The orchestra would pick up the tempo, at times getting frantic; and the dancers, with legs bowed and feet pointing out to the sides, would scuttle across the mats like terrified crabs. This helped for a while, but in the end Conrad had to get up.

He wandered around the perimeter of the grounds again, and was surprised to run into the young man, whom he assumed would have taken a ringside seat.

"It's meant to be hypnotic," he said after Conrad explained his trouble. "This is how Manora escapes in the end."

"Is this the end we're seeing, then?"

"Not even close," the young man laughed. "This is the part where the hunter, Bun, goes to the hut of Kassop, an old yogi who lives by the lake where the bird-women come to bathe. He gets him to reveal the secret of how to capture the bird-woman. Kassop tells him that he needs to get a noose, a noose made of a living serpent. And to do that, he's got to go down to the underworld and borrow it—or steal it—from the King of the Nagas. Once he has that noose, he can snare Manora. Provided she has removed her wings."

Conrad soon found himself back at the side gate where the man was still selling birds. They were small and undistinguished-looking, gray finches or brown wrens or something like that, and they fluttered impatiently back and forth against the bars.

A young Tambralingan couple, the man dressed in a stay-pressed polyester shirt and a long red and white sarong, the woman wearing a long-sleeved blouse and a green silk sarong, approached the vendor and negotiated a price for a bird. As Conrad watched, they carried the cage up to the gate of the temple and then opened it solemnly. The tiny bird hopped out and sat for a moment on the top of the cage. Then it stretched its neck and pushed off into the air, soaring in a wide circle around the couple, before shooting up into the sky. The young people watched, smiling, shading their eyes with their hands, as the bird disappeared into the sky. The vendor took the empty cage and stashed it with others against the compound wall. On impulse Conrad decided to free a bird of his own.

The man asked for fifty rials, but Conrad, having watched the last transaction, gave him twenty, knowing he was overpaying at that. The bird he got was completely manic, a cloud of feathers beating itself against the bars, a nasty little bill that drilled his fingertips as he struggled to open the cage door. The bird's frenzy proved contagious; Conrad's fingers nearly broke the cage apart before they got the door open. And as soon as it was open, the bird was gone. There was no trace of it in the sky above, nor in the treetops, nor anywhere on the ground.

"Gee, that was a fast one, huh?" Conrad said to the vendor, as the man took the empty cage out of his hands. Conrad could see at once that the man had no idea what he'd said; but he smiled anyway and replied in his own language, in soft and singsong tones.

As Conrad strolled back toward the dancers, the young man appeared at his side.

"Did you make a wish?" he asked. Apparently he'd seen the whole thing.

"No. I just let it go."

"You're supposed to make a wish. Takes your prayers up to heaven, like a messenger pigeon. Popular with couples trying to conceive."

"My wife and I gave up on that a while back," Conrad replied. "I just wanted it to escape."

He paused as they came up to where the spectators were sitting. Conrad craned his neck for a glimpse of Birgit in the crowd, but could not find her. The dancers suddenly assumed contorted poses, like the figures in the murals, and one of the musicians struck a large gong. The thought came to Conrad:

"They don't really escape, do they?"

"I'm afraid not," the young man said gently. He was trying to be kind. "Tomorrow the man will trap them again. The same traps. And a new bunch of pilgrims will release them."

"Oh." Conrad could not hide his disappointment, could not evade the feeling of being perpetually swindled.

The music stopped; the dancers quit in mid-stride. The rehearsal was over. In front of him, Eva stood, stretched, and yawned. She had been dreaming, she announced, with eyes open. Boon looked sleepy as well. Other spectators surged past them, streaming out through the temple gates. It seemed as if everyone had had enough, was in a hurry to descend the Naga staircase and catch the bemo back to town.

Conrad found his limbs weighed down with renewed lethargy. He watched Eva and Boon move lithely down the steps, sealed off from the rest of the crowd, it seemed, by their youth and beauty. He paused after the first couple of steps and yawned. Someone grabbed his left arm.

"I think this dancing is not so good for you," Birgit smiled up at him. "Now see, we are the last ones."

She announced in a loud voice that she was tired of the islands, sick of the exotic veneer. She'd made up her mind to go to the mainland, to look up her friend in Kuala Vimaya. She would see the "real" Tambralinga, by which she meant the struggle that was taking place there. She'd heard rumors of a general strike in the making, of students and workers and small farmers banding together. There were demonstrations almost daily.

Conrad looked at her. From what she'd told him already, the mainland sounded like a police-run kleptocracy, a bad place for a young woman to be traveling on her own.

"That's exactly why I want to go there," Birgit declared, turning her face toward Conrad. A sly pleasure illuminated her features. "But maybe I bring my bodyguard along for protection, yes?"

She leaned into him for a moment, squeezing his arm. Conrad was too surprised to speak.

Part Two

Sultan

9

The mainland town of Lingga Baharu is the major transit point along the route from Ko Banteay and the gulf islands up to the Lumbis Highlands. Most travelers going between the beaches of Ko Banteay and the jungle camps in Lumbis spend less than a day in Lingga Baharu. Yet there are more than enough attractions to keep an energetic sightseer busy for weeks. Begin with the ruins of **Rumah Berhala**, a tenth-century Hindu temple along the riverbank just on the outskirts of town. At present little more than a goat paddock with only the foundations of two towers and part of the causeway still visible, the Minister of Antiquities has announced that excavation of the site will begin sometime before 2004. The nearby **Wat Nakhon**, although small, is the only example of Khmer-influenced architecture in northern Tambralinga. The lone caretaker is an ancient monk and he is often away. Don't be disappointed if you find the place locked up the first time you drop by; your persistence will eventually be rewarded. On the upper slope of Mount Baguia, overlooking the harbor, check out the **Masjid Jamek**, the old Friday Mosque, said to be one of the finest examples of the Sumatran style. Just beyond Masjid Jamek is the **Lingga Baharu Historical Museum**. A quick walk up the hill brings you to the old **Portuguese Fort** and the ruins of the **Cathedral of the Assumption**, a sixteenth-century church that in the nineteenth century had the misfortune of being used as a gun powder storehouse by first the Dutch and then the British. —*Coswell's Guide to Tambralinga* (1997 ed.)

The ruins commanded a panoramic view of the harbor and the green hills to the south and looked directly down on the dome of Masjid Jamek and the red-tiled roof of the Historical Museum. Lucy, planning for the inevitable museum fatigue, had decided to visit twice, in forty-minute segments, first on her way up to the

Lumbis Highlands and then on her way back to the islands. But on her way up, she'd been in a hurry, anxious to see the "real jungle" along the shores of the big lake, Tasik Alang, and so she hadn't bothered with the museum. And now just the sight of its round roof, divided into eight sections, reminded her of a clock face, and she thought of how late in the day it was and how tired she felt.

The hotel she'd selected had no air-conditioning, but the rooms all had slow-turning fans in their high ceilings, and there was a small garden courtyard out front with flowering vines and small trees. She wished she were there now, drinking something cold and reading a book, any book, as long as it wasn't a guidebook or any kind of a book with maps and timetables in it. She'd seen the temple ruins, visited the tiny *wat*, snapped a few pictures of the mosque, and dutifully scaled the acropolis to see the fort. After what had happened at Tasik Alang, it seemed necessary to stay busy. But her sight-seeing did not cheer her, nor did it stifle the urge to flee back to the island. And now on top of her fatigue she felt a creeping nausea.

She pressed on anyway, descending along a rocky path to the base of the acropolis and rounding a few corners to the museum building. She discovered to her relief that it was closed. "Friday," she murmured to herself. The Muslim sabbath. She noted with some satisfaction that she had at least tried to get in. But then she realized that if she wanted to see the museum at all, she would have to delay her return to Ko Banteay, and this redoubled her fatigue.

Against her will, she pictured her husband in the hammock on the front porch of their bungalow, reading his dog-eared paperback, exactly as she had last seen him. It was absurd to picture him waiting for her; he had already left! And she knew that when he returned and found the note she'd left for him at the bungalow office, he would see it as a provocation, a declaration of war. If she went back now, would he even be there? And if he was there, would he speak to her?

She sat down on a stone bench in front of the museum's locked entrance and took the guidebook out of her bag. She looked briefly at the map insert. She could continue south along the coast, if she wanted. But now the names of the towns she would have to pass through looked strange and threatening, Sinubang, Kutang, Siantar, Kuala Vimaya, the names of fevers and venomous animals, of curved, slicing weapons and ingenious tortures. She shut the book.

As she made her way back to the hotel, she found herself beset by memories of Conrad, his large frame climbing the stairs from the street up to their flat, arms full of bagged groceries, or sitting at the dinner table, quickly sketching something on a scrap of paper to illustrate an idea he was trying to explain, or the calm voice he used when answering the telephone, or a hundred and one other things, the trivial things one remembers about a person. And it was like he was dead, or as if one of them were dead, passed into another world, forever out of reach.

The thought made her teary-eyed for a moment. She stopped to dig a handkerchief out of her bag. Across the street she noticed a hand-painted sign standing on the walkway in front of a small café: "Internet 400 Rls. 1 Hour," and she had a sudden urge to send a message to Conrad. She would send it to their mailbox at home, she would write something—she didn't know what—heartfelt and cheery. He might not pick up the message for weeks, not until they got back home, but what of it? She found herself putting the phrases together as she crossed the street. She would take care to sound neither hysterical nor coy. Her missive must be quick and to the point. But what point would that be? That she felt like reaching out to him, now that he was out of reach, passed on to another world? That she, the conscience-stricken widow, wished to obtain forgiveness from her departed husband's soul? Now that she thought about it, it wasn't clear which one of them had passed on; they were both outside of the bubble, both had fled the island, the magic circle of their marriage.

The café had three PCs and a printer on a long table. Three small boys were playing a game at one station, staring intently into the monitor, which pinged and buzzed and whirred back at them. A chalkboard menu in back of the service counter listed coffee, tea, cola, and orange soda, but there was no sign of a refrigerator or coffeepots or cups. Probably the drinks came from a restaurant down the street. Quickly she gave the boy behind the counter 400 rials and sat down at the opposite end of the long table from the boys. Conceivably Conrad would end up in a similar café, feeling very much the same way she felt now, and would decide to check his email. Was it possible to check your email at home from all the way over here? She didn't know. Perhaps it would make more sense to send the message to the hotel in Nagaseri, where she had suggested in her note that they meet up before flying back home. A moment of panic overcame her. What if he was already on his way back to Nagaseri, back to San Francisco?

She had the email address of the hotel written in her little datebook, but when she pulled it out of her bag, an ancient yellow sticky tag came loose and fluttered down into her lap. It was Antoine's email address, the one she'd used when they were first becoming involved. Jesus, she thought, what was that doing there?

She balled it up in her fist and dropped it on the floor, but then, thinking that a rude thing to do, picked it up again and put it in her bag. She brought up the application and entered the email address for the Nagaseri Hotel in the address field. She stared into the screen for a moment, trying to recall what she'd meant to write.

"Darling," she wrote. "I miss you awfully. So far my little jaunt has been sort of a disaster. Maybe I deserve it."

Christ, this wasn't how she wanted it to sound. She started again:

"I treated you awfully and now I miss you awfully. I'm sorry I couldn't, or rather we couldn't, seem to talk about things."

But, Jesus, he'd been so obstinate back at the bungalows, and so maddening in the ways he communicated his boredom, and so infuriating with his heroic cheeriness. And what really burned her was the way he'd put on that fixed little smile each morning, as if he was her nurse attendant and she an inpatient in a psych ward. She kept typing anyway:

I've been up to the jungle reserve at Tasik Alang. My first real adventure alone. I took the bus up from the coast to this resort that supposedly offered boat trips along the lake. Along the shores of the lake I'd heard that you could see monkeys, crocodiles, huge bats, exotic birds, and even orangutans and elephants. According to the guidebook, the bus was supposed to drop us less than a few hundred feet from the resort. But instead it dropped me at a crossroads where a bemo was supposed to stop and take me the rest of the way.

There was a young man waiting at this bus stop. He told me the resort I wanted was full, but that I could get a room at his hotel (which was very close by) and also get a tour of the lake (with him as guide) for a lot less money than the place the guidebook recommended. You know it's not like me to change horses in midstream, but there was

She stopped writing and looked for a moment at the address field. Then she pulled the crumpled sticky tag from her bag, unfolded it, and then looked again at the address field. She put the sticky tag on the tabletop and went back to typing.

there was this shiny, well-scrubbed look about his face that inspired confidence. He was wearing a basic sort of yellow turban, he was dark, compact, muscular.

She looked for the address field again, but found that it had scrolled out of sight.

I mean he really looked the part.

She stopped, scrolled up to the address field, removed the Hotel Nagaseri's address and replaced it with the one on the tag.

10

Antoine, why am I telling you this? There is a certain logic to it, don't you think? You're the one person I can be honest with, because you couldn't care less. So I'm going to tell you, without fear of annoying you too much, how beautiful he was. He seemed about twenty, dark eyes, muscular legs, creamy brown skin, a wispy mustache that gave him a sort of catlike appearance. And his movements were catlike, too, precise and relaxed, with this rippling sort of grace.

He'd already corralled some other tourists, an American couple whose names I've forgotten already. The man was a skinny, limp-wristed sort of programmer and the woman large, sweaty, and red-faced, with big glasses that made her look older and heavier than she really was. They claimed to be on their honeymoon, but had this weariness about them that made me think they'd been together for years.

The guide promised us a grand tour of Tasik Alang, which, he explained, was not one lake, but really a group of smaller lakes clustered around a common center. We could, if we wanted, spend the night in a rustic kampong house built on stilts right over the water. Beds, mosquito netting, coolers full of beer, meals, and so on, would all be provided. At dusk and at dawn, we would see all kinds of animals we wouldn't see otherwise, Sumatran rhinoceros, leopard cats, gibbons. The list went on and on as he led us off to the hotel. He had this infectious excitement in his voice, and this way of looking up at you suddenly while in the middle of a sentence, and making you feel like he was seeing you, really seeing you for the first time. And you would forget completely what he was saying. I felt like I'd been discovered, unearthed.

I mean, I didn't feel it all at once. It was a cumulative sort of thing. And by the time we set out on the tour the next morning, I had started to believe that he was sort of interested. On what was supposed to be the first day of our tour, we paddled all morning along a river that led into the lakes. We saw nothing, no jungle of any kind, just fields and rundown-looking villages, an occasional water buffalo. We began to put it together why this tour was so cheap—the canoe had no motor and it was going to take a hell of a long time to reach the reserve. The "newlyweds" began complaining, especially the woman, who looked miserable under that sun, in that humid, still air. After some arguing, the guide turned the boat around and began paddling us back up to the starting point. I assumed the trip was canceled, but then a bigger, motorized canoe overtook us and the guide hailed it and it stopped. The guide chatted with the men on the other boat for a few minutes and then indicated that the newlyweds would be taking this boat back to the hotel, while he and I pushed on. I was hesitant, of course, but he explained that it would be a shortened tour, that we'd be back to the hotel by dusk, that I must at least see some of the jungle.

He would lose face if I didn't go along with it. That was my rationale. I'd decided by this point that I couldn't stand the American couple, that I'd be damned if their obstinacy was going to rob me of my jungle tour. Before the other boat roared off, the pilot talked for some minutes at my guide, motioning with his hands at something way up the river, and making other gestures. My guide simply nodded his head now and then or grunted, and I "got" that he was getting directions from this other boatman, that in fact he had no clear idea of where exactly the jungle was.

I was too embarrassed to say anything about it or to get up and jump into that other boat with those awful people. I'd had a few words with the woman already. But I knew that I'd made a mistake. We set off down the river, paddling fast. Have you ever watched yourself do something you know is really stupid but been unable to make yourself stop? I paddled hard and every once in a while he would call my name and say "Okay?" and I would smile back over my shoulder as if to reassure him. But idiot that I am, I didn't see that he was becoming more than reassured.

After a punishing three hours, we came to a shallow lake full of reeds and a village of ramshackle huts built on stilts. He got excited when a white bird some distance away flew up against the sky. He insisted I take a picture of it, as if this was the moment I'd been waiting for all day. Was he trying to act like we'd arrived at the reserve? I stared at him, not believing, not wanting to believe. My shirt was drenched with sweat and there was sunblock running down in my eyes. Then I got furious with myself for being so easily taken in, for not sticking to my original plan, for not swallowing my pride and jumping ship with the newlyweds when I'd been given the chance.

We pulled up to one of the stilt houses and he shouted a greeting, but nobody was home. "We making meals here," he said, smiling again in that half-astonished way and for a flickering moment I believed it would be okay. He got the supplies out of the canoe, a kerosene stove and pots and some rice and canned meats, and set about making lunch. The owners of the house, he gave me to understand, were away fishing. For a small fee they let him bring guests in. The wife was a very good cook, a relative of his, some sort of second cousin. They brought home very big fish, he said, holding his arms apart. And I realized he was trying to talk me into spending the night.

I said I didn't think it was a good idea. I tried to be gentle about it, so he wouldn't lose face and all of that, but he took this as indecision on my part and all through lunch, which I barely touched, he kept describing the things we would see the next day, when, presumably, he would be able to locate the jungle. I got nervous, kept waiting for the owners of the house to show up with their fish, but then began noticing that the whole neighborhood was completely still, as if deserted. Finally I had to demand that he take me back. And that's when he made his move.

He was nice enough about it, I suppose: big, expectant eyes, mouth half-opened in anticipation. But as he brought his face close to mine, at that moment the only sound was of something creaking, some bamboo door or some abandoned boat rubbing against the stilts of a nearby house, only that sound and nothing else; and that sound made everything seem hollow. All my planning, my lists and itineraries, the phone calls to the travel agent, the faxes, the shopping for clothes and maps and first aid medicines, the hours spent on the airplane, those long silent arguments with Conrad, they all boiled down to this one cheap sensation. Here it was, the package that had been marketed to me, bit by bit, over the years: the exotic setting, the tall, dark stranger (well, dark, anyway), the mysterious power of nature. I pushed it away. I acted indignant, as if the very idea, etc. He seemed to take it well at first, but then as he packed the gear back into the boat, he kept making new attempts, and finally I put my hand over his face and shoved him back against the doorway.

A mistake! He grabbed my wrists and pinned me against the floor. The rage mounted in his face until I was certain he was going to kill me. Tambralingans are famous for their "cool hearts," but once they lose their tempers, they go "amok." And he could easily kill me and never get caught. Who would miss me? The honeymooners were probably halfway to Malaysia by this point, had probably already forgotten my name. I pictured Conrad waiting for me in the lobby of the Hotel Nagaseri four weeks hence, while somewhere on this lake, a fisherman pulled a crab-nibbled arm out of his net.

This was all of a moment. The next thing I knew, we were climbing back into the canoe and then paddling hard to get back to the hotel. I was seated in the bow, leaning forward anxiously over the water, as if that was going to speed us along. Whenever I felt him let up on the paddling, I'd look back over my shoulder, afraid of seeing him coming at me with his kris. But actually he was unarmed. He was just a boy, and I—under that sky, in that strange, baking landscape—was something less than that.

When we got back to the bungalows I was too scared to refuse when he demanded payment for the trip, the price we had negotiated for the full two days. Dimly I realized that he had no connection to the hotel I was staying in, that he was just a hustler, that I could have easily refused. But I paid him and he smiled at me that same way, lingering for a moment before he left, thinking perhaps that I might tip him.

I went to my room and cried, facedown in a dank pillow.

Late the next day I took the bus back to Lingga Baharu. I could have gone on to the recommended resort, but I was terrified of running into this guy again. I started wishing I would run into the American couple. Secretly I had despised them for being pathetic and ungainly, for spoiling all the wild beauty I had come to see with their flatfooted ugliness. Now I wanted to make it up to them. They seemed suddenly like beautiful, misunderstood people, well-meaning, fair-minded people who'd made a reasonable alliance, who were every bit as entitled to look for a bit of adventure as I was. I got teary-eyed thinking about them.

I don't know why I'm bothering to write this. You've long since gone deaf to the pluckiness of my banter. But, as they say, it was fun while it lasted. My one complaint (the major one, that is) is that I never had a chance to catch my breath while it was happening, never had anyone I could talk to about it, never had a chance to tell you the hundreds of things that I would see or think each day that I knew would make you laugh, that I knew you would love.

Here I am treading where I said I wouldn't. Don't worry, my sweets, I'm still reconciled to its being over. I had to write just this once. Feeling all alone and just needed to send a message, to feel that you were still somewhere out there, floating in the ether. Forgive me.

11

She didn't bother to reread the message, but decided instead to send it directly, while she still had the nerve. Afterward she felt silly, but also a little relieved, as if she'd lit a candle and said a prayer before an alabaster saint in the alcove of a cathedral.

Outside it was already getting dark. She felt the weakness come back into her legs. She'd eaten nothing since breakfast, besides tea and biscuits, and she knew from long experience that she would have to eat something immediately to fend off light-headedness and panic. Nearby was the night market, an open-air market that hosted scores of food stalls, each featuring a certain specialty. The clientele was entirely Tambralingan, according to the guidebook, and the food was unequaled for its exoticism and authenticity. Lucy lifted the chafing strap of her bag from her shoulder for a second, then set off for the market. One block away the air was already permeated with the scent of charred meat and roasted spices. But by the time she entered the market, it was almost seven o'clock, and the stalls were shutting down for evening prayers. She stared disbelieving as the mounds of blue rice and nasi goreng and trays of spitted meat and barbecued stingray disappeared. Even the non-Muslims, the Mon with their tom yam soup and the Chinese with their wok stands, were forced to shut down. The people left the market in droves, the aisles between the stalls clearing out in a matter of minutes. Lucy searched in vain for a vendor who might be willing to sell her a packet of cookies or a bottle of soda at the last minute.

She knew the prayers would last for less than an hour, but

this now seemed like an interminable and excruciating wait. The muezzin's voice blared down from the loudspeakers in the minarets of the Masjid Jamek, echoing in the narrow streets.

Allaahu Akbar! Allaahu Akbar!

She felt suddenly bereft and alone, a flimsy construction in the shape of a human being. She resisted the urge to cry, staggered back to the cab stand, and looked in vain for a cab. There were no cars on the street. The world had shut down. A long train of the faithful—the men decked in their Muslim caps and gold brocade sarongs or else in Arab-style turbans and robes, the women in their embroidered muslin veils—passed by on the way to the mosque. It all felt like part of an elaborate and cruel joke. Lucy understood no Arabic; the muezzin's mournful chant seemed to carry a mocking subtext:

Ashhadu Allah ilaaha illa-Leh!
(What you desire I have forbidden!)

Hayye alaa Salaah! Hayya ala Falaah!
(With sights and scents I torment you!)

Laa ilaaha illa-Lah!
(For by the whim of heaven, you are imprisoned forever.)

She fled in the direction of her hotel, walking against the flow of the faithful, who in the descending darkness seemed not to see her as they brushed past. She tried to keep her head up, but she was exhausted and dehydrated. As the muezzin's voice trailed off behind her, she found a new strength fueled by bitterness. The whole business of fasting and renunciation and compulsory worship took shape in her mind as a sort of conspiracy, something men did to keep women weak and off balance. It always went back to a book, whether the Bible or the Koran or what have you, always some goddamn book that claimed that the men should be in charge and women enslaved.

She stopped for a moment and moved her shoulder bag over to her left shoulder. She took momentary refuge in the thought that she was not enslaved, not yet anyway. Or rather, not anymore. And there, across the street, was a restaurant that seemed to be open.

"God bless the Chinese," she thought. "They never close."

There was only one other customer in the restaurant, also a woman, also a tourist. She sat at a table near the back, where the sweep of a large standing fan ruffled her peroxided hair at regular intervals. She paused between tiny spoonfuls of green sherbet as Lucy entered, then moved her head slightly as if trying to survey the street activity outside.

"This heat's just devastating," the woman said to Lucy, although she herself looked cool and poised. Lucy pushed a sweaty lock of hair off her forehead and grew apprehensive about her own appearance.

"Another refugee from the night market, I see," the woman said, and by her accent Lucy knew she was an American, probably from California.

"We're still a little too close to the mosque to get any decent mu shu pork," she went on, "but the beef with black bean sauce isn't bad. A little bland maybe, but if you don't mind that . . ." The remark sounded like an invitation, so Lucy sat down at the woman's table.

"I once got the best mu shu pork at this little place in San Francisco," the woman went on. "Out in the avenues. Have you ever been to San Francisco?"

"I live there," Lucy said. The woman's large blue eyes protruded slightly and an expression of delight swept over her face.

"I thought you were Dutch or something. My God, I haven't seen another American in days."

Her name was Jeannine and she was from Portland, Oregon. She'd been in the country for nearly two weeks, mostly on the islands. Like Lucy, she was now traveling on her own. At first glance she looked like she might be in her early thirties, although from certain angles she looked older. She and Lucy talked at first about the niggling annoyances they'd encountered around the town, Lucy about the confused English signage at the Cathedral and the mystifying hours of museums and government offices, Jeannine about the poor quality of the beer and the paucity of air-conditioning. When Lucy's dinner arrived, Jeannine sat with her, smoking cigarettes and talking about the "beach boys" on the island of Ko Neak Pean. There were a lot of them, she said. They worked the bungalow operations and the bars and pursued the tourist women on their days off. Lucy must have seen them where she was: young, long-haired, graceful as deer. They seemed delicate until you got closer and saw how muscular they were, especially in the thighs, like ballet dancers. Jeannine confessed to having a crush on one or two, of developing a taste for the "Asian type."

Lucy said she hadn't noticed any on her island, but then she was used to rather large men. She was afraid she might have colored a little as she said this: Antoine had not been large at all. Something about Jeannine began to intimidate her, something beyond her good looks. There was a quality of frankness about her, a certain bald innocence in her eyes. And she'd been places. Things had happened to her.

"I'm boring you," Jeannine said, snubbing out her cigarette.

"No, no," Lucy said quickly, afraid that the woman was going to leave. "I'm interested, really. I have noticed. What you said about the men. Now that you mention it."

She paused.

"Listen, to tell you the truth, I've had a bad couple of days."

12

Jeannine proved to be more than just good company. She was a revelation, a window thrown open on a blustery day. And Lucy began to feel something like a wind blowing through her chest, as if the open window were on her own person.

It had started the first night after their chance meeting in the restaurant. They had sat up in Jeannine's room until early morning, talking and smoking cigarettes and laughing at the excruciating noise being broadcast from the loudspeakers in the mosque up the street. Something beyond the usual call to prayer was going on over there. At five A.M. a subdued voice began speaking in Yawi, rather than singing verses in Arabic, as if delivering a lecture. Concealed behind the curtains on Jeannine's windows, Lucy and Jeannine gave themselves up to impious laughter. A sermon at five A.M.! In giddy voices they described to each other an empty mosque, a hunched man with oversized glasses reading quickly from prepared notes. A little man all alone in a tower—he seemed to be addressing them directly, admonishing them, an inept exorcist who cannot exorcise, but merely scold the offending demons. Lucy recognized that these same thoughts, a few hours earlier, would have depressed her. But in Jeannine's presence, she felt fortified, secure.

Over dinner she'd told Jeannine about her mishap with the guide; on their way back to the night market, she described her fights with Conrad; later in the hotel room, she confessed her affair with Antoine. How exhilarating to speak frankly to a complete stranger, to feel long-suppressed truths finally take shape in her mouth and fly out into the open air as simple declarations.

Jeannine was a good listener, her eyes steady and alert, her face registering each new revelation with an intrigued, slightly scandalized expression.

"You went to the hot tubs with him twice in the same day?" Her eyes were unusually large and her peroxided hair, while giving her something of a cheap look, also projected a disarming innocence.

"Different establishments," Lucy assured her. "But, yeah, that's how it was at first."

"Boy," Jeannine said, somehow managing a look of stolid, middle-class propriety, even with a bottle of rice whiskey in her hand. She'd grown up somewhere in Idaho and gone to nursing school in Oregon. She'd worked for a time at a hospital in a town called Beaverton, a name which, when uttered in that particular moment in that particular hotel room, sounded painfully funny, and gave them fits of laughter. Jeannine had had an affair with a doctor there, a married man with four children, but nothing had come of it. She sighed and looked at the floor as she related this, as if she'd perhaps had just this one experience of love. And Lucy, pleasantly disoriented with alcohol and nicotine, found herself ready to believe this. But then what about her comments over dinner, about the beach boys of Ko Neak Pean? Lucy decided that she liked the contradiction. She suppressed an urgent, elated impulse to declare that, one way or the other, everything was true.

"I envy anyone who gets to live in San Francisco," Jeannine went on. "I've always wanted to myself, but—well, for one thing, the cost of getting a place."

"I'll find you one," Lucy replied. "I'm an agent. I know that market cold. But I said that already, didn't I?"

"I like hearing it."

Jeannine seemed to enjoy much of what Lucy had to say. She listened with evident intent whenever Lucy alluded to the ancient Hindu kingdom of Tambralinga, or its conversion to Buddhism under the Khmers, or the invasions by the Bugis, the Achanese, the Portuguese, the Dutch, and all the others. And this was good,

for Lucy had read so many books on the country, that now and
then the pressure of her accumulated knowledge compelled her to
speak.

"I used to tell Conrad I was cramming for the entrance
exam," she explained to Jeannine on their second day together,
flushing at the realization that her lecturing had begun to tire her
friend. "It was electrifying—to plunge myself into this whole
other world, I mean. To see the possibility of another way of life,
the—what's the word? The connectedness of life. You know, the
people with the land, with nature, with the cosmos, with—
Sounds corny, I know."

"No, no," Jeannine said, touching Lucy's wrist. "Not when
you say it that way."

But Jeannine was clearly stunned when Lucy produced her
itinerary, all ten and a half pages of it, which listed not only the
places she wanted to visit, but also summaries of the salient facts
about each place and the reasons why anyone might want to visit.
Why should you have to look through the entire guidebook each
time you set off for a new destination? Lucy felt more than a little pride as she described how she'd designed each page to include
boxes in which she could record her comments about each portion of the trip.

"Gosh, that makes so much sense," Jeannine said. But then,
after examining the pages, she noted that Lucy had failed to write
anything about her jungle tour.

"No," Lucy admitted. "I'm still processing that."

It was fair to say that Lucy was still processing a lot of things.
On their third day of traveling together, as they stopped to buy
soft drinks at a stand near the entrance to the Cave of the Sleeping Buddha, Lucy noted that the woman working the stand had a
sleeping baby in a sling resting on her hip. It was a common sight
in Tambralinga, these tiny women, no more than seventeen or
eighteen years old, with newborns bundled onto their bodies. But
now the pitiful sigh this sight usually evoked was abruptly
eclipsed by an unexpected surge of envy. The girl had grown a
baby inside of her and had given birth while still young, without

a worry over graduate school and career path, without a thought to daycare or bottle feeding. There was no school for her and no prospects for a career, and no thought of either in the girl's head. The baby had not been discussed beforehand as an idea and then worked into a concrete proposal that had to be pitched to her husband. It had not been the subject of hours of anxious speculation. Most likely, it had simply erupted as a new certainty and had, day by day, worked itself into the slow rhythms of the girl's life. And the girl had carried the pregnancy as she was carrying the infant now, without a second thought, with the dumb, bovine faith of the ages.

Lucy gave her an extra bill for the sodas. It was the kind of tip that the guidebook had warned her not to dispense, but Lucy couldn't help it. The young mother regarded her with a puzzled expression. On the day that Lucy had given up trying to become a mother herself, had decided to release Conrad from the endless, humiliating visits to the urology clinic to produce "samples," she'd driven to a small motel north of San Francisco and impulsively taken a room. Sitting on a queen-sized bed in a room that stank of cigarettes, she'd lit one herself and then called her lover on her cell phone. He hadn't answered; she hadn't expected him to. He'd been keeping a low profile, protecting his options. Perhaps he'd been nervous about having fallen for an older woman—although at the time this thought had not occurred to her. As she'd hung up the phone, her renewed disappointment announced what should have been obvious for months: she wanted a child, yes, but not with Conrad. Having his baby would be somehow less than having none at all. Not that he would have made a bad father. No, he'd given every indication of being ready to cheerfully soldier on through this next life phase. Yet there was in Conrad an emptiness, a small void. Where others had a soul, Conrad had only a refined locus of control. Or so it seemed to Lucy. It was more than simply a matter of being unexciting. This thing within him cast doubt on the possibility of excitement even existing—beyond the framework of some grand illusion. It was this chill at his core that made her want to be done with him.

And this, then, this ridiculous vacation, was how she was going to do it. (She pulled on her straw and got air. How quickly all of that had been sucked up.) It was not a pattern she could bear to look at in its totality, but only in fleeting glimpses, like those of the limestone peak swaddled in shifting morning mists.

"Why do they call it the Sleeping Buddha?" Jeannine asked in a small voice as they began ascending the narrow path up the hillside. It was early and she was still not quite awake. The sun was fierce where they were, but up ahead, overhanging bits of the scrub forest offered some shade.

"It's actually called a Reclining Buddha, the image of the Buddha's last moment of life. But the people around here are all Muslim and can't tell the difference."

"In this heat I'm not surprised."

"It was carved by Mon monks in the middle of the fourteenth century. The stone is soft, easy to carve."

Jeannine stopped, placing a hand on her chest as she caught her breath. "Good," she said. "I'm glad."

Lucy looked up to where the path disappeared around a bend, pleased with her ability to summon relevant facts. For, having uttered them, the path no longer looked impossible but merely steep, and the forest no longer sinister but merely gloomy.

At the cave they found the statue surprisingly large, but badly weathered. The feet were blackened with campfires, the nose and lips broken off (by Malay iconoclasts in the seventeenth century, Lucy speculated). Jeannine found a dry spot on the rocky slope at the cave's entrance. She sat down and removed her shoes.

"I can see why this isn't such a popular sight," she said.

"Right." Lucy sat down next to her. She looked at her own feet and then asked for a cigarette.

"Trying to start?" Jeannine smiled as she lit one for Lucy.

"From a certain point of view, it might be considered an adaptive trait." Lucy applied the burning tip to a leech that had attached itself to her ankle.

"Oh my God!" Jeannine jumped up and took a step backward as the brown slug dropped from Lucy's ankle. It writhed among the chalk-white pebbles that covered the ground and then, regaining its composure, stood up on its hindquarters and moved its long, headless torso around and around, as if searching in the dark for a light switch.

"Aren't you going to squash it or something?"

"It'll just make a mess," Lucy replied. "Besides, it's got its quota of blood. Now it'll probably just lay its eggs and die."

"Eggs?" Jeannine asked, horrified. She picked up a big rock and sent it down on the worm. It exploded in a spurt of blood, which shone brilliantly on the white rocks and dotted the toes of Lucy's boots.

"Sorry," Jeannine said. "I just couldn't stand the idea—"

"Eggs," she said a moment later, shuddering.

In the following days Jeannine began to exhibit a pleasant reluctance to leave any hotel room or café or vista point where she was reasonably comfortable. There seemed to be a corresponding drop-off in her admiration for Lucy's command of cultural and historical facts. Lucy quickly discovered that discussing the next day's itinerary over dinner was now counterproductive, that the best she could hope for was a brief discussion after breakfast, and that she should consult her laser-printed itinerary only when alone. And now whenever Lucy indulged a didactic impulse, Jeannine's eyes would focus on something in the distance, as if she were at a depot, straining for a glimpse of a train long overdue. And as they moved down the coast, by bus and jitney, with the ultimate aim of getting to Sri Kala in time for the Festival of the Sea Goddess, item after item on Lucy's list was scratched out and abandoned because of Jeannine.

Things came to a head in Khota Dewa, with Lucy insisting they must visit the Museum Diraja and Jeannine wanting to spend the day close to the hotel, consuming iced coffees and writing postcards. The Museum Diraja, one of the many royal palaces that had been partially converted to a museum, was a Victorian mansion fashioned from tropical hardwoods, set out exactly as it had been 130 years earlier, with period furniture and hunting trophies and exquisite carvings from Japan, Java, and India. And though she cursed herself as a prating schoolgirl as she did it, Lucy read the passage from the guidebook that declared the Museum Diraja "a portal on a lost world, the world of the last Tambralingan Raja, preserved down to the last jeweled snuffbox and gold-plated serving tray."

"And is that *good*?" Jeannine replied, apparently distracted by the slowly rotating blades of the ceiling fan.

She was lying on her back on one of the twin beds that had been crammed into their hotel room. Her eyelids were puffy and dark. Lucy sat on the foot of the other bed, now and then gazing out the window. When the power had gone off the night before, they'd both found it impossible to sleep. The air, no longer agitated by the fan, had become gradually unbreathable. Like a soup that is heated but not stirred, the air had thickened at the bottom half of the room—or so Lucy had pictured it as she had lain awake. Was there really enough oxygen for two in this room? Even now it was sweltering. Never mind—she no more wanted to spend another night alone than she wanted to go sight-seeing alone. All these worries boiled down to a central urgency: Jeannine must not miss the wonders of the Museum Diraja.

"De Raja's Palace," as Jeannine called it, was situated in a parklike setting along the west bank of the Sungai Menam, close to where that river emptied into the sea. The grounds were covered in something that was not quite grass and planted with many kinds of palm trees and huge hardwoods with sprawling roots. The palace itself consisted of three buildings: a large building at the end of a long driveway, dazzling white in the late morning sun, a smaller building on a rise slightly above the first, with a veranda overhung with flowering vines, and an old guardhouse—now a ticket booth—standing between the two. Lucy found the ticket booth empty and a soldier with a rifle barring the entrance to the larger building. He hissed at her when she approached, meaning to try the door.

"But it can't be closed," Lucy blurted in English, for the guidebook had assured her that the palace was open on Sundays; and in the wake of her argument with Jeannine, Lucy could not believe the book had let her down yet again. As if in reply, the guard motioned with his rifle at the sign hanging in the door. It was composed of three lines, one in Paktai script, one in Arabic characters, and one in Chinese. A Rosetta stone of "no," Lucy thought bitterly. For a moment she felt on the verge of tears.

"Something the matter?" Jeannine called to her from up the drive. (She was a slow walker, as it turned out.)

"This part of it seems to be closed," Lucy called back over her shoulder. "I'm going to try the other building. That's probably the actual residence." She marched stiffly up the walk, trying to keep the anger out of her movements.

The doors were chained shut, the windows shuttered. The freshly painted surfaces suggested the massive indifference of white marble. She felt as if she were in a Greek temple, or at least a cheap replica of one; and, as she made her way back to Jeannine, she entertained dark thoughts about the vague deities she herself seemed to be worshiping, about all ideals being made of alabaster and being tolerated only long enough for something else, some living force—greed, lust, hatred—to take their place.

Jeannine shrugged when Lucy told her the situation. She liked the grounds in any case. She pointed to a bench down the slope and suggested that from that vantage point they might enjoy a pleasant view of the river.

The river was not much to look at, a sullen brown swath with a row of dull green trees lining its far shore. The air was dank and heavy, the sky darkening with thunderheads. Lucy suppressed her annoyance.

"I think you're working at this a little too hard," Jeannine said, pulling a strand of lank hair behind her ear. Sweat was beading up on her forehead. It was barely nine A.M.

"I'm here for a reason," Lucy said curtly. "I just don't know what it is yet."

When the clouds grew too threatening, they retreated to the palace entrance, hoping to find a taxi. The approach to the entrance was deserted, as was the narrow roadway that wound through the park beyond.

"Some kind of government holiday," Lucy speculated, as the first drops hit her nose.

Jeannine yawned.

"Maybe we should stand over there," she said, pointing to the covered walkway that joined the ticket booth to the two other buildings.

"A holiday," Lucy repeated. "That must be it."

The rain came down in sheets, forming little rivers that crisscrossed the long driveway. Clouds descended, obliterating their view of the park and the river. Now and then a wind gust knocked the rain into their faces.

"This is probably the worst of it," Lucy said, just before the lightning and thunder began. The first peal was so close, they both thought an artillery shell had struck the building. The rain redoubled its force and an immense puddle, newly formed, began encroaching upon the walkway where they stood.

"Maybe the guard will let us stand up on the porch," Lucy said.

Jeannine was laughing.

"I'm already soaked."

A white limousine appeared at the far end of the driveway and pulled up to the palace entrance. The guard stood at attention while a tall figure, a dark-haired man in a white linen suit, emerged from the car and walked up the front steps. He was inside the palace building for only a few minutes, but by the time he emerged, the rain had begun to slacken. He came out from under the covered drive-up and surveyed the grounds briefly, frowning, perhaps dismayed at the mud puddling along the walkway. As his gaze traveled up the walkway to where Lucy stood, his face registered surprise.

"Madam," he called out in English, "I'm afraid they have closed the museum for today. And now the storm has marooned you."

He spoke with a clipped, British-sounding accent. He was obviously a government official of some kind; the license plates on the limousine bore only two letters, and a small Tambralingan flag was attached to the rear antenna. But he looked Middle Eastern, rather than Yawi or Paktai.

Lucy called back that they were hoping to get a taxi, but that none had appeared. The dark-haired man turned and called out something to his driver, who emerged from the car and hustled toward them with a large black umbrella. The man turned back toward Lucy.

"Please, you must wait inside while we find you a taxi."

"And my friend, too," Lucy said, nodding toward the ticket booth, where Jeannine, mostly concealed, still stood.

"Oh, yes, of course," the man said. "I didn't see." And as he caught sight of Jeannine, he smiled broadly.

As they reached the palace entrance, the guard who before had shooed Lucy away now stood at attention and saluted. The chauffeur moved ahead and held the door open. When they entered the Museum Diraja, Lucy noted with satisfaction that it was resplendent after all. A crystal chandelier the size of a small Christmas tree hung from the high ceiling. It had been lowered almost to the teak floor. Three workmen, barefoot, quietly polished the hanging crystals with white cloths. They made a soft clinking sound as they worked. Hunting trophies studded the far wall, heads of tigers and leopards, bear and antelope, with muskets and spears and curved swords crossed beneath. Lucy's host turned and introduced himself as Rashid Omar Rahman, indicating with a self-deprecating smile that that was only a portion of his actual name, the easiest for foreigners to pronounce.

"I was just telling your friend," he said to Jeannine, "how sorry I am that you've come to all this trouble to visit our palace only to find it shut up. I'm afraid the prevailing holiday schedule in our facility is quite unreasonable, perhaps even sadistic. Actually there is to be a meeting here later this afternoon. State business, you see."

Jeannine assured him that she was happy to be there in any case. The grounds were heavenly, she said, the view fantastic, and the warm air, scented with flowers, had her bewitched. And as she said this, she turned away for a moment and stretched her body, a move that raised the hem of her wet skirt slightly above her knee.

"My mother was in fact Persian," Rashid said as they rode in his car back to the city center. "Persian by way of India, you might say. My father, the Sultan, preferred foreign-born wives. Also scotch whiskey. I was lucky in that respect. I was able to spend some of my school years in London." This was in reply to a question by Jeannine about his race, a question whose bluntness in Lucy's view bordered on insult. She'd felt herself contract when Jeannine blurted it out in her naïve way. With a little girl's expression, Lucy noted. This was how she managed not to be offensive.

"Your father is the Sultan? Does that make you a prince or a raja? I mean, how does that work?"

Rashid laughed. He seemed genuinely enchanted with her ignorance.

"I'm just a humble government minister. I'm seventh in line for the throne, for what that's worth. My father has other sons. Many, many sons."

"So he's a genuine powhattanite—I mean—what did I say?" Jeannine covered her mouth with her hand and laughed.

"Potentate," Rashid corrected gently. He went on:

"His powers are purely symbolic, I can assure you."

Lucy found herself beginning to be charmed by Rashid's manner, by his patience and attentiveness. She began to notice his handsome traits, the well-proportioned face, the dark eyes, the smooth, olive-toned skin, the comfortable way he moved in his clothing. And as she noticed these things, she realized that Jeannine had noticed them all along, had been playing to them, drawing them out. She sat back against the cushions, a little amazed, a little dismayed.

"Why do you call this white tea?" Jeannine asked. "It looks like mud."

"The color of Tambralingan rivers, I'm afraid," Rashid replied, glancing at Lucy. They were sitting in a nearly deserted restaurant of a large hotel, around a tray of cucumber sandwiches and a pot of tepid tea. Whatever business he was supposed to conduct for the state that day could apparently wait a while longer. His attentive civility had given way to a more relaxed manner. He leaned back into his chair, stirring the spoon lazily in his cup. A look of unabashed delight had settled over his face. Clearly he liked Jeannine, or at least liked looking at her.

Jeannine was telling him about her first husband, an architect, whom she'd married when she was very young. Lucy worked at containing her surprise. Jeannine hadn't mentioned to Lucy that she'd been married. And somehow she had worked into her frequent expressions of astonishment and her clear blue stares the insinuation that she'd hardly ever been farther than two hundred miles from Twin Falls, the city of her birth. Now it appeared that she'd married at nineteen somewhere on the East Coast, had lived in SoHo lofts and attended parties in Park Avenue penthouses.

Lucy looked out the window of the restaurant, at the parade of heavily draped Muslim women moving up and down the street. Some had handbags and high heels and colorful head scarves, and the cut of their dresses did not so much conceal their figures as drop pointed hints at how good they might be.

Her ex-husband had designed a famous building in Copenhagen, Jeannine explained, and another one in Cleveland.

Rashid confessed that he'd never been to Cleveland: Was it
nice?

"It's on a big lake," Jeannine replied. "So big it looks like the
sea."

"A sea of fresh water? Sounds enchanting, a fairy tale."

"It's not exactly fresh," Jeannine said quickly. "Two years before we got there, this river that feeds into the lake, it caught on
fire. Because of all the oil and pollution."

"The lake caught on fire you say?"

"The river that feeds it, the Kali-yuga or something."

"Cuyahoga," Lucy put in.

"Oh my," Rashid said, smiling. "Then I would have to say
that our rivers are not in such a bad way." He glanced at his cup.

"They call it white tea because of the condensed milk they
add," he went on. "They put the same thing in a cup of Nescafé
and call it 'café au lait.' And of course it tastes just the same as
the tea."

" 'If this is coffee, bring me tea; if this is tea, bring me coffee,' "
Lucy quipped.

Rashid looked at her quizzically. "I beg your pardon?"

"It's a quote from Abraham Lincoln."

"Oh, yes. I see." He gave her a schoolmaster's look of approval. "Very good."

Lucy felt her ears start to burn.

The building in Copenhagen was actually his best-known,
Jeannine went on. A factory and offices for an electronics company. The queen was there for the opening.

"The queen of Denmark?" Rashid asked.

"The queen of Thailand, too. She was visiting at the time. We
spoke to both of them for quite a while. John—my ex-husband—
thought for sure we'd be going off to Bangkok eventually to work
on a project for the queen, but it didn't pan out."

It occurred to Lucy that the Cuyahoga had caught on fire in

1969 and that if Jeannine had been there two years later as a married woman of nineteen or twenty, then she would have to be at least forty-five now. Lucy looked at her carefully, not quite believing what the numbers were telling her.

"I myself met Queen Sirikit for the first time only last year," Rashid was saying. "This is quite a coincidence!" He paused to sip his tea. Lucy followed his example. The flavor was ghastly, had gotten worse as the tea cooled. Rashid added a spoonful of sugar to his cup. Lucy, determined not to be left out of the conversation, pressed on.

"And what is it exactly that you do in the government here?" she asked.

Rashid stopped stirring his tea and touched the fingertips of his right hand to their counterparts on his left. He was an officer in the Ministry of Religious Education, he explained. Specifically, he was charged with enforcing certain laws about religious practice. He cleared his throat. But they should understand that these laws applied only to the practice of Islam. Only Muslims were under his jurisdiction.

An uneasy silence fell over the table. And then Jeannine asked: "You mean you're a Muslim?"

"By definition a sultan can be nothing but."

"Traditionally the sultan was more than just a king, or a raja," Lucy said quickly. "He was also supposed to be a religious leader."

"Well put," Rashid nodded. "And now that we are a democracy—and whether or not you call us a democracy will depend on how generous you're feeling—one of the last areas where the sultanate can exercise its power is in matters of faith."

Jeannine frowned.

"You mean you're actually forcing people to—"

"I don't administer the Religious Police. That's a different department altogether. Our ministry is charged with—refining—the religious practices of our Muslim citizens. This is difficult to explain, but Islam did not originally come to Tambralinga in a pure form. It's been bastardized, shall we say, by a hodgepodge of primitive superstitions, many of them sick, sadistic, all of them absurd. In certain districts they compromise things like public health and literacy."

He picked up his teacup, then put it down again.

"We have witch doctors who smear pregnant women with the blood of dead people to cure morning sickness, fathers who tattoo prayers across their hearts to make themselves immune to hepatitis or HIV."

"And you're so sure science has the answer," Jeannine put in.

"There are multitudes of poor people traveling to the tombs of so-called saints where they leave elaborate offerings to swarms of poisonous snakes. Do you really think the worship of snakes would be permitted in your country? In certain schools there are children who memorize long passages of the Koran without understanding the meaning of a single word."

He was speaking rapidly. His spoon lay on the tablecloth, above a spreading brown stain.

"What prevailed here for centuries was a sort of pantomime of Islamic civilization, a grotesque sort of aping of the form. We— the Ministry of Religious Education—have no intention of forcing religion on unbelievers. Yet applied correctly, religion can be a progressive force, a cleansing force, a force for building national unity, stability. That's what is required now, I believe."

"So your department works on hygiene issues?" Jeannine asked. Lucy shaded her eyes, glanced out the window. How could she ask such idiotic things?

"We are cleansing our religious *practice* so that *it* may act as a cleansing force on the rest of society, Muslim and non-Muslim alike."

Rashid stood up and spread his brown fingers across the white tablecloth. He looked from Jeannine to Lucy and back again. Then he sat back down. He produced a silver case from his coat pocket and opened it quickly.

"Cigarette?" he offered.

"Interesting character," Lucy said after Rashid left.

"And cute," Jeannine replied, inhaling the last of her cigarette. "I wish you hadn't started all that talk about religion. He might have stayed a bit longer."

"Me? You're the one that—"

"But you know what? You've got me kind of jazzed for more sight-seeing. What's next on your list? Let's have a look, girl."

Part Three

Imam

13

The Legend of Willow Leaf

In ancient times, Tambralinga was ruled by the Naga King's daughter, Liu-ye (Willow Leaf). One day Kaundinya, a Brahman prince from the land of Mo-Fu, sailed his ship toward the shores of Tambralinga, for a djinn had appeared to him in a dream and told him his destiny lay there. When Willow Leaf saw Kaundinya's ship approaching her shore, she led her own ships out to attack. In those days the custom in Tambralinga was to go about naked and tattooed, to wear the hair on top and to know neither upper nor lower garments. When Kaundinya saw this naked girl in command of her oarsmen, he fired an arrow from his magic bow. His arrow pierced the side of the vessel and Willow Leaf was greatly afraid, and so submitted to Kaundinya. Kaundinya then taught Willow Leaf to slip on a piece of cloth over her head, to never go about naked. Thus he took Willow Leaf to wife and made himself king of Tambralinga.

—*Coswell's Guide to Tambralinga* (1997 ed.)

Conrad sipped a drink from a green coconut and gazed at the waves muscling their way past each other in a rush to dash themselves on the shore. He was sitting in an open-air restaurant bar on Ligor Bay, a few kilometers outside of town, where Boon worked as a waiter and bartender. Eva sat next to him, working her long blond tresses with a fine-toothed comb, waiting silently for Boon to finish his shift. She'd begun spending her afternoons waiting for Boon. He preferred she wait for him where he could keep an eye on her, and he preferred that she sit with Conrad, so that other men, "beach boys" especially, wouldn't approach her. This Eva had explained to Conrad in a bare murmur, as though ashamed, her full, rounded lips hardly moving, her forehead contracted slightly, revealing to Conrad the places where furrows would eventually form and deepen. Conrad had agreed to help out. Watching her up close, he told himself, was poignant and fascinating, revived musings about beauty and time he hadn't thought of since adolescence. But the truth was he was lonely.

He'd been a long time on the island, away from Lucy. Four days earlier he had moved from the Cozy Comfort in town to a beach bungalow just a few hundred yards from where he sat now. When Eva and Birgit had moved out to Ligor Bay, he'd decided to follow at a discreet distance, choosing to stay at the bungalows a little way up the beach from theirs. It felt a bit awkward at first. He had only the flimsiest excuse for dropping by, the vague suggestion Birgit had made about traveling together. But maybe there was more between them than just that.

"And how is Birgit today?" Conrad asked. Since his arrival at the bungalows, he'd seen little of Birgit. She seemed to be ill, kept close to her bungalow during the day, appeared infrequently at the restaurant.

"Better, I think." Eva shrugged. She and Birgit were now rooming separately. Birgit, as far as Conrad knew, had never been to Boon's bar. And the last time they'd all sat down to dinner together, she had addressed not one word to Boon.

The wind picked up. Bits of plastic and paper scrambled across the beach in a corkscrew game of tag. A buoyant-breasted woman in a monokini frolicked alone in the waves. At least she seemed to be frolicking. She carried on as if she were with someone, sharing the exciting and novel sensations of warm surf and tropical sun. There was something not quite true about it. Conrad tried to remember if he had ever frolicked. *I hope you enjoy being on your own*, he remembered writing to Lucy. *I certainly intend to.*

"Oh no, here is this Tarzan guy." Eva nudged him. Conrad turned away from the ocean view and looked across the restaurant. At a counter that ran alongside the far wall of the place, the man had cornered a thin redhead in a gauzy sacklike dress. The girl looked bored; she'd taken up a handful of her own hair and begun scrutinizing their split ends. Whatever lines Tarzan was using didn't appear to be working. On the other hand, the man's technique probably had little to do with lines, Conrad decided. It was a purely visual presentation. All the work had been done months, years earlier in a weight room. When the Tarzan fellow pushed off from the counter and left, empty-handed, Conrad felt cheered. Obviously the girl had found him more ridiculous than virile. Conrad drained his coconut and tossed it on the sand. Empty coconuts littered the entire perimeter of the restaurant. He waved at Boon across the room and motioned for another.

"This guy is too much," Eva said as she watched the Tarzan character leave. "I think he's like the star in his own movie."

"Yes," Conrad replied. He noticed that Eva was still watching the man as he strode out onto the beach. He stood for a moment with his legs apart, fists knuckled into his waist. Conrad marveled at the preposterousness of the pose.

Boon arrived at their table with two drinks, "on house," as he put it. Eva protested that she hadn't ordered anything; Boon shouldn't waste his money buying her expensive drinks she didn't even want.

"Okay for my honey bunches," he said, patting her hand, and then offered some other mumbled approximations of English sweet talk before sauntering back to the bar. Eva made a face.

"Why in English do you always have to mix up love with sugar?" Eva asked Conrad. "Sweetheart, sugarpie—"

"That's true," Conrad agreed, as he slipped the straw into his mouth. "You'd think they'd compare it to more nutritious foods." He went back to watching the Great White Ape, who was now sauntering down the beach, turning his head this way and that, as if searching for more prey.

"He must stop spending money on me," Eva said quietly into Conrad's ear. "I feel terrible. He is borrowing money so he can take me out to dinner. And we always have to eat at the cheapest places. Last night was really bad. Now I must eat a big lunch so I'm not hungry at dinnertime."

"Maybe you shouldn't let him pay. Maybe you should insist."

"It would hurt him. He would lose face if a woman paid for him."

"Lose face?" Conrad said slowly. For no apparent reason, he pictured Lucy in the arms of a strange man, her naked body propped against the wall of a San Francisco motel room. He turned to Eva and wanted to say something else, but was afraid he would slur his words. He was not used to drinking, especially sweetened drinks, and some delivery mechanism in the sugar was expressing the alcohol straight to his brain.

"Well, I'm tiring of this," Eva said. "I will take a swim, I think." Conrad watched as she strolled out onto the sand, removed her long-sleeved blouse and her sarong and let them fall at her feet. She wore only a monokini underneath, like the other women on the beach, yet Conrad looked away, found himself staring at the floor, at the tiny ridges of sand drifted into the corners. His head seemed to be wrapped in a gauzy, diaphanous material that blocked his windpipe when he tried to inhale. When he finally looked up, Eva was already far offshore, arms windmilling through the glittering waters. There was no real reason he couldn't join her. His swimming trunks were back at his bungalow, but the pant legs on his nylon khaki trousers unzipped just above the knee. Yes, they converted quite easily into shorts, and they dried quickly. No doubt he could leave a matching pile of laundry on the sand right next to hers. But then there was the problem of what to do with the wallet.

Perhaps Boon would look after it, Conrad thought hopefully, looking back across the bar. But Boon was crouched over a broken glass with broom and dustpan, and Conrad noticed for the first time that the back of his T-shirt was riddled with holes. Why put temptation in his path?

Back on the beach the situation was deteriorating. Tarzan had returned and had sighted Eva. He waded through the gentle surf and then launched his body at her, moving through the water with the undulating grace of an otter. Tarzan closed the distance between himself and Eva in moments. Their silhouetted heads burst up from the shimmering blue surface simultaneously, as if coming together for a kiss.

Conrad looked away, placed a hand over some unpleasantness bubbling in his paunch. Behind him Boon sang along with a song playing on the stereo in a high, reedy voice. The gauze tightened around Conrad's head. So I've failed as a harem guard, Conrad thought. So what? He brought the straw to his lips, but then took it away again.

"Hey, where Eva go?" Boon called to him from across the bar.

"Just for a swim," Conrad tried to assure him.

Boon hurried out onto the sand, shading his eyes with his hand as he looked up and down the beach. But what could he do? Conrad wondered. Boon was a terrible swimmer (even the fishermen on the island didn't know how to swim) and only half the size of the Tarzan character, who was now knifing through the water alongside the backstroking Eva. Boon's hand came down to his side; his shoulders slumped for a moment. And then he was back at the bar, rinsing and drying glasses with fast, sharp movements.

Birgit entered, carrying a newspaper under her arm.

"Beer please," she asked Boon, as if he were a complete stranger. Boon put the opened bottle in front of her without looking up.

"On house," he said brusquely.

"I can pay," Birgit said loudly.

"No pay. Free!" Boon insisted.

"What is the problem with him?" Birgit asked, as she sat down next to Conrad. Conrad explained; Birgit laughed. Her laughter was deep and throaty.

"This cartoon man," she said. "I see him yesterday on the other beach, walking up and down in his little—what do you call it? Skirt? Talking to all the French girls. Very funny. He says he is English. Like the real Tarzan, yeah? Lord Greystoke."

"You said he was American. On the ferry, remember?"

Birgit ignored the point.

"I have found a newspaper today," she said, unfolding the paper on the counter. "In English. I thought you could like to see it."

"Does it have baseball scores?"

"I'm sorry?" she replied, not understanding.

"Just a bad joke. But what does this mean?" Conrad said, pointing to the headline. The headline read: THANAT ACCUSES AL-JABBAR OF CRIME LINKS.

Thanat, Birgit explained, was the so-called minister of justice. Al-Jabbar was the name of the opposition party, the Muslim majority party agitating for democratic reform.

"I thought this was supposed to be a democracy," Conrad said, slurring, despite his best efforts, the last word. Birgit seemed not to notice. This was the good thing about talking to foreigners.

"Only the one party is allowed to—make the political speeches and the advertisements—"

"To campaign? I see." This came out flawlessly, much to Conrad's relief. He took another pull on his drink.

"To make the campaign you must have the permit, and the government won't give. So they close up the offices of Al-Jabbar and put in jail these people who are—working to make the election. And now the minister is saying they are working with the Mafia and the other crime organizations."

"Oh, this is what you were trying to tell me the other day, wasn't it?" Conrad said. Involuntarily he touched the spot where Birgit had struck him. The sensation of swaddling around his head made him feel momentarily safe.

"Yes, yes," Birgit said eagerly, brushing a strand of hair from her eyes. She explained how the minister of justice had concocted the story that Al-Jabbar was working with Chinese gangs to smuggle Tambralingan children into hospitals in Peking or Shanghai where their organs could be harvested and then sold to wealthy and desperate patients from America and Europe.

"Most of the newspapers are saying it every day, as if it was proven fact. The TV and radio are always saying this story. This paper is the only one that doesn't say this story is for sure the truth, yeah?"

"They're skeptical," Conrad said, extending his index finger. He sat up straight and set his jaw determinedly. He might have slurred that last word; he couldn't be sure.

"The government censors the TV and radio, and the Yawi-language press. But they don't bother with this one, because it's in English and nobody reads it."

Conrad nodded cautiously and tossed his empty coconut out onto the sand. All of this sounded plausible. After a brief silence, he pointed to a picture on the front page.

"Who's that? Looks familiar," he said. He really was slurring badly now. Birgit offered him a handkerchief, with which he carefully dabbed the corners of his mouth.

"That's Usen Tatoh. They call him 'Sonny.' He is the main leader of Al-Jabbar. He has just returned to the country after a long exit."

"Okay." Conrad nodded. There was something wrong with her last statement, but he could not pinpoint the problem.

"I go to university with his cousin. That's why I go to the mainland, yeah? His cousin stays in Kuala Vimaya and I think if I go, maybe I meet Sonny."

"I like that name," Conrad said decisively.

"I saw him make a speech once. On video, you know? I didn't understand because he speaks it in Yawi. But I can see he is very—appealing. Everyone in the audience is very excited and some are yelling things to him and some are crying, and even passing up."

"Fainting?"

"Yes. Some women are fainting. If they get too close. He has the—what do you call it? Personal magnetism."

Conrad nodded, squinting. The sun had shifted slightly and now illuminated the dust motes swimming near the tip of his nose. Birgit looked down at the countertop, began doodling with her fingertip in a small puddle of ice water. Neither spoke for a minute.

"*Karisma!*" Conrad said, slapping the counter triumphantly. "That's the word."

Conrad found his new bungalow depressingly similar to the one he'd left in Ko Banteay. It featured a nearly identical papaya tree growing next to the porch as well as a similar view of the sea, the main difference being that this horizon had no islands on it. Conrad sat on the porch for the better part of an hour, nearly oblivious to the flies, searching without success for a reason to continue his stay on the island.

There was the Birgit factor, the preposterous notion of traveling through hostile territory with someone who was also vaguely hostile. Whatever experiences they might encounter would surely make for grand storytelling back home. But the prospect seemed less likely every day. On the other hand, the idea of returning home with nothing to tell was fairly depressing. He stared at a group of small children splashing in the water along the shore, feeling a heavy drowse come over him. His body grew warmer and heavier, his thoughts slow and confused. Or perhaps not confused so much as restructured in improbable ways: the splashing children were excavators, a road crew building a long tunnel, a tunnel that would lead to, and at the same time was, Birgit. The project would take years, would incur cost overrides, innumerable purchase orders, the training of teams of specialists, and an all but impossible coordination of schedules.

He sensed this Birgit-in-progress taking shape inside the stiff scaffolding of her pajama suit: the stocky but muscular legs, the lean torso, pancake-like breasts, arms built for javelin throwing. He recognized the absurdity of him, a man, contemplating her body; Birgit had that athletic sort of casing about her, that apparent boyish indifference to sensuality. Yet Conrad felt attracted anyway, pulled by the currents of hot and cold running through her. He pictured her face taking shape a mere seven inches in front of his own. Its cheek was turned toward him, as if inviting retribution. "Go ahead," was the implication. "Your best shot."

When he awoke, the children were gone, all but one, and the sun was much lower in the sky. The remaining child he recognized, after some minutes, as Philippe. The boy paddled back and forth along the shore, buoyed by a pair of bright yellow water wings. His mother, Rosanette, lay on the sand with a paperback. Conrad knew her at once from her dark mass of curly hair.

The discovery excited him, brought him decidedly awake. It was rather like sighting an exotic bird in the jungle canopy. He realized how little time he'd spent at the bungalows; Rosanette might have been there for days already.

It was some time before he worked up the courage to approach her. She had on only a bathing suit bottom, whereas before she'd worn the requisite white pajamas. Conrad circled around her a couple of times just to make sure there was no mistake. Rosanette lay on her stomach, paperback splayed before her, flip-flop dangling from her raised left foot. Her legs were chubbier than he'd imagined, but that was good in a way, made everything calmer. Her back was deeply tanned, making her look more Spanish than French, at least from behind, and as he knelt down beside her, heart pounding, silly images of guitars and roses filled his head.

She barely looked up when he announced himself. She was near the end of her book and seemed unable to break away. Conrad held his ground for moment, hoping for an opening. From the water, Philippe shouted something. Rosanette jumped to her feet. Conrad had a fleeting impression of flesh skirting the tip of his nose—perhaps a nipple, perhaps an elbow—and then she was in the water.

Philippe had begun swimming without his water wings, which seemed a good thing. But now the water wings had been snatched away by the serpentine currents and Rosanette was forced to swim after them. After she retrieved them, she tried to get Philippe to wear them again, but he refused. Mother and son exchanged some sharp words and then she dragged him out of the water, her breasts swaying from the effort. Conrad got off his knees and slowly stood. His timing had been bad, but now that he'd launched himself, he was unwilling to give up.

Rosanette dragged the boy up to the open-air restaurant and forced him to sit at one of the tables. The staff looked around uneasily, noticeably disturbed by the woman's nakedness. European beach attire couldn't be acceptable in the dining room, Conrad reasoned, and so he picked up the towel and paperback and brought them to Rosanette.

"Thank you so much," Rosanette said as she wrapped the towel around her. She made no attempt to turn away from Conrad as she did this. Philippe was not to swim without his water wings when no one else was in the water with him, Rosanette explained, as if apologizing. And then, in a more confidential tone, she explained that Philippe was a little bothered because his father had not yet returned from Ko Banteay.

"Oh, that's too bad," Conrad said automatically.

"But maybe it's better," she said absently.

What had she meant by that? Conrad wondered about it all through dinner, which he ended up eating with Rosanette and Philippe. They shared dishes, an odd succession of seafood curries, vegetable stews, chicken satays, and fried noodles, all of which were ordered in the hopes of pleasing Philippe and none of which did.

"This restaurant he doesn't like," Rosanette sighed. "I must take him to other place tomorrow."

"In this heat I'm not really that hungry myself," Conrad offered. His stomach was in fact a little queasy and he worried that Boon might have diluted his drinks with unbottled water. Rosanette looked at Conrad gratefully.

"Yes, I suppose."

"He is really a handsome boy," Conrad went on. "He has your mouth. And your eyes."

"Do you think so? Jean—my husband—thinks Philippe only looks like him. And his family."

"Oh no, no," Conrad said. The alcoholic haze that had hung over him all afternoon was now sufficiently dispersed for him to recognize his opening. "Look at his hair, those curls. Like one of those Greek statues. And the warm tones in his skin. It's all you."

Philippe had shoved his plate aside and was working feverishly with crayons and sketchpad, oblivious, or so Conrad hoped, to their conversation. Rosanette took hold of Conrad's wrist.

"We stay at this village on the mainland of the first few days. All the women in the village come to see Philippe. They have never seen anybody—child—like him before. He is like a—doll—to them. They all for pick him up and carrying him around the village and show to their friends. And he was so mad! He didn't like this carrying around. It was really funny."

She released her grip on Conrad's wrist, but then he grabbed hers.

"Did he fight them?" Conrad asked, feeling his circulatory system kick into high gear. She pulled her hand free.

"Yes, I suppose," she said. And then, more softly:

"Well, yes. He kicked the woman."

"Kicked her?" Conrad leaned forward. He had been leaning forward to begin with and this last adjustment required him to rise slightly from his seat. He couldn't say exactly what he meant to accomplish by this.

"Yes," Rosanette answered slowly. "It was really funny, very funny." Her eyes seemed fixed on something just above and behind Conrad's right shoulder, creating the impression that she was reading a cue card. She lowered her head suddenly, presenting Conrad with the curly mass on the top of her head. The scent rising from her scalp made him dizzy. He sat back down, his head spiraling upward through a cloud of pheromones.

"*Maman?*" Philippe asked in his plaintive voice. "*Je voudrais du gâteau.*"

"*Non.*" His mother shook her head.

"*Chocolat?*"

"*Non!*" And then to Conrad:

"He wants dessert, but I am being stiff."

"Oh, right," Conrad shook his head. "Got to be firm."

He looked around the restaurant as if awakening from a dream and was surprised to find himself there. Rosanette regarded him matter-of-factly.

"You sit in the sun today, I think," she said, and Conrad touched his forehead where it was no doubt red and glistening.

Philippe put his crayon down and left the table. He returned with a set of checkers and a board, which he'd gotten off the wooden shelf next to the kitchen door.

"Sure, I'll play you," Conrad said when Philippe asked. "*Chic alors!*"

Pleased that he had been able to recall this phrase, Conrad looked back at Rosanette for approval. But she was already bent over her paperback.

"He plays this with his father," she murmured without looking up.

Conrad decided to let the boy get well ahead, sometimes letting him take two turns in a row. Now and then Conrad sneaked a look at Rosanette, waiting for her to look up, but she never did. The window had closed as inexplicably as it had opened.

Conrad brooded.

When he jumped three of Philippe's kings in quick succession, the boy grabbed Conrad's finger and bit it. Conrad cried out, more out of surprise than pain, for the little bastard had scraped off a hangnail and made a bloody mess. He wasn't sure if the expression "little bastard" had actually crossed his lips. If it had, he supposed that he might pass it off as a term of affection.

"*Pardon! Je suis désolée,*" Rosanette said over and over as Conrad wrapped a tissue-thin napkin around his bloody nail.

"It's really nothing," he protested as Rosanette dragged Philippe off to their bungalow, the boy crying in that rhythmic way that is not actual crying, but mere protest.

Conrad watched them disappear up the beach, felt besieged

with a different kind of dizziness, a wonder at how quickly things had gotten out of hand.

One of the waiters, a young man who seemed to spend most of the day sitting in a corner, strumming a guitar, came over to scrutinize Conrad's finger.

"So lose her, eh?" he said, smiling.

"What did you say?" Conrad demanded, rising out of his seat. The young man stepped back.

"Sore loser," he repeated shyly. "This boy is one. I think so?"

"Yes, I think so," Conrad said, running his hand through his hair.

Conrad had not been back in his own bungalow five minutes before he heard a knock on the door. He swung it open, panicked, euphoric, certain that it was Rosanette.

"I saw you come in just now," Eva said. "I was going to the restaurant to look for you."

"Okay. Come in, sit down please."

She sat down on the edge of the bed—there was no place else.

"I'm surprised to see you," Conrad said, still standing by the door.

"Really? But we're so close by," Eva answered, lighting a cigarette. "They have better bungalows over here, I think."

"More expensive, too. Do you suppose I could have a cigarette?"

He sat down on the other side of the bed and lit up.

"I must ask you a favor," she began after a moment. "Do you remember what we talked about today?"

Conrad nodded.

"Boon won't let me take him out to dinner," Eva said. "He would lose face. But if another man paid, I don't think it would be such a big problem."

"An older man, you mean?"

"Birgit will come, too. You will invite us all, you see? I'll give you the money."

"Forget it. I'll take you."

"No, I must pay. I'm making you eat with us."

"You're not making me do anything," Conrad said, after taking another drag on his cigarette. "In fact, I was just thinking that I wanted to take you all out."

"But it is I who have asked you."

"Don't worry," he assured her. "I will take care of everything."

Eva hung her head.

"Please don't do this," she said, brushing her cheek with her fingertips. "I need your help and you make me feel trapped."

Conrad heard himself stammer. He hadn't meant it that way. He was the eldest, after all, the grown-up. He had more resources. The expense was really nothing. And he hated eating by himself.

"All right," he said finally. "However you want to do it. I'll be at your disposal. Just stop looking at me that way."

"What way?" she asked.

"I don't know. Like I'm trying to buy you—your friendship or—I don't know. It's hot tonight."

"Yes," Eva said, pressing the back of her hand against her forehead. "Tonight is too hot, I think." Her cheeks were flushed, but she was beginning to look relieved.

"Tomorrow night will be better," she said, standing up. "We will have a very good dinner. And afterward we will be good friends, you and me. Yeah?"

Later that night Conrad awoke with stomach cramps and mild diarrhea. When he couldn't get back to sleep, he decided to take a walk down by the water. Outside the monsoon was blowing. But was it the dry monsoon or one that would bring heavy rains? He couldn't remember what the guidebook had said and it chagrined him to realize that he didn't even know what season it was.

Trawlers rigged with bright lamps lit up parts of the black sea. It looked to Conrad like car dealerships scattered randomly across a flat, empty desert. He thought of the long drive across Nevada and Utah on the trip back to the Midwest to visit the time he and Lucy had driven straight through. According to the owner of the bungalows, the fishermen used the lamps to attract squid, which confused the light with the full moon and swarmed toward it, expecting to mate. It seemed to Conrad like a nasty trick to play on the squid. The amorous ones would ultimately be selected for extinction. The dullards would be left to reproduce in their own clumsy and halfhearted way; and of course, they wouldn't do it at nearly the same frequency as their doomed alpha counterparts. The whole species would soon be in deep trouble.

Heroic measures might have made Conrad a father. Surgical removal of the ovum, test-tube fertilizations, freezing and storage of embryos, eventual implantation, the expenditure of tens of thousands of dollars in doctors' fees, hospitalization, lab tests, special procedures. A process that could drag on for years. And for all that, the chances of failure still outweighed those of success. Much to Conrad's relief, Lucy had finally abandoned the project.

He supposed that he should feel grateful they had not conceived, now that things had begun unraveling.

They had once been the envy of their friends, the couple of legendary stability. While others waged bitter wars of conquest or independence, Conrad and Lucy had remained secure in their Swiss hilltop, cozy in their three-unit Victorian on Saturn Street (which he'd had the good sense to purchase in the mid-seventies, before real estate prices went through the roof). Conrad had fancied them the picture of happily ever after, at least in the eyes of their friends. Yet as the years went by, he'd begun to detect condescension in the faces of new acquaintances and a trace of mockery in their smiles whenever the longevity of their marriage was celebrated in toasts or introductions. Then, at Lucy's last birthday party, a girlfriend with too much champagne in her proclaimed Lucy "unrealized" and "a vast and untapped aquifer of potential." Only the way she pronounced "potential," after a long and poignant pause, gave it a sexual connotation.

Everyone laughed. They'd all drunk too much champagne. Another woman, a friend of Lucy's whom Conrad knew by sight only, admonished the first: Conrad was standing right there for goodness sakes. What about his feelings?

"Conrad doesn't have feelings," the drunk one replied. "He only has intentions."

"But they're really good intentions," Conrad responded, after another pause. And everyone laughed again, mostly from surprise that Conrad had managed a comeback all by himself.

It was, unfortunately, one of those conversations that gets played back endlessly, even months later. It came to represent for Conrad a sort of leak, a hint at the otherwise unspoken contempt with which his wife's friends regarded him. To them Conrad must seem less than real, not quite alive. Perhaps they saw in his demeanor a studied saintliness, a man who would put others' needs before his, but only out of habit and training. Was there any real conviction there? Any passion? Had Lucy married him simply because he was the first man who had been nice to her? It wasn't hard to imagine them debating the issue. And yet Conrad didn't kid himself that Lucy's friends spent much time on the question. To reach a tacit consensus required little more than a few remarks over the phone, a few nods at the dinner table.

A mosquito worried his ear for a moment, futilely fighting the steady wind from the sea. In the urgent beating of its wings Conrad heard something like complaining, then a gust took it away.

In the mass of stars above him he thought for a moment that he'd spotted Scorpio or maybe Draco—something serpent-like in any case. It was a toss-up as to which made him feel smaller, this vast field of stars or the knowledge that he was something of an afterthought to his wife and friends. There were two different kinds of smallness, he decided: the smallness of an insect and the smallness of a man who has failed in some basic way to be a man. The smallness of an insect was preferable, of course. It wasn't so personal.

14

In the morning Conrad awoke strangely refreshed, and soon after realized that he'd made a decision: he was going back to Ko Banteay.

He broke the news to Eva right after breakfast. He would meet them all for dinner that night as planned, but he would not spend another day sitting with her on the beach. The next day he would depart.

Conrad paid up his hotel bill and went into town to buy a ticket for the ferry. He'd hoped to catch a morning ferry, but the one-eyed man at the ticket booth insisted that the ferry only came in the evening. Conrad could not quite believe this, for he seemed to recall seeing boats in the harbor in the morning. He checked the ferry schedule, a blue piece of paper covered with faded print scotch-taped to the window, but found it indecipherable. In the end he decided to buy a ticket just to have it over with. It seemed a great relief.

By eleven A.M., with all of his business for the day complete, he found himself in town, with the greater part of the day still before him. Suddenly he was playing the tourist, strangely elated to be filling his hours with souvenir shopping and willing to listen to various touts make their respective pitches on motorboat cruises, jungle walks, and "culture tours" to the Yawi villages on the other side of the island.

"Shaman Heeling Cere-money Tonight" one flier read. Conrad was given to understand that for only twenty dollars U.S., a guide would drive him to a Yawi fishing village and take him to watch an actual shaman performing a cure. It was like a performance, a big show, the tout explained. The guide would translate everything so Conrad would be able to follow it. Conrad was feeling too expansive to reject the man outright.

"I don't think so," he said gently. "If it's like that bird dance, I'm afraid I'll fall asleep."

"Yes, much dancing," the tout nodded vigorously, not understanding.

"I don't think I'll be able to make it."

"If want, come eight-thirty here. Taxi here eight-thirty. You buy ticket then, if like, okay?"

It was market day again, just as it had been on his first day on the island. Conrad passed through the covered market with a new appreciation. The cries of fishmongers and produce vendors, the tiny transistor radios turned up way too loud, the barefoot men moving large barrels on rickety hand trucks, and the laughter of old women, veteran hagglers, mixing it up with the cries of the caged poultry. Here and there the concrete floor seethed with a mass of live eels or catfish, or was mounded with yellow vegetables and red fruits. And it all flowed past like a wrap-around movie spectacle, like a beautiful simulation in a theme-park ride.

On the other side of the market, he bought an orange soda at a vending cart and sat at a little table in the shade of a large umbrella and sipped his drink slowly. Everything was wonderful, he thought, because it was so fleeting.

In the next instant Conrad found this mood breaking apart. Two Australian tourists, both young men, sat down by the neighboring stand and ordered satays. The one had a loud voice, which he cranked up when the vendor failed to understand that he and his friend would pay separately. Conrad reflexively brushed the side of his head; it was very much like having a large fly buzzing around his ear. He thought of fleeing, but then decided instead to wait for them to move on, for he wanted to sip his drink slowly, and be massaged once more by the warm clamor of the marketplace.

But the voices of the two men persisted. The loud one had that deliberate, pompous way of speaking, as if issuing proclamations.

The other one talked in a staccato fashion that tended to abandon the ends of his sentences to the general clamor of the place.

"Princess Daha," this one said. "Last year at this time was quite a . . . on Saturday nights, this armada of boats—not just the ferries, but private motorboats, fishing boats . . . all these yahoos from the mainland . . . Muslims."

Conrad could see little of them. They were hidden partly behind the tilted umbrella that shaded the vendor's stand, and partly by the little woman working the grill.

"I was royally ticked when I walked in there the day before and find it's just a hotel," the loud one said. " 'Where's the girls?' I says straight out. And the little clerk says '*Gulls?* You like *gulls?*,' like we're on some sort of bird-watching trip."

"Shut down—Islamic government on the mainland—HIV, so they said—never got the hang of latex."

"I heard that later, yeah? But this clerk turns out to be a real nice guy, a real gentleman, you might say. And he sends me to this shop on the other side of town, to a guy named Iwan. All very low-key, discreet, yeah? Set me up with this gorgeous little Malay girl. What you call them here? Yawi?"

"That's one I haven't . . . of course probably great, but . . . nothing like a China doll."

"As far as looks, she's maybe an eight. But enthusiasm? Shoot me if she doesn't deliver superlative head. Best I've ever had, I reckon. Exponentially better than anything on Patpong."

"You're having me on."

"Blood oath, mate. I came in *quarts.*"

Conrad put his bottle on the table. There was none left to sip. The bottle was still cold. He wiped some of its sweat onto his hand and then touched it to his forehead.

"Café Indra," the loud one was saying. "Iwan—this little guy with a mustache."

Conrad ordered another soda and turned his chair so that his back was to the Australians. The loud guy was fat; he was sure of it. A swag-bellied lout boasting about tepid sexual encounters to some other lout. That was the way of it. Once you've gone through with it, you needed to parade the fact in front of someone else.

The loud guy became less loud. In a confidential voice, he began supplying the details of his encounter. There'd been a great massage to start with, then the little hands working their way up his thighs, then the subtle movements of lips and tongue along the shaft, then the tiny fingers opening him up like a flower. Conrad felt a panic growing inside him, wriggling like a tapeworm.

"—and to get an actual Yawi girl is rare. Most are Chinese, you know."

Conrad cleared his throat loudly, suppressing the urge to flee. He took a swig from his new bottle. He was not going to let this thing push him around.

15

Eva wore a silk sarong of purple and yellow and a black halter top that showed her smooth brown shoulders. As she glided across the street to greet him, she seemed like a figure from summers long past. The dusk was alive with the buzzing of motor scooters and the jingling of bicycle bells and the voices of small children, and somehow she had marshaled all of this behind the flowing movement of her body. She called his name. She was coming for him; her smile was for him. And for a dizzying second, the swirl of foreign sensations that included the sight of the barefoot, turbaned women carrying baskets on their heads, and the scent of burning charcoal and fried bananas permeating the dank, languid air, and the twittering of bats flocking in a large tree overhanging the street, and the alpenglow of the cream-colored buildings across the street—all of this took on the flavor of home, of a half-remembered childhood, and Conrad felt himself to be someone else entirely, someone with a different past, and following a very different trajectory.

But then the moment passed, and she was pressing a wad of bills, Tambralingan rials, into his hand.

"There," she said. "Now you can be my sugar papa, okay?"

Conrad again assured her he was at her service, and dutifully followed her down the street toward the restaurant. As they passed a café, the sign caught his eye: Café Idris. Why did that name seem familiar?

"Birgit will be there," Eva said over her shoulder. She was walking fast and Conrad, still distracted by her physicality, found himself lagging a half step behind.

"She seems better today, I think."

"Not so angry with you?" Conrad suggested. Because he was leaving, he could be perfectly blunt. Eva smiled at him confidentially.

"I think she has dropped this idea of Kuala Vimaya. We stay here some more days and then I think we go to Sri Kala in the south and see the festival. Everyone is going. It only happens every seven years and last time you couldn't get into the country for all the fighting."

"Maybe I'll make it down there," Conrad said. Although in truth he hadn't the slightest interest in seeing any more of the country, and planned to set off in the opposite direction in the morning.

Boon and Birgit were already seated, smoking and talking amicably, when Conrad and Eva arrived. Conrad began to thank them for inviting him, and then remembered that he was supposed to have invited them.

"A terrific place," he said to their blank faces. "Best on the island." And indeed the large chalkboard menu offered a range of dishes, Yawi, Chinese, Paktai, and South Indian, Conrad had not seen before.

"I hope you are right," Eva said to him.

They dined on shrimp curry and tea-smoked duck and green beans cooked with shredded coconut. Conversation was sparse at first, but everyone ate with gusto. Some kind of truce had been established, and Birgit made a point of addressing Conrad in warm, conspiratorial tones.

"I'm disappointed that we don't go to the mainland together," she said to him. "I meet this American guy yesterday who is going. And he is talking about the—shrines—where the Muslim saints are in the ground—buried. They have two rocks for each grave—one for head, one for feet."

"Gravestones, you mean?"

"Yes. And when you have this holy man buried in this grave, the distance between the stone for the head and the stone for the feet has grown little bit each year, until now at this shrine, the distance is four or five meters between the markers. If you visit the shrine, you can make the wish, yeah? And the spirit of the holy man will give it to you."

Conrad nodded, but could not quite follow these remarks. He found himself distracted by the idea of returning to Lucy. After a week and a half of waiting for him, he imagined that she would be furious; but far more distracting was the realization that he could no longer picture Lucy—not all of her anyway, not the totality of her. He could only summon bits: the thin upper lip, the long, tapering fingers, the deft curve about her waist. Her face he could not see clearly, but only overlaid with features from other faces, bits of Eva and Liv Ullmann and Rosanette. He felt a moment of panic. Where was she? Where had she gone?

Yet how clearly he could picture the masseuse that the braying Australian had described to his friend! He could see the cut and styling of her hair, gauge the space between her eyebrows, match the slope of her nose with that of her breasts, see the shaft of male flesh disappear between her pouting lips.

They ordered a bottle of wine, which proved undrinkable, then settled for Thai beer, which Birgit declared she needed, even though it upset her stomach. Conrad drank greedily. He was very thirsty.

Birgit was still talking. She'd become quite talkative, sitting next to Boon, who seemed a little withdrawn, even sullen. Things were going her way, Conrad realized. She and Eva would be leaving.

Birgit went on to describe the American she'd met: a young filmmaker who'd come to Tambralinga to make a documentary of sorts about the changing culture.

"Beachside discos?" Conrad asked.

"No," Birgit replied. "Not Ligor Bay. Traditional culture. If you go to other parts of the island, you see villages still the same as before. As—twenty, thirty years before. He goes tonight to film a shaman ritual in a Yawi village on the other side of the island."

"I thought it was all Mon and Paktai on the islands," Eva said.

Boon corrected her. There were three Yawi villages on the island, he explained—small fishing villages. The fishermen tended to be more traditional than the Yawis on the mainland. Many still practiced magic, communicated with the spirits in the earth and sea, practices which were forbidden in mainland communities that followed a stricter form of Islam.

"In fact," Boon said with an emphasis that suggested he'd just acquired the phrase, "police on mainland don't let these magics happen, so *pawangs* must come Ko Neak Pean to make their magics and cure somebody."

"The police?" Eva asked.

"The religious authorities," Birgit said. "The imams and mullahs."

There was a pause while everyone soaked up this irony. Then Conrad remembered the flier in his pocket. When he showed it to them, Eva got excited. They should go, she declared. They could all share the cab and the guide. It would be a wonderful change.

"Is good," Boon said hesitantly. "But maybe goes too long." He touched his lip thoughtfully.

Probably counting the nights he had left with Eva, Conrad speculated. Who wouldn't? He drained his beer and ordered another.

Birgit began shaking her head.

"Why do we have to make every part of their culture some kind of business?" she asked. "I think it would be very interesting, yes. But maybe we should leave them alone this time."

Eva looked dismayed. She confessed to being tired of hanging around the beach day after day.

"It wasn't my idea," Birgit said, looking away.

"Nothing is ever your idea," Eva shot back. "You can only criticize!"

"My idea was to go to Kuala Vimaya and leave this—this tourist stuff." Birgit turned her gaze toward Boon.

"Your idea is to say one negative thing after another until I am sick of hearing your voice," Eva replied. "If you don't want to go, fine. Just Conrad and I will go."

Everyone looked at Conrad. He stopped the progress of his bottle, which was exactly halfway between the tabletop and his lips.

"Well," he said after a moment. "I wanted—that is, I—" He knew he was supposed to say something conciliatory, something to defuse the tension, but the alcohol had slowed his mind and at the same time directed his attention to an undertow of blunt desire.

"Well, sure," he said finally, stung by the knowledge that he would go anywhere with Eva, even if it was to sit through a long, tedious ceremony, just to be alone with her. But by the time the words struggled across his lips, they had become irrelevant. The discussion had moved on, was running far ahead, jumping from English to Swedish and back.

"All right, then," Birgit was saying. "We will all of us go."

Words were still coming from Conrad's mouth, but no one was listening. He closed his lips. All of his reactions seemed to be on a five-second delay. He watched his disappointment approach like the dark edge of a storm front.

The check came and Conrad paid with Eva's money, as planned.

It would be wise to go set things up with the driver and the guide as soon as possible, Eva said as she got to her feet. The others stood up. Conrad remained seated. He explained that he was a little tired, that he was going to sit at the table awhile longer, with another beer, and write some postcards. He would meet them at the departure spot near the marketplace.

"You are coming, though?" Eva asked.

"Yes, yes," Conrad said, closing his eyes. For a moment he was falling through a shower of purple and yellow flowers, like those patterned on Eva's sarong; but then he took hold of himself, and fearing that he was appearing rude, opened his eyes.

"All right," he said, blinking hard. But they were already through the door.

He was a little drunk. More than a little, he realized, as he tried to explain to himself exactly what he was doing. He pushed off down the street and aimed himself at the door of the Café Idris. He found the inside dark and smoky, awash with the aromas of chicken and lamb satay. A short man with a black cap stood behind the display case in the back. Behind the glass were different sample plates, mosaics of yellow rice and fried greens and red curry sauces. Conrad stood in the doorway for a moment, staring. He felt his frustration ebbing away. What was he doing in another restaurant? Something about the name: Café Idris. The Australian had said it. Café Idris, ask for Evan—wasn't it?

Not Evan, he corrected himself, but Imam. Ask for Imam.

The place was empty but for a few couples sprinkled around the tables. The proprietor put a cigarette to his lips as Conrad approached. Sobered, Conrad remembered not to be in a hurry, not to seem too businesslike or brusque.

The man cocked his head back as Conrad greeted him.

"Imam?" Conrad asked slowly. "Are you Imam?" The man smiled strangely, touched his weathered cheeks. He might have been sixty, maybe even older.

"How can I help you, mister?" the man asked. He pronounced each word carefully, with didactic precision. Chatting him up would take a while.

Conrad explained that he'd heard the Café Idris was a special place. The man pointed to the different platters in the display case, describing the contents. His eyes smiled inwardly, as if he had already guessed Conrad's purpose, but was enjoying the charade. Conrad praised each platter in turn: This one was like a mandala, this one a flower, and that one was a real beauty.

"You are men—a man—with refined tasteds," the man told Conrad. "You are like—" he paused, reaching for a word. "The artist."

"I like beauty," Conrad replied. "And beautiful—things."

The man seemed to like this reply. He smiled, exposing a row of perfect teeth. Conrad went on to ask how long he'd been in the business and how the "staff" was working out, and what time of year was the busiest. After some while, Conrad thought he detected a perplexed air about the man, and so decided to get to the point.

"You are American, I think," the man said. "But more friendly than American mens. But why you ask for imam?"

"Imam? I heard he would help me—find someone."

"Yes?"

"A girl," Conrad said quickly, looking away. "Are there any available tonight?"

"Tonight?" the man asked slowly.

"Yes. Now, actually. The sooner the better."

There. He'd said it. The throttle was thrown wide open on his atrium, the artery in his neck pulsed savagely. Conrad turned his gaze back to the man and waited for the result.

The man looked at him for a minute and then drew up as close to Conrad's face as his height would allow.

"You asking me to get you girl? This is no bad house, mister. This is for good peoples, not for like you. You Western people think you can buy everything. Money is everything for you. If you get girl here, she is—not free—she is a sleeve."

"Slave," Conrad whispered.

"You want easy girl, but she is no easy. Not for her. She is catched like animal. Men keep her in cage. Maybe her father sell her. Maybe men catched her. And boys come and pay. They don't know about this. But man like you, I think you know about this. You, you are big man. You know about this."

The man looked down at his feet for a moment and finding a box, stood up on it, so that he was closer to Conrad's height. His voice had been getting steadily louder all along, and one of the couples at a side table turned to watch. Conrad stared at the man in disbelief. The logical thing would be to excuse himself and leave, but the enormity of his error left him paralyzed. He kept waiting for the man to smile again, to wink and let him know it was all a joke, but the man simply kept on, with his slow and careful pronunciation. The West had corrupted everything with its filthy money. Tambralinga was poor, but that was no shame, nothing compared to the parade of wantonness coming out of the West.

Conrad sat down on a stool. The man looked down at him and shook his finger slowly. This is a cartoon, Conrad thought, a bad dream. He rubbed his eyes instinctively. His back began to itch. He imagined eruptions of rashes and boils. Still the man prated on in his quacking schoolmaster's voice, about sisters and mothers and all the good things that were taught by Jesus. Surely he'd been to church, to worship the Christ.

Would it help to order dinner? Conrad thought. Would that shut him up? What he'd really like was a beer, but he doubted that the man served alcohol.

Everyone in the place was watching.

Rosanette came in, with Philippe in tow. Philippe was complaining bitterly about something, but she shushed him and dragged him by the wrist up to the counter. A bowl of rice, she told the man quickly. Plain rice, no sauce on it. But the exasperation in her voice had distorted her already heavily accented speech. The proprietor looked at her blankly, the way one would look at a barking dog. The boy yanked himself free and made for the door; his mother gave chase. Conrad watched. Here was his opening. Just follow the kid out the door.

Instead he turned toward the proprietor.

"She wants a bowl of rice," he said carefully, trying to keep the tremors from his voice. "Just rice. Nothing else."

The proprietor blinked.

"And a pot of tea, please," Conrad went on, fishing a bill from his pocket. The money here was small, like the country. The ten-rial note was little bigger than a calling card. The man's gaze went down to the bill, then back to Conrad's face. For a moment Conrad feared that the man would strike him, but instead he removed his cap and turned away, busying himself with the aluminum pots on the stove.

Conrad stared at the man's back, at the dingy bottom of his polo shirt, at the comb-over on the back of his head. He was free to go now, he realized. Relations had been normalized. He wanted to say something conciliatory, "Sorry about the mix-up," or something like that, something tossed off in an airy tone over his departing shoulder. But he knew his voice would fail him at the critical moment, and so he pushed off from the counter without another word.

"You are sick?" Rosanette asked Conrad as he turned around. She touched his smoldering forehead, then the pulsing artery in his neck. He knew his face must be showing emotion, but what emotion could it be? For they all flickered before him, like stills in a peep show: fear, anger, embarrassment, lust, loneliness, frustration.

"Rosanette," he said, then hesitated, surprised at finding her name on his lips. "It's just you," he went on, struggling for some semblance of a smile, but not certain if it was to be sincere or ironic or just sarcastic. "Seeing you again."

Okay, sarcasm it would be. He kissed her hand quickly and then went past her into the street.

As he hurried down the street, the full extent of his humiliation began to sink in. The couples who'd been watching would surely talk about the incident. It would become a wonderful anecdote to be told and retold over the breakfast tables of dozens of hotel and bungalow cafés across the island. Who knows, maybe one of the couples was traveling on to Ko Banteay the next day and Lucy would end up hearing about it, laughing in her pointed way, not knowing the miserable slob in the story was her own husband. On the other hand, even a general physical description, if included in the retelling, might betray his connection to the matter. Conrad pondered this with some alarm. He was taller and older

than most, he could easily be spotted in a crowd. It was not hard
to imagine one of these couples turning up on Ko Banteay, brushing up against him at a souvenir shop. People might point at him
from across the beach or nudge each other when he entered a
restaurant.

Conrad turned a corner on impulse, not quite ready to arrive
at the taxi stand and face Eva and Birgit again. For them to learn
about it seemed worse than Lucy's finding out, and it was not a
far-fetched idea by any means. Conrad turned another corner and
found himself in an unfamiliar alley. Crude shops lined the narrow passageway. Hand-painted signs hung over the doorways,
some in Thai, some in Chinese, some in Roman letters. Sober
faces peered at him from doorways and windows, an old man in
a black cap buying cigarettes, a Chinese woman unfolding the
gate across the shop window, a moon-faced child crouched over a
brazier cover with smoking satays. Everywhere small yellow dogs
slunk about. And there at the end of the alley was a small café,
little more than a crude bar with a few stools in front of it. The
sign above it read CAFÉ INDRA. A second, smaller sign hung below
it: ASK FOR IWAN.

Conrad stopped to look inside the café. A short man with a
sparse goatee leaned against the counter, supporting his weight on
folded arms, talking animatedly to a tourist, a fat man swaddled
in sweaty white pajamas.

"Yeah, sure," the man was saying with swooping motions of
his head. "No problem. Tonight. Tomorrow night." He made a
fluttering motion with his fingers. At that moment his gaze turned
in Conrad's direction and he raised up his hand.

"*Selamat malam, Tuan!* Yes, mister, how are you doing?"

Café *Indra*! Conrad thought. Ask for *Iwan*! This was the
place, a little cave in a brick wall, lit by a single dingy bulb. He
felt himself tucking in his shirt, squaring his shoulders. Christ,
this was it.

Part Four

Semengat

16

If you're headed upriver, check out the hilltop shrine in **Karimunja**, where droves of Yawi villagers come every year after harvest to make offerings at the foot of an ancient tree. Four tiny altars have been built into the trunk, each one facing one of the cardinal points. At one time each altar housed a small statue, but recent changes in the law have forbidden the public display of graven images. Nonetheless, believers say the spot is charged with *semengat*, a vital energy that can allegedly restore one's health, attractiveness, and sexual vigor. Lighting a candle at each altar is likewise guaranteed to make you lucky in business or gambling.

—*Coswell's Guide to Tambralinga* (1997 ed.)

Jeannine looked at Lucy wryly as she read this description aloud from the guidebook.

"Semen-got?" she asked. "They really call it that? Imagine the billboards along the highway: 'Got Semen?' "

"It's not pronounced that way," Lucy replied in a tone that put an end to Jeannine's laughter.

Lucy explained that the shrine was not the real draw for her, but rather the people who came to make offerings. Some came from as far away as Nagaseri. Some nights there were long processions up to the shrine, farmers, fishermen, laborers setting out barefoot, with flickering candles, each candle just long enough to last the walk up to the shrine. Lucy liked the idea of the candles lasting only long enough, although in the inevitable follow-through of her thinking, she worried about how the return trip was managed. Also appealing was the possibility that the ritual was a throwback to ancient times, when perhaps a temple stood on that spot and young girls, dancers in shimmering sarongs, led

the processions. Although she didn't admit this to Jeannine, she
found the idea of ancient rituals partially remembered, imper-
fectly reenacted, especially pleasing, mysteriously linked to the
vague yearnings that always came upon her at dusk.

The route up the hill proved less romantic, however. The steps
hewn from solid rock that Lucy had pictured were glaringly ab-
sent. (Where had *that* notion come from?) The path, instead, was
a tangle of thick roots and creepers, every other one of them
swarming with ants. At the top of the hill they could find no sign
of the shrine, although they looked and looked. There were only
a few tree stumps and, down the far side of the hill, a smoldering
burn pile.

"Wrong hill, Luce," Jeannine said, laughing.

Lucy looked doubtfully at the guidebook. The directions had
been so clear.

"Disappointing," she managed to say.

"Give it a rest, sweetheart." The note of condescension in
Jeannine's voice had been sounded one too many times that day
for Lucy's taste. Jeannine's initial deference to Lucy as team
leader had evaporated. Jeannine trekked back down the hill with
an annoying air of self-possession. "Better than you," the back of
the blond head seemed to declare. "Longer legs, more youthful
skin, more grace, more experience. I could not care less about the
sights. I am the sight. Maybe not the one people come to see, but
absolutely the one they remember."

Lucy recalled certain girls in high school who displayed this
kind of poise, girls who moved in stratospheric social circles, surrounded by athletic boys and admiring followers. It had been a
simple matter to dismiss their ascendancy as merely adolescent, to
leapfrog their little status-sphere by aiming for mature relationships
with grown-up men in far-off universities. And so she had come to
California and met Conrad, Conrad the grown-up, the serious one.

The young man behind the desk at the Karimunja Inn gave rather
elliptical answers to Lucy's questions about the shrine, or so it

seemed to her. "Nobody goes up there for a long time now. Maybe bad lucks follow." He seemed not to understand the word "procession," nodding at first as if it were some kind of slogan that had sparked his enthusiasm, then looking suddenly uneasy as Lucy described the dancers and the candles.

"No, missus. Sore-ree," he said, twisting his hand back and forth in the air as if trying an invisible doorknob.

"No more procession?" she asked.

"Pross-gression," he repeated uncertainly.

"He thinks you said 'progress,' " Jeannine said.

"Progress," the clerk said, nodding.

In the Karaoke Bar, they ran into Rashid. He sat at a table with two other men, one of them dressed in a policeman's uniform, talking animatedly through a cloud of smoke. All three were drinking white tea. Rashid showed no surprise at seeing them again. As they entered the room, he got up from his seat, smiling warmly, as if expecting them; but then immediately sat back down as they passed by toward the bar. Maybe it was not that unusual to find an officer from the Ministry of Religious Education in a bar, Lucy decided. No place else was open after eight o'clock and in fact the karaoke machine had not yet been turned on.

As a rule Lucy drank only wine, but the selection here was poor—tepid-sounding whites from Australia and Chile, and nothing at all from California. She followed Jeannine's lead and ordered a gin and tonic. It was a slow night, a Sunday. Someone at the hotel had told her there was a logging camp nearby, but the loggers wouldn't get paid for another five days and would stay out of town until then. She listened more intently to the men's conversation than she wanted, followed its rhythmic cadences as though it were a drum solo. One of the men, the one not wearing a uniform, was in the habit of ending every outburst with a rising-pitch sigh, after which a brief silence would fall over the table. What was he lamenting, Lucy wondered. The fact that the loggers weren't here to spend money? That his wife had run off with another man, a policeman perhaps? The others seemed to listen in pitying silence. Did he irritate them, she wondered, or merely express what all three were feeling? Maybe he was telling a story. Yes, that was it. He was taking the part of a character in the story he was telling, one of those fairy tales in which the character makes the same question or complaint three different times. And on the third time, something unexpected happens. She listened for the shift in tone that would confirm her theory, an outburst of laughter from the others, a sudden switch to a new voice. But nothing changed. The voice continued to sigh, twice, three times, four times more. And each time the subsequent silence deepened.

They were all bored with this guy, Lucy decided, just as she was growing bored of Jeannine. She poked at the ice in the bottom of her glass. Next to her she sensed a dangling sandal flapping gently against the bottom of Jeannine's foot. Lucy looked over at her companion, who was also stirring the ice in her otherwise empty glass.

"I'm going to have them put more lime in the next one." Jeannine smiled. And Lucy wondered why she wanted another one. They were both so obviously bored. Why not leave? What were they waiting for?

And then it occurred to her that they were both waiting for the other men to leave, for Rashid to come over and join them. And to see which one he would sit next to.

17

The view was of rice fields and stands of oil palms and the serrated profiles of limestone ridges against the reddening western sky, but somehow Lucy felt she was back in America. It must have something to do with the smoothness of the ride; the newness of the highway. It was also the spaciousness of her seat and its plush upholstery. Yes, and the way the world slid by untouched, under glass. That's what America was like.

She was in the backseat of Rashid's limousine, the guidebook in her lap. They were on their way to Kuala Vimaya, still more than two days away, and she had grown tired of checking their progress along the dotted line in the guidebook's map that was meant to show a highway under construction. It cut a straight line through the Sangra hills and across the alluvial plain of the Vimaya River, unlike the old road, still unpaved in many parts, which slavishly mirrored the river's meandering course. The thought of missing that part of the trip saddened her. It was not so much that she would have savored being crammed into an ancient bus and hauled along rutted dirt roads as she would have enjoyed telling about it afterward. Physical hardship cheerfully endured was a necessary ingredient to any good travel story. All in all, discomfort had been in short supply on this trip, and this was beginning to bother her. As the road curved to the left, the sun's new angle afforded Lucy a glimpse of her own reflection in the window—a sudden materialization of her slender forearm, her short, straight nose, the brim of her sun hat—that momentarily blotted out the countryside. She looked down at her nails and then began searching her bag for an emery board.

Next to Lucy sat Rashid and next to him, Jeannine. Rashid

held Jeannine's palm in his hand and appeared to study it. A great
uncle, someone on his mother's side, had taught him how to read
palms when he was still a boy. Or so he claimed.

"You have a long life line," he said to Jeannine, tracing the tip
of his index finger across the heel of her palm and on up her
wrist. She laughed skittishly.

"Not quite *that* long," she insisted.

"This line is very deep. Strong heart. Open." His fingers
moved across her palm again, appeared to caress her fingers
briefly. Lucy wondered why Rashid had bothered to invite her
along at all. Was he too much the gentleman to simply "cut one
out of the herd"? Jesus, she thought. That was Antoine's expression.

What annoyed Lucy most was the way Jeannine pretended not
to understand what was happening, and how willingly Rashid
seemed to swallow this pretense. It seemed part of a dance, the
steps of which Lucy had never learned and which she was now
condemned to watch from the sidelines. She'd been married too
young. She'd married an older man. She'd been in a hurry to
prove herself a grown-up. And the thing with Antoine had come
on so suddenly. Before she knew it, they were spending all their
time together hiding out in hotel rooms or private hot tubs. There
had never been this flourishing of tail feathers, this display of
swans' necks twining around each other in public.

Public, she wondered. Am I their public?

But no, Rashid seemed to want to include her. He took her
hand and gently brought it, palm up, next to Jeannine's.

"What a complex web of fine lines," he said. "What a contrast
to your friend's! Where your friend's are simple and clearly
etched, yours are mysterious, enigmatic. It's—what's the word? A
labyrinth! A labyrinth of poetic impulses, of very deep emotions."

Even though she knew better, Lucy felt stirred by this flattery.
The man was sounding all the warm tones in his voice, was playing them like a xylophone. He squeezed her hand slightly and
squinted at the folds this made in her palm. She felt herself
coloring.

Rashid continued to scrutinize the palm. "There was an old man who sometimes came to the Sultan's court when I was a boy. We called him 'uncle,' but he was no blood relative. He was a famous *pawang*, a sorcerer—much feared in the northern part of the country. When the Japanese invaded, he killed seventeen of their officers with just his sorcery."

Lucy managed to meet his gaze. "Really?"

Rashid smiled. She noticed a patch of pockmarked skin near his left temple and a small scar under his left eye. Neither of these things seemed unattractive.

"It was generally believed that he had the power to raise the dead. That in fact, the reason he was honored at court was because he had the power to bring the dead back to life."

Rashid began stroking her palm with his free hand, as if trying to smooth out the folds he'd made with the other.

"I find that hard to believe," Lucy stammered, shy now of looking away from his gaze, of appearing frightened by his forwardness.

"Oh, he couldn't bring just anyone back to life. It was my uncle, you see. When my uncle was a very young man, not more than sixteen years of age, he and my grandfather had a bitter argument. My uncle left the house in an absolute fury and mounted his horse and rode off. It was his favorite horse, but in his agitated state, he caused the horse to run faster and faster and it finally threw him. When the servants found him, he had stopped breathing. The court physician pronounced him dead. My grandfather was heartbroken."

Lucy looked down at her hand, at the gentle rhythmic motion of the man's finger across her palm. She felt like an alligator that had been wrestled into submission.

"He and my father were very close, you see," Rashid continued when she was again able to look at his face. "He was the old Sultan's favorite, his heir. Quite spoiled."

A momentary panic seized her: Did he mean to have both of them? The idea exerted a queasy fascination.

"The *pawang* was at court when the accident happened. My

grandfather called him in, screamed at him, threatened him, begged him, wept. You can imagine the scene. The *pawang* said that he could bring him back, but only for a short while—less than an hour, in fact. And my grandfather would pay a heavy price: his own life."

"So your uncle had to die all over again?" Jeannine asked, her voice taking on a familiar brassy edge. "That's kind of rough, isn't it? I mean, twice in the same week!"

"Shush," Lucy said quietly. She gave Rashid's hand a quick squeeze as if to encourage him to continue the story.

"This is the story I heard growing up. You may draw your own conclusions, as they say." Rashid continued. "The *pawang* went into a deep trance and began speaking in the language of the djinns. He danced around the room where my uncle lay, grappling with the spirits, talking in many different voices. And then he ordered my grandfather to walk clockwise three times around my uncle's bed, reciting a particular verse from the Koran, pledging his life to Allah. My uncle revived, he sat up, he smiled. The Sultan wept, threw his arms around the boy's feet, begged his forgiveness. My uncle cried also, also begged for mercy. And so they were reunited very briefly, but their joy was beyond anything known in this world.

"Three days later my grandfather took to his bed. Six months after that, he died. And my father was named Sultan."

Rashid patted Lucy's hand and then released it. Rashid turned toward Jeannine, whose face was suddenly covered in tears.

"It's so sad," she murmured.

"Not everyone believes that story," he said, directing the sweep of his large brown eyes back toward Lucy. "Do you believe it?"

"I believe," Lucy said, swallowing, "that you believe it."

"Some have suggested," Rashid said slowly, "that the Sultan obtained the throne through intrigue, even murder." Lucy forced herself to meet his gaze, bearing down on the tremors that threatened to commandeer her legs.

18

The ticket booth that stood at the end of the ferry dock appeared abandoned. The flimsy door swung feebly in the evening breeze.

Conrad slung his half-filled duffel over his shoulder and hiked up to the end of the dock, where a small group of passengers waited. He was early. He was eager to get back to Ko Banteay, to San Francisco, to put an early end to this so-called vacation.

A stocky, bow-legged man in a white cap nodded to Conrad as he approached the group. Conrad acknowledged the greeting shyly, trying to conceal his aversion. The cap, he now realized, flagged the man as a Muslim. There were racial characteristics as well—the somewhat darker hue to the skin, the somewhat wider eyes—that distinguished this man from his Buddhist countrymen. Before the incident at the Café Idris, Conrad had been only dimly aware of the differences, Birgit having mentioned them in passing. Now they seemed glaringly obvious.

Conrad inquired, by means of gestures and sentence fragments, whether the man was going to Ko Banteay. The Muslim seemed to agree.

"Kuala Vimaya," he said cautiously, "Lingga Baharu, Ko Banteay."

The list of place names reminded Conrad how little he knew of the country's geography. He brushed the ticket nervously against the palm of his hand.

"Ko Banteay?" he asked again, just to make sure. The Muslim smiled and gestured to the north.

"Ko Banteay," he said. Then, pointing south, "Vimaya, Sri Kala."

The issue was getting muddled. Was the man going to Ko Banteay or not? Or was he saying that the boat was coming from Ko Banteay? Conrad squinted at the horizon for a sign of the boat. Behind him a boisterous group of tourists approached, speaking loudly in German. They undoubtedly knew the ferry's destination, but Conrad noticed two of the women in the party looking in his direction and laughing in a confidential way. Had they heard about his debacle at the Idris or maybe even witnessed it? He drew in his belly. With luck the boat would be crowded and he would sit far away from these chattering young people. He'd decided to wait for the evening ferry in hopes of minimizing his exposure. He would return to Ko Banteay under cover of darkness, slip back into his lodging at Dak's Bungalows unseen.

Yes, and what then?

Conrad's throat tightened. When he got his breath back, all of the anger returned, a searing vapor that went through his head like Japanese horseradish.

He calmed himself with the thought that Lucy might not be there. Nonetheless, he kept picturing the look of surprise on her face.

The girl Iwan had sent him to the night before possessed dark skin and large eyes—a Yawi, Iwan had assured him. And although he would not at first admit it, Conrad succumbed to a cheap twinge of triumph at having apparently snared a Muslim girl.

The girl's thighs were a little chubby, her breasts small, but that had been fine with Conrad. He wasn't trophy hunting. This wasn't a shopping expedition, not really. He was only asking her to perform a service.

But when Conrad entered her tiny room, his first impulse was to hurry back to Iwan and make other arrangements. Iwan had insisted that Conrad would be under no obligation. He'd even apologized for not having other girls available that night. The girl smiled sweetly at him and Conrad immediately felt sorry for her, and worried that a rejection by him might put her in bad straits with her boss. Conrad returned her smile. He wouldn't permit the transaction to make a boor out of him.

The girl stepped back to allow Conrad to enter, bending the thin plywood wall behind her. The tiny bulb in the ceiling gave off a weak yellowish light; her great round cheeks shone like twin moons in the semi-dark. Just being in close proximity to a strange body should be sufficiently stimulating, Conrad told himself.

"You like naked massage?" she asked, and he nodded, not knowing exactly what was meant by the term, but reassured by her cheerfulness. Quickly it became apparent that "naked massage" meant that she would remove her clothes immediately and charge him an additional fifty rials. But that was okay with him. That was perfectly fine.

His own clothes he took off and hung on one of the nails sticking out of the plywood wall, mentally cataloguing each item as he did so: the stain-resistant, rip-stop nylon pants that converted to shorts, the wrinkle-free rayon-polyester shirt, the gray cotton-poly underpants with the pouch in the front for extra comfort (not really necessary), the formerly white cotton socks.

She gestured for him to lie down on the bed. He flopped down on his stomach without looking at her, suddenly apprehensive. He half-expected her to start searching his clothes for extra money. He'd seen that in a movie once, one of those foreign films. Instead she turned on a small radio. A soft tenor voice issued from it, quavering against a background of strings and woodwinds, moving slowly up a pentatonic scale.

"You like music?" she asked, and he said that he did, because he could hear voices coming from another room.

"You like candle?" And when Conrad agreed, she lit a candle on the small stand in the corner of the room and turned off the overhead light. Then she began rubbing oil on his back and humming along with the radio. She could be washing the floor, Conrad thought. Or doing the ironing. The thought relaxed him.

She moved down his back, to his buttocks and thighs. She

seemed to know what she was doing. She worked her way down to his calves and the soles of his feet, then straddled him across the waist and started on his shoulders and neck. He felt her pelvis against his back as she leaned into a stroke, felt her warm breath against the back of his neck. A delicate aroma engulfed him. He began to imagine that he was in the hands of some other woman, a different sort altogether, one synthesized from the peripheral glimpses of arm, breast, and thigh, and the steady stream of stereotyped images—the insinuations of billboards and television commercials, the blatant come-ons of pornographic magazines— flowing from some secret reservoir in his brain. Her body at first felt pliant, but in quick stages grew muscular and fierce.

She had him lie on his side and began lightly working his chest and midriff, then his stomach and inner thighs. As his penis began to engorge, he grew shy, wanting, on the one hand, to roll back on his stomach and on the other hand, to turn toward her and look her full in the face. But he could do neither.

"You want me play your willy?" she asked quietly.

"Yes."

As her hand closed around his shaft, the stream of images began rushing before his closed eyes, and for one rapturous moment Conrad believed everything would be permitted. He rolled on to his back, ready in the next instant to grab her up in his arms. But as he turned his head around, Conrad caught sight of her vulva nearly at eye level.

He stopped, his hand hovering near her waist. In the dim light he couldn't quite tell what he was looking at, only that something was off.

"What is that?" he whispered.

The girl looked down at him serenely. Conrad reached for the candle that sat on the stand and brought it near the girl's naked thighs. She had no pubic hair to speak of, no labia, and no clitoris. But for a tiny hole, her entire vagina seemed to have been erased. When he felt the hot wax running onto his skin, Conrad started, dropping the candle.

"Jesus!" he exclaimed, jumping off the bed. He backed into

the plywood wall, found the light switch and flipped it on. Under the hard light the girl picked up the candle and put it back on the stand. She lit it and then turned to Conrad.

"Want lay down some more?" she asked, as if nothing had happened. Beneath her placid smile, Conrad's erection wilted away.

"Were you born that way?" Conrad asked and immediately realized what a foolish question it was.

The girl didn't seem to mind when he started putting his clothes back on.

"You pay me now, okay?"

Conrad paid her.

How would he describe it one day? The term "circumcision" could not encompass what he'd seen. And where was his parlor with the sliding French doors? Where were the brandy and the cigars? Conrad could no longer conjure them. He hummed to himself as he scanned the horizon.

By the time Conrad noticed the ferryboat, it was already at the mouth of the inlet and he was unable to tell from which direction it had come. More passengers crowded up to the end of the pier, motley groups of old men in turbans and sarongs, younger men in polyester shirts and dark glasses, peasant women carrying baskets of produce on their heads. In their midst was a young man, a Westerner, who looked somewhat familiar. Conrad hailed him.

"Didn't we meet up at the temple the week before last?" Conrad asked.

"Wat Tara Sek? Right." The young man extended his hand. "Conrad, isn't it? I'm Romney Gavin."

"Right." Conrad reached for Romney's hand, forgetting the ticket he held in his own.

"Let's not lose our ticket, eh?" the young man said as the ticket fluttered down onto the pier. Conrad snatched at it and missed, but Romney plucked it out of the air.

"Off to Kuala Vimaya or going all the way to Sri Kala?" Romney asked as he handed the ticket back to Conrad.

"I'm going back to Ko Banteay. Isn't this the right boat?"

"Well," Romney said, taking a closer look at the ticket. "This ticket is for this boat, but this boat doesn't go directly to Ko Banteay. You have to change boats in Kuala Vimaya. It's something like twenty-three hours if you go that route. There is a morning ferry to Ko Banteay, I think."

"The man in the ticket booth said the ferry only comes in the evening."

"*His* ferry only comes in the evening. There's more than one line, you see."

Conrad hummed, tried to appear nonchalant. He took the ticket back and crammed it in his pants pocket.

"There is an evening ferry that goes directly to Ko Banteay," Romney continued. "But it's very slow and it only runs a couple nights a week. Not tonight."

"I'm confused. So there's a morning ferry and an evening ferry tomorrow, but none tonight?"

"Another of the Orient's great mysteries." The young man shrugged.

The ferry approached the dock, its prow riding low in the water, its deck a few meters lower than the boards where Conrad stood. A small ladder was set up and the passengers, mostly tourists, began disembarking.

"Most of the tourists get off here," Romney nodded. "The mainland's a bit tense right now, at least around Kuala Vimaya. There've been a few riots lately."

"And that's where you're going? Cola what?"

"Kuala Vimaya," Romney said with a note of impatience. "Actually I'm going to a village a good ways beyond Kuala Vimaya, a place called Airabu. There's a famous shrine there I'm eager to see. It's been compared to Lourdes—miraculous cures and all that."

"I could use a trip to Lourdes," Conrad said quietly.

"Well, you do have a ticket," Romney said, stretching. "I could help you find a safe hotel. Relatively safe."

"Safe?"

"Like I said, there's been some disturbances over there. I wouldn't be surprised if some of our fellow passengers are going to the mainland to join the protest. Notice how they're mostly Muslims?"

When Conrad asked what the protests were about, Romney sighed with obvious annoyance. It was so hard to explain in a few sentences, he told Conrad. There was the devaluation of the Tambralingan rial, the end of government food subsidies, the brutality of the Paktai police and army, the bribery scandal in the Sultan's family, the militant Muslims calling for a separate Islamic state. And a charismatic leader, a young man who was mobilizing the students and the peasants in a sort of democracy movement. The rhetoric was full of conflicting symbols, of liberty and jihad, of the "purification" of the nation, and the great stew of languages, cultures, and religions that gave Tambralinga its soul.

The stream of passengers leaving the boat tapered off. Two old women slowly climbed the ladder. Coming up behind them was a young Buddhist monk dragging a large chest. The chest appeared heavy; the young man stopped when he got to the foot of the ladder, apparently out of breath. Passengers waiting to board now began scrambling down the ladder. There was something of a race to stake out desirable deck space, Romney explained, as the trip took most of the night. Romney himself seemed to be in no hurry. He clearly enjoyed watching the people jockey for space.

"Oh, hello!" He nudged Conrad. "Look at this guy." Conrad followed the general direction of Romney's nod and saw the Tarzan character striding up the dock, with bare chest and bare feet, as usual. He wore a troubled expression, rendered somewhat more cerebral by his round, wire-rimmed glasses. The face of a chimpanzee deep in thought, Conrad observed.

"Jane's gone missing, from the look of things." Romney smirked. "Now watch how these Yawi women react."

Conrad watched as the big man climbed down to the deck. The women, clustered mostly on one side of the boat, at first turned their veiled heads toward the new arrival and then looked quickly away. A wide swath of deck space opened up as the man put his rucksack down. The young women sitting next to him pulled their scarves closer around their faces. Some put their heads together, seeming to laugh. Romney also seemed to laugh, emitting a high-pitched squeal through his nose.

"This promises to be an interesting trip," he said.

"I don't know," Conrad said. It was hard to look at the body-builder, and equally hard not to look at him, at the obscene way his skin glistened, as though covered with oil. Conrad's gaze wandered back to the young monk.

"Not in a big rush to get off the boat," Conrad remarked.

"Probably waiting for someone to hoist his trunk up on the dock," Romney said. "And look how they all ignore him. He's not a real monk, you see. Just a beggar dressed as one. Thailand's full of them. It's what one does when one has no money or job prospects."

"How can you be so sure?"

"For one thing, he's too dirty to be a proper monk. And he's wearing leather sandals. And, of course, he's smoking."

It was true. The monk had a cigarette dangling from his lips and was bending over, struggling to light it.

"Maybe he's on vacation," Conrad suggested. "Everyone breaks the rules once in a while."

Romney touched his gel-stiffened hair.

"Of course with two hundred and twenty-seven vows you're going to get some fudging. But I would argue that the total package we're being presented with is a bogus one."

Conrad looked at Romney, at his thin cotton pants that faintly resembled jodhpurs, the lace-up jungle boots, the green camo T-shirt. Then he looked back at the monk, who was in the process of bringing his cigarette to his lips. Conrad noticed then that the monk was missing most of his left arm, that the robe had been draped skillfully to hide this handicap.

"Need a hand?" Conrad called down to him. The monk gave him a severe look and Conrad realized that he'd said something stupid.

"I mean with your trunk," Conrad clarified. He climbed down to the deck and took hold of a handle on the chest.

"You are getting off here, right?" Conrad asked. The monk did not answer. He climbed the ladder and, without looking back, set off down the pier, apparently confident that Conrad would follow.

"He's put you to work in a hurry," Romney called as Conrad hoisted the trunk up to a middle rung in the ladder. The thing was heavy, and it made clinking noises.

"Sounds like dinnerware," Romney observed. "Maybe he sells place settings door-to-door." Conrad heaved the trunk noisily up onto the next rung and for an awful moment, almost dropped it. The monk, already several paces up the pier, turned around at the noise.

"Ta-ta-ta!" he admonished, gesturing impatiently with his single hand.

"Careful, old boy," Romney cheered. "You've got his whole livelihood in there."

"Would you help me, please?" Conrad held on to the ladder and took a deep breath. It was easy to work up a sweat in this climate.

"And bring my duffel, would you?" he called up to Romney.

"Decided to stay and make yourself useful, eh?" Romney said as he leaned over to take a trunk handle. Together he and Conrad hoisted the trunk over the last rung and onto the dock.

"I'm a little disappointed. I was looking forward to— But it's probably a wise choice. Listen, for God's sake don't give that guy any money."

"He didn't ask for any."

"He didn't ask you to carry his luggage either."

The boy at the back of the ferry blew the all-clear on his whistle. Romney jumped aboard. The boat shuddered and hissed before shoving off. Conrad pulled the trunk along the pier, taking great care when going over rough spots. The monk walked several paces ahead, chin raised, tattered robes swaying. No doubt his arrogance was typical of ecclesiastics in this country, Conrad consoled himself. The touts, ragged Muslim boys, laughed as Conrad and the monk passed through them. Conrad flushed, and then felt annoyed with himself for doing so. Was this his punishment, then? But what precisely had he done besides give a poor woman the equivalent of thirty U.S. dollars?

When they reached the taxi stand, Conrad faced another crisis: where to go next. He could not stand the idea of another night in Pak Sai. An agent from one of the beach resorts was showing an album of promotional photos to a group of young backpackers, quietly urging them into one of the crowded bemos. This alternative also set Conrad's teeth on edge.

At the monk's direction, Conrad lifted the trunk into the back of a small bemo. The monk climbed in after and perched on the side of the bench next to his luggage. From a small woven bag slung over his good shoulder he produced cigarettes and a slim box of matches.

"Say," Conrad said, approaching the side of the bemo where the monk was seated. "Mind if I smoke one?"

The monk looked at him. Conrad mimed his desire for a smoke. The monk tossed him the pack and the matches. The cigarettes were the local brand, but the matches were from a restaurant in San Francisco. "Café du Retour" was printed in raised golden letters across a background of black velvet. Conrad ran his thumb over it.

"Been to San Francisco?" he asked the monk, holding up the matchbox and underscoring the city's name with his index finger.

"I know this place. I ate dinner there once." Conrad pointed to the name of the restaurant, tried to get across the idea that it was a restaurant.

"Café Detour," the monk said slowly.

"No. Café du Retour," Conrad corrected as he lit his cigarette. Another passenger, an old woman in a faded turban, climbed into the back of the bemo with a sack of something that might have been rice. The driver touched Conrad's shoulder.

"Lanka Suka?" he asked. It was the last call. Conrad looked at the matchbox again.

"All right," he said, tossing his duffel bag inside.

"You got these from an American woman on Ko Banteay, didn't you?" Conrad asked as he turned the matchbox over in his hand. The bemo had taken them beyond the edge of the small town and already the pavement had ended. The trunk jiggled and clinked as the road began to wind its way into the hills. Conrad had no idea where Lanka Suka was. He hoped it was someplace remote.

The monk inhaled on his Willow Leaf and looked at Conrad.

"You have trouble with wife?" he asked. "I can fix for you."

"You're a marriage counselor?"

His question was almost sincere. The monk seemed not to understand. He took the matches from Conrad and tried to decipher the golden letters.

"Du Retour," he said out loud.

The anniversary dinner had happened there. Lucy had been happy, gushing. Possibly oozing with another man's semen. And Conrad had promised to take her somewhere: Europe, Greece, the Aegean. He inhaled on the cigarette and for the first time it felt good going down. He wondered, as the plumes trailed from his nostrils, if there might not be some other dimension to smoke that had escaped his notice, a contemplative property that let one step outside of time. Perhaps by impersonating the flow of time itself, it gave one the illusion of watching it from the outside. Conrad inhaled again and, as the bemo hit a large hole, grew suddenly dizzy and sick.

Lanka Suka turned out to be a Muslim fishing village on the far side of the island. The driver let off the old woman in the village and then drove on to a small *wat* on the top of a nearby hill. The monk climbed out of the bemo. Conrad dutifully pulled the trunk off the back of the bemo and lowered it carefully to the ground. Some sort of elaborate greeting was taking place between the one-armed monk and the monks of the *wat*. All the while, two large temple dogs circled them, barking angrily. It seemed that Romney was wrong about this beggar, Conrad noted. But then the driver touched his shoulder and Conrad realized he was expected to pay. *For God's sake don't give him any money.* But what were sixteen rials, anyway? Somewhat half of what they were a week ago.

When the greeting was over, Conrad obediently shouldered the trunk and followed the monk through the front gate of the temple compound. Neither of the other two monks made a move to help; this kind of thing no longer bothered Conrad. He followed the monks past the monks' dormitory, a long, one-story building with a thatched roof, and then past some smaller houses to a very small house, no more than a hut on stilts, at the far end of the compound. A little way beyond the hut, at the edge of the scrub forest, was a raised platform made of bricks, which, with its black burn marks, looked like it might have been used for large cooking fires.

The one-armed monk conferred with the other two monks in a soft voice as they approached the last hut. Conrad groaned as he lowered the trunk onto the narrow bamboo platform that served as a porch for the tiny house. With that last bit of effort he felt something give in his lower back.

"What is in that trunk?" Conrad interrupted the monk's conversation in a loud voice. One of the host monks, a bulky man with black-framed glasses, stepped forward and addressed Conrad in reasonably clear English:

"Our friend and guest, Kraivichien, is a healer. In this chest he carries his medicines."

"I'm sorry. Crave itch what?" Conrad asked.

"Kraivichien," the older monk replied. "You may call him Moo. When Muslim mens come for cure, they call him Tuan Moo."

Kraivichien and the older monk exchanged a smile.

"Moo, do you have anything for a sore back?" Conrad asked, rubbing the lower part of his spine. Moo shook his head. Massage was the best thing for a sore back. Conrad would have to return to Pak Sai for that.

Conrad did not go back to Pak Sai, not that night, nor the next.

He was given a room of sorts at the *wat*, a space in the dormitory where he could unroll his sleeping bag on the floor. Conrad learned that monks never turned away anyone in need of shelter; it would violate some sort of precept. To be sure, the dormitory was mostly empty. Many of the monks seemed to live by themselves in small huts in the forest, staying away from the main compound for days or even weeks at a time, apparently skipping the single meal the monks were permitted each day. Conrad was never completely clear on how all of this worked, as the monks ate only in the early morning, when he was still asleep. Conrad took his meals in the village, at the headman's house.

The headman had grand plans for constructing bungalows along the beach just up the coast from the village, and was enthusiastic about having Conrad take meals at his house, perhaps seeing in Conrad's arrival a portent of tourist hordes to come. He let Conrad know there already was a bungalow operation nearby, south of the village. But he hastened to point out that it was quite small (only three huts) and always full. And it was run by Mon Chinese, whose cooking was not up to Yawi standards. In fact, their guests often came to the headman's house to eat because they were bored with the food, or so he claimed. And it was not a short hike by any means.

All of this was communicated to Conrad through gestures and fragments of English supplied by the headman's youngest son, who attended school from time to time in Pak Sai. Conrad assured the headman and his son that Mon Chinese cuisine sounded very dull indeed. Furthermore, he had no desire to even look at another bungalow operation.

Having to bed down on the rough boards of the monks' dormitory, knowing that he would not sleep until the moon set and the dogs stopped baying, was annoying at first. Also annoying were the visits from young novice monks who wanted to improve their English by discussing American movies they'd seen in Nagaseri, action flicks with lots of semiautomatics and big-breasted women who had trouble keeping their clothes on. Becoming a monk apparently did not require a lifelong commitment. It was more of a summer job. The boys were alternately fascinated and repelled by Conrad's shirts, fascinated with their Teflon properties and repelled by their smell. The young monks convulsed with laughter when one of them held the shirt at arm's length and waved his hand in front of his face.

And yet the second day, when Conrad woke at first light to the sound of temple bells being rung on the far side of the compound, he found that the urge to rejoin his wife, to resume their subtle and frosty warfare, had left him.

19

The Shrine of Airabu

Many years ago, a pious Moslem, a goldsmith, came to Tambralinga from Java. Some say his father was an Arab from Mecca. He settled in the village of Airabu and married. One day while digging in his garden, he struck a large lump of gold, but when he pulled it out of the ground it turned coal black. When he died, he was buried in a small tomb on the same spot where he'd found the gold. His wife, burdened with many debts, was forced to sell the property. The new owner and his wife, Cik Puteh, built a house opposite the tomb of the dead goldsmith.

A bearded saint in Arab garb appeared to Cik in a dream and commanded her to guard the tomb in the garden, promising great rewards. Cik guarded the tomb for many years, and one day seven large snakes appeared on the roof of her house. Two hours later, silver and copper coins rained down on the roof. They fell every fifteen minutes for an entire hour. Cik Puteh fell to the ground, apparently dead. Her terrified neighbors prayed out loud: "If this be the tomb of a *wali*, a saint, let this woman recover." Straightaway, Cik regained consciousness and sat up.

The word went out that a miracle had occurred, that the tomb was a place of spiritual power, of *semengat*. Pilgrims began coming to the shrine, looking for cures for sickness or infertility, or hoping just to change their luck. Cik Puteh eventually came to be regarded as a living saint herself. At this writing she is quite old—some say over 100—but still lives in the house next to the shrine, and dresses only in yellow, the color of Tambralingan royalty.

—*Coswell's Guide to Tambralinga* (1997 ed.)

They took a detour off the highway and traveled down a dirt road to a small village. The driver stopped the car before a squat, whitewashed building in front of which a lank Tambralingan flag

hung from an ancient flagpole. Rashid explained hurriedly that he
had to attend to some official business before they went on to
Kuala Vimaya. He apologized for the delay and hoped that it
would not be too long.

A short man in a khaki uniform came out of the building as
Rashid approached, gestured for him to enter, and then followed
him back inside. As the door shut behind the two men, Lucy became aware of the crushing stillness that weighed upon the village. The streets were empty. There were no cafés or restaurants
that Lucy could see. A small shop on one of the adjacent corners
offered only produce and canned goods. There was nothing to do
but wait in the car.

Lucy dug a book out of her bag, a well-worn biography of the
British explorer Richard Burton. But just as she found her place,
Rashid emerged from the building and got back into the car.

"One more stop, I'm afraid," he said as the driver put the car
into gear. They drove a short distance beyond the village, down a
rutted track that petered out at the base of a low hill planted with
sick-looking banana trees.

"Please bear with me," Rashid said, giving Jeannine's hand a
squeeze as he climbed out of the car again.

Lucy stared dumbly as Rashid walked briskly down the dirt
track and disappeared behind the hill. Did I really see that? Lucy
asked herself. She played back the image of Rashid's hand coming
down on Jeannine's. There was a carelessness about it, as if he
had only meant to graze the knuckles with the barest touch, then
somehow become ensnared in the impulse to grasp. *Please bear
with me.* He'd been talking directly to Jeannine, as if she were the
only other person in the car.

Lucy had shared a room with Jeannine the night before, same
as always. And Rashid had stayed in a different hotel up the road.
Still, the careful way Rashid and Jeannine addressed each other in
the morning seemed more than suspicious to Lucy, who was now
able to picture a dozen different ways they might have trysted
while she slept. Tonight she might insist on her own room. Keep
things simple.

Lucy drummed her fingers on the cover of the paperback in her lap, as if this would somehow diminish the anguish coiling up in the pit of her stomach. She opened the book and squinted at the lines of print.

Jeannine lit a cigarette and blew the smoke out of her open window. Neither she nor Lucy spoke. A hot wind blew through the window. The engine was still running, the air-conditioning was on. The windows in the front began to steam up. Lucy wanted to ask Jeannine to smoke outside. She imagined her request would start an argument and she played it out, line by line, in her head. It ended with Jeannine slamming the door and shouting: "You make your*self* miserable!" And then Lucy struggling to concentrate on the lines of text before her, which she kept reading over and over (as she was doing now in actual fact) without any meaning coming through.

An hour went by, or what felt like an hour. A jeep full of soldiers dressed in rumpled khaki uniforms pulled up next to them. The soldiers looked incredibly young; they were laughing and chattering, like Boy Scouts on their way to a cookout. Slowly they got out of the jeep and proceeded on foot along the same path that Rashid had taken, making no attempt to form a column or proceed with anything resembling a march. One of them held his rifle by the tip of the barrel and dragged it along the ground behind him.

Lucy allowed her gaze to cross Jeannine's face, perhaps hoping for a moment of shared amusement, a glimpse of their former camaraderie. But Jeannine was looking elsewhere.

"He's been gone a long time, don't you think?" was all she said.

Lucy nodded. She opened her door and plunged face forward into the hot wind. She glanced back at Jeannine as if to declare her intent to go after Rashid. Jeannine climbed out and followed. As they trudged around the hill, the path became a crude walkway made of rough-hewn planks laid across the muddy ground. On the far side of the hill, they came to a house. In back of the house stood a small building, which looked to Lucy like a minia-

ture replica of a mosque: four walls of brick and crumbling
stucco with an onion-shaped dome on top. The whole thing was
covered with lichens and moss, but here and there on the dome a
streak of gold paint was visible. Lucy guessed it was some kind of
shrine, perhaps a tomb. Behind it grew an enormous tree, whose
roots spread out from the base and along the top of the ground
like huge buttresses, and whose branches overhung the little
building.

A group of men, shirtless, their sarongs hoisted above their
knees and swaddled around their loins like diapers, worked a
shallow trench in front of the structure with shovels and pick-
axes. A pile of wooden posts lay nearby. Neither Rashid nor the
soldiers were anywhere in sight.

They moved past the little house and approached the place
where the men were working, Lucy walking ahead with hard
strides, Jeannine hanging back a few steps.

"They're setting up some kind of perimeter around that building, looks like," Lucy said. It was the first time either of them had
spoken since leaving the car, and Lucy's voice sounded strained to
her own ears.

So what if Rashid preferred Jeannine, she told herself. That
had been clear from the get-go. She would just have to get over it.
But what was harder for Lucy was to acknowledge herself to be
in open competition with Jeannine. And for what? The most fleeting, most illusory sort of indulgence possible.

"Barbed wire," Jeannine responded, pointing to glittering rolls
of the stuff lying here and there along the trench. Her tone was
matter-of-fact, her face expressionless. So she was holding back,
on her guard, Lucy noted. This tacit acknowledgment that they
were at war came as a relief; it was easier to accept defeat at the
hands of one who at least was trying to win, who at least saw
herself as a threat.

"They're putting up a fence so they can charge admission,
right?" Jeannine went on. "But what's that?"

She pointed to a hand-painted sign lying broken on the ground
next to the path. Lucy had missed it entirely. It had both Roman

and Arabic letters, presumably spelling out the same word: AIRABU. Lucy recognized the name from the guidebook insert.

"It's the shrine," she said. "It looks different than I imagined. Smaller."

She stopped. Jeannine passed her, walked ahead toward the domed shrine. The workmen stopped and stared at her. She had neglected to wear a headscarf, as the guidebook recommended when visiting rural areas, her skirt exposed far too much of her calves, and her arms were uncovered almost to the shoulders. She was not a young woman, but Lucy could tell by the expressions on the workmen's faces that they could not see that, that they were transfixed by the sudden appearance of all that pale skin, and the glints of sun in bleached hair. Jeannine greeted them, mangling the pronunciation of the Yawi words almost beyond recognition. None of the men laughed, as Lucy expected, but instead nodded as if to show their approval of Jeannine's effort.

"*Selamat pagi!*" one of them replied. He seemed to be the youngest among them, and Lucy wondered if his image of Jeannine didn't correspond to some apparition of Western carnality conjured from glimpses of American magazines or videos. Perhaps there was an American swimsuit calendar in the local barbershop. Lucy wondered whether things like calendars and magazines and videos had already penetrated this far, had rained down on the natives like an artillery barrage. Maybe she and Jeannine were the advance guard that came next, soon to be followed by the full-scale invasion. We will wipe them out, every last bucolic farmer, she told herself. We'll turn them all into taxi drivers and forest guides and beach boys.

Lucy noticed soldiers among the banana trees behind the house. One was apparently relieving himself against a tree. Another stood nearby, smoking. She looked briefly for signs of Rashid among them. She had the uneasy sensation that something unpleasant was taking shape. She hurried to catch up with Jeannine.

The trail ended at a small well at the edge of a scrub forest. They had just reached the end when the first shot rang out. Somewhere amid the banana trees two soldiers ran after a chicken; another soldier emerged from the field holding a dead rooster by the tail.

"Shit," Jeannine whispered. And on her face Lucy read her own thought: Where there's pillage, there's rape.

"I wouldn't worry too much about it," a man called to them from behind. Lucy turned around. He was sitting in the shade a few yards away, on the very edge of the forest. It was difficult to see him at first; he seemed to be wearing camouflage. When he stood up and brushed the back of his trousers, Lucy could see he was a Westerner, a young man.

"The soldiers are heavily supervised. Today, anyway," the man said. He had something like a British accent. "Some sort of government official is overseeing the whole operation."

Where is he? Lucy almost said, but stopped herself and asked instead, "What operation is that?"

"The Ministry of Religious Education has condemned the shrine as un-Islamic. One of their deputies is serving the papers to the landowner. The soldiers are here just as a show of force. But the owner won't put up much resistance. She's something like eighty years old."

"She?" Jeannine asked as another shot was fired.

"Cik Puteh, the keeper of the shrine," the young man replied, yawning. "This is a shrine, the tomb of a Muslim saint. The locals regard Cik as a sort of saint herself. People come here with their problems and she lights a candle or burns incense for them, sometimes dispenses advice."

"But what's wrong with that?"

"The government says it's a public health matter. The old woman was keeping venomous snakes in a cage by the tree. A pilgrim was bitten. Or so they say."

"She kept snakes?"

"The government took them away last year. But pilgrims still come here, and that bothers them. Islam isn't really supposed to have saints. You're not supposed to pray to them. Especially not the ones associated with snakes. So now they're appropriating her land. They're going to demolish her house as well. They can't destroy the tomb; that would be a desecration. So they're going to put a barbed-wire fence around it."

"Oh," Jeannine said, looking back toward the shrine, where the workmen had begun to set the fence posts.

"I don't blame them for getting rid of the snakes," Lucy said. "I mean, it is a public health issue, isn't it? A person comes here for a cure and gets bitten instead?"

"The snakes were said to have miraculous properties. I've read fairly credible reports—from anthropologists and others—that claim certain ailments were cured when the patient simply touched the serpent's skin."

"Snake oil?" Lucy asked.

"Ha-ha," he pronounced slowly. "Some of us were hoping for a chance to investigate."

"I mean," Lucy went on. "If this country is ever going to get on its feet—I mean, if the superstitions are affecting people's lives—I mean, it's too bad for the tourists, but what else can they do?"

The young man shaded his eyes and looked at something over Lucy's shoulder. She turned around slowly, afraid, for some reason, that it was Rashid. A man in white Arab-style robes was approaching the shrine. The workers stopped and listened. It was the village imam, the young man explained. The leader of the mosque who had, no doubt, recruited the men for the job.

"How many years has he been waiting for this day, I wonder?" the young man mused.

"What do you mean?" Jeannine asked.

"With the old woman gone, he'll be the undisputed religious authority in the area. And since the Sultan's man has removed her for him, his loyalties will tend to lie with the Sultan. The Sultan's men are doing this sort of thing all over the country, rooting out the last vestiges of the old Hindu culture, banning shamans from holding public seances, even closing down shadow-puppet theater. They're trying to get the loyalty of the Islamists, trying to undercut Al-Jabbar's appeal."

"Wait. What is Al-Jabbar?"

"The opposition movement. The people who want to change the government. At the moment it's got a broad base of support among a whole range of factions. Hence the name, Al-Jabbar, the giant. They have their charismatic leader, of course, a young man. You may have heard of him: Sonny Tatoh."

"I think I saw his picture," Jeannine said.

"A lot of the Islamists support the reform movement," the young man went on. "Sonny Tatoh talks their language. And if he succeeds in bringing a Muslim majority government to power, the sultanate becomes pretty much irrelevant. Probably a lot of his men will end up in jail."

"Whose men? The Sultan's?"

The young man nodded.

"If there's any justice, yes."

"My head is swimming," Jeannine said.

Lucy touched her own forehead. She felt vaguely ill. She recalled her own fruitless search for the tree at Karimunja, and her plan to visit the festival at Sri Kala.

The door of the small stilt house opened and two men emerged. One was in uniform. The other was Rashid.

Rashid looked dazzling in his light gray suit as he stepped down from the little platform and into the full force of the midday sun. He towered over the other man, yet kept his head slightly bowed as he spoke, as if showing respect. The aura of nobility about him now came into focus as the workmen bowed slightly at his approach. Flanked by the imam and the police chief, he began delivering a little speech.

"The Sultan's man is thanking them for their hard work, making vague promises about the benefits their village will soon receive," the young man commented.

"You understand Yawi?" Jeannine asked. She was looking at him with some interest.

"Yes. Also Malay and Indonesian." The young man's interest seemed to come awake as well, as if Jeannine had flipped a switch somewhere. There was a trick to it, Lucy felt sure, and it annoyed her that she couldn't see how it was done.

An old woman dressed in yellow appeared in the doorway of the stilt house and called out in an admonishing tone. Rashid stopped his speech and turned around, but it was one of the workmen who answered in a plaintive voice. The others turned away or looked at the ground.

"The old woman is an aunt of sorts to this guy," the young man translated. "Apparently she cured his wife of something. Kidney disease, I think."

"Gee," Jeannine said. "So why are they out to get her?"

The young man shrugged.

"Because the shrine is magic and magic is bad for religion. Because magic is about the self, about individual enterprise, and religion is all about group control. The Sultan's man is control."

Then Jeannine brought up the very thing Lucy had been hoping she wouldn't.

"When we first met him, he didn't seem that way at all."

"You know this guy?"

Jeannine explained at some length how they had arrived there and what Rashid had told them about himself.

"Him? The Sultan's son?" the young man asked incredulously. "He's an Indian."

Lucy looked about in a sort of panic. Rashid had resumed his speech. The workmen had their heads bowed. Perhaps he was reciting a prayer.

"He said his mother was from Persia," Lucy explained quickly. "His father preferred foreign wives."

Lucy felt foolish hearing herself say this, and worse as the young man looked over at Jeannine and then back at her.

"Yes, I imagine so," he replied.

Lucy felt a wave of shame pass over her, as if she'd suddenly found herself naked and chained to a rock for all the world to see.

20

The town of **Kuala Vimaya** lies along the shores of the **Vimaya River**. Tourists will find little of interest in this former boomtown. The logging and mining companies came through here big time in the 1980s; the tin mines gave out about the same time the surrounding hills lost the last of their forests. The fishing villages that once dotted the beaches up and down the coast are now mostly gone; huge trawlers sweep the coast, and most of the mangroves have been cleared away to make room for shrimp farms.

A large island at the mouth of the river holds one of the Sultan's many country estates, the **Istana Vimaya**, a grand Victorian-style mansion, the area's only certifiable historic landmark. Unfortunately it is not yet open to the public.

—*Coswell's Guide to Tambralinga* (1997 ed.)

With some trepidation Lucy watched the road unwind itself as they passed through the hills and onto the alluvial plain of the Vimaya. Kuala Vimaya, Rashid had assured them, was a miserable place. They would please consider staying at the Istana as his guests for a few days. They could then continue their tour by taking the ferry over to Ko Neak Pean or down to Sri Kala, as they preferred. Lucy perceived a subtle gruffness in his voice as he made this invitation; to tell the truth, it sounded more like a command. He seemed to be losing patience with them. Neither of them had said much of anything since leaving Airabu.

"What do you think, Luce?" Jeannine asked, her tone cautious for once.

"Let's think about it for a little while," Lucy replied tepidly.

Rashid appeared to focus on something in the distance, seemed to grow grim and weary. She recalled with alarm the young man's assessment. What if Rashid was just a bureaucrat with keys to the limo, bent on seducing foreign women with absurd stories about his royal pedigree? He could easily be in sales, now that she thought about it. It wouldn't be the first time she'd fallen for a salesman.

Rashid had seen them wandering around the grounds of the tiny shrine, had seen them talking to the young anthropologist, if that's what he was, had been aware of them watching him make his speech to the workmen who were dismantling the shrine. Lucy imagined that the reasons for their long silences were not a mystery to him.

The fact that the Istana was on an island began to worry her. How easy would it be to get off the island should a sudden departure become necessary? She opened her guidebook and read the half-page on Kuala Vimaya. The island was accessible only by boat. That couldn't be good.

"There's only one hotel in the entire city which you might find acceptable," Rashid said, glancing at Lucy's guidebook. He took a small notebook from the pocket of his suit jacket and quickly wrote something in it.

"I can have the driver drop you there if you like. But I'm afraid you'll find it rather confining. It's not really safe for a young woman to wander around in the city. On the island you'll at least be free to come and go, although I must confess that business will keep me from being a very good host. You'll be left rather to your own devices."

He reads minds as well as palms, Lucy thought, and she looked at Jeannine for confirmation of this, but Jeannine's eyes were closed, her head back against the headrest.

Lucy gazed out the window at the wide, green rice fields. Not safe for a young woman, he'd said. Did he really see her that way? Who was it that had pegged thirty-six as the age at which a woman's looks start to go? Urban folklore, she decided. For some reason, Lucy thought of the young man in the camouflage T-shirt again. His haughtiness had annoyed her, yet the fact that he'd shown no sign of being intimidated by Rashid's position or style was kind of admirable. He'd gone right up to Rashid and introduced himself, engaging him in an animated discussion for several minutes, most of it in Yawi. And at the end of their chat, the young man had handed Rashid a card, which struck her as odd, now that she thought about it—an ethnographer with a business card? But maybe she was simply showing her age. Kids today seemed more serious than those she'd hung out with when she was young; more focused on careers. How Conrad had stood out against that crowd! A man with a career, a plan, a purpose—*substance*, that was the word.

"Perhaps we should take you by the hotel and you can look it over," Rashid said after a long silence. "If it meets your standards, then—"

"That sounds reasonable," Jeannine murmured sleepily. But as the limo turned onto a wide, four-lane road, a sort of bypass that swept around the edge of the city and over toward the island at the mouth of the river, Lucy got a clear view of the town. Rashid had not dissembled about that. It was dismal looking. Lucy could discern the outlines of individual buildings along the waterfront and the rain-scoured furrows in the clearcut hills beyond. A row of faceless concrete boxes dominated the center of the city; shanties clustered on its fringes. Glimpses of cranes and water towers and the dull gold dome of a large mosque swung into view as the highway curved and crossed a short bridge. That the road was virtually empty of other traffic gave the entire landscape a haunted look. Strange that they would build a bypass when there seemed to be no traffic, Lucy thought. Then she noticed Jeannine leaning forward to get a better view of the island, and the white-washed gables of the Istana Vimaya. Lucy realized that Jeannine wanted to go to the Istana, but was waiting for Lucy's approval.

"Not many people on the road today," Lucy ventured.

"No," Rashid agreed. "There is a curfew in effect. I'm afraid the police are expecting some disturbance."

"Al-Gibber? The democracy movement?" Jeannine asked.

Oh God, she's said it, Lucy thought. She felt herself shrink up before the coming confrontation.

"There are many citizens who are angry about the end of government subsidies for bread and rice and other staples," Rashid answered carefully. "And there are those who are willing to exploit that anger for political gain. I'm not certain you would call them 'democratic.' Do you know what? I happen to have a tape recording of a lecture given by one of the so-called spiritual leaders of Al-Jabbar, a certain Haji Da-Oh Udzir. Would you like to hear it?"

The women agreed. Rashid had the driver stop and fetch the tape from a piece of luggage in the trunk. He inserted it into a tape deck mounted in the console next to the driver's seat, adjusted the volume, and sat back in the seat. The old man's voice that came over the speakers creaked and broke in places, uttering a string of incomprehensible syllables.

"Is that Yawi?" Lucy asked. Rashid rolled his eyes and sat up abruptly.

"Forgive me," he sighed. "I forgot it wasn't in English. Stupid of me."

He looked exhausted.

"Why don't you just tell us what he's saying?" Lucy suggested.

"Translate a little of it," Jeannine agreed.

"Okay. He's talking about circumcision. Female circumcision." Rashid paused. "This is difficult to say. I'd prefer that he said it himself." He lit a cigarette and went on. "But okay, this is what he says: Female sexuality must be controlled so men won't be tempted. Men are easily tempted from their religious and social duties. When they neglect their duties, social chaos—what the Arabs call *fitna*—results. Female circumcision is necessary to prevent *fitna*.

"Okay, here's the part—a woman can be aroused at any minute, he says. Even if a woman is riding in a car, if she hits a few bumps, she can become sexually aroused. Her unbridled lust would then cause the man to lose control.

"What would then happen to the children, to the families of the men she would unwittingly draw to her? Consider the blood feuds that would grow up between men, between families."

He paused, inhaled on his cigarette.

"So you see this practice certainly is not meant to punish women—but it is necessary for preserving society. And—well, he goes on like this."

Rashid turned the tape machine off.

"I believe I've made my point."

Lucy looked out the window. An uncomfortable silence settled over the cab once more. If this talk of clitoridectomies was meant to assuage her fears, it was having rather the opposite effect. She found herself huddling up against the side of the car, chin down, elbows close against her sides, knees pressed together. But then the car hit a bump and Jeannine began to laugh.

The Istana Vimaya stood on a low bluff above the river, its light-colored wood dazzling in the late afternoon sun. It looked to Lucy like a smaller replica of the Sultan's palace in Nagaseri, which she had glimpsed on the bus ride from the airport, a three-story Victorian with tall, shuttered windows and Moorish arches supporting the roof of the wrap-around veranda. A series of carved panels were attached to the eaves of the portico, forming a delicate latticework, and this, Lucy recognized at once, bestowed a much-needed airiness and lightness to the massive house.

Servants stood at the doorway as they entered, smiling, looking relaxed in their white cotton shirts and red sarongs. At a word from Rashid, they bowed quickly and went outside to collect the luggage. The guest rooms, he explained, were in the rotunda, which afforded views of the river and the town. He took them into the kitchen and introduced them to the cook and his assistant, who he insisted would prepare a meal or snack anytime upon request. Breakfast would be brought to their rooms if they wished. He showed them the dining hall, the library, the study, the meeting hall, the conference room. He introduced them to the laundress and explained that she did laundry daily, by hand, and that articles given to her in the morning would be returned to their rooms spotless and pressed by late afternoon. He hoped they would find the bathrooms tolerable; it was an older building and the plumbing was a little on the primitive side.

Then he excused himself; work would keep him busy until dinner. He suggested that they avail themselves of the piano in the great hall, if either of them had a musical bent, or the library, which contained many books about the history and exploration of his country by European adventurers. Or, when it cooled down a little, they might take a stroll around the grounds and down along the river. But they must take care not to let the macaques approach them; these monkeys foraged in the garbage heaps back in the woods and had lately become a nuisance. Some of them carried rabies. Clapping and shouting was usually enough to scare them away, but one should not act too aggressively toward them.

Jeannine gave Lucy an odd look as they wandered back through the house, across the large dining room and the library and into the ceremonial meeting hall.

"It's a beautiful space," Lucy said, breaking the silence. "But if I was selling this house, I'd insist the owner change the window treatment. Those drapes look like they haven't been cleaned since 1930." The windows were oversized, constructed on a scale to match the grandeur of the hall. Yet the drapes were dark and heavy and covered the windows almost completely.

"The place could stand a little fresh air," Jeannine agreed. A ceiling fan was spinning high above them, but Lucy felt no breeze from it. Jeannine offered Lucy a cigarette, then lit one herself.

"I feel like that woman that used to be on TV, the one with the cigarette holder," Lucy said. She struck a pose, holding the cigarette in her right hand, resting her right elbow in her left palm.

"The one that said '*Dah*-ling!' all the time? Like with a drawl? When we were kids, you mean."

It sounded funny to hear Jeanine say "when we were kids," as if they'd grown up together, and this made Lucy hesitate.

"No, not with a drawl. She was dressed all in black and lived in a creepy house."

"Oh! You mean what's-her-name, on *The Addams Family*? She didn't smoke cigarettes, darling. She just *smoked*, remember? From the armpits or something."

"I remember a cigarette holder. But I was only six or seven at the time. I didn't understand that she was supposed to be creepy. She just seemed self-possessed. I really liked that about her."

"You're confusing her with someone else," Jeannine insisted. "Audrey Hepburn, perhaps." As she said this, Jeannine swept across the room with exaggerated grandness, then stopped and pivoted delicately on the balls of her feet. The cigarette came up to her lips with a finishing flourish. It was all part of the same gesture. Lucy clapped.

"Yes! I remember that. Where was that from?"

Jeannine lifted her chin and looked around the room in mock disdain, as if the question had insulted her.

"Really, Miss Hawkins, if the Ambersons expect to sell this place, they must do something about the dust. This house has been on the market how many weeks did you say?"

"Oh, well—a little over ten weeks," Lucy said, straightening up and placing her hands behind her back. "More like eleven weeks, if you count the holiday."

"And how many offers?"

"Well, none, really. But we've had a lot of interest. Let me show you the dining room."

Lucy led her into the next room and, taking a breath, began in earnest:

"The formal dining room easily seats sixty or more guests and connects to the kitchen down this short hallway." She clasped her hands in front of her with both index fingers extended and pointed to the hallway. "The main hall of course is accessed via this arched doorway. Guests can be greeted in the main hall with cocktails and hors d'oeuvres and later seated at this fifty-foot mahogany and rosewood dining table, which can be included in the total sale."

"Fascinating," Jeannine said in a bored tone. Lucy smiled professionally.

"The fireplace—rarely used for the last hundred years—is constructed of Tuscany marble quarried just outside of Siena. The chandeliers were custom-built in Antwerp, and you'll notice the banister on the grand staircase is, believe it or not, Canadian maple. Now what looks like mother-of-pearl inlay is, in fact—"

Jeannine snorted, suppressing a laugh.

"This wall will really have to go," she said, visibly struggling to stay in character. "Makes it like a dungeon in here—so dark and—"

"It's really quite remarkable that you should bring that up! As a matter of fact, the owners have been wanting to reconfigure much of the space on the ground floor for some time, and had plans drawn up just last week."

"Stop," Jeannine said, laughing. "I can't stand it anymore. Jesus, you're good."

"Every property is unique," Lucy said, running her hand along the banister. She thought of her own house on Saturn Street in San Francisco and the summer many years before when she'd spent two weeks sanding and refinishing the hardwood floors. When she first moved in with Conrad, the floors had been covered with gray paint, which had already begun chipping off. How satisfying to see the stuff disappear under the sander! Nearly two years had passed before she'd found the time and money to get started. She recalled the relish with which she'd attacked the job, the muscles that began showing up in her arms and shoulders, the pains in her back. But her house was a showplace now, a graceful blue and gray Edwardian with views of the Bay and the Oakland hills beyond. She felt a twinge, a yearning to relive the familiar sensation of entering her own home after a long day, that moment when she would step out of the cold west wind and into the snuggling warmth of their flat. Her parents' house had never been so inviting, so economical in its balance of utility and luxury. How pleasant to come up the long flight of stairs to the landing, to touch the white wainscoting, the metal handle of the old door opener, and to hear Conrad at the other end of the flat, searching for a station on the radio or drawing a bath. She loved those moments when he was not yet aware that she had arrived, when she could sense his warm, lumbering presence down the hall or behind the closed pocket doors of the parlor. Solitude without loneliness. This had always been a big part of Conrad's appeal, the personal space he instinctively afforded her. Yet at the same time, during those first rickety years of their marriage, when nothing else seemed to be going right in her life, his enfolding arms could contain the worst of her anxiety attacks, could steady the palpitations of heart and lungs. She felt again the ocean swell of tenderness Conrad used to stir in her—tenderness, she now realized, but not love, exactly. She wished somehow that they could still live together when they got back to San Francisco. Perhaps they could partition the flat. Or maybe she could persuade him to take the unit on the second floor.

She felt something huge turn inside of her. She was going to leave Conrad. She was in the middle of doing just that. It was too awful and too wonderful to believe. Tears ran down her cheeks. Jeannine, examining a red Persian carpet, didn't notice.

"I don't know what this means, his inviting us here," Jeannine was saying. "God, I wish it was cooler. I feel like sitting in a bathtub. I haven't seen a bathtub since I came to this country."

"Let's draw a bath anyway," Lucy said, wiping her cheeks. "It doesn't have to be hot, does it?"

They went upstairs to the bathroom closest to their rooms. A tepid stream trickled out of the tap. "This will take hours to fill," Jeannine complained, running her hand absentmindedly around the rim of the great, claw-foot tub. "Be better off taking a dip in the river."

Lucy made a face. The color of the river water, she reminded Jeannine, was the same as that of their milk tea.

Jeannine splashed water on her face.

"You know that guy at Airabu, the anthropologist? He was kind of cute," she told Lucy.

"Oh?" Lucy said, suddenly alert.

Jeannine shook her hands and reached for one of the white towels hanging on the wall. One of the maids, a short, dark woman with a wide face, knocked on the door and brought in a tray of bath items—soaps, sponges, bottles of shampoos and bath oils in crystal bottles. She smiled warmly, with averted eyes, as she set the tray on the table next to the tub.

"Thank you very much," the maid said in a soft voice.

"You're very welcome," Jeannine replied. The maid looked up, as if surprised at getting a reply, and then shut the door quickly behind her.

"This guy looked rather Asian, body-wise. Lean. Not too tall. I bet he's built like an Asian. Muscular, but still—what's the word?"

"Gracile?" Lucy suggested, wondering where these disclosures were leading. Was Jeannine saying that she didn't want Rashid? But who would after seeing what they'd seen at the shrine? No wonder he'd suggested they wait in the car! Still the idea that Jeannine might be withdrawing from the competition sent an anxious chill up the small of Lucy's back. Examining one's real desires was like trying to observe the sun, she decided; one only dared attempt it at long intervals and oblique angles.

"Gracile," Jeannine said quietly. "That's the word. I never really appreciated that in a man until I met this guy on Ko Neak Pean."

"Yes, so you told me. When we first met."

"That's right." Jeannine turned around and laid a hand on each of Lucy's shoulders. "I did, didn't I?"

21

They ate dinner not in the dining room but in a small alcove in the library where the staff had set up a table for the three of them. The servants—all men, dressed in white, loose-fitting uniforms and white caps that resembled those worn by Moslem hadjis—set before them a series of dishes: roast duck, rice pilaf, chicken with lemongrass, vegetables in curry sauce, chili prawns, carrots, and potatoes. Rashid apologized for the lack of wine but did manage to provide a liter bottle of Thai beer, which Lucy and Jeannine shared. The air had cooled, but was still muggy. When one of the servants opened a nearby window, Lucy was surprised to see that it had no screen. Mosquitoes were not a problem at this time of year, Rashid explained. The rains were never heavy and the bats on the island kept the insect population down.

"Bats?" Lucy asked.

"Yes, a small colony of them in a cave on the other end of the island. I could show it to you after dinner if you like."

Lucy didn't care to see the bats, but the three of them went out after dinner anyway and walked along the water. It was twilight, and on the other side of the river lights were coming on in the city. Lucy thought she heard a voice echoing in the distance. A loudspeaker, perhaps, but it was too tinny and distant for her to be certain. The path was crudely paved. One of the servants walked ahead, sweeping the area with a flashlight. Checking for snakes, Rashid explained. Jeannine inhaled through her teeth.

"It's not really a problem," Rashid assured her. "But with my honored guests, I must take no chances." His hand came up to her shoulder, then dropped away. Had he hugged her? Lucy

strained to decipher Jeannine's reaction, but the light was too dim to be certain of anything.

Whenever she looked up, Lucy could see the silhouettes of bats flashing here and there against the reddened sky. The path was descending; she sensed the water getting closer.

The servant stopped the sweep of his flashlight, called something over his shoulder. Rashid answered quietly.

"We've found something for you," Rashid said to Lucy and Jeannine, but before he could go on, the servant jumped back with a startled cry and the flashlight beam zipped around the path and then up into the trees. Something hissed, something large scuttled across the stones just ahead of them. The flashlight beam swung down from the trees and illuminated a huge snout and a long forked tongue.

"Jesus!" Jeannine cried.

"Monitor lizard," Rashid said quickly.

"God, I thought it was a crocodile."

Lucy came closer, fascinated. The lizard stood completely still, transfixed by the light. Counting its tail, she figured the thing had to be at least six feet long. The servant leaned forward slowly, extended a long stick toward the lizard, and poked it suddenly in the flank. The thing scrambled off the path and into the brush with hard, thrashing movements. Jeannine cried out as if she'd been stabbed.

Rashid spoke harshly to his servant.

"He didn't mean to scare you," Rashid explained. "He has a fear of monitors. One nearly took his foot off when he was a child."

"That's it. I'm sorry. I have to go back," Jeannine said. "I'm just not comfortable with this."

"Oh, but we're nearly to the beach. I'd hoped to show you some sea turtles. They come here to lay their eggs, you see."

There was no way. Lucy could feel Jeannine trembling when she laid a hand on her shoulder. She could feel Rashid's hand there as well, was surprised at how familiar the sensation had become.

It was decided that the servant would take Jeannine back to the house; Rashid and Lucy would proceed the remaining distance to the beach and, employing Lucy's own pocket flashlight, attempt to spot the turtles. Her second thoughts arrived only minutes later, as a branch brushed across her face and shadows of the forest seemed to close around her.

"Just a short while yet," Rashid promised. "With the hawksbill turtles you don't have to wait so long." There was a tremor in his voice. So he felt himself to be on shaky ground as well.

The night is suddenly gorgeous, the darkness closing around Lucy like the soft petals of an immense flower. When they reach the sand, she turns off the feeble beam, feels herself move through the balmy air like a spirit. The sound of the river lapping on the shore is strangely transporting, almost hypnotic. Has she been drugged? No, it feels nothing like that.

"I think I see one," Rashid whispers. His hand comes out to stop her progress. "Perhaps we should sit here."

The sand is still warm, gloriously so. She slips her hands under it. She makes no attempt to turn the flashlight back on.

"When they come—you won't believe how large they are," Rashid whispers. "Like something prehistoric, from the bottom of the sea."

A wonderful image, Lucy thinks, but she can no longer resist the urge to lie down on the sand and gaze up at the sky. Stars emerge from between long fingers of dark cloud. She thinks she can hear popping sounds in the distance, as if somebody is bursting balloons far up the path. She pushes her arms into the sand. What must it be like to be hatched into the midst of the stuff like a baby turtle? To dig your way up to the surface? She moves her hand through the sand and bumps into something, another hand.

When Rashid leans over to kiss her, it feels like a meteorological event, the culmination of atmospheric tensions, the inevitable rain that follows the buildup of thunderheads. As she kisses his chest, it seems perfectly natural that he's already removed his

shirt. Her own clothes come off with agonizing slowness. He seems bent on playing the gentleman to the last. How surprising, then, when after briefly nibbling her breasts, he abruptly hoists her up onto her hands and knees and mounts her from behind. She feels her body thrash back and forth and side to side, as if she's grown a long tail and snaps it, whiplike, at her enemies. She goes down on her elbows and bellows, her voice low and strange to her own ears. Across the water someone seems to answer, perhaps more than one, perhaps a chorus. Little flashes appear in the cityscape, like the stars that swim before her eyes when she is really excited, panting, close to hyperventilating. With each little flash, there comes a popping sound, a second or two later. And then suddenly many, many flashes and subsequent popping noises, and she feels herself gush, the way she had the first time with Antoine, and she thinks someone must be setting off fireworks, cat-o'-nine-tails, and sky rockets, and how perfect that is, how very perfect.

22

On his third night in Lanka Suka, Conrad ate a wretched dinner of dried fish and rice, cooked by the headman himself. The man put the meal before Conrad with an apologetic air. He gave Conrad to understand that his wife had taken ill, that she was nearly paralyzed with shooting pains in her arms and legs. She'd had this condition many times before and he'd twice taken her to the clinic in town for treatment, but to no avail. The doctor had been unable to find anything wrong.

Arthritis? Sciatica? The headman was not familiar with these terms. He seemed to think that she'd been attacked by spirits, by the *phii* that lived out upon the water. Fortunately the monk staying up at the *wat* was known to be a powerful healer. They would consult with him, even though he was not a Muslim.

"Spirits here mostly Bud-dha spirits," the youngest son explained. "Bud-dha spirits live around Bud-dha *wat*. So monk is best med-cine for us."

Conrad was just awake when the headman and his sons brought the ailing wife into the temple grounds the next morning. The dogs set up their predictable chorus as the tiny woman, leaning now against her husband, now against her son, limped toward Moo's hut. She made no sound, but the anguish was obvious on her face. In the early morning light she reminded Conrad of a neighbor who formerly lived down the block from his building in San Francisco, a stocky woman not yet forty, her round face not yet wrinkled in any significant way.

As Tuan Moo emerged from his hut, the headman placed his

palms together and bowed his head in greeting. The one-armed monk returned the salute as best he could, then led the headman and his family into the courtyard of the main temple. The temple itself was tiny, not much bigger than a chapel, but the surrounding courtyard was large. In a far corner, under the shade of an immense tree, Moo gestured for the family to sit on the tattered mat that seemed to have been placed there for that reason. Flanked by two other monks, he sat on a short bench in front of the family. Conrad seated himself on a large paving stone a discreet distance away. The big monk with glasses came up to Conrad.

"You'll get very warm sitting there," he said in a soft voice. "Come sit in the shade with me." And he showed Conrad to another bench closer to the tree.

At a sign from Moo, the monks began chanting, palms together, eyes lowered. They went on for a long time, never looking up, as if nobody else were there. Now and then the headman threw an uneasy glance over his shoulder at the main hall, where a good-sized statue of the meditating Buddha was visible through the open door. Proximity to the gold statue, to the writhing serpents and winged creatures carved into the temple doors, seemed to make him nervous. He was decked out in his white cap and his short coat, as if to protect himself from pernicious influences.

Moo asked the headman's wife a number of questions. She replied in a soft voice, almost a whisper. Now and then her husband shook his head.

"Do you understand Yawi?" the big monk whispered to Conrad. "No? Well, this is what is happening: husband has other women in town. We say 'little wife.' When this husband first get his little wife, the first wife gets sick. Now she is sick again and husband is afraid little wife has hired sorcerer to make first wife sick."

"Why?"

"Little wife jealous. Wants husband all to herself. This is what husband says."

"Little wife," Conrad repeated. He liked the sound of this.

"Tuan Moo," the headman said in a tremulous voice. He lowered his head and placed his palms together and then placed them on top of his head. Moo began speaking in a loud voice. Instructions were being issued. Then the headman leaned forward and touched his palms to the mat three times. The wife, with some difficulty, followed suit. The consultation appeared to be over.

"Purify," the big monk said to Conrad as the couple rose slowly to their feet. "They must purify their house. Burn incense, drive away bad magic."

"That'll be a big help," Conrad said. He hadn't meant to say this out loud. The monk gave no sign of having detected the sarcasm.

"They will return tomorrow," the monk concluded.

"Mister," Moo called to Conrad. "I speak you inside." He gestured for Conrad to follow, but Conrad, annoyed by the man's imperious style, ignored him. The monk called a second and then a third time, and finally Conrad could not disregard the urgency in his voice.

The trunk lay open on the floor. The light coming through the doorway illuminated an odd array of tiny bottles—clear, opaque, brown, green, red—each stopped with a piece of cork or a bit of rag. The bottles were arranged in stacking wooden trays that perhaps once held silverware or woodcarving tools. Each seemed to hold a dark, muddy-looking liquid. A vaguely rancid smell hung over the collection, a smell that oscillated between cow dung and an old refrigerator that has been left empty too long.

"You help make missus better?" Moo asked, arranging the folds of his robe to better conceal the absence of his forearm.

Conrad agreed to the idea in principle. The monk bent over the chest and removed one of the trays. Conrad grew alarmed at the prospect of being asked to administer one of the tinctures to the headman's wife, his head suddenly split with visions of convulsions and vomited blood. What the monk pulled from the trunk was not a bottle of so-called medicine, however, but a crude doll made of rice straw. It had a body—arms, legs, torso—but no face. A red thread was wrapped about the waist. The monk untied the thread and then wrapped it around the legs.

"Put under house," he said to Conrad. "Tonight after dinner."

"What did you say?"

"Just throw under house," Moo repeated. "Night time. Nobody see you. Help missus."

Conrad looked at the doll skeptically. And just why should he get involved in this bit of voodoo nonsense, he wondered.

"I help you later," Moo said, as if reading his thoughts. "Get wife back from udder mans."

Conrad stared at the monk's pockmarked face. Did he actually want Lucy back? The question was like the twist of a knife in his stomach.

"I don't know that you need to do that," he mumbled, turning away. He felt he might throw up, or, worse, start to cry. He walked out of the hut.

"Ta-ta-ta-ta-ta!" the monk called after him. "Please hide this thing!" Conrad still had the doll in his hand. He stuffed it quickly in his shirt. In front of him he saw the headman and his son escorting the headman's wife back through the gate. Already she was walking a little better.

Like all the traditional houses in Tambralinga, the headman's house was raised on stilts. A flick of the wrist was all that was required to send the straw effigy underneath, but Conrad felt foolish and a little ashamed, as if he'd tossed a rock through a neighbor's window. The headman seemed surprised to see Conrad, because Conrad had waited until it was quite dark before approaching the house. Dinner seemed to be over.

"We think you eat at bungalows," the youngest son explained. In fact Conrad had trekked past the village and down the coast to the South Beach bungalows, hoping to find something palatable on the menu. But the first glimpse of the bungalows made him do a quick about-face. He understood then that he wished to think of Lanka Suka as a world apart from anything resembling a beach resort. This surprised him. And when the headman scraped together something like a meal—some leftover rice, a suspicious-looking soup, a couple of withered red bananas—Conrad put aside his usual fears of contamination and consumed all with grim determination.

At the second consultation, the headman placed the straw figure at Moo's feet with an air of relief. Here, at long last, the problem had been identified.

It was evening. The headman's family and a number of monks were seated around a small fire in the middle of the temple compound.

The monk picked up the doll and examined it carefully, turning it over and over, tugging on the red thread, plucking at the straw here and there, as if much could be gleaned from doing so.

A sorcerer had used this doll to cause a spirit attack on the wife, Moo announced. He glanced at Conrad as he said this, but did not smile. Conrad looked at the fire. Here was the smoke, but where were the mirrors?

Moo ordered the headman's wife to kneel before him, and then he sprinkled her with holy water and whispered incantations over her head. This went on for a long while, the monk gradually lowering his head until his lips were nearly touching the top of the wife's head, the headman growing twitchy and tense. Conrad struggled to keep awake. Finally, Moo invited the attacking spirit to take possession of the woman and identify itself.

The woman's eyes bulged. She began to choke, and then to speak in a strangled voice, little more than a whisper.

"My name is Sang Kala!" she announced and then jumped to her feet. Her face contorted with rage. She picked up a bamboo stick and began slashing the air in front of her. The headman and his son looked terrified. Moo remained unperturbed.

"Sang Kala," he asked, "who sent you to attack this innocent woman?"

At first the spirit refused to say, continuing to snarl and drool and writhe around on the ground. Conrad lowered his head and began inching away from his place on the mat. Inexplicably, he felt certain the woman would come after him, and knew he was too weak and weary to deal with it.

She did come after him. Perhaps it was the way he was moving; perhaps it showed fear. In any case, she attacked, bringing the stick down on Conrad's shoulders and back. Fortunately for Conrad, the bamboo was not heavy or thick. It was hollow and on impact made a loud cracking sound which the monks found hilarious.

Moo stood up and in a loud voice commanded the spirit to stop. The headman's wife stopped and then turned in the direction of her family, who bowed their heads and covered them with their hands. Conrad crept back to his seat next to the big monk, but remained tensed for the next onslaught.

"I was sent by a sorcerer in Ligor," the spirit announced finally. "A sorcerer in the pay of the headman's little wife."

"A monstrous woman, a cruel woman," Moo prompted, and the spirit shouted its agreement, causing the wife's face to twitch and break into a manic grin. Then Moo and the spirit conversed for a long time, and Conrad had no idea what was being said until the big monk sitting next to him explained to him that powerful, malignant spirits like Sang Kala required long and complicated negotiations before they would agree to release their victims. In the end, the husband promised to throw a big feast in honor of the spirit, and during the feast, offerings were to be left for Sang Kala in a shrine set up by the water's edge. The spirit demanded, among other things, slices of smoked pork and bottles of Thai beer. The prospect of having to handle these substances made the headman miserable, compounding the humiliation of having to seek help from a Buddhist priest in the first place. All of this was visible on his face when he lifted his head to thank Tuan Moo.

Real or forced, the headman's gratitude was not wasted. Moo stood up and commanded the spirit to leave the wife's body. The woman shook her head a few times, looked around her as though the fact that she was standing surprised her, and then quietly sat down. The pain in her arms and legs was gone, she reported. Conrad's shoulders and back were throbbing and he began to wonder if he was bleeding anywhere.

Moo held up a tiny vial of brownish liquid and told the wife that she was to put a drop on each earlobe, on each cheek just beneath the eyes, on the tip of the nose, just under her lower lip, and, finally, next to the other two of her body's openings. She was to do this every night for seven nights, just before going to sleep. During this time, she was to refrain from intercourse with her husband. This would prevent the spirit from reentering her body.

On the eighth day, she was to cast the bottle into the sea while reciting a secret prayer that Moo would give her directly. He motioned for her to approach his bench and then, cupping his hand next to her ear (without actually touching it), he whispered something quickly. The woman's eyes widened for a second, as if scandalized, but then her face grew placid once more and, bowing to the monk, she took the vial, which he had placed on the bench next to him.

The company rose as the headman and his wife took their leave. Conrad noticed a certain levity in the looks the monks exchanged as the headman and his wife passed under the gates. The headman slouched, his jerky movements betraying a growing sense of apprehension; his wife floated serenely after him. She was cured. The expense of the feast and the long-planned construction of the beach bungalows would undoubtedly leave her husband with no means for supporting a little wife. This thought barely registered before Conrad awakened to the streams of sweat running off his forehead and to a sharp, turning pain in his nether regions. He stood up beneath the orange sunset and limped toward the latrine.

By circumstance he'd only been to the monk's toilet once before and was uncertain as to its exact location. But in subsequent days its location became permanently fixed in his consciousness, like the pole star, and he learned the intricacies of squatting over its noisome hole without soiling his clothes, even while close to fainting. He learned to pull the chain with just the right amount of tension, to refill the overhead tank with the plastic bucket from the leaky spigot down the path, and to clean himself without benefit of paper, using just a small can of water and his left hand. Very quickly this sequence became the entirety of his universe, what he did with his day. It was not real dysentery, he assured himself, perhaps not even giardia. If he kept replenishing his fluids, it would pass. And yet there was the unpleasant fact of the fever, which came and went, sometimes torturing him with its malarial affectations. There was also the unbearable exhaustion as his body refused first vegetables, then rice, and then even tea. After the fifth day, he could no longer drink a cup of water without having to crawl to the toilet fifteen minutes later. It seemed too late to seek medical help in Pak Sai. Leaving the *wat* seemed a laudable but unattainable goal, like climbing the Matterhorn. It became inconceivable to Conrad that one could do anything else besides stare at the geckos gobbling the mosquitoes that danced tentatively against the thatch of his ceiling.

Elaborate and troublesome dreams visited him during the day and all through the night. He believed that his mother and father had come back to life and were reinforcing the walls of the hut with brick and mortar, but without consideration of the doors and windows. Breathing became difficult. Trips to the bathroom began to require assistance from the monks—or, rather, the unsmiling volunteers from nearby villages who worked the temple grounds. Eventually someone placed a plastic bucket just outside Conrad's door, and this usually sufficed. Now and then Conrad had glimpses of Lucy in the doorway, but she wasn't speaking to him. She had a small child with her, little more than an infant, which she carried around on her hip. She swept through the room as if Conrad wasn't there, discussing in a loud voice where they would knock down a wall or install a window, declaiming the absolute necessity of opening up the dining room. She put an arm around Moo and kissed his shaved head. Had they just been married? No, it had been going on forever, for twenty years. Then Lucy got in bed with him, which seemed a neat trick, since the bed was impossibly narrow, not even a single mattress width. She rubbed his sweaty forehead, was actually rubbing something into his skin, something that smelled awful. And no wonder—it wasn't Lucy at all, but the one-armed monk with one of his vile little bottles.

When the fever broke, it was the middle of the night, and Conrad came awake to a chill in the air. Urgent voices conferred outside his hut. Men grunted as if carrying something heavy. The howling dogs approached, but then were driven off. The men talked for a long time. Now and then one of them groaned loudly. Conrad crawled to the doorway and looked outside. His plastic bucket shone white, icelike in the moonlight. A man lay on the ground, bandaged about the head and arms. Monks stood around the recumbent form, but Conrad could not make out their faces. They talked earnestly, with nervous gestures. The wounded man cried out, turning on his side toward Conrad, his hands under his cheek. Conrad's weakened mind sought to explain the scene with gothic melodrama. The body was him, Conrad, at the moment of death. He was already a ghost, watching from the outside. But there was the matter of his bowels and the sudden need to access the white bucket. As Conrad squatted over the brim, close to fainting, he noticed the wounded man's face was Tambralingan— Yawi—and there was a grim familiarity about it.

Hours later, he woke up again. The night was silent, but a stench, something like burning plastic, filled the air. Conrad imagined himself well again but broke into a sweat when he got to his feet. He staggered out into the compound. Stars blazed overhead; the moon had set. A small fire was burning on the brick pad behind Moo's hut. As Conrad approached it, the smell grew worse. Billows of smoke made big holes in the starry firmament, but the flames themselves were meager. It wasn't until Conrad was almost on top of the pad that he could see what was happening.

A body lay on the brick pad, being consumed by a slow-burning fire. Moo sat on the ground next to the pad, feeding the fire with small sticks. The fire centered on the chest. The ribs were exposed, but the head and limbs were still intact. Next to Moo were several widemouthed jars, some partly filled with a yellowish oil.

Moo waved Conrad away.

"No! Not for you. Go back! Make sick again."

23

The Puja Pantai, or the Feasting of the Spirits of the Sea, is held only once every seven years in a small group of villages just 10 kilometers north of Sri Kala. At one time celebrations went on for seven days and nights, but pressure from the powerful Ministry of Religious Education has reduced the festival to three days and two nights. That the festival has not died out altogether is due to the efforts of the new Minister of Tourism, who cites the festival's special appeal to the foreign tourist: the natural setting, the colorful rituals, the carnival atmosphere, the showcase of traditional arts, the mock sea battle commemorating Kaundinya's conquest. Efforts are under way to reach a compromise and eventually a sanitized version of the festival—one without the bloody sacrifice of a white water buffalo before the elaborate shrine of the Sea Goddess—may be staged in a soccer stadium in the capital. Visitors will then have an opportunity to view the festival without the bother of a trip down country.   —*Coswell's Guide to Tambralinga* (1997 ed.)

When Conrad next awoke, it was not yet light. He could hear the monks chanting in the great hall, hear the birds gathering in the courtyard tree. He wondered aloud what day it was. And he knew that because he could formulate such a question, he was much recovered.

His stomach was quiet. He found himself only slightly light-headed when he started across the temple grounds. How many days since he'd eaten? Here was another question that reassured him. His limbs tingled with a peculiar energy. He found the water spigot near the dormitory, turned it on and began to wash himself. At the other end of the compound he saw a pile of ashes smoldering on the brick pad.

A hundred years seemed to have passed during his sleep. His

body, like a desiccated sponge, began slowly swelling back into its regular shape in the presence of moisture. What had passed for living before now seemed the dreariest of daydreams. It hurt his eyes to view certain colors. The green of the banana leaves, the azure of the sea, the orange flesh of the papaya. He left the chanting of the monks behind, went down the rutted road toward the village, pausing now and then to rest against a buttress root of a giant meranti tree or steady himself against a boulder. Fleeing the place where sickness has kept one prisoner seemed a natural enough impulse, but it was somehow more than that. Conrad felt himself in the tow of an irresistible attraction, a pull, not a push, something that seemed to float him above the ground, allowing him to waft like a fragrance through the morning air. Perhaps it was that the lack of food over the last several days had left his sense of smell in a hyperattenuated state, and that the force leading him down to the headman's house was the smell of breakfast being cooked. This theory gained ascendance as he called a greeting to the headman's wife. She seemed astonished at his arrival, as if she'd long ago ruled out that possibility. Her hens had produced an abundance of eggs, which she seemed happy enough to cook for him. She also had leftover rice, which she made into an overly sweetened porridge.

And so Conrad passed from delirium into a beguiling dream of village life. He discovered in Lanka Suka a saturating stillness, an atmosphere in which peace might be shown to possess physical properties, like humidity, if measured with the right sort of gauge. Palms swayed in the wind with decided dreaminess. Fishermen called to each other from their boats, hints of melody resonating in their voices. The most mundane perceptions, a rooster's crow, the scent of burning charcoal, the sight of a two-man saw resting on a woodpile, seemed luminous, gemlike. With rapt attention, Conrad observed villagers mending fishing nets, harvesting coconuts, tending their garden plots. He watched small children make toys for themselves, fashion paddlewheel boats from bits of wood and leaves and rubber bands, kites from newspapers and sticks. Was this what Lucy had in mind all along? Getting to this point of tranquility—was that what had driven her list-making, her obsession with jetting off into unknown regions? He stared at this likelihood in dull amazement.

Conrad was sitting on the sand, resting his back against the painted hull of a beached *kolek*, when Eva arrived. He didn't see her at first because of where the sun was.

"Hello," she said. "They didn't have any room for me at the bungalows, but they say that there are these tourists sleeping on the beach just outside the village."

"I'm them." He did not feel at all surprised to see her. "I was staying at the local *wat*. But last night I decided to stay down here."

Eva dropped her pack in the sand next to Conrad and then sat down. She sighed heavily and coughed. Smoker's cough, Conrad noted.

"Surprise to see you," she said, touching his shoulder. Conrad thought she looked sad. "So you didn't leave the island after all. Or did you just come back?"

Conrad explained his circumstances.

"I was sick, too!" Eva said. "It was that last dinner we had, all of us, together, I think. On the ferry boat I became very ill."

"Sorry about that," Conrad said.

"Why? I took us out, remember?"

"Right."

They exchanged sidelong glances. Conrad watched something in the waves that might have been a turtle. Neither of them spoke for a long minute.

"Birgit and I, we have—separated," Eva said.

"I wasn't going to ask."

"We had a falling down over this festival in Sri Kala. For me, this was the whole point of the trip. They hold it only once every seven years and it has all of the—what is it? Magic? Of the place. But Birgit is only concerned about her politics and to see this Sonny Tatoh leading the demonstrations in Kuala Vimaya."

"Right," Conrad said, nodding. "Sonny."

"I told her that if she wanted to meet this Sonny guy so bad—Birgit knew his cousin at university—she should just stay in Kuala Vimaya. And I would go on to Sri Kala alone. But she didn't like that idea, so she came. And Sri Kala was a disaster."

"How so?"

"They have shut it down. The government, I mean, these religious people. They came in with police and put up these signs everywhere. You can't see the dances anymore, or the shadow plays, or any kind of ritual—what is the word? invocation?—of spirits of the sea. It's all against Islam, they say. Forbidden to Muslims by an act of Parliament."

"But you are not a Muslim."

"No, but the people who make the festival, the dancers, the puppet masters, the musicians, the *pawangs* who make the ritual, they are all Muslims."

"They are? But the dancers were rehearsing at the big temple on the hill here. I thought—"

"They are all officially Muslims," she said, shaking her head. "It was a different kind of Islam they had here originally. But now the government wants to change it, make it like it is in Arabia."

"So the government just shut everything down?"

She shook her head again. The tourists would still have their colorful festival to photograph, she explained. All of the locals would get dressed up. There would be kite-flying contests and bird-singing contests and assorted crafts and textiles for sale. But carnival rides were being substituted for the banned rituals. Pop bands from Thailand and Malaysia and Singapore were being brought in to perform on large sound stages. A small exposition featuring products manufactured in Tambralinga was being set up. Busloads of tourists were still coming down from Nagaseri, and many vendors were there to sell them food and drink. The religious authorities were not stupid. The changes in the festival would ultimately benefit the local economy.

"You know, I began to think that Birgit was right, that this thing we are trying to find here is not really here. When we were in Kuala Vimaya, we see posters everywhere of Sonny Tatoh. The police were taking them down, but more kept going up. There were homemade banners with his picture painted on it hanging between the streetlights or else across the tops of apartment buildings. You could feel in the air this electricity, like something was going to happen."

"So you went back to Kuala Vimaya?"

Eva hesitated, afraid perhaps that she was telling too much too fast. Afraid of being overwhelmed by the feeling of easy intimacy that seemed to come over travelers far removed from their normal routines.

"No," she continued. "We didn't. I mean, I didn't."

"And Birgit?"

"She made me angry. Her sarcasm. 'The government will fall,' she says. 'The people will rise up as one, as the giant, Al-Jabbar. But we won't bother with it because they don't wear the funny clothes and play the gamelan music.' So I came back on my own."

She looked up and down the deserted beach.

"It's nice here," she said. "I could get comfortable here."

They spent the afternoon taking a long walk, up the shoreline, close to where the beach ended and a steep, jungle-covered hill began. They didn't attempt the hill but instead found a path that meandered inland, through groves of coconut trees and peanut farms, to a small Paktai village filled with ragged children and skinny dogs. The place was crisscrossed with what looked like clotheslines from which the brown bodies of squid and cuttlefish had been hung out to dry in the sun. The smell was overpowering.

They climbed a small hill just beyond the village, and on the gentle slope of its far side came upon a group of farmers standing in a big circle. Their arms were stretched out so that each man nearly touched the fingertips of his neighbor, and they were yelling excitedly, as fans might yell at a football match. In the center of the ring two large water buffaloes paced, as if about to face off. Behind each bull stood a little man, shirtless and barefoot, like all of the others, holding a long switch.

"What are they doing?" Eva asked.

"It's a fight," Conrad said. "A buffalo fight."

It seemed a preposterous sight, this arrangement of painfully skinny men in long checkered sarongs staked out like fenceposts around what was meant to be a fight ring. One of the buffaloes moved nervously back and forth, clearly wanting to leave the ring, but shy of the noisy, gesticulating men. The point between Eva's eyebrows puckered, rippling the placid, curving surface of her forehead.

"They're making bets, aren't they? As in a cockfight. And these animals will gore each other." She covered her eyes and turned away for a moment. Conrad watched, enrapt with the faces of the men, men desperate for something, anything to happen; and more than that, with the way their desperation was set against the painful green of the vegetation, the uncompromising blue of the sea, the dark peaks of clouds erupting along the horizon. Surely their boredom was as hard and sharp as these primary colors. At a signal the little men began lashing the buffaloes' hindquarters, urging them forward with high-pitched cries. The nervous bull began to prance, then charged. The other buffalo turned and ran, scattering the wall of screaming men, rushing down the hill and into the brush at the edge of the field. The other bull came charging after, closely followed by the two screaming owners.

It was impossible not to laugh at such a scene. Eva laid a hand on Conrad's shoulder and pressed her forehead against it. Conrad's laughter came in deep swells, rising slowly from his belly. He was beginning to like the place.

They ate dinner together at the headman's house, Conrad warning Eva sternly not to drink the lemon squash set before them— he was certain it was the drink that had made him ill. But Eva put a small tablet in each glass and assured Conrad that it would be fine to drink after ten minutes or so. Other than that they were silent. Nonetheless it was entirely different for Conrad to have another person at the meal who didn't speak Yawi, who could sit with him in the semi-dark while the headman and his wife exchanged staccato bursts of verbiage, like opposing soldiers firing at each other across a disputed frontier.

"Is this your daughter, then?" the headman's son asked Conrad. Conrad checked himself before issuing a full denial. Surely they would be scandalized if Conrad confessed that he and Eva were "just friends," hardly more than acquaintances. Conrad decided instead to call Eva his niece, his sister's daughter. Once translated, this revelation was received with visible relief by the headman and his wife; the burden of ambiguity had been lifted from their shoulders, and Conrad realized how tense they'd been all through the meal.

Eva showed no sign of being disturbed by Conrad's fiction, no sign, in fact, of having been listening at all. She sat up straight and raised her arms above her head in a prolonged stretch.

"Where do we sleep tonight?" she asked matter-of-factly. "Outside?"

Conrad nodded slowly, startled to find himself once more part of a "we."

"You say the mosquitoes are not so bad?"

"They'll go away in a minute," Conrad answered. She had unrolled her sleeping bag right next to his. Not halfway down the beach, not three feet away, but right next to him.

When Conrad dared to look at her, Eva was already in her bag, lying on her side, facing him. Her face, partly framed by her long blond hair, appeared ghostly white in the cloud-filtered moonlight, the play of shadows on her brooding features rendering them sepulchral one moment, alive with nestled warmth the next. Conrad stayed on his back, hands clasped behind his head, looking up at the encroaching mass of clouds. Eva asked him in a whisper if it would rain. And Conrad, hearing a plea for comfort in her voice, said that it wouldn't.

"When the moon goes down, the stars are quite bright," he added, as if this was a little-known fact. Eva sighed, apparently soothed by this banality. Conrad found his thoughts starting to race, circling endlessly around the terms "niece" and "uncle." When he dared look at her again, he saw that her eyes were still open, that her face resembled more than ever that of Liv Ullmann, the brooding Liv Ullmann of *Persona* and that other movie the title of which he could not remember. Who was it that had said the movie stars of one's middle years can only ever be actors, while those of one's youth will always seem like gods?

"Conrad," she asked in a bare whisper. "Have you ever been in love?"

Conrad found himself unable to look away.

"I'm not sure," he said.

"With me as well," she said. She pushed a strand of hair out of her eyes, and although he could see only part of her face, this motion of wrist and fingers revealed the perfection of her body.

"But what about your wife?" Eva went on. "When you first get married?"

"I wanted her," Conrad said. "She was a prize I didn't dare believe I could ever have." Conrad was surprised to hear himself voice these words.

"But then you get tired of her?"

It hadn't been that way at all. He'd guarded her jealously, nurtured her, husbanded her. Yet for all of that, he'd never really possessed her, not for a moment. A familiar swell of resentment rushed these thoughts forward. It took a moment for Conrad to formulate an answer.

"I couldn't please her," he said finally. "She started seeing another man. At least, I think she did."

The breeze picked up, dispersed the mosquitoes. Eva lifted herself up on an elbow.

"In Sri Kala—Birgit and I—we had this terrible fight. I told her she had been ruining this trip for me. Her bad moods and her thing with politics—what is the word?"

"Obsession."

"Yes. And she says I am superficial, that I care nothing but for my own pleasure. 'These beach boys,' she says. 'You are paying them to fuck you.' And I say that it's just that we have more money than they do and so we must share it. And she says that I don't understand anything, that I'm an idiot. And so I say that if I am such an idiot, you don't need to go with me anymore. And she begins to cry, to beg me not to go."

Eva rolled onto her back. She seemed to be sobbing. Conrad tried to say something comforting.

"When I first saw you today, I was so glad," Eva began again. "I felt this relief."

"Thanks," Conrad said, not sure what this meant. Eva draped an arm around his neck and hugged him clumsily, nearly cutting off his wind.

"Birgit said she loved me," Eva went on after she'd released Conrad from the choke hold. "She said that she has always loved me, that I'm so beautiful—"

"Yes," Conrad said, wiping her tears from his grizzled chin.

"I realized then that I really don't like her anymore, and that I must get away. Then we hear about the riots in Kuala Vimaya and that this Sonny Tatoh was shot. And Birgit gets mad that she hadn't been there, that she'll never get to meet this guy."

"Shot? This protest leader?"

"Yes. That's what they were saying. The soldiers came and shot at everyone."

They were quiet for a moment.

"And Birgit gets mad also because I'm saying that we should be apart for a while. She begins to insult me again, saying I'm superficial and all of that. So then I don't feel bad anymore about leaving."

Eva grew quiet once more. Conrad listened to the lapping of the waves, which was growing louder as the wind picked up.

"But when I started to leave, she hits me. Gives me a mark on my cheek."

"She hits hard," Conrad murmured.

"Did you ever hit your wife?"

"No," he said after a long pause.

"I just broke things," he confessed. "Furniture mostly."

"What furniture?"

"Expensive things. An English antique dresser with beveled mirror. A Shaker chair."

"What is 'Shaker'?"

"The Shakers were a religious sect. They lived in big communal farms. They were great craftsmen. But they were all celibates, and so when they died—"

"Oh yes, like the Puritans," Eva interrupted.

"The Puritans were not celibates," Conrad started to say, but then stopped to wonder why this misconception felt like such an affront. He turned instead toward the promise of sleep that now extended from the sound of the waves. He grew weightless, as if floating out to sea with the tide. Overhead the clouds broke apart and the sky brimmed with the brilliance of the stars. It seemed to Conrad that other bodies floated next to his, jostled by the waves. He thought of the movie with Liv Ullmann that ended with her in a lifeboat surrounded by floating corpses. There'd been a massacre in Kuala Vimaya. Conrad imagined it to be like the scene in the movie: gray, silent, permeated with despair. Yet he felt no despair himself, only the weightlessness, the relief of not having to struggle. Sonny Tatoh—he remembered the face from a poster in Pak Sai. Now it would have a funereal look about it, like Che Guevara's portrait. But was this man actually dead? Eva had said only "shot," and that could mean so many things.

Eva's voice spoke to him from a long way off.

"We did sleep together, Birgit and I—in Sweden a few times, and then once when we first came to Tambralinga. I didn't know if I wanted to keep doing it. I wasn't sure. So I told her that, and she said she felt the same way. That we could just be friends like

before and everything would be—but it wasn't like before. I felt
like I was in this little, enclosed space."

"Bubble."

"That keeps getting smaller. And I had to break out. That's
how I felt when we met Boon that first night.

"Do you mind me telling you this? I can't help it right now. I
feel that we should be able to say anything. We should be able to
do what we want without all of these judgments coming from
other people."

Conrad opened his eyes and found himself resting on solid
ground once more.

"It would be nice," he agreed.

"Did you break this furniture because your wife was seeing
this other man?"

"No. I didn't know then." He paused. "Or maybe I did, but
didn't want to admit it."

"It's strange, this jealousy. Isn't it? At the university they say it
is all Darwin, about passing on your genes. But can it be only
that?"

"I started thinking how my wife might become his wife," Conrad whispered after a long minute. "That all of the friends we had
as a couple would become his friends. That our house might become his house. That after six months or one year or two, it
would be like he'd always been there and like I had never existed."

Conrad propped his head up with hand and elbow. The moon
was behind her, making her recumbent form appear as a range of
distant hills. He waited for her to say something else, but then realized she was asleep, exhaling with a steady rhythm that neatly
echoed the lapping of the waves. He watched her for a long time.

The sun was already high in the sky, just above the bank of gray
clouds building along the eastern horizon when Conrad awoke.
Eva's sleeping bag lay next to him, empty. The voices of village
men, laughing in their high-pitched way, came to him from somewhere up the beach. Conrad squirmed around in his sleeping bag

in a long search for his underpants, somewhat embarrassed at the fact that he'd awakened with an erection. That hadn't happened in a long time. Two villagers, wiry men with turbans, each balancing a load of bamboo poles on his head, suddenly emerged from the stand of coconut trees just a few yards away. One of them sang a phrase from a song.

"*Selamat pagi!*" they called to Conrad. Conrad waved back, then grabbed his folded trousers, which were lying on the sand next to him, and, when the men had gone by, stood to shake them out. But as Conrad held up his pants, a familiar-looking woman appeared between the trunks of the leaning palms.

"Good morning!" Rosanette called to him. Philippe followed her out onto the beach. "I've heard from your friend that you are here, so I come to say hello."

"Hello," said Conrad, hopping a little to get his right leg into his pants. He turned his back as he attempted the left leg and lost his balance.

"Oh, pardon me!" Rosanette said, grasping his arm to steady him. She held on as he finished pulling up his pants.

"I see your friend at breakfast," she said. "We stay at Chum's—the South Beach bungalows, yes? She said you were sick."

"I'm better," Conrad said.

"You look different. Darker."

"I've lost weight."

"You have the beard now," Rosanette went on. "You're like the sheep-wreaked seaman."

"Is it gray?" Conrad asked.

She smiled, coming closer. She picked up the amulet that was hanging around his neck.

"Buddha," she said, holding the amulet in the palm of her hand. The amulet consisted of a tiny image of the seated Buddha suspended in a dark, oily liquid, sealed in a triangular plastic case. "The monks give you this for good luck, yes?"

"Yes, when I was sick," Conrad said with growing nervousness, for the scent of her hair was sending tiny ripples through his solar plexus and this distressed him. Conrad looked up the beach to where the two villagers had dumped their load of bamboo. Maybe that was where the headman would build his bungalows. How quickly his little refuge was vanishing!

"But what is this—oil?" Rosanette asked as she let go of the amulet, rubbing her thumb and forefinger together. A small amount of oil had leaked around the edges of the plastic casing where the seal was not secure. Rosanette sniffed her fingers and declared that the oil smelled of roast pork. She pressed her finger under Conrad's nose, then let it brush against his lip.

"Not pork," Conrad said, as he took her hand and pulled it away from his face, for the scent of the oil had awakened unpleasant memories. Rosanette winced.

"My hand," she whispered and Conrad, startled, released his grip. Still, she clung to his wrist.

"You must come down to the bungalows and eat some breakfast. Chum makes the good omelettes."

"I guess I'm not hungry," Conrad said, pulling on a T-shirt. He had no clean clothes left. Why did she continue to linger?

"They tell me this place in the hills, in the jungle near here, you can swim in the fresh water. It's a small lake—pond—with the waterfall."

"Waterfall?"

"Yes, and nobody of the people goes there." She came close to him again and picked a tiny insect out of his hair. "They say it is hunted by the guests of dead people."

"Haunted, you mean? By ghosts?"

"Yes. So it's—quiet. Not so busy."

He bent over to brush the sand off of his pant legs. There was sand inside the pants as well.

"We can go sometime," Rosanette said. "When Philippe has his nap. I have this girl at Chum's watching him, yes? And maybe we go then together, alone."

"Maybe." He couldn't wait for her to leave. But why did he still have an erection?

"I need to go into Pak Sai," he said abruptly. "My laundry—"

"They do laundry at South Beach bungalows."

"I have to go to the post office too, to get a message to my wife. And change money." Conrad frowned. He didn't want to think about Lucy.

The scent of burning oil from the moiling engine enveloped Conrad as the scooter crested the first hill. The driver sounded the horn—just a loud, scabrous buzzer—as they came up behind a small boy driving a water buffalo forward with a switch. The buffalo moved aside, but not before the scooter hit a rut that nearly tumbled Conrad and his bag of laundry off the back of the bike. The driver smiled at Conrad over his shoulder, as if to say, "Tighten your grip!" And Conrad held tighter to the edge of his seat, but could not overcome the feeling that even this was less than solid.

Pak Sai had changed. Soldiers were everywhere, cherub-faced young men in green fatigues marching in double time up the main thoroughfares, rifles extended. Soldiers were posted along the ferry docks, in front of the post office, around the banks. Soldiers sat in the lobby of the Cozy Comfort smoking cigarettes and drinking tea, bulging leather holsters hanging from their belts. The manager of the Cozy Comfort only smiled when Conrad asked him what the soldiers were doing there.

The laundress that served the hotel had not yet picked up that day's laundry. Conrad negotiated a price with the manager, who promised his clothes would be finished by five P.M. Included in the price was the use of the shower and the shared bathroom on the second floor. (The stares of the other guests had convinced Conrad that a shower and a shave were now essential.)

As he removed his T-shirt in the bathroom, he noticed a grease spot where the amulet had touched it. He had an impulse to ditch the thing, but then, as he stepped into the tepid shower, grew distracted with thoughts of Lucy.

He could not imagine she was still waiting for him on Ko Banteay. The only conceivable way he might get a message to her was through the Hotel Nagaseri, where they had planned to rest up for a few days before taking the long flight back to San Francisco. Possibly she was crazy with worry, was regularly calling the front desk, hoping for a message. Would she roundhouse him the next time they met? It seemed a real possibility. Conrad hung his head and let the jet of water rinse the back of his neck. Of course it was questionable whether the term "jet" could be applied to the flaccid stream that he usually obtained from Tambralingan showers. And just as this thought crossed Conrad's mind, the water pressure dropped to a bare trickle. He shook the lathered shampoo from his hands, grateful that he had not already applied it to his hair, for he knew the water tanks on the roof had emptied and would take the better part of an hour to refill. It could have been so much worse, he thought as he slipped the amulet back over his neck. Maybe his luck was changing.

Long-distance calls could be made from a single phone at the post office. One had only to pay the clerk behind the counter, then at a given signal proceed to the booth in the corner of the lobby and dial a number. There was a line for the phone when Conrad arrived. A barrel-chested German was wedged into the booth, angrily repeating the same phrase over and over.

While Conrad waited, he suddenly recognized Romney Gavin standing at the *poste restante* window. Without thinking, Conrad hailed him, and thus became embroiled in an absurd conversation, absurd because it required yelling trivial remarks halfway across the room, over the heads of the placid islanders lined up at the other windows.

"I said," Conrad repeated at an uncomfortable volume (he hated to shout), " 'how was your trip to the mainland?' "

"Bloody awful," the young man yelled back in his excruciating accent. He seemed bent on claiming English origins by giving a nasal treatment to certain vowels. This tendency seemed to have worsened since the last time they spoke.

"I was lucky to get out of there alive," Romney went on.

"How do you mean?"

"I'll tell you when you're finished with your call."

The young Yawi woman at the long-distance counter wore no veil, but did not return Conrad's smile. She grew distracted when Conrad asked to place a call to Nagaseri, twice giving him the wrong change. Her discomfort grew when it became obvious that she would have to show Conrad how the phone worked, and when she actually got into the booth with Conrad's large head leaning in over her shoulder, her voice grew strained and nervous. She darted out of the booth before Conrad could get a fix on what she was saying, shoving the phonecard into his hand. Conrad carried on as best he could, attempting at first to insert the card into the phone and then, when that failed, to dial the hotel directly. Only Romney's timely intervention got the call completed.

"Punch in this number here. That gives you the long-distance operator. Then enter this code. When you hear the tone, dial your number, okay?"

But talking to the receptionist at the hotel was like talking to an echo. Every one of Conrad's statements came back to him as a question, and this seemed to require that Conrad issue an additional confirming statement, which the receptionist repeated as a question and so on. In the end Conrad was nearly shouting:

"Not 'Berry Hill'! Very ill. I've been very ill."

He wiped at the sweat running down his face with the back of his hand.

"Right. And I will meet you at the hotel on the twenty-second—No! At the hotel. On the twenty-second!"

By the time Conrad hung up the phone, everyone in line was looking at him.

"Pay no heed," Romney murmured to him confidentially. "Just look straight ahead and march out of here. You look like you could use a drink."

On the way to get a drink, they passed the shrine of the four-headed god, whose many arms were draped with garlands of white and yellow flowers. Two soldiers stood in the street nearby, rifles propped against their shoulders, as if standing guard.

"Do you know what this is about?" Conrad asked, nodding toward the shrine.

"That's a statue of Brahma. Buddhist worship in this part of the world incorporates some Hindu elements, probably because the Indian traders that first colonized—"

"No, no. I mean the soldiers."

"Good God, man, where have you been?"

"I've been pretty isolated. On the other side of the island. And sick, too."

"Sorry," Romney said. "You do look thinner than the last time I saw you. A good deal thinner.

"Well," he went on, "there was a bit of an uproar on the mainland some days ago. The police called it a riot, but it was really more of a massacre. The big opposition party held a night rally in Kuala Vimaya and the army surrounded them and opened fire. They shot the leader, but apparently didn't kill him."

"Sonny somebody, right?"

"Usen 'Sonny' Tatoh, right. So you have heard?"

"A little."

They came to a restaurant/bar housed in a sort of garage. Romney called to the waitress in Paktai as he and Conrad crossed the concrete floor and sat down at a white plastic table.

"The latest rumor is that Sonny escaped by boat to one of the islands, perhaps this one," Romney continued. "Or that he's still offshore somewhere, waiting for a chance to land."

"But he's Yawi, isn't he?"

"He has supporters here. Most of the islanders, I should think. Hence the government's eagerness to have him snuffed."

A waitress, dark and birdlike, arrived at the table with the beer. Conrad studied her small hands as they gripped the necks of the bottles and set them on the tabletop. Romney was speaking about something else, but Conrad was not listening. He watched the waitress move on to the next table, fixated on the narrowness of her waist and neck. A squadron of soldiers appeared in the street, moving briskly past the restaurant, three abreast.

"—and I got to Airabu just as the shrine was being dismantled," Romney was saying when Conrad was again able to concentrate on his words. "Right before my very eyes. The thing that I'd come to see, to investigate, rubbed out."

"Terrible," Conrad commented absently. He was thinking about the girl in the post office, how terrified she'd been of getting close to him. He drank from his bottle, stared out at the street.

"—somebody calling himself the Minister of Religious Education," Romney went on. "He was one of these unctuous Indians you see in the civil service here. But the amusing thing was that this bureaucrat, this gopher, had these two American women traveling with him. He'd fed them some story about being a prince, one of the Sultan's heirs. And they had apparently devoured every word."

"Two women, did you say?" Conrad asked, sipping his beer.

"Two women fighting over one man, from the looks of it. Two reasonably attractive women—one quite striking, actually. But completely enthralled by his aura of authority, his big car, his Italian suit. You could see it a mile away, the way they looked at him, the way they followed him around the site at a discreet distance. And the way they would look at each other! Any minute you expected them to draw knives and go at it."

Conrad laughed along with Romney, not quite certain what was so funny. The waitress slowly approached their table, momentarily meeting Conrad's gaze with a frankly curious expression.

"Now, why did you go there exactly?" Conrad asked, turning toward Romney.

"The shrine was supposed to have healing properties. Miracle cures. I study that sort of thing." He glanced over his shoulder as the waitress drifted past, and then back at Conrad.

"Well, I got cured by a monk." Conrad drained his beer.

"Really? Not the one from the ferry? With the trunk?"

Conrad nodded. Romney moved his chair closer to the table.

"Tell me about it, then," he said, signaling the waitress to bring more beer.

"Do you know what this is?" Romney said as he held the amulet between thumb and forefinger. "I mean, how could you? You're a software consultant, not an ethnographer." His elbow bumped an empty beer bottle, sent it wobbling across the slippery tabletop. When it failed to fall over, Romney smiled at Conrad and brought his palms together.

"Luck. It's my lucky day. There are certain mythical substances that one reads about in the literature but doesn't have a prayer of encountering in the field. For example *lek lay*, a magical metal alloy that gangsters claim protects them from bullets. Or *phlay dam*, a root whose extracts will sharpen a man's vision to the point where he can see through solid objects, like closed doors or the backs of playing cards. Or the dresses of beautiful women. And then there is 'corpse oil,' the rendered fat taken from a murdered man. From the chin, usually. It's considered extremely dangerous if it's not used properly. Causes insanity in some people."

"Insanity?"

"Yes. Or love."

"I don't understand."

"It's a love charm. The oil of a murdered man. Somehow his essence, his life force—the *semengat* they call it—gets distilled into the oil."

Romney held the amulet up to the light. The Buddha image inside glistened as the amulet swayed gently at the end of the chain.

"Makes a beautiful bath for our little friend in there," Romney said.

"Why would it be rare?" Conrad asked. "Aren't there lots of murdered men around?"

"All murdered men are not created equal," Romney smiled. "Some have more *semengat* than others. Or so the folklore tells us. Besides, in order to cast the right sort of spell, you have to know the murdered man's name."

Conrad took back his amulet, stared at the featureless face of the Buddha image inside.

"So what's this one's name, I wonder?" Conrad asked.

"Sonny Tatoh," Romney said, without skipping a beat.

Romney had heard Sonny Tatoh speak the night of the massacre. Unwisely Romney had worked his way into the middle of the crowd that filled the great public green on the banks of the Vimaya, drawn in by the hypnotic rhetoric of Sonny Tatoh. He was not a fiery orator—he didn't have the big delivery of a Hitler or a Martin Luther King. Rather, the warmth in his voice pulled one in with promises of tranquility, somehow stirred up in the listener an urgent need to get closer. And so Romney began wending his way through the mass of white-capped hadjis, the barefoot rickshaw drivers, the masses of unemployed laborers, the white-collar workers in their polyester shirts and checked sarongs, entire families with grandparents and children and mothers and aunts straining to see. Usen quietly exhorted the crowd to prepare for the new day, the rising of the people to peacefully reclaim their country and their government. His was the usual prescription: hard work, selfless dedication, diligence. But it was the soft, gonglike tones in his voice that swayed the people, that forced individuals here and there to throw up their arms and declare that God was great.

God *was* great. The suffering on the faces in the crowd was so vivid, Romney could not help but be swept up in the mysterious violence of that statement. And when the army units replied, unambiguously, with automatic rifles, Romney found himself swept up again, riding the crest of a wave of bodies that went crashing back across the field. Old women, men with turbans, girls in long

white smocks, these anguished faces, these flailing limbs,
the handholds and footholds that delivered Romney fro
crush. Over the top he went, all hesitation gone, all guilt
quished, feeling only gratitude for the traction his Vibram so.
provided.

Breaking free of the mass, he zigzagged across the field, unable
to see where the soldiers were deployed. Here it came again, the
crackle of gunfire, the dull rhythmic thud of his feet against the
earth, the elbows of other men running alongside. He'd never run
this fast in his life. And this was his life, this was all there was to
it, and now it was going to end. Faces emerged from the dark—
contorted, alien faces. He struck them down, crying out. *Aie-yee!*
Women, he realized too late, and then they were behind him, and
he was glad they were out of the way.

Guns went off somewhere behind him. Other guns answered
somewhere to his right and then to his left. It was a conversation,
boys yelling to each other over a fence, a hedge, a parking lot.
Ollie-ollie-oxen-free! Two men, shirtless, screaming, knocked him
over. He decided to stay down, to proceed on all fours. Yes, that's
what they tell you in a holdup: keep your head down, don't look
up. And pray the police come. The smell of mud and rotting vegetation filled his nostrils and he knew he'd stumbled into the
unofficial garbage dump at the edge of the river. The headlights
of a truck came on then, and he glimpsed the soldiers' helmets
silhouetted in the glare. He ran along the river, expecting to be
cut down, but the shots never came. Truckloads of soldiers were
now rumbling across the commons, bodies flitted back and forth
in the crossed headlight beams. Somewhere a loudspeaker issued
commands, a call for calm, for order, and the amplified voice
echoed off the buildings that bordered the rapidly emptying
green.

Romney paused to swig his beer. Beer came in big bottles here
and was more potent than American brands. Conrad glanced at
the amulet, which was lying on the table before him. He picked it

up and gazed into it, as if expecting to glimpse the scenes that Romney had described.

"Jesus Christ," he said, putting the amulet back down on the table and wiping his hands on his pants.

"Don't lose that," Romney advised. "It might be worth something."

"It's leaking," Conrad said, feeling his stomach turn.

"Maybe it's meant to. Timed-release, you know?"

He took out a small notebook and quickly wrote something in it.

"What did you say that monk's name was?" he asked Conrad.

"Moo. Tuan Moo."

"Master Pig?" Romney was incredulous. He explained that "Moo" was a Thai word for pig, and that children in rural Thailand were usually saddled with these sorts of nicknames. "Tuan" on the other hand, was the honorific Malay title.

"A joke at the expense of his Muslim clientele perhaps."

"But I don't see why they would bring a wounded fugitive all the way out here and then leave him at some little *wat*. I mean, by the time I saw the body, it could have been anybody's."

"Cremations are public ceremonies held in the daytime," Romney sighed, bringing the bottle to his lips. "What you saw was body disposal. Big secret, little fire."

It wasn't hard to imagine a boat taking Sonny to the far side of Ko Neak Pean, Romney went on. Nor was it hard to imagine the villagers panicked over the possibility of Sonny's grave being found near their village. Muslim fishermen were often skipped in the official census. The disappearance of one or two families, even an entire village, would hardly be noticed in Nagaseri.

"I've heard enough," Conrad said, standing up, images of the burning corpse rising before him. Briefly he beheld the flickering possibility that the body had still been breathing as Moo fanned the flames. He staggered, watched a curtain of purple stars descend from the ceiling. Too many beers.

"Don't forget your Buddha," Romney said. "Your *semengat* seems a bit low."

"Keep it," Conrad said. He went to the counter with the intention of paying for the beer, but the waitress was nowhere to be seen.

"She's hiding from you, old man," Romney teased. "She doesn't trust herself around you. But I'll pick up the tab, don't worry. Since you're being so generous, I mean."

Conrad went out without giving Romney a second look. He wanted no more part in this business.

Or did he?

When he reached the hotel, he discovered that the laundry was not ready, would not be ready until the next day. He began to ask for a room at the hotel, but then grew inexplicably perturbed at the thought. Exhausted, he sat down on a chair in the lobby and stared at the grease spot on his shirt.

When he closed his eyes, he saw Rosanette's looming face turning in his direction, a smile spread just for him. But he no longer wanted this, probably never had. Why, then, was his heart racing? What he really wanted was the night before, the tranquility of the beach under the stars, the quiet lapping of the waves merging with Eva's voice.

Conrad opened his eyes. A fat gecko was peeking out from behind the gilded frame of a large mirror that hung on the wall. He pictured Eva rubbing thumb and forefinger together, then sniffing.

"Smells like pork," he heard her saying.

He found Romney sitting at the same table, writing in his notebook. A young couple sat at the end of the bar. Otherwise the place was deserted. The amulet still lay on the table. Conrad snatched it up.

"Changed my mind," he said to Romney's startled expression.

"Of course," Romney stuttered. "But I wonder if I might get a chance to study it before—"

"Maybe in a couple of days."

Conrad held himself erect as he strode out of the bar and down the street toward the taxi stand. A squad of soldiers, smooth-faced boys who might pass for middle school students back home, looked at him as he walked past. As a movie star might indulge a gaggle of gaping fans, Conrad smiled and placed his palms together in a Buddhist salute.

"Sawatdee!" they called back at him, grinning and laughing as if they shared with him a secret joke.

Part Five

Child's Play

24

As he walked away with the amulet, with that hard certainty enclosed in his fist, Conrad permitted himself a moment of wonder. His luck was changing. The way forward was growing clear. The evening sky stretched before him like a great banner emblazoned with declarations of his triumph. There was a reason why he'd come to Tambralinga after all, a real reason, a secret reason. He would squelch the fresh currents of doubt already circulating through him, the inevitably unsavory linkage between his vision of paradise and Usen Tatoh's dying face. There was simply nothing to be done about it. It was all quite beyond his control.

Conrad arrived back in Lanka Suka just after sundown. As he climbed off the back of the scooter, a small group of village men were gathering outside of the headman's house. The headman and a few others prostrated themselves on mats facing the setting sun. An old man with a stringy beard and a dirty white cap appeared to lead the prayer. Conrad stood still until the men were finished praying.

"Please you come dinner now," the headman's son said as he hurried past Conrad. "Tonight big dinner. Everyone come."

It was the feast the spirit Sang Kala had demanded during the séance. The headman's wife and sister had been working all day to prepare the food, and now the boy was going around to all the houses in the village issuing invitations. Conrad watched the boy go from house to house and noticed the wife and sister coming from the headman's house with platters of food and stacks of banana leaves.

The feast was laid out on woven mats on the ground. As the guests began arriving, they seated themselves in a wide circle, some sitting on floor mats brought from home, others sitting directly on the sand. Sticks of incense were lit and stuck in the sand in the center of the circle near the food.

Conrad watched the scene for some minutes before making a move. He'd ridden into the village with the conviction that Eva would be waiting for him, and that after dinner they would walk off down the beach together and watch the stars rise out of the sea. But Eva was not there.

"Yes, you come now," the headman's son called to Conrad a second time, as he went to the last house. It appeared that anyone invited was supposed to drop whatever he was doing and come. Conrad swallowed his disappointment, found himself moving to join the circle.

All the guests were men. They sat down solemnly, legs folded beneath them, backs ramrod straight, as if waiting to participate in a karate match. Conrad attempted to follow their example, but found sitting on his heels unbearably painful. He teetered momentarily in an awkward crouch, afraid that he might topple forward onto the mat, but then squirmed into a cross-legged position. Nobody seemed to notice. All eyes were focused on the food. The center of the feast was a mound of rice shaped like a pyramid, which was ringed by balls of sticky rice. The circle of rice balls was in turn surrounded by dishes of fish, meat, and vegetables. The entire display was illuminated by two kerosene lanterns.

"Hello," Rosanette said quietly in Conrad's left ear. "Are we too late for dinner?"

"Oh, hi," Conrad replied. "It's not the usual dinner."

"Why are you whispering?" She was kneeling down in the sand next to him. Philippe was running back and forth somewhere behind them.

"It's a ceremony. I think you have to be invited."

"Oh. The boy here, he invites us. Just now. We are walking by the boats and he comes. I think it is bad to refuse, yes? But we have eaten already and Philippe is—"

"I'm not hungry either."

"Never hungry, eh? But why are they having this feast now?"

Conrad explained, in a progressively quieter voice, the situation with the headman's wife and the cure that Moo had provided.

"Ah, they feast the spirits so! I like this." She settled down next to him and smiled at the display.

"Spirits don't get to eat very much of it."

"But no! They eat the *parfum*—the smell of this wonderful food. I wish I could live on just the—fragrances. Is that the word?"

"Yes."

"But we must go out and kill the animals and the fish and get fat eating all of them." She made a face, rubbing her fingers together. "It's degrading."

"You think so?"

"No, I'm joking." She squeezed his biceps. The man sitting on Rosanette's left looked over at them.

"I think it's starting," Conrad said.

The headman, seated on the opposite side of the circle, began speaking. His voice sounded solemn, as if he were reciting a practiced speech, and when he paused, all the men in the circle muttered something, as if in agreement. The headman continued speaking, his voice taking on a mechanical, rhythmic cadence.

"I think they are praying," Rosanette whispered. Then she turned and shushed Philippe, who was making a noise like a bird. The boy came and sat down in his mother's lap and stared at the feast with wide, blank eyes.

"His father was supposed to come back two days ago," Rosanette whispered slowly. "Then he writes saying we should come to Ko Banteay. So I get ready to go and he writes again. No, don't come yet. So I come here instead." She shrugged. So things were far worse between her and her husband than she had let on.

"I'm sorry," he said. She blew some air through her lips.

"It's okay. Maybe it's better we have different holidays."

The headman stopped talking, and the old man in the white cap began singing in a plaintive voice.

"It sounds like the mosque." Rosanette straightened up.

She was right, Conrad thought. It did sound like a different language altogether, a flowing, mellifluous language from some far-off place, a far-off place other than the one in which he was now situated. Conrad looked around the circle of faces. Did any of them grasp the meaning of the words, or were they simply savoring the underlying music that sent the words aloft? Perhaps the singer had no idea what the words meant either. Perhaps the chant was equally incomprehensible to everyone present. It was a comforting thought.

But now the singer paused and all the men chanted "Amin."

"Amen," Conrad said quickly, and then, imitating his neighbor, turned his palms toward the sky and lifted his face as if expecting a gift from God. The singer continued and then paused again.

"Amin," Conrad said with all of the others, keeping his face tilted skyward. But then he noticed that the other men were now staring down at their palms, and at the next "amin," they covered their faces with their hands.

Philippe whispered furtively, squirming in Rosanette's lap. Rosanette whispered something quickly, to which the boy replied with a distinct *"Non!"* The men sitting near Rosanette looked at her, as if to ask why she didn't remove herself and her child. But she seemed reluctant to leave Conrad's side, and so let the boy wander off instead.

The singing stopped. The men rubbed their faces with their palms, as if waking from a long dream. The headman's son went around with a pot of tea and filled everyone's glass. Two of the guests rose and stepped into the circle and began serving up the food. For each guest, they ladled a portion from each dish onto a banana leaf. Conrad's dish was heaped with rice porridge and fish curries and meat in red sauce, and chicken in yellow gravy. At a sign from the headman, everyone began eating.

The men scooped the rice up hurriedly with their fingers, as if the meal were part of a contest, an event to get through quickly. Conrad picked up his glass of tea and sipped it. Nobody spoke.

After a few minutes, Conrad noticed all the men had stopped eating and were looking at him and Rosanette.

"The fish is very good," Rosanette said to him, before she noticed the men staring.

"What did I do wrong?" she whispered to Conrad.

"Maybe we're supposed to stop eating."

It seemed unlikely. The banana leaves were still nearly full. None of the men had eaten more than a few bites of his dinner. But Conrad stopped anyway and shook the rice from his fingers.

One of the guests immediately stood up and bowed to the host, apparently taking his leave. The headman nodded and the guest quickly wrapped up his leftovers in his banana leaf and departed. One by one, the other guests repeated the performance, until most of the guests had gone.

"I think they taking this food home for their families," Rosanette whispered after a minute.

"Yes."

At that moment Philippe returned from the outer darkness dragging a basket. He chattered in cheery tones as he pulled items out of the basket to show to Rosanette. Here was a ball of yellow rice, a pack of cigarettes, a bottle of rice whiskey. A bobbin from a sewing machine with a bit of blue thread on it, a bunch of tiny bananas, a tiny comb, a tiny cardboard box, a package of brass pins, a small mirror, a broken harmonica. Rosanette smiled placidly, oblivious to the horrified expressions on the faces of the remaining guests.

"Where did he get these things?" she said, laughing. The headman's son came over to them.

"Excuse, sir," he said to Conrad with his hands clasped behind his back. "This no good. Basket is for *hantu*. Is for Sang Kala, not for your son play."

It was a few moments before Conrad grasped what had happened. Philippe had come across the makeshift shrine that the

headman had set up near the water's edge and had made off with
the basket offerings. The headman gasped when he saw what
Philippe had done. The rest of the company was too reserved or
too shocked to utter a sound.

To Conrad, Philippe's mistake seemed immediately understandable, marauding spirits apparently being placated with
many of the same things that appealed to small children—broken
objects that have no use but still glitter, toys that resembled tools
or luxury items, objects normally forbidden them. But it was too
late to try to explain this. Philippe turned the basket upside down
and emptied the remaining contents on the sand. The headman
rose up with a birdlike cry and, eyes popping, lunged at the boy.
Philippe, thinking it a game, ran laughing back toward the water,
behind the curtain of darkness that circled the little gathering.
One of the guests knelt next to Rosanette and began reassembling
the basket. The headman stood at the edge of the circle of light
and called out something in Yawi, as if scolding the waves,
which, Conrad could see as his eyes adjusted to the dark, glowed
with a faint phosphorescence.

Conrad whispered to Rosanette that they had best leave.
Rosanette agreed.

"Everyone looks freaked up," she replied, not quite able to
contain her laughter. As Conrad stood up, he noticed that the
offering basket was nearly all back together. He bowed to his
host and to the rest of the company, but no one returned the
salutation.

"Now we are invisible again," Rosanette laughed as they
walked away from the feast. "They have exercised us." She let
her hand brush against Conrad's.

"Invisible," he repeated, surprised at the bitterness in his own
voice. As they approached the water's edge, he looked up at the
night sky. The three stars in Orion's belt shone brightly against a
field of much fainter stars. But where was Orion's club? That was
the part Conrad could never make out. Again Rosanette's hand
brushed against his, and this time he took it. Instantly, he regretted it.

Rosanette swung around in front of Conrad and looked up into his face. Philippe circled them in the dark, involved in some game of his own, uttering high-pitched cries and flapping his arms as if they were wings. Conrad understood that he was supposed to kiss her, that an unusual alignment of celestial bodies had decreed it. He let the moment pass.

Philippe wrapped his arms around Conrad's legs, mistaking them in the dark for those of his mother. When he discovered his mistake, the boy recoiled and ran off down the beach, giggling. Rosanette gave chase, calling out in rhyming French. The laughter of mother and son trailed off down the beach, swallowed by the sound of lapping waves.

Conrad turned in the other direction and found a spot along the beach where he could hide in the shadows of the coconut trees. And then later, when it was clear that Rosanette was not coming after him, he came out to the water's edge and watched the waves breaking for a long time.

25

The clouds threatened rain as Conrad unrolled his sleeping bag, but then thinned and disappeared. He fingered the amulet for a little while, recalling Eva's hug of the previous night. Her absence pained but did not surprise him. He grew certain that he would never see her again, that the unseen machinery which had wheeled her across his path had already moved her out of reach. He clutched the amulet in his palm again, as if to squeeze out the last drop of oil. Absurd hope! Whatever magic existed would still be mitigated by his own obtuseness. Would he even have noticed that people were acting differently toward him if Romney hadn't pointed it out?

Gradually his heart stopped pounding and his breathing became more relaxed.

Eva was there next to him when he woke up, the shock of yellow hair spilling from the top of her sleeping bag onto the sand.

"Oh, I was dreaming something so strange," she said, as if they were already in the middle of a long conversation. Her lips pursed thoughtfully.

"I was trekking in the jungle with Birgit and Boon. It was some kind of big tour. There were others. You were there. With your wife, I think. But you were in the back of the group.

"We went long ways through the forest, until we found a big rock, maybe the size of a table. And flat, or little bit curved across the top. And the guides get their big sticks under this rock and pry it up. It's flat on the bottom, yeah? Underneath is—miniature city—houses and big office buildings and trains and cars and things, shining in the evening light. We see it for a moment only and then it turns to dust. They say, the guides say, it has something to do with oxygen.

"We trek on to another spot and the guides lift up another stone and there's another city underneath and everybody has their cameras out this time and they're all snapping pictures before the city dissolves. By the time we reach the fourth or fifth stone, I am telling the guides please don't, don't dig up the next one. I can't stand to see it destroyed.

"And they say, 'But you're the one that said we must dig up all the stones. You're the one that organized this whole expedition.' And I realize that they are right, I am the one. Then I wake up."

"Huh," Conrad said, after a long moment. He grew self-conscious of the graying hair on his chest and pulled the sleeping bag up to his neck.

"I met this German guy yesterday," Eva went on.

"A guy?" Conrad asked.

"Older man," Eva said. "About thirty or so."

"Oh," Conrad said, lying back down. He had not even gotten out of his bag yet and already the day was in shambles.

"He was a foreign-aid worker staying near Kuala Vimaya. He had to leave because of the crackdown. We walked up in the hills around here and all through these villages some kilometers from here."

"You were with him all day?"

"We talked about the political situation." She rolled her eyes. "For hours.

"Missed you yesterday," she said a moment later.

"I had to go into Pak Sai," Conrad said, pushing himself up on his elbow. He was wide awake now.

"I was afraid I'd made you angry yesterday," she went on. "And that's why you disappeared."

"No, no," said Conrad. "No, no." He sat up, tried not to stare. She smiled at him in a way that made his heart throttle up. Was it the oil doing this, Conrad wondered.

"I feel like it's Christmas morning," Conrad said suddenly. "And I'm seven years old."

They ate breakfast at the South Beach bungalows, for Conrad was wary of approaching the headman's house that morning, and Eva had expressed a desire for pancakes.

Rosanette sat down at their table just as they finished, expressed astonishment at their being up so early.

"There's no shade where we are," Eva explained. Conrad noticed Rosanette looking up at the word "we." Conrad was tempted to reinforce this: *Yes, we haven't found a bungalow yet.* In fact Conrad was dismayed to be sitting in yet another beachside restaurant, looking over at another cluster of tourist huts. In addition to the three existing huts, another four were under construction. The dining area was decidedly primitive, plastic chairs set around one long wooden table; but it seemed only a matter of time before a new concrete pad would be poured and regular tables and chairs acquired.

Chum, the small, dark-skinned woman who owned the place, came to clear Conrad and Eva's plates. When Conrad smiled at her, declaring her cooking "lovely," she misunderstood, apparently thinking that he was flirting with her. She retreated in an embarrassed silence behind the bamboo screen that concealed the outside cooking area.

"Conrad," Eva chided. "You must not—what is the expression? make eyes?—all of the time."

"I wasn't," Conrad insisted. "I'm just glad to be alive."

"Conrad says there is this place to swim up in the hills." Eva turned to Rosanette. "With a waterfall and the jungle all around, very private. So I think we walk up there today."

"Yes," Rosanette replied slowly. "I heard as well this place is good." When he could bring himself to do so, Conrad looked in Rosanette's direction. She moved her fingers over the space on the tabletop as if arranging a napkin, but in fact there was no napkin.

"Come with us, then," Eva urged cheerfully, probably because Rosanette looked so miserable.

Eva's invitation made Rosanette brighten, but to Conrad it felt like a punch in the stomach. To be alone with Eva—that above all else! He touched his forehead where his hairline used to start. Maybe he would try to get a bungalow. How simple it would be if he and Eva could retire there after breakfast. But somehow the thought revolted him.

"I don't think it's possible," Rosanette answered. "Philippe cannot walk so far, and he must sleep little bit in the afternoon."

"Come when he's having his nap then. Maybe Chum can watch him." Eva smiled. And Conrad saw that she wanted to please everyone, that she couldn't help it any more than sand could help being blown about in the wind, and that maybe he loved her for it.

The trail to the waterfall begins a good distance up the beach and almost immediately turns into a series of switchbacks along a steep hillside. Bamboo thickets come next, then a forest of huge trees, many of which are covered with thick vines.

Eva's ass is wider than Conrad is at first willing to acknowledge. He has had only fleeting glimpses of it before, instinctively avoiding anything that smacked of voyeurism, and he tried to cast these impressions in the best possible light. It seemed the polite thing to do, given the fact that as a man he was condemned to imagine her in various postures without clothing. But now that he is following her up the slope and into the forest, the precise dimensions of her posterior confront him at every turn. She wears a long, sleeveless dress that comes down over her knees. There are damp, sandy patches on the seat from sitting on the beach.

But what of it? Whenever she glances back over her shoulder, he peers into the eyes of his own youth; he feels a discharge of something like electricity in the humid air around him.

His own youth was squandered in laboratories and libraries under harsh fluorescent lights, in glass buildings where the windows didn't open, where he flowcharted his future, drawing arrows from one empty box to another on an endless sheet of graph paper. Yet how could it have been otherwise? The world required that youth and vitality be processed into food and shelter, demanded a progression of ever-larger paychecks, of newer and more expensive acquisitions. Even the production of children was synchronized with this industrial model, each newborn requiring progressively better equipment: car seats, baby strollers, high chairs, diapers, monitoring systems. The nurturing of infants, having taken on the trappings of a science, now seemed to require constant refinement, reinvention. And so each toddler left in his wake a string of broken toys and discarded theories, lurching forward on untried legs.

But what of it? A stillness gathers above the treetops and presses down with palpable weight, squelching all thoughts. Now Conrad is the unarmed child, moving from one empty box to another, celebrating the emptiness, the space, the weightless volume of light that fills his heart.

The path disappears beneath a tangle of tree roots. Conrad stumbles, trying not to step on the dark lines of ants that crisscross the trail. Incredibly, Eva is barefoot, her toes appearing to grip the roots as she moves up the hill. The trail grows steep. They hold on to roots and vines to pull themselves up. At the top of the rise, Eva pauses to catch her breath. A large butterfly alights on her head. She looks back at Conrad, smiling, unaware of the thing hanging from her yellow hair, slowly opening and closing its metallic blue wings.

"We're here!" she says. "I see it!"

It's like a set from a Tarzan picture, one of the old Johnny Weissmuller movies that flickered across the blue screen of his childhood TV. A long ribbon of white water pours over the top of a twenty-foot cliff, feathering as it reaches the surface of the dark pool. The water in the pool is clear, the shapes of rocks visible through the spreading ripples. Huge trees, their trunks wrapped with the thick, woody vines of strangler figs, tower over the pool. Nearby, sunlight breaks through the canopy where a big tree has fallen.

Eva drops her little daypack on the ground and turns about on her heel with arms outstretched.

"Fantastic!" she declares. "Isn't it?" And Conrad smiles, intimidated by the scene's Technicolor perfection. Who was it that had decided the place was haunted? What sort of grim event had happened here? These questions push their way to the front of the noisy queue in his head. His heart pounds for no apparent reason.

"Conrad!" Eva turns to him. "I have not felt this good in a long time. I'm so glad it's just us here."

"Yes," Conrad forces himself to utter. He feels for a moment as if he can't move, but then Eva motions for him to sit next to her on a big rock by the water's edge, and that he manages without a hitch.

"You are red, Conrad. The back of your shirt is all sweaty," she says, taking hold of his shirtsleeve between thumb and forefinger. "But the front is dry. Your body gives off heat like a refrigerator, I think."

Conrad laughs nervously, begins to shiver.

"It's too hot to keep these things on," she says, pulling her dress off over her head. She has a swimsuit on underneath. Conrad removes his own shirt slowly, shy about the state of his body, terrified of disappointment. He stares straight ahead and tries not to think about what will come next.

What comes next is that Eva removes the rest of her clothing and stretches out on the rock. Conrad watches from the corner of his eye, hugging his knees to his chest.

"Conrad," she says dreamily. "I feel so strange. The atmosphere here. Do you feel it?"

"Yes." Conrad swallows.

She sits up. Tiny bees circle her head like stars as she rummages through her little backpack. She pulls out a bit of dried green leaf from a plastic bag and a tiny brass pipe and then nods at Conrad with an inviting smile.

"Marijuana?" Conrad asks. He leans back on his arm, hoping to project a relaxed image. The arm begins to tremble, threatens collapse.

"Bought it in the marketplace in Pak Sai. In wide daylight. Can you believe it?"

"I thought the guidebook said it—"

"The guidebook!" Eva snorts. "Everyone saying the guidebook says *this* or the guidebook says *that*."

Five years in prison, Conrad thinks, looking over his shoulder as if expecting to find police coming up the path. Funny the stuff you remember.

He had smoked a little pot in college; everyone had at one time or another. Whether he'd enjoyed it was less certain. In the intervening years, the pipe had become a symbol of subversive pleasure, pleasure that cannot be earned, but only stolen.

"Come smoke with me," Eva says. "Just a little, yeah?"

He tells himself he will only puff, not inhale. But the proximity of all that exposed skin confuses him. He inhales on the pipe as she inserts it into his mouth, transfixed by her dreamy expression, by her half-closed eyes. She touches a fresh match to the bowl and tells him to suck harder. He does. Her face becomes the sky, the movement of eyelid and lip register as celestial events. She leans back, arms extended behind her, her aureoles like astonished eyes mirroring his own bewilderment. Conrad places a hand on her waist, but it might be a tree trunk or a weathered rock. The old categories have been swept away.

Eva stands, ties her hair. Conrad studies her profile, the slight upturn of her nose reflected in the swell of her lips, and then again in the way her breasts arch gently upward. Her entire body seems but a series of repetitions of this same gentle curve, the curve of the prow of a *kolek*, or the roofline of the temple pagoda. Eva dives into the pool headfirst, disappearing beneath the reflected green.

She stays under for a long time.

Conrad leans over the edge of the pool. A pensiveness settles over him, as if she has abandoned him. He swishes a twig over the surface of the water, not entirely certain, from one moment to the next, if it is water.

Eva comes up quietly next to where Conrad sits, her face breaking the surface without apparent noise, and reaches for him with her long, well-formed arms. He lets himself be drawn down for a kiss, then realizes too late that she means to tumble him into the water.

"Why do you keep your trousers on, old man?" she laughs, splashing water in his face as he dog-paddles around the pool, sputtering and coughing. He climbs out of the pool and removes his wrinkle-resistant slacks and his jockeys. Hurriedly he climbs back into the water, for already he has the beginnings of an erection.

"You are so big," Eva says in a teasing voice. "How big are you?"

And Conrad shakes his head, not wanting to admit that he's ever taken the trouble to measure his erection. In fact he has done so more than once, and has committed the measurements to memory—just to reassure himself that he is in the range of what might be considered normal. The length is six and a quarter inches, if measured from the curving underside, but not quite five and a half if measured from the top side. Conrad believes that he can claim six and three quarters or even seven inches without eliciting too much controversy. The circumference he finds a bit more reassuring, a solid six inches there.

"How big?" Eva presses him.

"Seven inches."

She makes a face.

"I mean, around that. Roughly," Conrad clarifies.

"What is that in centimeters?" Eva asks.

Conrad looks up at the treetops. Of course, she only knows the metric system. One inch is about 2.54 centimeters, so seven inches would be close to eighteen centimeters. But Conrad figures that probably he is closer to fifteen and a half, so he compromises and calls it sixteen. Eva is incredulous.

"You are sixteen centimeters tall?" she laughs.

"No, no. You said big—" But she has already seen through the mix-up and is helpless with laughter. She swallows some water, then clings to a rock at the side of the pool. Conrad glances down at the Buddha dangling from his neck, treads water with vigorous strokes as if trying to beat back the panic.

He swims up to her and attempts an experimental kiss. She allows his lips to brush against hers, but then laughs again.

"I don't know what is happening to me," Eva says finally. "I have never felt this way before."

Does she mean what is happening between them or just the pot, Conrad wonders. His own pulse sounds like the beating of very big wings, like monstrous raptors descending upon his head. She drapes her arms around his neck for a moment and presses her forehead against his. He would look into her eyes, but they are too close to his own. They appear as a single eye, an eye with two pupils.

Conrad pulls away, leaning into a backstroke.

"I must get out for a minute," Eva says. While Conrad paddles around, she pulls herself out of the pool, unrolls her towel on the rock and lies down.

Rosanette's voice calls up to them from the steep path.

"Hello—oh! Is it good today?"

26

"A warning shot across the bow" was how Conrad heard himself describe this sudden announcement. "She seemed afraid of catching us in the act. And I suppose I was grateful that at least *she* thought it a real possibility."

Conrad saw himself sitting in the parlor of his third-story flat on Saturn Street, drinking cup after cup of English tea.

Rosanette for him had become the embodiment of the inevitable punishment that follows moments of bliss. Conrad thought of weather systems, of high-pressure areas giving way to cold fronts, of nature correcting an imbalance in the ecology of pleasure and pain. Had he made her any promises, dropped any hints? He could think of none. Yet as she stood on the large rock, purposefully not looking at Conrad's naked form treading water at her feet, a chill came into the air. Every shift in her shoulders, every toss of her head felt like an indictment, seemed to bear witness to the pulpy creature that dwelled in his secret core.

Eva greeted Rosanette happily. They conversed in French, exchanging forced laughter. Conrad paddled toward the far side of the waterfall, the thing inside him turning, gnawing. He watched the two women from a distance. Eva once more produced her pipe. Rosanette sat down cross-legged on the rock, stiffly at first, but then with growing ease. Gradually her clothing came off, sandals first, then the blouse, then the sarong. Eva, as if seeing Conrad for the first time, waved him over.

The three of them sat quite close together on the rock, Conrad and Eva face-to-face, Rosanette in between, shoulders, arms, outer thighs touching as they huddled around the pipe. Rosanette looked at Conrad with simple sadness, plaintively, as if mentally cataloguing the pleasures they might have shared. She brought the pipe to his lips and murmured approvingly as the last bit of bud glowed in the bowl and then went dark. Conrad exhaled with relief. Perhaps everything would be okay after all.

The pipe was reloaded; Conrad drew on it once more. Everything seemed drowned in the midday stillness. No one spoke for a long time, as if the three of them had become statues or were playing at being statues, like the gold- and silver-painted actors who struck poses on the park benches around Union Square in San Francisco. Conrad wondered how he would ever make it back down to the village, back home.

"Back home," he said out loud and laughed. The women looked up at him as if startled from a deep, silent communion.

"Back home," Conrad said again, as if to beat back the encroaching stillness. He fingered the amulet that hung about his neck. He should take these women home with him, back to San Francisco. That's what he should do.

"Life in a bauble," he said a moment later. It was the punch line of a well-known joke, but nobody laughed. Nonetheless, Rosanette laid her head against his shoulder and patted his leg just above the knee.

Eva looked on placidly. Rosanette's hand traveled up and down Conrad's thigh. A distant alarm sounded. She was staking her claim. Conrad's heart did something like a hiccup. He wanted to raise his voice against the sad inevitability of it all, but part of him, the bigger part, still didn't believe any of it was happening.

It was happening. Eva smiled at them indulgently. She stood and stretched. For the last time Conrad scaled her body's wonderful escarpment with his eyes. It was the granite face of El Capitan or the Matterhorn. He felt tiny and helpless before it.

"Are you going?" he heard himself ask. Eva smiled down on him from a great distance as she slipped her dress back on. She made some vague excuse for leaving. The sense of her words did not register.

After Eva left, Conrad remained seated for a long time with Rosanette's head resting on his shoulder. The weight of her head suggested a sadness contained within. The realization that she felt wretched and alone came as no surprise; it had been there all along. Conrad had simply been unable to feel it before. Somebody had decreed that they should be each other's consolation. But Conrad was not in the mood to be consoled.

Rosanette's hand discreetly withdrew from his leg. He sensed her growing trepidation, shame at her own forwardness. Reflexively he stroked her hair, as if to reassure her. But this she interpreted as a caress, and slowly brought her hand back to his thigh.

Sweat began trickling down behind his ear. Why couldn't he untangle himself? He would break free, dig a cigarette out of his shirt pocket and contemplate his misery behind a screen of smoke. It distressed him that the unwanted hand could work the same changes on his body as the desired one. That an oblique glimpse of Rosanette's lolling breasts created much the same effect in him as the prolonged frontal viewing of Eva's torso. That Eva's condescending smile had fixed his place in the firmament of sexual relations, and that the motions he'd gone through were not his own, but merely the turning of the celestial sphere to which he found himself bound.

Rosanette tilted her expectant face up toward Conrad's. He let her lips press against his in a tentative way. He wondered just how far, out of sheer politeness, he would let things go.

"I didn't sleep last night," she said. "Seeing your face . . ."

"I'm sorry," Conrad apologized. He pulled himself away from her and fetched his cigarettes. He lit one for her and then for himself and they reclined on the flat rock, heads pillowed by their mounded clothing. Conrad struggled to say something, to explain himself, but the cannabis was too strong, and so he stared up at the canopy and said nothing.

Rosanette seemed to sleep. Something like an hour went by, maybe a year.

A large bird, black with a huge curving beak and a red and yellow casque, like a horn, growing out of its bill, swooped down from the treetops and landed on the other side of the pool. It cocked its head back and forth as if viewing Conrad from several different angles; and then, when Conrad moved his hand to brush a bug away, the great bird took off with a peculiar honking noise. The noise awoke Rosanette.

"What was that?" She started up. "Is it late?"

"I can't tell," Conrad admitted. "I need to wake up."

Conrad stretched and then slipped into the water.

"Hey, we will swim to the bottom, yes?" Rosanette said, jumping in beside him.

Conrad treaded water for a moment, and then followed her down. She signaled to him to lie next to her on the bottom, to gaze up with her at the sky, as if they were sunbathing. She laughed; large bubbles escaped from her mouth as she settled down on her back, hands clasped behind her head. Too buoyant to join her, Conrad clung to a rock; he was afraid to release the air in his lungs, afraid he would forget where he was and try to inhale the water. Rosanette tugged on his wrist, gestured for him to look up.

The rippling surface seemed miles away, a distant dome of green glass. The disorientation Conrad feared crept over him. Everything felt normal, as if he sat in his own living room looking up through a skylight. But then a figure appeared in that skylight. He saw the dark outline of a head, face obscured in shadow. An optical illusion? he wondered. A contorted reflection of his own face? He looked to Rosanette for confirmation. Huge bubbles escaped from her mouth—more laughter. And then Conrad's air was used up and he found himself rushing to the surface.

Waterfall, rocks, sky, jungle—the familiar categories reasserted themselves as Conrad breached. Looking down on him from the big flat rock was Eva.

"You came back!" Conrad nearly shouted.

"Rosanette," Eva said, looking past Conrad to where

Rosanette now surfaced. "There is a problem back at the bunga-lows. You must come quickly."

She said something else in French and abruptly Rosanette climbed out of the water and threw on her clothes without both-ering to dry off.

27

They vanished down the trail before I had a clue what was going on," Conrad heard himself saying back in his parlor, by his fireplace, while fronds and branches came whipping past him. "I knew something awful had happened, and I couldn't stand the idea of her suffering."

For no reason he pictured the white crown molding in his re-Victorianized parlor. Twenty-five dollars a foot it had cost him, and the antique chandelier Lucy had "scored" at a salvage yard in Berkeley was no bargain, either. It seemed to Conrad that he was piloting a helicopter, flying low over the forest canopy, or simply watching video images from the camera mounted in the chopper's nose. The jungle below him looked immense, suitable for dinosaurs, although it was really (let's be clear about this) just some underbrush he was wading through. The fireplace in the parlor was not really much, either, a shallow, decorative affair originally meant for burning coal. Perhaps he could fix it so that it would burn coal again, hard lumps of black coal, producing a fire appropriate for brandy in expensive snifters. Not that he usually drank brandy, or much of anything else, at least not before arriving on this island. Always the Boy Scout, somebody had to drive. And wasn't it dangerous to be running down the hill at this speed? Weren't there protruding roots or snakes to consider? But he was a hunter, tracking the wonderful swirl of textures and smells receding before him.

"The voice of reason called for caution, but I pressed on, a man possessed." Obviously untrue, if he could simultaneously experience the thing and recount it, but there was the fact of the dank grittiness of his trousers shifting around his running legs

and the displaced panic rising in him that wasn't so much a feeling as a large parcel that was still in the process of being delivered. The forest gave way to banana plants, the bananas to coconut groves, and then he was on the beach, running in the direction of the bungalows. His pace slowed when he hit the sand. He saw no sign of Rosanette or Eva. For a moment he doubted he was running in the right direction, or even on the right beach.

But it was just the cannabis making short distances longer. The village appeared and rolled past, and then the bungalows appeared amid the ocean-leaning palms. Rosanette's was the first.

Conrad stopped at her bungalow, forgetting at first why he'd come. Inside he saw two beds, platforms with thin foam mattresses. Philippe's was the one with the crayons and the sketchbooks scattered across the sheets. Conrad sat on the edge of the bed and thumbed through one of the sketchbooks. Lots of undersea pictures, scuba divers, and sea serpents. And here was a seven-headed snake from Wat Tara what-do-you-call-it.

"Why am I here?" he asked out loud, and then recalled Eva's breathless return to the waterfall. All this seemed like years ago. The shadowy places in the hut were alive with swirling sparks, the cannabis again. Outside he heard Rosanette's voice, calling for Philippe. She sounded far off. Conrad could just make out her son's name. Inexplicably, he pictured the boy biting someone. Conrad became convinced that this was the nature of the emergency, but at the same time could not think why he was so certain. After a moment, Conrad recognized his prediction as a memory. Of course! The boy had bitten him. But that was ancient history.

"Philippe!" Rosanette's voice sounded louder. Conrad went outside.

Farther down the beach, past the house where the owners lived, a small group of people, both tourists and Tambralingans, stood at the water's edge. From their midst came a high-pitched wail, unmistakably Rosanette's. Philippe lay sprawled on the sand before her, his face white, bloodless.

A glance conveyed the whole story: the young man who

worked at the restaurant stood next to Rosanette, holding the de-
flated water wings. The boy had awakened from his nap early,
had apparently become bored and swum out past the coral, somehow puncturing his water wings. It had been midday and Chum's
girl, or whoever Rosanette had charged with watching the boy,
had been asleep herself. No one had seen Philippe struggling in
the water. Or perhaps the young man had seen, but being unable
to swim could not help.

Rosanette, still crouching by the body, turned and yelled something in French at the top of her lungs. The young man gazed at
her serenely. One of the other Tambralingans smiled. Somewhere
in the convoluted folds of Conrad's cortex, he registered that this
was not a happy smile, but some other kind of smile, a smile that
wasn't used in the West.

Rosanette focused on Conrad.

"You!" she cried. "You!"

Conrad staggered. The boy was dead.

"You!" she cried again.

"An accident—" he started to say, and then accepted the
blame, like a blow to the gut. Yes, his fault, his conniving. He put
his hand on his stomach. But I'm not a villain, he thought.

"You! You! You!" This was apparently the only English word
Rosanette could remember at the moment. She signaled Conrad
to come to her. Conrad touched his fingers to his chest as if to ask
if it was he she wanted. She nodded furiously, pointing to the
boy's ashen face. Suddenly it clicked.

Conrad knelt in the sand and lifted the boy's head so that air
might pass easily through the trachea. He put his lips on the boy's
mouth and blew. The little chest inflated. He took another breath
and blew again. The boy's lips were cold, like the mouthpiece of a
snorkel. Rosanette put her ear to the chest and then prodded it.
Conrad blew again and again, until he grew dizzy, then pressed
gently on the chest with one hand.

"Harder!" Rosanette urged him, forcing his hand down.

"No," Conrad said. "It'll break his ribs." Her lips drew back
to reveal her teeth, her eyes glistened like an animal's.

"Faster, then!" She pushed on Conrad's hand.

"No!" he shouted. "You're crushing him, for Christ's sake!" It occurred to Conrad that she had no idea how to do CPR, that no one else on the beach had the slightest idea of how to proceed, that the body—that is, the boy—had lain on the beach for God knows how long before anyone had noticed.

He delivered another breath, then spread the boy's arms out. A little water dribbled out of Philippe's mouth. Rosanette cried out, something midway between hope and terror.

"Okay, a little faster then," Conrad said as he pushed repeatedly on the boy's chest. Rosanette began to calm down. Conrad's own heart pounded as the ugly reality of the scene sunk in. Again the rubber lips against his, the taste of seawater and regurgitated noodles, again the hand on the chest pressing down, again folding the arms over, then the lips again and the impression of the entire mouth shriveling, growing colder. How long had he been doing this? It felt like hours.

He pushed on, Rosanette fairly yelling in his ear, pleading with him, with God, in French. She hovered so close, she seemed to be on top of him, and in a weird moment of wandering attention, he pictured her mounted on his back, flourishing a riding crop. Gradually it became clear that his efforts were not going to suffice. When he sat up to rest for a moment, Rosanette held the boy's chin and slapped his cheek. She slapped it again, noticeably harder, and there was nothing, not even a red mark in the ashen skin. But then, how could there be a red mark, Conrad thought. That would mean the heart was working. On the other hand, some kind of circulation had to be going on, some kind of respiration had to be occurring in the boy's cells.

Rosanette slapped the boy again, yelling loudly in his ear. Conrad took hold of her wrist.

"You'll break his jaw," he said.

"What! What can I do?" She yelled this in his face.

They must take the boy to a hospital or a clinic, Conrad explained. Some place that had the electric paddles they used to shock the heart back into action. Much of this he had to pantomime to Rosanette in between delivering breaths to the body. To the Tambralingans it must have looked like some kind of ritual. But Rosanette got the idea and ran off to find a vehicle that would take them into town.

Miraculously, the bemo had just arrived minutes before. Conrad scooped up the body, rushed with it up to the road where Rosanette was waiting with the bemo. Conrad scrambled in the back and resumed CPR. The frantic Rosanette was coaxed into taking a seat next to the driver. The bemo lurched as the driver threw it into first—new clutches seemed to be illegal in this country—just as Conrad lowered his head to deliver another breath. The boy's teeth came up hard against Conrad's lips. The taste of blood at first brought hope, until Conrad realized that it was his own and not the boy's blood that felt so warm against his tongue.

As he attempted to deliver another breath, the boy's mouth jumped up again, harder this time, and as the head fell back, the face looked pinched and nasty, a hatchet carved in the likeness of a face.

Jesus, Conrad thought. I've never been this high before.

28

Conrad loses his seat on the next bump, first slamming his head against the bemo's ceiling, then sprawling on the metal floor with the boy's body splayed across his chest. He puts the body back on the bench and then kneels before it, bare knees on the metal floor. A bolt in the floor catches his eye, and he stares at it for a moment as it orbits around in its hole. The boy's lips feel like plastic. Breathing into plastic lips, this is what he does for a living. He's been at it for twenty years or more.

He delivers another breath. The little chin jabs his nose as he pulls away. It's a tough job, one that requires perseverance and timing. Timing above all else.

He delivers another breath, a long one, while the bemo rattles over what must be a field of rubble, and the little arms flail around his head, boxing his ears. It's a tough job, but someone has to do it. God knows he is ready for a vacation, a long sabbatical.

The drive will not be quick. Conrad remembers how the road meanders through rocky hills, in places blocked with fallen trees or rain-filled potholes so big one might expect to find ducks and fish in them.

From time to time the horror of what he is doing gathers inside him. He is kissing a corpse, and he must go on kissing it for all eternity. Because not to kiss it means that it is all his fault that the corpse is a corpse and not a boy, means that Conrad will have to tell the mother riding up front that it is a corpse. But the horror soon fades before the challenge of the task, and slowly the whole experience changes into something different, a set of motions divorced from any purpose, an elaborate ritual in which the body is only a prop.

Conrad pushes on the chest and it seems to him that something cracks. It's hard to be certain with the background noise of screeching metal, the struggling engine, the spinning tires as the bemo rattles uphill. The body is coming apart, he thinks. The bemo is shaking to pieces. Everything is disintegrating. He works the little arms, which are no longer arms, but more like stems of kelp, cold rubbery appendages. And now a cry issues from the little mouth; or is it bolts in the floor squeaking? He looks through the back window of the cab, at Rosanette's face plastered against the glass, staring, grimacing, lips moving silently, praying perhaps. On with the show, he thinks.

He inhales and delivers another breath to the boy's body. The process suddenly ceases being familiar. Now each act becomes utterly novel, as if he is performing it for the very first time. My lips on his lips, he thinks—how absurd! The air streaming out of my body and into his—who would believe it possible? Now I bring his hands together. Is he applauding? Everything is changed now. From now on everything will be different. Every sensation, every thought, every event will be something entirely new.

The horn sounds, announcing their arrival at the outskirts of town. The bemo comes to a halt before a farmer driving a flock of ducks across the road. Tiny children, naked from the waist down, wave from the roadside.

"Bye-bye!" they scream. Their one word of English, the seed from which their future livelihoods will grow, Conrad hears himself think. *Welcome in Ko Neak Pean! Have best and cheapest hotel for you! Have nice day!* The bemo lurches forward again, but soon they are on pavement and the ride grows smooth.

Conrad returns to his work, pushes faster on the boy's chest. Peripherally he is aware of the buildings alongside the road and the bemo turning one way and then another and the smell of the harbor and the noise of traffic and then the glass doors of the medical clinic behind them. The bemo stops and still Conrad continues with the CPR. Who knows? It might just make the difference. And then two stocky nurses appear at the open back of the bemo, and at the sight of their starched white caps, caps Conrad hasn't seen since his own childhood, Conrad feels his grip on the boy relax and something like hope fills his chest. He delivers a final breath and then hands the boy to the nurses. Their plump warm fingers brush against his own; he senses competence, strength, safety in their touch. For Christ's sake, everything is going to be okay. They've made it in time.

He climbs out of the bemo and faces Rosanette for a moment. It seems like a year since he has been able to stand up straight. Perhaps he has never stood at his full height before. In her face he sees the same hope he feels, and for a moment thinks she means to embrace him. But she brushes by him instead and he thinks, Of course, of course. She thinks I'm the cause of all of this. Why would she embrace me? The monstrous weight of what's happened settles on his shoulders and he slumps after her, through the glass doors of the clinic building, past the unmanned front desk, and into an examining room in the back.

Everything is clean and cool inside, a sanitary oasis in the midst of the dirty little town. Everything says safety, says control. The walls are painted a light yellow, cheerful without seeming flippant. Fluorescent lights hang from the ceilings, off at the moment, their long tubes like cylinders of ice. It's a little dark in here, but the nurses seem unconcerned. They're used to it. Conserving electricity and all that.

Philippe is placed on an examining table and one of the nurses feels his pulse. At any minute the technician will arrive with the paddles and someone will yell "Clear!" or the local equivalent, and the boy will start breathing on his own and then Conrad will think about getting himself something to eat.

The other nurse comes around to the foot of the table and takes Philippe's foot and begins massaging it. Probably some Oriental thing that's going to help his kidneys, Conrad thinks. The shock of the paddles probably has some side effects. It takes a minute for Conrad to remember that no one has yet produced the paddles. He watches the panic grow on Rosanette's face. She speaks rapidly in French, which no one understands. The nurse at the head of the table leans down and listens to Philippe's chest. Conrad feels his delicate optimism start to disintegrate.

"The paddles," he says to the head nurse. He grasps two imaginary paddles in his hands and then mimes their application to the boy's chest. They look at him, uncomprehending.

"The paddles," he says again, although he knows it's not the right word. "You know—the electric—electricity?"

The nurse at the head of the table shakes her head.

"No electric. To-day black-out. Toe-tall."

She actually smiles as she says this. Everyone smiles in this country. Part of the language. A whole lexicon of grin. This one says: "Sorry, we can only go through the motions."

Rosanette also goes through the motions, tearing her hair, pounding on the wall, screaming at the placid Tambralingan faces gathered around the table. Conrad, not believing, reaches for the light switch. He flicks it and looks up dumbly at the fluorescent bulbs, expecting them to flicker on. See, he will tell them. Problem solved.

But there is no light. In fact, the room is quickly darkening as the sun slips behind the mountain. Someone appears with a kerosene lantern.

"Sore-ree," the head nurse is saying to Rosanette. She signals to the other nurse to stop massaging the boy's feet. It's over, then, Conrad thinks as the sheet is pulled over the body. Maybe he's been dead all along. For hours maybe. How long were they at the waterfall? An eternity. He cannot get a grasp on time just now. The cannabis, of course. All of those synapses firing. Irrelevant thoughts. Inappropriate thoughts. He looks at Rosanette and remembers how she looks with her clothes off, and then how hungry he is. The guilt is more a physical sensation, a sort of napalm eating away at his stomach. He touches his stomach, is surprised to find it intact.

The boy is placed on a cart and wheeled into another room. Conrad looks at Rosanette, who has collapsed on the floor, sobbing. No one has made a move to help her. The Tambralingans stand around looking embarrassed. This is not the way to behave. Conrad finds himself following the body.

"Where are you taking him?" he calls out, confused. It occurs to him again that the boy is dead, that in one sense it doesn't matter where they take him. The nurse pushing the cart replies over her shoulder with something that sounds like "bathroom," but which Conrad later figures out is "back room." He follows her down a short hallway and into a large, dark room. It's little more than a shed attached to the back of the building. The walls are made of woven bamboo; he can see the diminished sunlight shining through the slats. The floor is not even concrete but pounded earth. Tiny flies swarm in the thin shafts of light shining through the bamboo walls. A faint barnyard smell pervades the area.

"What is this?" Conrad asks. "Somebody's garage?"

"Back room, back room," the nurse replies sharply.

"What happens now?" Conrad asks.

"Monks come," she says, touching her throat. "Take to *wat*."

Conrad pictures a big fire on a brick platform. A little pot of ashes, packed in their luggage with their souvenirs.

"No. They won't want that," he says, blinking, as his eyes adjust to the semi-darkness. The nurse's nose and lips are small and well formed, like those on a doll's face. The vein in her throat pulses visibly. The effect of the oil? Or has he been staring at her like this from the start?

Conrad turns to the cart with the sheet draped over it. He notices a window at the far end of the room and the outline of what might be a door. He's in no hurry to return to the examining room, to Rosanette's howling. It's easier in here. Everything has been resolved. He wanders around the perimeter of the room, running his hand along the bamboo until he comes to the door. He tries it. It opens onto a little street. Of course, he thinks, all the streets in this town are little. Maybe the monks come through this door. Maybe they arrive in the middle of the night and take whatever's available for cremating.

The nurse makes a shushing noise. Some sort of admonishment. He turns and smiles at her and she backs her way out of the room. He'd prefer to be cremated himself when the time comes, but Rosanette is undoubtedly a Catholic. She'll want the body.

29

Conrad found his way back into the clinic building. Rosanette was now in the front room, seated in a chair, very quiet. An official-looking man stood at the front desk, holding what looked like a passport.

"Ah—Mr. Lamb-burro?" the official asked.

"It's Lamoureux," Rosanette corrected. Conrad looked past Rosanette to the street sloping down to the waterfront. The clinic building afforded a wonderful view of the harbor. One could walk right out the door and down to the pier and wait for the ferry to Ko Banteay. If one had one's money and passport with one.

"Mr. Lamoureux," the official said. Conrad looked at him, then at Rosanette. Her eyes had dark circles around them, the mask of a raccoon.

"I am grieved for your son," the official said. He placed his palms together and bowed slightly. Did that mean he was a Buddhist? How did the Moslems do it, he wondered.

"My son—" Conrad said slowly. This was not the time to go into the particulars of his relationship with Rosanette.

"Sorry now bring this up to you, but tomorrow police here." The official straightened his tie and turned his eyes upward for a moment, as if straining for a word. He smiled briefly at Conrad, a smile that said he couldn't think of the words and that this caused him some embarrassment, given the situation. He turned around and pulled some forms from a plastic rack hanging on the wall.

"Oh. Paperwork," Conrad said. He remembered vividly the long line in the consulate in San Francisco, and the long minutes he'd spent filling out the visa forms. Leaving the country with a body must involve an entirely different set of papers.

"Yes, paperwork," the official said.

"He doesn't understand what I say," Rosanette said. Her voice was flat, empty.

Conrad spelled "Philippe Lamoureux" for the man twice, very slowly. He spelled "Belgium" also, taking great care to differentiate "g" from "e." There was also the father's name (Jean), and the father's father's name, and the father's mother's name. Likewise with the other side of the family. There was date of birth, weight, height, and color of hair and eyes. Religion. Cause of death. Circumstances surrounding. Emergency measures taken. The question of exactly where the boy died. All these questions Rosanette answered slowly and Conrad rephrased carefully and the official recorded meticulously, word for word.

Conrad tensed his knees and then his abdomen, bearing down on an upwell of panic. The questions would never stop. The cannabis, initially energizing, now pressed down on him with a great weight.

"Please sign," the official said with a little smile, no doubt meant to convey sympathy and regret, but which nevertheless to Conrad suggested sadistic pleasure. Rosanette got up from her chair and signed the bottom of the form, then urged Conrad to do the same.

"Jean Lamoureux," she dictated softly. "Just do it, please. I must get the body on the plane quickly. The heat and flies—" She inhaled audibly and held her breath for a moment. "I can't wait for Jean to come back here."

"Okay, okay." Conrad stared at the paper. It seemed that he was being asked to sign a confession, to state categorically his part in the boy's death. He began to sign his own name, but then caught himself. How was it his fault exactly? Never mind, the body was no doubt already beginning to rot. He had to be quick. He wrote the name of Rosanette's husband carefully across the bottom of the page, skillfully covering over the partial name he'd written earlier. He found himself speculating how exactly the body would be packaged for its journey home. Innumerable times he'd heard of "arrangements" being made to transport "remains," but never a hint as to the gritty details of the process.

Rosanette turned her wonderfully large eyes toward him and for the first time since the waterfall really looked at him. It was not a withering look. It did not condemn. It merely asked in blank wonder: Who are you, anyway?

More forms followed: one for permission to transport the body by air. Another for police headquarters in the capital. Another form to be given to Belgian customs. And finally, a statement that the body would not be used as a container for transporting drugs or weapons or any other contraband, and that the signatories understood that the body might be X-rayed, examined, and "aggressively probed" prior to loading.

The official began explaining how the body should be transported to the mainland. They would need to find a suitable box— preferably of wood, but cardboard would do. After the police checked the body and signed the papers, they would have to find a fisherman who would take them to the mainland. This would be expensive. Fishermen were superstitious and didn't like transporting bodies, especially those of drowning victims. Often it was necessary for the police to force them.

"But now is no possible for fish'men boat leave Ko Neak Pean. Army say no boats come and go. Is—blockade—this island. Only ferryboats can sail."

The army had blockaded the sea around the island, Conrad realized. Looking for the fugitive.

"Don't the police or army have a boat?" Rosanette demanded.

The official explained, in his tortured English, that the police were every bit as superstitious as the fishermen, although they would not admit it. They would offer some other excuse, but they wouldn't take the boy.

"I will talk to them," Rosanette declared flatly. Her face was hard.

"Why not just take him on the ferry?" Conrad asked. The official smiled at him in a wincing fashion.

"Not permitted, sir," he said softly.

"When is the blockade finished, then?" Rosanette demanded.

"Two day," the official smiled, holding up two fingers. "Maybe three day." He looked to Conrad like he was giving the victory sign or flipping him off British style. For a slight fee, he added, the monks at Wat Tara Sek would cremate the body and provide customary funeral rites. Then it would be much easier finding a boat.

Rosanette poured her glistened face into her hands. Conrad sensed the whitewater of rage and nausea churning inside her. He felt it, too, as he stammered his protests, and started mentally listing the resources available to him: his U.S. citizenship, his credit cards, his relatively imposing physical stature. The official beamed at him, a smile of supplication and meditative amusement. It recalled for Conrad the condescending smiles of beaded women in long skirts who worked the health-food stores of his youth, peering at him through half-closed lids, all snuggled up with their esoteric know-how. Where were these showcases of self-possession now, he wondered. Somewhere in Oregon selling Chinese herbs out of the trunks of their Volvos? Retailing organic impotence drugs over the Web?

"I will do everything done," the official said firmly.

"He says he will do everything possible to speed up the process," Conrad translated. And then, softly, in French, he apologized to her. The small voice that came from his mouth sounded pitiful to his own ears. A little boy asking to be excused.

She didn't seem to hear him, and that was good. When Conrad tried to take her hand, she pushed his away violently. That was also good. In fact, it made him feel better.

"We have to go," he said softly. She let him guide her out of the office. Moist, sultry air came up the street from the ocean, pulsing against their faces with the slightest pressure. The street was alive with young people, new arrivals in their languid pajamas. Some in white, others hued in tropical colors, they waved their arms around in amazement, calling to each other in German or English or French. How wonderful, Conrad thought, to be arriving just now.

30

Henceforth the scene outside the clinic would be the setting for many of Conrad's dreams. And each of these dreams would inevitably produce the same revelation, that the boy was not dead, but merely unconscious. Some versions had Philippe falling into a coma from the bite of a venomous sea snake. Conrad would escort Rosanette outside only to find the streets flooded, wriggling with snakes, and he would exclaim something like "Of course!" or "Eureka!" In other versions it would simply occur to Conrad that they'd made a terrible mistake and, rushing back into the morgue, he would find Philippe sitting up, wailing with terror. In any case, the shock would be enough to wake Conrad, and he would spend the rest of the night sitting up in a chair, afraid of closing his eyes.

Conrad would console himself with the notion that dreamers often revisit traumas they were unable to fully assimilate at the time of their occurrence. But in his case, the sense of reality that pervaded these dreams was far greater than the one that was with him when he stepped out into the street. Eva's Thai stick was still with him; he imagined his lungs might be permanently coated with the residue, for now and then all sense of volition would evaporate and he would feel himself turning into something like a rubber ball, ricocheting from wall to wall.

Obsessively, his mind arranged and rearranged events. And sometimes a pattern would emerge in which all evil began with his snatching the amulet back from Romney, with the joyful certainty he'd felt as his fist closed around it.

For Rosanette, the reality seemed much simpler. She spoke only of the body, of saving the body, of getting the body off the is-

land before it was devoured by vermin or cremated accidentally through some kind of misunderstanding.

"But he's dead," Conrad wanted to say to her as they went down the street toward no place in particular. "What does it matter now?"

She followed him past the marketplace and up the hill. My shadow, Conrad thought. Why was she doing this? Surely she could see that he'd already provided what help he could. That he'd suffered enough.

"I can't wait for Jean," Rosanette repeated endlessly, as they climbed the hill. "I must go find my husband." And then, as the Princess Daha came into view, she took hold of his arm. They must steal the body, she said, conceal it in a box or a bag and take it on the ferry back to Ko Banteay. Her nails seemed to penetrate his shirt. That very night, before anyone was the wiser. On Ko Banteay she would find Jean and get a speedboat back to Nagaseri.

She brought her face close to Conrad's, so that once again he could detect her scent. Conrad recognized the bond between them, something as tenuous and tough as spider silk, felt her looping it around him with deft movements of eyes and lips.

"I'll do it," he said finally. "Whatever it takes."

The absurdity of their plan did not occur to Conrad until they arrived back at Lanka Suka. He could barely look at Eva, even as he hugged her goodbye. "I will see you in Nagaseri?" she'd asked tearfully and he'd said of course, I'll be at the Hotel Butterworth, a name he drew out of thin air.

As they put Conrad's duffel and Rosanette's luggage in the trunk of the waiting taxi, a small group of villagers gathered to watch. The story had gone around that Philippe had offended Sang Kala, the demon that ruled during midday, dusk, and midnight—this according to Eva. Conrad began to worry that the story might get to the ferry before they did, that they would be spotted and apprehended before they even got close to the boat.

Rosanette wept softly all the way back to Pak Sai, and Conrad was left alone with his worries, which, like exhausted runners, limped around the same track again and again. Perhaps he fell asleep on the way back. In any event, he was still groggy when he and Rosanette went to buy the ferry tickets at the little booth near the pier. He let Rosanette do the talking, listened dumbly to the tortured conversation with the ticket seller, the confusing details of price and schedule, the predictable mangling of syntax and pronunciation. Yet eventually the moment arrived when the transaction was finished and Rosanette was shoving a ticket at him.

"And now go away, please. I see you on the ship. Right now— I haven't more patience to—" She rolled her hand in the air as she tried to summon the words. "See you again."

"She hates me," Conrad realized. It astonished him that she could hate him when he was trying so hard to help. But as he walked away, shoulders rising into a familiar hunch, it began to make sense again.

He found a restaurant nearby, a Chinese place that sold noodle soups and tall bottles of beer, and decided to wait there until nightfall. He was hungry and exhausted and soaked with sweat. He stared hopefully at the big fan in the doorway, waiting for the power to come back on.

The plan was simple. He would enter the morgue through the alley doorway and stuff the body into his duffel. The body was quite small, the duffel only partly full. He could arrange the sleeping bag inside the duffel to minimize the odd bulges the body would make. Then out the back door and down to the pier just as the ferry took off. If anyone tried to stop him, he still had all of the official papers on him. He would act the bereaved father, wave the papers around in a desperate show of grief. And if they asked to see his passport, he might summon a look of outrage and push past. It could work. But why would anyone stop him?

In the street a squadron of soldiers moved slowly past, automatic rifles slung low, barrels angled toward the ground. One of the soldiers paused to peer into the restaurant, craning his neck as if looking for somebody. Conrad slumped a little in his chair, felt the absurd fear that they were looking for him, the oversized foreigner. What he and Rosanette were attempting suddenly seemed like complete madness. But there it was; he'd promised her. She'd be waiting on the boat.

About the time the noodle soup arrived, Romney came into the restaurant, looking flushed. He glanced nervously over his shoulder as he sat down at Conrad's table.

Army units looking for Sonny Tatoh, he explained after a perfunctory greeting. He'd heard that they'd landed all over the island, that they were making a sweep of the town and all the villages.

"They shoot people," Romney confided as he lit a cigarette, "somewhat arbitrarily."

"Tourists?"

"They don't like journalists."

"You're not a journalist?"

"No, but I ask a lot of questions. It amounts to the same thing."

Conrad slurped his noodles thoughtfully.

"And they're after this Sonny character because he led a protest?"

"They say his organization traffics in human beings. Sex slaves, organ donors. Children. They say they have evidence. Bodies."

Conrad drank his beer slowly. He took his amulet off and laid it on the table.

"You wanted this. Why? You really believe it's got some kind of power?"

Romney shrugged, picked up the piece nonchalantly.

"I'm an ethno-pharmacologist. I study things like this. I thought I'd told you. I have a theory about murdered man oil."

Conrad took a sip of beer.

"About it being like an aphrodisiac?" he asked.

Romney tilted his head back and laughed at the ceiling fan.

"If only it were that simple. It might be that certain compounds appear in the tissues of dying men who have undergone some sort of massive trauma. Perhaps certain organic molecules absorbed through the skin or through the mouth might subtly change a person's chemistry, imbue them with 'chemistry,' if you will."

"And I suppose you've got a grant from some university to study this?"

"They laughed at me at the university," Romney said, tapping his finger against his cheek. "They said I was mad."

"Oh," Conrad said after a moment. "You're making a joke."

More soldiers went by, a big loud bunch of them.

"They seem happy to be off the mainland," Romney said, holding the amulet up in front of his face. "Probably think they're going to get laid tonight."

He looked at Conrad as if expecting a response to this remark, but Conrad did not provide one.

"There may be some commercial potential here," Romney went on. He made a face at the amulet still dangling in front of him, as if he'd discovered some sort of flaw in it. He wasn't advocating mass-production, of course. Heaven forbid! He'd been thinking solely in terms of niche marketing—very small, very specialized.

Conrad looked at his watch and then at the smooth, intent young face. He grasped his bottle by its neck and lifted it an inch off the table. The bottle was still nearly full. He put it back down and then got out of his chair.

"Well, good luck," he said, extending his hand. "Whatever you decide to do with it."

The darkening street filled with soldiers as Conrad approached the clinic building. Where was the access to the back alley? As he attempted to circle around to the back of the building, he came across a group of soldiers who seemed to be guarding the alley. They looked at Conrad curiously as he turned in their direction. Their apparent leader, a slight man not more than five feet tall dressed in green fatigues, stood in the center of the alley, arms held behind his back. He had no gun. He simply smiled at Conrad and that was enough.

What seemed like several minutes passed before Conrad was able to make himself enter the clinic through the front door.

31

Conrad knelt by the cot, which now held only some of his dirty laundry bunched together under a sheet, and pretended to pray, just in case someone came in and found him there. He had not yet worked up the nerve to hoist the boy, now hidden in his duffel, over his shoulder and to walk back out into the street. He was stalling, afraid that if he left too soon, the fraud would be discovered and the soldiers would seize him as he tried to board the ferry. In California there were laws against hauling corpses around. At least, he expected that there would be. If her son had drowned there, Rosanette would have been cited for criminal negligence at the very least. That's the way Americans were about accidents. It had to be an adult's fault. Tambralingans blamed spirits. The important thing was that someone got blamed, that accidents were not allowed to remain random events.

Two nurses entered, wheeling in another body, an old woman. They stared at Conrad for a moment, at his attitude of prayer. Conrad looked back dumbly over his shoulder, taking in the white coats, the starched caps, the black-framed glasses. Nurses here certainly dressed the part, anyway. Remembering that he was supposed to be praying, Conrad turned back to the pile of clothes under the sheet and began mumbling.

"Oh Heavenly Father, please bless thy gifts which we are about to receive . . ."

He repeated the prayer three times before recognizing it as the one his grandfather used to say over Thanksgiving dinner. He stopped, certain that the nurses had overheard and seen through his little ruse, that the matronly one would in the next instant yank the sheet back and call for a guard.

He resumed his praying in a louder voice. Pray that neither of the nurses can understand English, he thought. Pray that neither has been trained in a Catholic hospital, that neither of them notices I don't remember how to cross myself properly, that sweat is rolling off my neck and down my back.

The nurses began washing the new arrival and Conrad realized that it was time. He slung the duffel over his shoulder. It was important not to let the body get all bunched up at one end. He could not quite believe he was actually going through with it, but the body was so light, it felt like nothing at all. Conrad unzipped the bag at one end. Letting the air circulate seemed like a good idea, especially if he was going to cart the thing around for the next several hours. He steeled himself for a hasty exit out the front, but just as he started to leave, one of the nurses hailed him.

"Ex-cuse me, sir," she said.

Conrad turned around slowly.

"We need you take away the body," the nurse said. "You have box?"

"Oh," Conrad said, shaking his head. "I can't leave it here, huh? I mean, I can't leave the body here?"

"Sore-ree. Better you take."

"I will find a box. Can I leave it here until morning?" Conrad asked uneasily.

"Okay, okay. Till more-ning."

"Thank you. Thank you very much. God bless you."

The ferryboat was already docked when Conrad reached the pier. He hurried, afraid to run, afraid of rousing the suspicions of the two soldiers who were strolling up the pier ahead of him. Looking for Sonny, Conrad thought. The essence of Sonny.

Conrad made it aboard just as the boy hanging off the bow blew his shrill whistle and the other boy on the pier tossed the towline aboard. A one-eyed man took Conrad's ticket, slipped it into a cloth pouch hanging from his shoulder. And they were off.

The boat was ancient and slow, completely different from the one he'd taken to get to Ko Neak Pean. There was no air-conditioned cabin for well-to-do tourists, just a single enclosed deck packed with poor villagers and farmers.

Conrad waded through wicker baskets of chickens, sacks of peanuts, and netted coconuts to secure a spot far away from the other passengers. In the back by the engine housing, amid some large bundles bound with cloth and rope, he found space to un-roll his sleeping bag, which he carefully drew from his duffel. The Tambralingans didn't care to ride next to the engine, which smelled strongly of diesel, but instead placed themselves near the front and around the sides, where a few of the windows still opened. The men, Conrad noticed, seemed to prefer the sides. They talked loudly in their quacking language, struggling to make themselves heard over the ancient engine, engaged in a game that looked like dice. The women bunched together on the deck near the front, wrapped in cotton blankets. Conrad failed to see Rosanette among them.

That she might have gotten on the wrong ferry did not at first occur to Conrad. Rosanette was simply someplace else, perhaps in the little outhouse hanging off the end of the boat. But by the time the shoreline of Ko Neak Pean began rolling away into the darkness, it was clear to Conrad that Rosanette wasn't on the boat.

If she's changed her mind, she should have met me at the dock, Conrad thought as he peered through the smudged glass. It came to him then that Rosanette had boarded the ferry to Kuala Vi-maya, the one that came earlier in the evening, the one Conrad himself had nearly taken twelve days earlier.

Conrad moved back and forth before the little window, a leop-ard pacing an inadequately sized cage. How could he have let this happen? When the shoreline disappeared, Conrad went after the ticket-taker, hurling questions across the deck in a loud voice. The one-eyed man met Conrad's agitation with a somber expression. The ferry, he explained, would take nearly all night to reach Ko Banteay; the ship was full to capacity and they had to take care not to burn out the engine.

Conrad went back to his sleeping bag and lay down. He took off his money belt, rolled it up in a T-shirt, and slipped it into the sleeping bag's stuff sack. As usual, this would be his pillow. And then, in the noise of the churning engine, Conrad sought out and found a sheltering stupor, a counterweight to the growing conviction that this entire business would never end.

Conrad woke up sometime later and looked around the dimly lit interior of the boat. The other passengers had all gone to sleep. A light breeze from one of the windows cooled his forehead, which was damp with sweat. The air smelled of approaching rain. He spent a moment in anxious speculation as to how the boat might perform in a storm. The engine churned on, unperturbed. He felt for the duffel, and for a terrified moment couldn't find it. Once he had found it, he took a small flashlight from one of its side pouches, opened the bag slowly, and shined the light inside. The body, the boy, lay on his side, like one asleep. Conrad stifled a cry and switched off the light. What had he expected to find? Surely not a person, this cream-colored face, the features in their proportions still displaying the perfection of early childhood, the dark hair, now dry, striped with seaweed.

He stood up and made his way to the back of the boat. He couldn't stand to be next to the boy right now. He passed through a door that led to a narrow exterior deck in the rear. He climbed a short ladder to the top of the boat, a long flat deck piled at the center with more bits of odd cargo, tied up under tarps. The light was poor; the moon was down, and to the west a dark mass approached, swallowing up the stars. Overhead, Orion struggled against serpentine swaths of blackness.

He had to urinate. He moved to the rear starboard side and unzipped. As an afterthought he raised a moistened finger above his head. Close enough, he figured, and let fly.

The wind changed. The arc of urine swung violently to the right, then started to return to its point of origin. Conrad tried to compensate by shifting his stance, but then felt his stream break up before sudden warm gusts. There was a sound of water hitting vinyl; a long bundle on the port side was getting it. The bundle began to move. Christ! It was a person. He swung around toward the west, but the wind shifted on him again, driving him back. He bent over slightly, stood helplessly as his bladder discharged onto the deck.

The bundle sat up, looked around. Conrad zipped up hurriedly. After a minute the bundle said:

"Do you know what time it is? I think it's going to rain."

She seemed to be Australian. Conrad put out his hand.

"I guess I felt a few drops."

The bundle shifted. Conrad heard the crackling of a vinyl poncho, the unzipping of a sleeping bag. A silhouette dislodged itself from the lumps on the deck and made its way toward Conrad.

"Do you have a light? Oh, never mind. Here we go." A match flared up in her cupped hands, thrusting bits of a face from the shadows: a sharp chin, Roman nose, eyes of startling green, swatches of dirty blond hair.

"I don't sleep so well in the rain. How about you?"

Conrad explained that he was down below, that he'd just come up for air, that he'd been awakened by a nightmare.

"Yeah? About what?"

"About snakes. Finding a nest of them in my bag."

"Ugh!" she shuddered. "*Phii am*—the gibberish of the *phii*. That's what the locals call nightmares."

"Pee?" Conrad repeated uncertainly. "Oh. The spirits."

"Every little patch of ground has spirits living in it, you know. You used to see little shrines for them everywhere, those little pagoda-things on pedestals, like birdhouses."

"Right," Conrad said, remembering suddenly. "I guess I never really looked at them."

"Used to be if you got invited into a Tambralingan house, they would make an offering to the spirits so they won't attack you, make you sick. Or give you nightmares. But the people have been letting their traditions slide, yeah? And the spirits are starting to let them know that this isn't cool. Cigarette?"

"No, thanks."

"They're starting to go after tourists now. Like the kid that drowned on Ko Neak Pean. Norwegian, I think. Strong swimmer, not even far from shore, his mother and father right there. He goes down, like he's been struck by lightning. Did you hear about it?"

"Something about it."

"I heard about it in Pak Sai, from one of the locals that drive you about on their scooters? He saw the whole thing. Just took an instant, he said. The parents swam out to him as fast as they could, but it was no good."

"Maybe I'll have that cigarette if you're still offering."

Conrad lit up, saw the wavering flame reflected in her eyes. She seemed big-framed in a wholesome sort of way, and her face, Conrad decided after the flame went out, was pleasant enough. The stud in her nostril, though, reminded him of a particularly pugnacious zit.

"Spirits." Conrad exhaled. "Why would they punish a little boy over something like—"

"Not punish. It's never about punishment, exactly."

The boat hit some choppy water and lurched. The girl staggered against Conrad. He steadied her, catching a faint whiff of urine in her hair. When she regained her balance, she seemed to be standing closer to him.

A light rain commenced. They squatted down on the deck, Conrad steering her away from the area where he'd been standing, their backs to the wind. The dim light coming from inside the cabin below illuminated the rear deck and offered tantalizing hints of white-foamed waves cresting in the boat's wake.

She explained that she was coming back from Sri Kala, that she was on her way to Nagaseri. Conrad explained that he wouldn't be traveling any farther south, that he had to rendezvous with a friend on Ko Banteay. The girl said it was a shame and gave him a nudge.

He reclined, supporting himself on an elbow. The girl mirrored his position. Couldn't she see how old he was? Probably not.

They talked on. He admitted to being an American; she preferred to think of him as being from Texas, because of his size.
She asked him what he did for a living and he answered briefly
and afterward allowed her to believe he was some sort of programmer. She had worked in a travel agency in Perth and dabbled
in gemology. She'd purchased some fake sapphires in Thailand
and planned to have them set, maybe study jewelry-making herself. It didn't bother her that the stones were fakes. To the naked
eye they were indistinguishable from the real thing. The only
thing a microscopic inspection would turn up was the fact that
they had no flaw. That was how one told the difference. The real
ones had flaws.

"But you'll know they aren't real," Conrad insisted. "It's the
feeling, the belief that they're real—that's what people pay for,
isn't it?"

"I didn't actually pay for them," the girl said, leaning her head
closer to his. "Not that much, anyway." She offered him another
cigarette. He sucked on it greedily.

"What kind of car do you have?" she asked. Conrad thought
for a moment.

"A Jaguar," he lied. "Green."

"Nice!" she said. "What do you think I drive?"

"A scooter. A Vespa."

She laughed.

"That's funny. I had an Escort. I knew someone with a Vespa.
But she got hit one day. Broke both her legs."

"That's awful."

"Not really. She was kind of a bitch. Stole my boyfriend, actually. And the accident was her fault entirely."

"What hit her?"

"An Escort."

They laughed. Conrad drew her to him. She did not resist.

"That was nice," she said as their lips parted. But he could
not tell by the way she pronounced the word if it had been a
"give-me-more" nice or a "that-will-do" nice. What was worse,
he couldn't say whether or not he'd enjoyed the kiss. He lay down

on his back and felt the rain on his face. He felt the emptiness of the sea below him, the boat's bubble-like frailty. For a moment he could not locate a reason for his being there. It seemed like he'd always been floating in the darkness.

"Sleepy?" she asked, and kissed him again. So she had liked it. But what had she liked, exactly? His shadow? The sound of his voice? A profound calm settled over him. He stuck his tongue out and tasted the rain. The worst had already happened. A child was dead. And through the mechanics of a tortured syllogism, the blame had been shifted onto him, Conrad. The voices of little angels protesting his innocence had been swallowed up by a sinister thrumming, a vibration akin to the churning of the ship's engine. And from that feeling, that smoldering certainty in the pit of his stomach, he drew a peculiar strength.

She let her fingertips stray across his knuckles. He reached for her other arm, could not find it, settled for her waist. Its narrowness surprised him. She squealed in protest, maneuvered unconvincingly to elude his grasp. As she slithered against his arms, his hands found her breasts, her thighs, and began fumbling with the drawstring to her baggy cotton pants. He paused, releasing his hold, and waited, the fine rain sprinkling his expectant face. She sat up and rustled around with poncho and T-shirt. Then she leaned over him and they were both enclosed in the darkness of her poncho and her lips were brushing against his face. There was a gamy smell about her, a convoluted mixture of sweet onions and butterscotch and overripe cantaloupe, and the flesh of some fragile sea creature that was just about to go bad.

"My God," he whispered.

Her fingers forced their way into his mouth and he found himself thrusting up in mean, hard jabs. There was no thought of prolonging her pleasure with clever maneuvers of glans and fingers. Somewhere inside her was the orgasm and the race was on to claim it. Conrad's breaths came deep and fast; he felt a certain iron enter his legs and buttocks, his arms and chest. The girl rode on, unperturbed, interrupting the rhythm occasionally to bear down with a hard clasp, accompanied by a high-pitched wheezing noise, not unlike her laughter. He felt a warm seepage about his thighs, and with this came the sudden fear of infection and images of the dozen or so unsheathed cocks she might have taken inside of her since leaving home. But the mechanism of worry broke under her weight, and with it went the coherence of his perceptions. They came at him in fragments—a bit of hair, a flick of tongue, the heavy air, engine noise, squeeze of muscle, grappling fingers—like pieces of someone else's mind, shrapnel from an exploding head.

He awoke to the warmth puddling up beneath him and a hissing sound inside of his head, like that of a glass being filled with seltzer. The girl still squatted over him, still held him inside. It seemed like he'd been asleep for hours, for his entire life. The poncho flew up, admitting the rain and wind. She stood up and Conrad felt his cock plop down on his stomach.

"Jesus it's dark," she said, walking over to the other side of the deck. Conrad stared straight up, stunned and tingling. His limbs slinkied back from wherever they had scattered themselves and slowly reattached to his body.

"I guess you didn't wake anybody," she continued, yawning. "But you're a loud one." She made a sound as if she were stretching.

"I blacked out," Conrad mumbled. The rain stopped. He sat up. He looked in her direction, at the movement of her silhouette against the starless sky, or what he imagined to be her silhouette. It was all just shifting fields of black.

"Jesus it's dark out here," she said again and this kindled in Conrad an adolescent fear that she might be ugly, that the one glimpse of her face had deceived him, that he'd been suckered somehow. He felt around for his trousers, found her T-shirt and panties. It had been nothing to her, a routine encounter, a momentary blip on the sonar screen. As it would have been for any number of people.

He began to tremble.

She was a rare one, he told himself. The one in a million. She had to be.

"Hey, is my shirt over by you?" she asked. The nasal quality of her accent suddenly irritated him. He stopped trembling and tossed the shirt in her direction.

Freedom, he thought. Liberation.

He found his pants a few feet away, bunched up in a puddle. Not to worry—they were impervious to stains. Lucy had assured him of that. Conrad pictured his wife, first at the sales counter, then on a hotel mattress with her fingernails plunged into the salesman's back. How trivial these images seemed now! Conrad looked in the girl's direction and watched the areas of darkness moving against each other as he struggled back into his trousers. The trousers were wet in the seat and in the knees. He tried to re-member the last time he and Lucy had been naked together. The weekend before they'd left on this trip, wasn't it? All flushed with anticipation?

He excused himself and went below.

Everything looked the same. The Tambralingans stretched out on the deck, inert. The duffel bag next to his sleeping bag, just as he'd left it. He dug out his flashlight and looked at the boy's face again. The strange thing was not so much that the boy was dead, but that he had ever been alive. Conrad put the flashlight away. He ran his fingers through his thinning hair, remembering the fer-tility clinic in San Francisco, the cool-eyed nurse handing him stacks of magazines, unrepentant porn filled with shots of leather-garbed blondes taking it simultaneously in mouth, ass, and pussy, of Aryan poster boys getting rimmed and fellated by teams of East Asian beauties, of taut young bodies daisy-chained around a living room. Conrad remembered the ejaculate spilling into the plastic cup, his attention veering from the splayed centerfolds and into an odd chain of images, of bowling alleys and tournaments, and thoughts about how the whole project of conception was like bowling, attempting the impossible spare, the seven-and-ten-pin combination, how he was one pin and Lucy the other, rotating, wobbling, but not ready to fall down.

Conrad lay down on his sleeping bag and shut his eyes. After several minutes he realized he wouldn't sleep, couldn't sleep, as long as the thing next to him was a boy and not just a bag. He went back up top and crouched next to the girl, who had stretched herself out beneath her poncho as before.

"Can I sleep here?" Conrad asked. She grunted and turned on her side, murmuring something unintelligible. Conrad stretched out on his back. The deck was wet and felt cold at first—but then, later, quite warm.

Part Six

The Western Gate

Part Six

The Western Gate

32

The shadow puppet master always begins a performance by singing verses from the Quran. Without the blessings of Allah, my guide explains, the master would be at the mercy of the spirits he must call down to animate the puppets. As he ends his prayer to Allah and begins salutations to the spirits of the four corners of the earth, the master switches from Arabic to archaic Malay, now and then throwing in a Javanese, Pali, or Sanskrit word for good measure. It's a language whose meaning only the spirits fully apprehend. The master faces North to greet the Spirits of the Sea, South for the Spirits of the Jungle, West for the Spirits of the Dead and to the East for the chief of all Spirits, Azal Lalu Champin. "But I," the master declares, "shall remain the supreme power throughout the performance and no spirit shall dare disturb the company gathered here."

Lucy closed the book and plopped it onto the pillow next to hers. Adolf Coswell's *Travels in Tambralinga*, 1912 edition. Morning light, muted by a thin overcast, had begun to creep up the far wall of the chamber, illuminating the bulging eyes and tusks of carved masks hung halfway up. The wall closest to her was covered with antique shadow puppets, queerly angular figures of wood and buffalo hide, brilliantly painted. On the opposite wall was mounted a crude bow and a quiver of arrows Rashid said came originally from a Negrito pygmy tribe living in a highland jungle. "Vanished now, of course," he'd said.

"The tribe or the jungle?" she'd asked, surprised at her own cynicism.

Lucy sat up in bed and lit a cigarette. She'd certainly bought the whole package this time, she thought as she watched the exhaled smoke fan out across the bedsheet. A large bird perched on the windowsill briefly, and Lucy thought at first it was a rhinoceros hornbill, but then decided it was probably a crow. No matter—she could recall it as a hornbill if she wanted. She closed her eyes and attempted to fix the image in her mind.

"Hornbill," she said three times, as if chanting an incantation.

She looked over at the book, which she had taken from the library downstairs. Reading in bed she found difficult when the air was so humid; in this climate, you did not curl up with a book but rather held it at arm's length. In fact, all of the books in the library had to be kept in ziplock bags to protect them from the humidity and the nesting habits of certain insects.

Rashid was always gone when she woke up in the morning, but was usually back by now. She stretched and took another drag on the cigarette. Strange to connect words like "always" and "usually" with Rashid. They'd only been together a few days and always (that word again!) with the expectation that tomorrow would be the end. She picked up the book and found her place.

Seated on the ground around me are mothers in their red and blue shawls, babes clutched to their breasts or cradled in their arms, the older children seated next to them, gazing raptly at the screen. Further back the men of the village stand, hands clasped behind their backs, silent with expectation. Against the screen the silhouette of a king appears with much fanfare. It is Ratu Daha, Lord of Ingkandri, the master's voice announces. Ratu is bewailing the fact that he and his queen are unable to have children. He fears for his lonely old age, his empty palace rooms, his helplessness before young usurpers who will surely seek to displace him.

In a cloud of lightning and thunder, the god Indra appears. The screen billows gently in the night wind, the shadow of Lord Indra growing suddenly larger. One of the children cries out. In the sky above lightning flickers and in the distance come faint rumblings of thunder.

"Ratu Daha!" Indra tells the king. "You shall be blessed with children. But you must agree to sacrifice 40 bulls and to give your first-born daughter to the great hero Cheke Wanang Pati!" Ratu Daha agrees and as time goes by, his queen produces a daughter, Radin Galoh Chendra Krina, and then a son Radin Parabuan, and then another son, Radin Gunong Sari.

Lucy found her eyes drifting off the page, her thoughts returning to her lover's surprisingly supple body. Rashid was perhaps not the most graceful lover she'd ever had, but he was undoubtedly the most ardent. (Had she really had so many lovers that she could start comparing them? It gave her a mild buzz to think so.) He was worth waiting for, in any case. Yesterday Jeannine had sounded a note of impatience, wanting to know when they would be off to Sri Kala. Rashid kept extending his stay at the Istana, citing some sort of unpleasant business in the city. Yet he seemed to have much of the mornings free and managed to dine with Lucy and Jeannine in the evening.

"What's the big rush?" Lucy had asked Jeannine. "Are you afraid it will be gone by the time we get there?"

Jeannine had looked at her strangely, a thoughtful mixture of annoyance and jealousy. Later on she'd asked to be allowed to prepare lunch. No doubt watching someone else's fling was somewhat less exciting than keeping house.

Lying on her back, Lucy raised the old volume above her head so that the sun's lateral rays sharply illuminated the open page:

Years go by, but the king does not sacrifice the 40 bulls. Neither does he marry his daughter Krina, Princess of Daha, to Cheke when she comes of age. Lord Indra, much incensed, sends the demon Bota to steal the princess away. The audience shrieks when the form of the terrifying demon appears on the screen. But the monster does not descend upon the girl and devour her. Instead, he speaks beguiling words to the young girl and persuades her to follow him into the throbbing underworld of the demon, deep into the mountain called Gunong Sila Maling.

There was a knock on the door. Lucy pulled the sheet over her.

"Rashid?" she asked, but it was only the servant inquiring about breakfast. Lucy declined the offer. The room was heating up and she'd been lolling too long to have much appetite.

A second knock came a moment later.

"I said no thank you," Lucy said in a loud voice.

"It's me," Jeannine said. She came in with her day bag slung over her shoulder, panting from the heat.

"I went to the city this morning," she explained. "The boatman gave me a ride. I had to get off the island for a bit. There's a big open-air market right along the waterfront. I thought I'd pick up some fruit and things there. And I found this newspaper. I didn't realize they had an English-language press here."

She unfolded the newspaper on the bed. The headline read:

VIMAYA CALLED "MASSACRE"
Calls for Inquiry into Police Actions

"There was a massacre in Kuala Vimaya the night we got here. Something like three hundred people got killed. There was a demonstration and the army just started shooting everybody."

"Three hundred people?" Lucy asked.

"A guess. Nobody knows. The army is saying something like fifteen. But look at this part on page seven."

"I don't really want to know what's going on in the world right now," Lucy said, folding the paper shut.

"It was just across the river." Jeannine looked annoyed. "But on page seven—"

"I know you're restless," Lucy said. "And I guess I am, too."

"Are you?" Jeannine asked, sitting down on the bed. "Really?" She sounded hopeful, but also sad.

"Maybe we should go on to Sri Kala," Lucy suggested quietly.

"It's more than being restless. I'm a little afraid," Jeannine said.

"Of what?"

She looked down at the bedspread and smoothed it with her hand.

"That you're getting in over your head. That things aren't exactly kosher here. I mean, whenever I'm in the kitchen—"

"Don't be intimidated by servants, Jeannine. You just have to use the right tone of voice."

"Hey, I was there for that lecture too, if you'll recall."

"Look, all I meant was—"

"I don't know why you feel you need to counsel me," Jeannine interrupted, voice shaking. "Like you're the queen of the goddamn Nile or something."

Jeannine paused, looked down at her hands, which quickly folded themselves in her lap.

"And here I thought you were trying to counsel me," Lucy said stiffly. "I know it's all make-believe, if that's what you're worried about."

She looked at the lines in her palm.

33

Located some 2,000 feet above sea level in the heavily forested Singhora valley, the ancient city of Tambralinga is only accessible by four-wheel-drive vehicle. For those determined few ready to make the five-hour, bone-rattling bus ride from Sri Kala or lay out 200 dollars U.S. for a guide and jeep, the rewards are many, the first being the chance to enjoy the quiet elegance of the ruins in a pristine jungle setting, far away from the crowds one usually encounters in Pagan and Angkor.

Standing at the western gate at sunset, it is easy to picture the scene described in the seventh-century Chinese chronicles: "As the king goes forth upon a white elephant, shaded with the seven-tiered parasol, leading a company of soldiers and courtiers replete with banners, fly-whisks, flags and drums, the common people along the route prostrate before him as though he were a god."

—*Coswell's Guide to Tambralinga* (1997 ed.)

The long approach to the ruined city is lined with thick vines hanging from the forest canopy, strangler figs that have long ago killed their respective hosts and now coil around thin air. Using each vine to mark the contours of the original tree, Lucy finds herself filling in the blank spaces, resurrecting the forest as she moves up the path. She has arrived only a short while ago in a Landcruiser belonging to the Ministry of Religious Education. More than half of the road from Sri Kala is newly paved, making a round-trip possible in a single day. The Landcruiser has had no trouble ascending the precipitous slopes of the Singhora Mountains, nor in finding a shaded spot in the new parking lot.

Lucy lingers over a spot on the forest floor where the bud of a *Rafflesia priceii* is nosing its way up through the leaf litter. Within a fortnight the bud may grow to a blossom three feet across, with a carrion stench that will draw pollinating flies from miles around. At the moment it is not much to look at, and in fact reminds Lucy of a rotting red cabbage she once extricated from the back of her refrigerator. She lingers over it anyway, allowing Rashid and his driver to go on without her, to disappear around a turn in the path. Lucy wants to be alone when she passes through the gates of the ancient city, wishes now that she'd arranged to come by herself, that she'd given herself a day to wander in solitude among the remnants of palace and temple.

In high school Lucy had entertained blatantly romantic notions of becoming an archaeologist; at the university she came to understand that the discipline was less about the pleasure of ruins and more about the memorization of pottery sequences, and that to become an excavator of ancient buildings required something like a vow of poverty. Lucy had promised herself a very different sort of future, egged on, in part, by the memory of her mother, newly widowed, struggling to make mortgage payments, only to lose the house to back taxes. And by the time Lucy entered the university, she'd become wary of mere academic success. The classroom's best and brightest seemed to suffer financial penalties later in life, apparently obliged to pay a price for knowing more than anyone else. But surely, Lucy had reasoned, there were also financial rewards for knowing more, and ways of getting to the pot of gold without the rainbow's dubious endorsement. And so she pursued a series of hardheaded goals that led at first into marketing (for which, sadly, she had no facility) and then into real estate, where her childhood enthusiasm for ancient architecture resurfaced as an ongoing obsession with Victorian houses. She found that she could talk forcefully, even passionately, about the history of a given property. Every house had a story, a text written into the roofline, the foundations, even the plumbing. Lucy's pitches inevitably leaned toward the elegiac; more than one buyer commented upon the sense of yearning at the core of her storytelling. Lucy nursed this yearning, recognizing in it a contagion capable of infecting certain buyers, of sparking bidding wars.

Lucy crouches next to the dark red bud and runs her fingers

over it. She makes a mental note to point it out to Jeannine on the way back. Jeannine is also up ahead, walking with her new swain, Owen, a preposterous-looking bodybuilder from London. That Jeannine would pick up a man like this, Lucy sees as a mark of desperation.

Lucy and Jeannine had set off for Sri Kala a few nights before, agreeing to meet Rashid there and then make a side trip with him up to the ruins. The much-vaunted Festival of the Sea Goddess turned out to be a depressing little carnival, but there was at least a beach, where Jeannine spent the early hours of the day dozing in the sun while Lucy composed cryptic postcard messages.

Mary and Bob—
    Hi! Well, the bloom may be off the rose, but the lotuses are tastier than ever!

Bill and Jody—
    Conrad and I have decide to take the paths of least and greatest resistance, respectively.

Chris and Michelle—
    Yesterday while snorkeling, I found myself in the midst of a school of jellyfish, which turned out to be clear plastic bags jettisoned by a cruise ship. Believed I'd discovered the origins of life, until the daiquiri wore off.

It had been, for a few hours at least, much like the first euphoric days Lucy had spent with Jeannine. (How long ago that seemed now!) But then a busload of tourists coming from the islands by way of Kuala Vimaya arrived, depositing, among many others, a man wearing little more than a loincloth.

"The creep from the deep," was how Jeannine described him, because when they first saw him walking along the water's edge, he was stopping to chat up each unescorted woman he came across.

"At least he walks on two legs," Lucy had replied. But when he had come closer to where they lay, Jeannine's interest had awakened. Owen proved affable enough and spoke with an endearing speech impediment. And so, after coaxing him into a shirt and longer sarong, Jeannine brought him along on the trip up to the ancient capital.

The gates are little more than piles of bricks still overgrown with a tangle of creepers and the roots of young trees. But farther on, Lucy comes to a well-preserved portion of the terrace wall, in which huge figures of Hindu gods have been carved. Each god rides his sacred mount in a long procession led by Agni on a one-horned rhinoceros. The guidebook remarks that normally one finds Agni bringing up the rear of such processions, as he is closely linked to death and the last day of the week. Very likely the relief depicts the planetary sequence of a particular date in which Saturn, Agni's planet, rose first. Lucy stops to examine the features of the god's face, which stand out in the slanting rays of the late afternoon sun.

"Excuse me, madam?" A slim young woman approaches. She is Tambralingan, probably Paktai, but dressed in khaki slacks and a white blouse.

"We are filming here today. This area is actually closed right now. I'm sorry, but you understand we are trying to record everything here before they flood the valley."

Coming up the path behind her are two men carrying tripods, lights, and cameras.

"Of course," Lucy says, blinking awake.

"I apologize for the inconvenience," the young woman says. She sounds like she's spent time in Cambridge or someplace like that.

"I was just going, really," Lucy says.

"Thank you for understanding. It's a huge undertaking, and I'm afraid it's going to come down to the wire."

Lucy hurries up the path, which was once a boulevard of sorts, dubbed "the Avenue of Agni" by the guidebook. Lucy opens the guidebook and checks her progress against the map of the city in the back. The Avenue of Agni should take her directly to the western gate, where she will meet Rashid to watch the sunset. She had wanted a little time alone in the ruins, to savor its atmosphere, but now she feels anxious and a little bit lost. She does not like being told she is in the way.

She comes to the courtyard of a large temple. Massive blocks of stone are tumbled along one side where the outer wall once stood. The temple itself is in the tentacled grip of the strangler figs, whose roots hold the structure together in a tight net even as they pry the individual stones apart. The lintel block over the entrance is carved with the stylized head of Kala, a grinning leonine figure with huge mouth and teeth, that seems to be consuming the elaborate floral arabesques that make up its own body. But the guidebook says that these floral arabesques are really nagas, stylized snakes that Kala holds in its claws. Lucy strains to make these out. Are her eyes going? No, if she stands far to the left and looks up at the lintel at an oblique angle, she can see the heads of the snakes. So the image really is of a lion's head eating snakes, "the merging of solar and lunar principles," as the guidebook reverentially puts it. Yet the image of Kala is a cruel one, with its impersonal, insect-like eyes, its cold grin.

Lucy puts aside the nagging urge to locate Rashid and enters the temple. She finds herself in another courtyard, a great rectangular space that apparently once held water, for there are elevated paths leading to a small building in the center of the courtyard which Lucy realizes must house the Central Sanctuary. She is momentarily carried away with the antiquity of the place, with half-formed impressions of ancient pageantry, of kings arriving on elephants, of bare-breasted dancers moving in long processions around the temple, while the priests remove the god from the inner sanctum and prepare to parade it around the city. She sees the seven-tiered parasols held over the king and queen, hears the drumming and the gongs, smells the smoke of the sacrificial fires.

As she approaches the entrance of the central sanctuary, she sees Owen and Jeannine emerge from behind the building and climb the steps to the entrance. Owen's shirt is open to the navel. But it is not his heavily muscled chest she notices in the slanting light, but rather the bald spot emerging from his blond wisps.

Neither Jeannine nor Owen sees Lucy, and so she dawdles, not wanting to join them. A clammy sensation crawls over her. She feels ashamed for Jeannine, for the perfunctory way Jeannine has picked up this man, as if meaning to prove something. *I might have taken Rashid instead, had I wanted to.* The implication makes Lucy uncomfortable. One must not equate Owen with Rashid, and the kinds of relationship possible with each.

Lucy recalls the look of embarrassment on Rashid's face when Jeannine first introduced him to Owen—embarrassment over the man's determination to wear his musculature. Even after Jeannine puts a shirt on him, even when he sits quietly in the backseat and smokes his fat cigarettes, the sheer bulk of his pointedly engineered arms and torso is impossible to ignore. It seems to Lucy that one cannot look at a body like his without confronting the intent behind its structure.

Lucy looks back at the walls of the inner courtyard. One is supposed to study the friezes, identify the Hindu pantheon, the celestial bodies, and compare the wall's measurements in cubits with the number of days between equinoxes. The avenues that intersect at the temple are aligned with the rising of the sun on the winter and summer solstices. This or that constellation may be seen directly overhead at the beginning of the New Year. The entire cosmos is here reproduced in stone, according to the guidebook. Apparently there was never any doubt in the minds of the ancients about where things stood.

"This?" Owen's voice booms from inside the sanctuary. "This is what they worshiped? This post?"

"It's a lingam." Jeannine's voice is less audible. "A phallus. Symbol of Siva."

It strikes Lucy odd to hear Jeannine adopt a didactic tone.

"Do you mean they actually came in here and worshiped it in bwoad daylight?" the man goes on. "And how did they do that then?"

"They poured ghee or coconut oil on it," Jeannine replies.

"Lubwicant?" Owen laughs.

Jeannine clears her throat and reads from Owen's guidebook. There is currently much controversy over who actually built the city, renegade princes from the Khmer empire or Mon peoples coming down from the north.

"Personally," Owen says after a moment, "I like the idea of the phallus being worshiped by the mons."

Jeannine says nothing for a long moment. Lucy reaches the entrance, touches the side of the doorway and peeks inside. Jeannine stands before the shrine, holding the book up in a shaft of light coming from the other entrance. She holds the book open and turns the pages as if trying to find a passage.

"First of all, Owen, the plural is 'Mon.' "

"What's the singuwar, then? Mon-ey? Did they migwate here fwom Cash-mir?"

Jeannine produces a strained laugh.

"What's the matter? Did I make you mad just now?" Owen demands of the silence that follows.

"Not at all," Jeannine says, turning away from Owen and looking in Lucy's direction. Lucy pulls her head back around the corner of the doorway. She fights off the urge to run back down the path, the surge of shame at nearly being caught eavesdropping. Why am I doing this, she wonders, but then slowly moves her head back around the doorway.

Jeannine seems to be adjusting the front of Owen's sarong. He places a hand on top of her head and leans back against the temple wall. No need to watch any more of this, Lucy advises herself, but then continues to stare as Jeannine draws the man's engorged penis through the folds of the sarong and begins delivering long, twisting strokes that cause the thing to telescope out to a length that strikes Lucy as unprecedented.

Lucy jerks her head back, overwhelmed with a sensation she later decides is disgust. It's like a fountain inside of her, an uprush from a dozen different jets, the streams converging and then separating, over and over. She makes her way carefully back across the courtyard, which is now deep in shadow. Her legs tremble; she needs to eat something. And she begins to doubt what she's seen, to hypothesize a deceptive play of slanting rays and long shadows. It seems likely that what she'd glimpsed was really Owen's bare foot and that Jeannine's ministrations had been directed at a thorn or a sliver on one of the toes. Finally she concludes, without much conviction, that it doesn't matter either way.

"Lucy," Rashid pronounces her name slowly. "Loo-see. The name of the first woman, I think."

"You mean Eve."

"*Lucy.* It's the fossil from Ethiopia. Australopithecus, I think. Oldest known ancestor, isn't it?"

"The oldest one with a Christian name, I suppose." Lucy lays her head against Rashid's shoulder. They stand at the western gate of the city, watching the sun slide behind the mountaintop. All the surrounding peaks rise up with startling precipitousness, with near-vertical limestone cliffs and jungly toupees crowning the tops. In front of them a deep rectangular tank has been dug out of the earth and lined with stone blocks. Once it held water, probably fish, and perhaps (who knew?) even the corpses of sacrificial victims. From the wall of the granite and brick temple on the other side of the tank, a huge face, draped in shadow, smiles down at them. It's a wide face, framed by an elaborate crown, with heavily lidded eyes that make it impossible to tell exactly in which direction the face is looking.

A guard in a disheveled khaki uniform appears and motions with his hand that it is time for visitors to leave the ruins. Rashid utters something rapid and sharp in Yawi and the guard smiles apologetically and shuffles off.

Lucy takes Rashid's hand in hers and with the finger of her other hand gently strokes the inside of his forearm. The skin is smooth like a child's skin. A man with this kind of skin should be a young man.

"Loo-see. First woman," Rashid says. "And I am the first man. First in the world." He takes a strand of her red hair and gently rubs it between his fingers. She wants to think that he's never been with a redhead before. Too bad it isn't quite her true color, she thinks.

"It does feel like the beginning of time all right." Lucy sighs. The approaching darkness fills her with a sense of peace. She remembers the summer evenings of her childhood back in Minnesota, the extended twilight, the slow seepage of shadow and darkness across the landscape. Tambralinga wasn't very big on twilight, she reminds herself. It seemed very eager to get on with nightfall. The sun is orange and fuzzy as it slips out from behind the peak for a moment. The air seems dense with reddish haze. Birds shuttle anxiously across the remaining portions of undarkened sky, shrieking over some last-minute bit of business. She had been worried about coming out to the ruins so late in the day, but Rashid was right, they had to be seen at sunset.

"Is this a wedding ring?" Rashid asks, feeling the band with his finger. "It's gold, I think."

"Yes."

"But you're not married anymore?"

"No. Not anymore."

"Was he very rich, your husband?"

"He's not poor. But generous, I guess you'd say. He liked doling out gifts."

"And where did you get this necklace?" Rashid asks, fingering the thin gold chain on her neck.

"I bought it in Lingga Baharu. You like it?"

"You bought this there, too?" he asks, as his fingers find the amulet attached to the end of the chain.

"No. A monk gave that to me on Ko Banteay. For luck."

Rashid lets go of the amulet and laughs.

"Buddhist monks are supposed to be very unlucky for Muslims. We're supposed to keep away. Their magic is said to be dangerous. They talk with the dead, you know."

She kisses him. Gently he encircles her with his arms, moving one hand slowly up and down her back. There is nothing timid about his gentleness, she notes. It's all very precise. She lets her hands slip from around his neck down to his waist, then to his hips. The mosquitoes are coming out, but she isn't concerned.

"This man—your husband," Rashid asks, touching the ring on her finger again. "Did he give you a house as well?"

"I paid half the mortgage," Lucy says. "Last year I made more money than he did. For the last two years, in fact."

"Oh! This is why you left him, isn't it?"

The features of the stone face dissolve into shadow, the temple becomes a dark hillock. Lucy feels a certain coziness at being out of the giant's field of vision.

"I didn't want to be married anymore," Lucy says dreamily. "Not like that. Not like being put to sleep. Being put into a box."

In the silence that follows she senses Rashid's confusion.

"You didn't like to sleep with him?" he asks.

"That's not what I mean. I mean—well, you could say that, I guess. I guess you could."

She stands up and stretches, opening her arms. Does it look silly to him? she wonders. Like I'm embracing the sunset or something? She feels like Manora, the bird-woman, beginning her twelve dances before the sacrificial bonfire. She sees herself stepping through her twelve dances, one for each month of the year. She swirls the tattered days of her calendar around her like confetti, bringing down a blizzard upon her audience that will freeze them in their seats. And as the last embers of the bonfire flicker out, she rises into heaven, not as the ghost of the sacrificial victim, but whole, restored, free.

She does a pirouette and faces her lover. "I'm Manora," she tells him. "I've escaped to heaven." Rashid confesses that he doesn't know the story, that he's never had the patience to sit through an entire performance. His voice sounds suddenly morose. He slouches in the defeated way of middle-aged men. Lucy brings her arms down to her sides.

"I forgot you went to school in London," she says.

"Singapore, mostly. London only for a short time. I was ordered to come home."

To get married, Lucy realizes. Childhood betrothal. Of course! It had been hanging over everything from the start, the unrecognized constellation slowly moving across the sky. The veiled missus tucked away in some compound near Nagaseri, an unspecified number of sons decked out in black felt hats and Arab-style robes, enrolled in religious schools. It is all there in his slouch.

Instead of bringing this up, she asks:

"What did you study in London?"

Rashid shrugs.

"Classics. The Greeks. In Singapore I studied business, but I had no facility for it." He produces his cigarette case and finds a cigarette. The glow of the match is like a tiny campfire on the face of a clouded mountain.

"My father thought I was studying political science, public administration, that sort of thing. When word got back, there was a bit of a row. He wanted me to get a government job."

"Are all of the Sultan's sons supposed to work in the government?" Lucy asks.

Rashid clears his throat, but doesn't answer.

Damn me, Lucy thinks, as she feels their intimacy bleeding away. But in the end it had to bleed away, had to come under the knife.

"I must tell you the story of Manora," she says eventually.

"Oh, no, it's okay. My mother told me when I was a boy. I just can't remember now."

"You must hear this story," she insists. The moroseness in his voice has deepened. She spreads her arms out and begins to tell him.

"Oh, yes, I remember now," Rashid says when she gets

halfway through it. "They want to burn her, but she tricks them and flies away. Yes, yes."

"Now you tell me a story."

"A Tambralingan myth? I don't know any."

"A Greek myth, then. You studied the Greeks, you said."

Rashid exhales slowly. "All right," he says after a moment. "Do you know about the birth of Orion?"

"Orion?"

"There," he points to the constellation overhead.

"Oh!" she says, recognizing the belt.

"Well, there is a story that his mother couldn't have a baby. She grew old and died. Then his father, also very old, received a visit from the gods Zeus and Hermes, who were traveling in disguise. Although he was just a poor farmer and beekeeper, he shared what he had with the two gods. They were touched by his hospitality, so they offered to grant him a wish.

" 'Oh, but it is too late!' he says. 'What I really want is a son, but I'm an old man and my wife is gone.'

"But the gods, being gods, know the magical loopholes that are written into the contract of life and death. And so they advise him: Sacrifice a bull, make water on its hide, then bury it in your wife's grave. The farmer does this and nine months later, a son is born to him: Orion. Or, according to Ovid, 'Urion'—'he who makes water.' And the only reason I remember this story is because somebody told me that in the Mediterranean both the rising and the setting of this constellation bring rain."

Lucy watches the glowing cigarette tip trace a curve through the darkness.

"I don't like that story," she says. "Urinating on his wife's grave. It's disgusting."

"Not really the grave," Rashid starts to explain, but then stops, apparently too tired to argue the point.

"So when the little boy grows up, he thinks it's okay to urinate on women in general, is that it?"

Rashid seems to shrug.

"The rain falls on everyone, saint and sinner alike, they say."

"They? Who are 'they'? Some committee of old *men*?"

"Orion gets killed in the end, if that makes you feel better."

Lucy feels herself calming down. Once again the darkness is soothing, but it is no longer seductive.

"It's still disgusting," she says.

"I'm sorry, Lucy. You wanted a myth. This is the one I know."

34

When Jeannine met them in the parking lot, she was alone. Owen was taking the bus back, she announced in a tone that invited no further questions. Rashid expressed a tepid concern for Owen's comfort.

"We parted on good terms," Jeannine assured him.

"Well, I'm glad of it," Rashid nodded. Lucy was too surprised to say anything. And then it was just the three of them again, heading down the road for what felt like the last time.

As they neared Sri Kala, Rashid announced that he would have to return to the Istana Vimaya that night by himself.

"Affairs of state . . ." he began, and then, apologizing with a flutter of his hand, "I don't mean to sound pompous. It's really no big deal. A meeting I must attend. A cabinet minister and his wife. I may be changing jobs, you see."

"I understand," Lucy said, touching his hand.

"I'll return tomorrow night," Rashid continued. "If you're planning to still be there."

Lucy was surprised to find her breath taken away. It wasn't as though this was unexpected.

"Not sure, eh?" Rashid said. "Well, I'll just plan on coming anyway, then. I mean, barring some sort of emergency."

"Emergency?" Lucy whispered.

"The government is in a bit of an uproar at the moment. The deputy minister of justice has been forced to resign."

"Because of the massacre?" Lucy asked, finding her voice. She pushed some hair away from her forehead, quelled the swelling in her tear glands.

"There was a disturbance which some are calling a massacre. In Kuala Vimaya."

"We saw it, didn't we? Across the river. That night."

"Yes."

"And people were being shot."

"It was a horrible thing."

The car hit a bump and Lucy focused for a moment on the road unwinding before them. The headlights pried the darkness apart slightly, revealing a wall of vegetation swishing by on either side, the leaves strangely colorless, as though coated with ash.

"A shocking tragedy," Rashid was saying. ". . . a full investigation . . . those individuals on both sides . . . held fully accountable."

Whenever Lucy sensed a pause in Rashid's speech, she interjected something like "You're right, of course," or "I couldn't agree more," launching her comments in the manner of the newly deaf, without certainty about where they might fit or if they were necessary at all.

It was without a doubt a bad time to begin assessing one's life, future, and ultimate goals, but the process was under way before Lucy was really paying attention, and once begun, the process took on an irresistible momentum.

When they pulled up to the hotel in Sri Kala, Jeannine asked Lucy if she would mind sharing a room with her that night. Lucy felt a sudden rush of tenderness: Jeannine was going to stay with her. She dabbed her eye with her sleeve.

"I'm sorry I must rush off," Rashid was saying when they pulled up to the hotel. "I should love to have dinner with both of you, but I really have no choice, I'm afraid."

He held Lucy's hand for a long moment while Jeannine climbed out.

"Onward!" Lucy said at last, somehow managing a flippant tone. She jumped out of the vehicle, landing lightly on her feet.

"I shall send you a postcard from San Francisco," she called back to Rashid as she slipped the necklace and amulet from around her neck. "And here—a keepsake!" She tossed the necklace through the open door. Rashid caught it with one hand.

"If you ever feel depressed, you can dip it into a glass of water and then drink the water. Also cures glaucoma—at least according to one of the books in your study."

"Next time I feel lonely," Rashid said, his small smile illuminated in the car's overhead light. He brought his open hand close to his face in a gesture midway between a wave and a salute. And then the door swung closed and he was gone.

As Jeannine unpacked her bag, she laid the newspaper, now four days old, on the floor of the hotel room. The word "massacre," in large caps, caught Lucy's eye.

"Are you still carrying that around with you?" she asked Jeannine.

"It doesn't matter now. I was going to show you something."

"Something about Rashid? You're right, it doesn't matter."

She picked up a brush and began untangling her windblown hair. The trip was over. Whatever was supposed to have happened had already done so. She supposed the logical thing to do would be to return to Nagaseri and wait for Conrad. If he wasn't already there.

She imagined he would be furious with her, furious, but nonetheless incapable of uttering a discouraging word. She sighed as the brush became snagged. She doubted that she had any patience left for Conrad's timed-release hostilities. Couldn't they just come clean for once and admit they no longer liked each other? Make a clean breast of things? Honesty for once—yes, why not? If there was no longer a marriage to preserve, there was no longer a need to lie.

She noticed the newspaper again. What an odd souvenir it would make. *The night he made me see fireworks.*

But what was it Jeannine had wanted to show her? Lucy leaned over and picked up the paper. She read the beginning of the article on the front page and then turned to the back for the rest. On page seven she came across the part that Jeannine had meant to show her:

> . . . Rashid Abdul bin Rahman, Deputy Minister for Religious Education, said the Sultan stands by the actions of the army. "There is no evidence that the army acted inappropriately," the Deputy Minister Abdul said. "The entire blame for this tragedy rests with Sonny Tatoh, who unfortunately is still at large." Following talks with archconservative Muslim cleric Haji Da-Oh Udzir, the Deputy Minister hinted that the Sultan was in the process of forming a coalition of Islamic conservatives opposed to the Al-Jabbar movement. Amid cheers of "God is Great!" from the small crowd, Abdul promised that the Sultan's forces will be unleashed against "the agents of chaos and the enemies of Sharia."

Lucy put the paper down and picked up her brush. Slowly she worked the snarl out of her hair, while gazing at nothing, at the space on the wall where the mirror might have hung if the hotel had been that sort.

"I couldn't decide," Jeannine said from across the room. "Whether to tell you about it or not. I was afraid something awful was going to happen."

"You did the right thing," Lucy said. She turned toward Jeannine, who was shaking out a pair of slacks. Lucy watched her for a long time, noting the care with which Jeannine handled the fabric, the precise way she folded the slacks and hung them on a hanger.

"I wasn't sure," Jeannine said into the long silence, "how much you wanted to know."

Right, thought Lucy. That is the question.

35

The ancient bus shuddered as it pulled up next to the ferry terminal building. The driver stomped on the brake pedal and yanked on the emergency simultaneously. The sound of metal grinding against metal momentarily eclipsed all Lucy's other perceptions. She waited for the crush of passengers to exit the bus, then pulled her bag out from under her seat and disembarked. There was no need to rush. The ferry to Nagaseri didn't leave for another two hours.

The waterfront teemed with soldiers. The stench of the harbor, of rotting fish and diesel fumes, hung heavy in the air. The terminal building housed a dozen different ticket offices; Lucy found the one that handled ferry tickets to Nagaseri; she knew enough words in Yawi to ask directions. A young woman in a gauzy veil sold her a complicated-looking ticket, one made of three different pieces of paper, each bearing a different stamp, and stapled together.

A squad of soldiers, boys barely past puberty from the look of them, stood in the vague semblance of a line across the entrance to the ferry dock. A few carried rifles. The others stood with their hands clasped behind their backs, chatting with each other, now and then glancing at the ferry passengers lining up in the early morning rain. They seemed to be waiting for someone. Lucy walked along the line of soldiers and across the parking lot toward a small tea stand, where she hoped to get a coffee or a white tea. Beyond the ferry dock she glimpsed the mouth of the river and the island of the Istana Vimaya. A ferryboat was coming in, one of the slow-moving night boats from the islands. She stopped to watch, wishing (pointlessly, she realized) that it was her ferry arriving early.

A beggar woman holding a ragged bundle brushed up against her. The beggar extended her free hand in Lucy's direction, hoisting the bundle up against her shoulder as if it were a baby. But Lucy wasn't fooled. She walked past the woman as if she weren't there. At the tea stand she bought an overly sweetened glass of something and a kind of crêpe with jam in the middle, sat on a small stool, and attempted to eat. After a few minutes, she decided that the queasiness in her stomach might be actual nausea, rather than a suppressed urge to cry.

Lucy had spent the previous night in a small hotel near the central bus station, an unspeakably dirty place where the bathroom was down the end of a long corridor and offered no hot water. She'd slept on top of the bed, afraid to get in between the synthetic sheets, which had grown nubbly from repeated washings. When she turned off the light, the mattress seemed to come alive with crawling insects—all traces of which vanished whenever she switched the light back on.

The beggar woman approached her again, muttering something in a low, gravelly voice, like a prayer or an incantation. She seemed ready to make an offering. The woman's eye was infected; she squeezed it to produce a munificence of pus and then thrust her face in close to Lucy's.

Lucy pushed the woman back, yelling things that she scarcely believed could be coming out of her own mouth. She wished to go home now, to be there instantly, and the thought of the ordeal ahead of her—the boat ride, the long wait at the airport, the twenty-six hours on the plane—became unbearable. She wept into her napkin, which was, after all, not a napkin, but a piece of tissue, toilet paper to be exact. One of the boy soldiers, seeing her distress, left his place in the line and shooed the beggar woman away. He made a loud "ch-ch-ch" sound, as if the woman was one of the scruffy dogs slinking about the garbage pail. Lucy sat back down on her stool, mortified to find herself allied with the armed forces. Why hadn't she simply given the poor woman a few rials? She turned her back on the pier and the dogs and the soldiers and stared into her white tea.

A little later Lucy glanced over her shoulder at a noisy procession of elderly island women coming down the pier from the ferry that had just docked, the effulgent colors of their turbans and sarongs suggesting a resplendence usually associated with funerals or weddings. Which is it, Lucy wondered. And how odd that the sight of exotic dress still stirred something in her.

Behind the train of island women came a lone Westerner, a short woman with a great mass of dark, tangled hair. She shuffled past the line of soldiers, looking around the pier area as if not quite sure where she was. But when she saw Lucy, she seemed to wake up, and made a direct line for her. She spoke in heavily accented English, in a rush of broken sentences and tormented phrases that took Lucy some minutes to untangle.

"I've been stolen," the woman said over and over, eyes shifting about like those of a newly caged animal, and it finally dawned on Lucy that the woman had been robbed on the night ferry while she slept—of money, passport, and most of her luggage.

"And I have taken the wrong boat," the woman said, pressing two small fists into her forehead. "I must get to Ko Banteay! I should already be there!"

Lucy felt her throat closing up.

"It's going to be okay," she said quickly, before her voice failed her. "We'll get you there. I promise. I promise."

36

Finding a box for the body proved relatively easy, but the problem of the odor, which by noon had grown serious, was not so easily addressed. Conrad's duffel had captured the interest of more than one of the dogs working the waterfront at Ko Banteay, and as he walked up the narrow main street, they followed at a discreet distance. Conrad dared not leave the bag on the street to go into a restaurant or a café, yet taking the stinking package inside with him was clearly out of the question.

Originally Conrad planned to pack the body in a box with a great deal of ice, and while he found large cardboard shipping boxes available at Banteay Handicraft Company, ice proved to be in short supply on the island. Furthermore, he quickly realized that ice would not survive the heat of the day, and that as it melted, the bottom of the cardboard box would surely disintegrate.

The solution to his dilemma arrived unexpectedly in the form of a small boy on a bicycle, balancing a sack of durians on the handlebars.

"How much—*berapa ini*?" Conrad asked, almost proud that he had managed to learn this much Yawi in just a few short weeks. But the boy responded with a smile of sheer bafflement. Conrad's pronunciation was flawed, or else the child spoke only Paktai. As a clarification, Conrad opened his wallet and waved a large bill in the air. The little boy smiled sheepishly and then grabbed the money, dropping the bag as he pushed off with his bike.

There was a waterfront café that offered a view of the ferry dock. Conrad waited there for the rest of the afternoon, sipping

beer and soft drinks, watching the restless clouds alternately mass
and break apart. The shipping box that now held his duffel and a
number of durians sat on the walkway in the sun, just outside. A
single durian, cracked and oozing, lay on the ground next to the
box. Whenever the breeze came off the sea, the stench came with
it. But Conrad was used to the smell by now. The dogs he drove
away whenever they got too close. He had only to make a hard
shushing sound and they trotted off, whimpering. As the afternoon wore on, a sort of game developed between Conrad and the
dogs. He sat still and let them approach the box, and then, when
they got quite close, he hissed softly, gradually increasing the volume until the dogs flinched and scurried away. The object of the
game became to drive the dogs away with the minimum amount
of noise, without making any other threat, without moving a single muscle. He got quite good at it.

Toward evening, other tourists began showing up along the
waterfront and the dogs went away. Conrad scanned the horizon
pensively. He had nothing to read. His one book was in the duffel
bag with the body, which was now inside the box.

When the boat finally churned into view, Conrad allowed himself a moment of exuberant relief. If Rosanette was on the boat,
in a short time she would find her husband, and Conrad's own
part in this unfortunate business would be finished.

A rush of happy thoughts ensued as the boat tied up at the
dock. For Conrad felt that the first leg in his long journey home
had begun, and however difficult his reunion with Lucy would
be, they would nonetheless climb into an airplane together and allow this dismal interlude to recede rapidly behind them. And he
could put off confronting the burden of shame now growing inside of him, make a deal with himself to pay off the debt in easy
monthly installments, bit by bit, layered into the quiet sameness
of his life in California.

But was Rosanette on the boat, Conrad wondered as the passengers began to disembark.

She did not keep him in suspense for long. Rosanette was one
of the first passengers off the boat, walking briskly down the

dock, arms moving with what might be suppressed rage. Next to her was another, much taller woman, whose visual elements eventually arranged themselves into a figure of breathtaking familiarity. Before the two women reached the end of the dock, Conrad found himself rushing to meet them.

"Over here!" Conrad yelled, waving. And when Rosanette took Lucy by the arm and pointed at Conrad, he knew that the women had shared confidences on that long boat ride, and that there would be no going back, no easy monthly payments. The crumbling edifice that had been his life was now simply a pile of brick and dust, and there seemed little point in worrying about it any longer.

37

What made listening to Rosanette's story so excruciating for Lucy was the impossibility of saying anything comforting—or anything at all—without sounding like either some flippant little narcissist or an utter buffoon. The crushing gravity of Rosanette's story banished all thought of flight, even flights of fancy and flights of fancy language. It felt futile to Lucy to offer sympathy, to suggest somehow that others knew what she, Rosanette, must be going through. They didn't know. How could they? The low, white buildings of Ko Banteay harbor slid past the point of the bow as the ferry slowly turned toward the pier. Lucy registered a wildly inappropriate surge of envy. I will never know her loss, she thought. Never know what it's like to have a child in the first place.

Rosanette paused to blow her nose on a tissue, the last tissue in the small pack Lucy had given her fifteen minutes earlier. Rosanette was halfway through the third retelling of her calamity, stuck on the part about how insane she'd become over this man.

"Young man?" Lucy prompted, for that's how she pictured it the first two times. Rosanette squinted at the approaching shore.

"He has about him—the feeling—of young. And I want this feeling. I was so—" And here she lowered her eyes, shaking her head. And this also fed Lucy's envy, which in turn set off in her mind a shrill sort of debate about whether or not such feelings were shameful.

"He must have been something," Lucy said, for she could not imagine leaving her own child, her only child, alone in a small hut by the sea, more than a hundred miles from the nearest hospital in this fragile approximation of a country. There were worlds of experience she would never know, no matter how far and freely she roamed. She put an arm around Rosanette and lightly rubbed the woman's tan, rounded shoulder. Rosanette resumed her weeping. With her free hand Lucy pulled another packet of tissues from her pocket and gave it to Rosanette.

As the ferry aligned itself with the pier, Lucy sensed a range of moods and emotions presenting themselves to her as a sort of color wheel. And she selected from this rotating kaleidoscope a simple faded blue, a quiet sadness that she couldn't help but compare to the thrill, the exalted naughtiness she'd experienced when she'd embarked from this same pier almost a month earlier. How trivial and pointless her own travails seemed when set next to Rosanette's catastrophe, how pallid her own passions. What was worse, seeping into her consciousness were growing doubts about life with Conrad being all that bad. He was at least predictable, a known quantity.

Rosanette gripped Lucy's arm as the side of the boat bumped up against the row of tires lashed to the pier.

"I don't know what I do if he—this man—is not there. And if he is there, it's bad also."

"You hate him?"

"Yes. Now I hate him. He has not done anything, yet—I can't explain it."

"Don't try," Lucy said and then stopped herself from saying "I know just what you mean."

A group of young German women were just ahead of them as they disembarked. A resurgent envy overtook Lucy once more as she watched the girls swing their packs up off the pier and onto their backs. Their gear looked new; the girls seemed emboldened by the primary colors of their backpacks. As they set off on their long, sturdy German legs, their packs swayed slightly, as if animated with happy anticipation.

"If he's not waiting for you down there," Lucy said to Rosanette as they hurried after the Germans, "maybe we should get something to eat and then, you know, plan our next move."

Rosanette nodded, eyes pointed somewhere in the vicinity of

her feet. Lucy wondered if she had spoken too quickly for Rosanette to follow.

"Or I find Jean first." Rosanette turned her puffy eyes toward Lucy. Lucy averted her gaze and looked ahead toward the foot of the pier where touts gathered to greet the arriving tourists.

"Certainly," she said to Rosanette. "Whatever you think best. I want you to know that I'll be with you until—"

"Over here!" a voice called to her. Rosanette grabbed Lucy's arm and pointed at a tall figure waving at them from the foot of the pier. An expression of surprise failed to fully take shape in Lucy's mouth. For coming toward her in sagging nylon khaki shorts and a formerly white rayon-polyester short sleeve shirt she had once purchased on sale at Stonestown, was a disheveled, highly attenuated version of her husband, badly in need of a shave. He did not embrace her, or even greet her.

"My God" was all Lucy could think to say. Relief, joy, anger—in vain she sought a label for the convulsive thrills passing through her. Conrad nodded to Rosanette, and then, like an apparition who lacked authorization to speak, pointed at a nearby cluster of tables and broad umbrellas that marked an outdoor café.

"There," Conrad said eventually.

By this time they were following him onto the café patio. That is, Rosanette was following him and Lucy was following Rosanette, and the portion of Lucy's brain that captioned the images coming in from the eyes had temporarily shut down.

"Durians," it finally registered. "Dogs."

Conrad shouted at the skinny black dog sniffing about the cardboard box, clapping his hands to frighten it away. Lucy felt like the subject of a stage hypnotist, awakening from a trance.

"My God, Conrad," she said, looking from him to Rosanette and back again. "I didn't know it was *you*."

Part Seven

Cremation

38

. . . and interestingly, reports from twelfth-century Chinese travelers suggest the king's hold on power was always tenuous at best: "In the Palace there is a tower of gold where the king retires every night. There the Naga, the seven-headed serpent that rules the soil, appears in the shape of a woman. During the first watch, the king couples with her. At the second watch, he leaves the tower and then he may sleep with his wives and concubines. The king must perform this duty every night or risk great misfortune. And if it happens that the spirit of the Naga does not appear, the king's servants immediately begin preparing his funeral pyre."
—*Coswell's Guide to Tambralinga* (1997 ed.)

There is a moment in the Nagaseri airport during which Conrad believes his old life might yet be resurrected. He and Lucy peer through the window of the transit lounge, a small waiting room in the single terminal that constitutes the Nagaseri airport, watching gray clouds mass in the eastern sky. The clouds seem strangely amorphous, lacking the sculpted profiles of rain-laden thunderheads. A thin white haze fills the rest of the sky. The dark clouds approach with the urgency of a cyclone, descending like a gray curtain over the sea, reducing it by degrees to a glittering blue stripe just off the end of the runway.

"I hope the flight isn't delayed." Conrad glances at the wrist where his watch formerly resided (he somehow mislaid it on the ferryboat). Lucy nods and then gives his hand a squeeze.

"We'll get home okay."

Her reassurances are a tacit acknowledgment of the fact that Conrad dislikes flying, and that to dislike flying is neither unusual nor necessarily unwise. Conrad is surprised. It's the first time since their reunion that Lucy has deigned to touch him, and he has expected all along that when she chose to break the ice, she would do so with a clout. *There!* she might have said. *That's for your little Belgian!* More than once Lucy has alluded to Conrad and Rosanette's extended affair, for this is apparently the way Rosanette's broken and tear-choked English had reconstructed their relationship. Conrad recognizes the futility of contesting the official version of events at this particular moment, and lets pass without comment the naïve insinuation that his whole purpose in traveling to Ko Neak Pean had been to accomplish just the sort of sexual adventure Rosanette has described. Certainly at the beginning, Conrad reminds himself, there was little thought of outright adventure; he wanted only to make a purchase. But now the mere thought of his embarkation—the promise of the distant island, the memory of that vertiginous, anticipatory surge in his belly— releases a tremor of shame that ripples down the length of his body. Mysteriously, Lucy shows little sign of being especially angered by the whole business. Cool and distant, yes, and sometimes a little astonished, but not angry.

About her own trip Lucy has said very little, beyond her meeting another American woman and ultimately seeing almost everything she'd set out to see, everything on her list. And so the last two nights, one at Dak's Bungalows and one in the Hotel Nagaseri, where none of the available rooms had a working fan, have passed in sticky silence, Conrad finding himself in yet another sort of limbo, waiting quietly for Lucy to start talking about the separation of property and who will sleep where when they get back home. But so far she has said nothing.

The young woman in the airline office agreed to change their reservations so that they might fly home a few days early, so that they might board the flight to Seoul this very afternoon, and from there take the early morning flight to Los Angeles, and then on to San Francisco. It seems imperative to rush off, to strap themselves into the great apparatus of international travel, to climb into the taxis, push on through the terminals, passport control, customs, and then onto the aircraft, to place themselves behind the folding tray tables and the tiny video screens, to call the flight attendant for an extra glass of wine, to squeeze into the bathroom lines, to check and recheck their progress on the world map in the back of the in-flight magazine. Conrad tells himself the momentum will restore their equilibrium. But as he considers his wife's sphinxlike demeanor, "their" equilibrium no longer looks like an issue. He cannot remember seeing Lucy looking so calm, as if relieved of a great burden—of the necessity perhaps of having to make a particularly troubling decision.

So the squeeze of the hand might simply mean goodbye? Or, worse, the commencement of hostilities? The image of Lucy disappearing behind a phalanx of lawyers, of becoming not just an enemy but an utter stranger, briefly torments Conrad.

"If you want a divorce," he says, "let's at least not go to war over it, okay?" Lucy looks at him with mild shock, for this utterance has arrived without a hint of warning. As her eyes lock onto his face, Conrad finds, amazingly, that he need not look away. Lucy appears to consider the request.

"Agreed," she says finally, and the evenness of her tone bestows a moment's peace during which Conrad finds himself entertaining impossible visions of a renewed life on Saturn Street. But why impossible? Talks have commenced. A preliminary agreement will surely be hammered out in a matter of days.

"Agreed," Lucy says, focusing on a spot between Conrad's eyebrows, for she can't bear to meet his gaze just yet. The contraction in her middle that might be longing or anticipation, or simple nausea, slowly uncoils itself. She feels lighter; her head and shoulders seem poised to lift off, to break away from the rest of her body.

"I need to use the ladies'," she says, wanting very much to be alone.

In front of the washroom mirror she pretends to apply makeup. The small voice that reflexively inventories flaws of face and hair is conspicuously silent. For the moment she no longer wishes for larger eyes and irises of a definite color, or a face that is perfectly oval and devoid of all hints of rectangularity, or hair that is naturally red. Her face is simply a face, an arrangement of planes and curving surfaces, of shadow and light.

She sees again the face of Rosanette's husband, Jean, in the moment just before Rosanette gives him the news about Philippe. The reddish light of the setting sun is doing odd things to his hair, burnishing the crests of its waves, tinting the shadows of the troughs with a sort of green. His face is disarmingly boyish and open. There is just the right amount of space between the eyes, and a pleasingly chiseled quality about the nose and lips.

The greeting is still on those lips when the first signs of alarm register in his eyes. As Rosanette's message sinks in, a predictable succession of expressions sweep across his face: shock, disbelief, rage, grief, numbness. It is like a waterfall of masks. Lucy knows she should turn away, let the couple be alone with each other. But she finds she cannot look away.

Lucy holds the mascara wand in front of her for a moment and studies the tips of its tiny bristles. Again the sequence of grimaces passes over the man's face, and Lucy finds herself restored to the sequence of her own life. I'm in the airport, she reminds herself. My trip is over.

"Over," she whispers, pursing her lips at the mirror.

She'd ridden halfway across the island with Rosanette in a sort of taxi, arriving just before sunset, at the dive resort where Jean was staying. The director of the resort, a Dutchman who jumped from English to French to Yawi with astonishing ease, assured Lucy that he would have no trouble getting a boat to take Rosanette and her husband back to Nagaseri, that very night if necessary. The taxi driver was sent back to Banteay Harbor to collect the body, as well as Conrad, who'd been left behind to continue his vigil.

Poor Conrad, Lucy thinks, slipping the mascara back into her purse. Sitting all day with that body, and then into the night. Strange how good he'd looked climbing out of that taxi, his face

all craggy and sunburned, as if he were just back from the ends of the earth. At that moment she'd caught a glimmer of what Rosanette had been talking about—perhaps more than a glimmer. But it could barely penetrate the seething overcast that had descended upon her at the ferry dock, the confused outrage at finding that her husband was not the fixed star she'd always believed him to be. Was it sexual jealousy? Yes, partly, if she had to be honest. There seemed little point in maintaining a deception at this stage. And as long as she was being honest, she had to admit there was no justification for getting angry—Conrad having done nothing that she hadn't done herself. But it seemed cruelly unjust that he should give himself to another woman with such ferocity and depths of tenderness, qualities that she, his wife of fifteen years, never knew he possessed. How could she not feel cheated?

She applies lipstick to her upper lip, then gently rolls her lips together. Conrad had been the first to leave the island, she reminds herself. The first to effectively declare a separation. She bares her teeth at the glass, wipes a bit of lipstick from an incisor. But now that the D-word has finally been uttered, a new feeling moves inside of Lucy, a sad camaraderie with this new Conrad, a fellow refugee from a suffocating marriage.

Over his shoulder Conrad finally glimpses Lucy returning, her willowy form moving unhurriedly against a stream of anxious travelers, her limbs communicating a sensuality that he's never noticed before. He turns toward the large window and tries to summon a look of intense concentration as she approaches. A small jet taxies across the runway and positions itself for takeoff. The clouds descend upon the far end of the runway, obliterating the ocean and the silhouettes of distant palm trees.

"Uh-oh!" a passenger standing behind Conrad says. "Looks like this could be the last flight of the day." Conrad turns to see who has spoken, grateful for something else to look at. The speaker turns out to be another American, a younger man who

still looks to be in his thirties. The auburn hair cresting his forehead has a familiar swoop about it; the red goatee also looks
familiar.

"Is this Conrad Shermer?" the man says, removing his
sunglasses.

"Breen. Larry Breen. What are you doing here?"

"I might ask you the same."

"I'm on sabbatical."

"Vacationing *here*? You're kidding. The place is a powder
keg."

Conrad resists the temptation to declare it all his wife's doing,
and instead pretends to laugh off the suggestion of danger.

"Lucy, this is Larry Breen. Larry worked as a sales consultant
at Dogwood Systems back when I was product manager for
giantSTEP. giantSTEP was that e-commerce hub solution, remember?"

"Vaguely."

"Wow, even I can't remember that one," Breen says to Lucy. "I
do remember Conrad being the point man for every sales consultant in the firm, though. The guy that really had a handle on the
business side of the technology."

"That's still the case," Conrad assures him.

"You came through the re-org all right, then?"

"Re-org?"

"They announced it almost two weeks ago. Didn't you hear?
It was all over the *Mercury*. Oh, but you've been—"

"I've been out of touch. This is—what? Our fifth week here."

Breen opens his mouth in a look of mock astonishment.

"Five weeks in Tambralinga? Conrad Shermer? Are we talking
about the same guy here? This is incredible! But, say, I don't
mean to be the bearer of bad tidings. I'm sure Chang or Murrow
would have told you before you left if you were going to be af-
fected by it."

"Right, right," Conrad says. "Actually both Chang and Murrow left in December. But enough about me . . ." He glances back
at the runway, the far end of which is disappearing into the gray

curtain. The small jet still waits to take off. What did Breen just say about it being the last flight of the day?

"I've been working with X-Saulte Corp for the past two years," Breen explains to Lucy. "And when they told me we had a client who was having trouble in Tambralinga, I'm, like, 'Excuse me? Where?' And it turns out to be the government, the so-called Ministry of Justice. Huge database customer. Who knew?"

"So what was the problem?" Conrad turns away from the window with a growing sense of apprehension.

"Oh, the apps they built with our DBMS kept crashing, they were losing all kinds of data. And this weenie in tech support gets the idea that we should sell them on a failover site in Mountain View—you know, have a duplicate database in California running in synch with the one out here, so that all the lost data can get recovered. Also buys some insurance against arson, truck bombs, all the usual terrorist stuff."

He looks at Conrad knowingly and Conrad recognizes in this a call for commiserating laughter. But the grim inevitability of their flight being delayed proves too distracting and Conrad can only stare.

"But that won't stop the system from crashing," Breen continues. "The problem is that they didn't purchase the GUI module for some reason."

"God, no."

"Yes. So the DB manager's basically flying blind. I told them that we'll be glad to sell them all the HA functionality they want, but if the guy at the controls can't see where he's going—right?"

"Absolutely."

A pause follows, during which Conrad feels himself being sized up.

"Oh, hey, sorry about the geekspeak," Breen says, turning toward Lucy. "Five minutes of that will make your ears numb, eh?"

"Do you have a light?" Lucy asks him.

"Sure," Breen says, fishing a book of matches from his pocket.

"Anyway," Breen says turning back toward Conrad, "they bought the whole package: GUI, failover functionality, training.

Created a big row on the budget committee, but, hey, you got to break a lot of eggs for an omelette this big."

"Omelette," Lucy says. "There's a word I know."

Conrad watches her pull a cigarette from her pack and then, against his better judgment, asks her for one. Their eyes meet for a moment as she hands him the pack.

"Smoking in the airport," Breen says, lighting the match for both cigarettes. "What a country!"

Outside, the sky is turning completely gray. Half of the runway has now disappeared. The small jet backs out of its takeoff position and taxies back the way it came.

"Shoot. That's it, I'll bet," Breen says. "I was hoping to get out of here tonight."

"They're not going to cancel the flight over this," Lucy protests. "There's no rain, no lightning, hardly any wind. I wouldn't even call it a storm."

"I wouldn't, either," Breen says. He smiles.

"I'm sorry, I've forgotten your name."

"Lucy."

"Lucy, yes. Beautiful name. It's not a storm, Lucy. It's smoke."

By the time they reclaim their luggage and find a taxi back into the city, the gray cloud has begun raining white ash over the entire airport. Half of the country is on fire, Breen reports as the taxi driver experiments with his windshield wipers. The monsoon forests of the west provinces are burning; the wet season was not wet enough, and now the dry season is really dry. Fires set to clear jungle for new plantations have been burning out of control for days. The smoke, coaxed by prevailing winds, is snaking its way down from the mountains and coiling itself around the capital. And it may get worse. Yesterday in Lingga Baharu it was pitch black in the middle of the day. You literally could not see your hand in front of your face.

"But if I'm going to be stuck here, you know what?" Breen smiles at Conrad and Lucy from the front passenger seat. "I'm going to run up the biggest damn tab I can. This hotel has an incredible restaurant and I want you both to be my guests for dinner."

Lucy's lips purse in a way that tells Conrad she is intrigued. Her chin angles slightly, as she turns her head toward the window, where an old man on a bicycle looms up out of the smoke and then disappears. The driver leans on his horn.

"Agreed," Conrad says.

The Hotel Soma Vamsa was not in their original budget, but budget hardly seems to matter now. A sign in English advising tourists that 1997 is Visit Tambralinga Year stands on an easel just inside the glass doors. Beyond, something like an acre of carpeting stretches from the reception desk over to the hotel bar entrance. Somewhere in the middle a gaunt, elderly man sits at a large piano making an odd sort of music that Conrad at first takes to be Bartok, and then some dreadful sort of avant-garde jazz, but finally decides is neither. The vivid whorls and arabesques in the carpet's pattern somehow evoke both the stylized serpents of the Buddhist temple and Arabic calligraphy, at least according to Lucy. And who is to say differently? She's smiling, really smiling, for the first time in days. She tells Breen that she loves the way the man at the piano seems to play only with two fingers, as if striking the keys with little hammers. And Breen, who's been staying at this same hotel for over a week, explains that the pianist has a grant from the Ministry of Tourism to showcase classical Tambralingan music, music originally composed for gamelan orchestras.

"That's why he sounds as if he's playing with hammers. And why sometimes it sounds like he's only using the black keys."

"Debussy's music was influenced by gamelan, wasn't it?" Lucy asks.

"Was it? How wild. You know, this guy plays a lot of Debussy."

They exchange a smile.

The strap on Lucy's sandal chooses that moment to break, but Breen is right there, catching her by the elbow as she stumbles.

When they reach the reception desk, Breen steps aside, allowing Conrad and Lucy to register first. It bothers Conrad that Breen is within earshot when Lucy asks for two separate rooms.

"Adjoining?" the clerk asks, his accent truncating the word so that at first it sounds like "A-johnny." Conrad, thinking the term refers to bathrooms, begins to answer that a shared bath might work. Lucy cuts him off just as he realizes his mistake.

"Adjoining if possible," she says. In a somewhat louder voice, Lucy explains that the last few nights her insomnia has kept them both awake and that her husband badly needs his sleep. The clerk produces the usual smile. He has two rooms on the same floor, but that is as close as he can get them.

The TV in Conrad's room shows clips of soldiers on maneuvers with tanks and jeeps. Superimposed over these are alternating images of mosque and *wat*, the reclining Buddha, the Muslim prayer rug. A Paktai soldier shares his binoculars with a Yawi soldier in a close-up that has the two gazing uneasily over the sandbagged rim of a foxhole, presumably monitoring the off-screen advances of the enemies of the nation. On the sound track, a brass band staggers through what must be the national anthem, slurring the notes as if the musicians are all drunk, or just exhausted. But the effect must be deliberate, Conrad thinks before changing the channel, an attempt to include quarter notes and semitones, articulations outside the usual language of Western music. He despairs of ever understanding the point of it all. He settles into the chair next to the TV. Some sort of roundtable talk show is in progress. All of the panel members wear Muslim caps and seem to be speaking Yawi. Conrad closes his eyes to confront a diaphanous recollection of Eva by the waterfall, a memory he only dares view from oblique angles. Eva's face no longer resembles that of the young Liv Ullmann. Traces of another face now infect Eva's image, the face illuminated in the match flame on the night ferry. Eva had no stud in her left nostril, no overly pronounced groove above her upper lip, no hint of the equine in the bone structure of her face. In vain Conrad tries to restore the original Eva, to separate her from the Australian girl, whose name Conrad cannot remember. There is no way to separate the two, nor unlink either from the reptilian mouth of the dead child, that now lurches at Conrad with teeth bared after every bump in the road.

Conrad wakes up on the bed sometime later. (Apparently Lucy was right; he did need rest.) The TV percolates with the high-volume chatter of a Bangkok game show, and Conrad recalls that he is supposed to meet Lucy and Breen downstairs for drinks and dinner. The digital clock on the nightstand tells him that he is almost thirty minutes late, and this sends him rushing out into the hallway, groggy and alarmed. He changes directions twice before locating the elevator.

Before he is halfway across the lobby, he sees them, his former colleague, his soon-to-be ex-wife, sitting at the hotel bar. The bar is packed, the lobby buzzing. This is where people go when the airport is closed. Through the large plate-glass window Conrad sees that the streetlights have come on; flurries of ash twirl in the headlight beams of passing cars. Conrad is not sure if the sun has actually set or not.

Breen drums his index fingers on the bar as he talks. Then he draws an invisible circle on his glass and stabs its center repeatedly with his index finger. Lucy accepts a fresh drink from the bartender, something tall and canopied with a preposterous pink umbrella. She turns back toward Breen, draping one arm loosely along the end of the bar. She touches her hair with a gesture that betrays her self-consciousness. Conrad sees Breen as a woman might, as a decent prospect, a man not yet forty, lean, hair still intact, face as yet uncompromised by gravity. He is a cyclist, if Conrad remembers correctly, and sometimes rides fifty or sixty miles at a stretch. He's been married once, back when he still raced stock cars. But now he works with networks and databases, and he knows how to talk to people.

Conrad takes a seat in the cube-shaped armchair next to the

piano. The chairs near the piano, where the pianist sways back and forth as he plays, are mostly empty, the other guests preferring to congregate near the windows. On the street outside, sirens wail with the seesaw rhythm Conrad thinks of as European. Police cars roll by; a truck full of soldiers follows close behind.

Back in the bar it looks as though Lucy and Breen have linked up, that invisible filaments connect their bodies at wrist, shoulder, knee, and ankle. Breen laughs at something Lucy says, leans back in his chair, shaking his head. Lucy leans forward boldly, hands in front of her, and for one very cold moment Conrad feels certain that she will put her hand on the man's thigh.

He closes his eyes. *Plink-plink-plink*. The pianist hammers the keys with nervous insistence. His music permits no escape from the moment, lacks the forward tilt of a march or a sonata. It is music that features chords of a sort and a certain momentum; but there is nothing like a chord progression, or any kind of progression at all—just an interlocking pattern of arabesques and flourishes that repeat again and again, as if meant to go on forever.

ACKNOWLEDGMENTS

Tambralinga is a wholly fictitious country that should not be confused with any existent nation or province, but which does feature some of the social and economic problems—as well as the great natural beauty—abundant in many parts of Southeast Asia. In constructing the particulars of Tambralingan cultural life, I am much indebted to the rich ethnographic literature on Southeast Asia, especially Clifford Geertz's *The Religion of Java*, Louis Golomb's *An Anthropology of Curing in Multiethnic Thailand*, Carol Laderman's *Taming the Wind of Desire*, Mohammed Taib Osman's *Malay Folk Beliefs*, S. J. Tambiah's *The Buddhist Saints of the Forest and the Cult of Amulets*, and Stewart Wavell's *The Naga King's Daughter*.

Toni Graham's critical insights and moral support proved invaluable to the completion of this book. I am also indebted to Maxine Chernoff for her close reading of the manuscript and cogent editing suggestions. I would also like to offer special thanks to my agent, Caron Knauer, and to my editor, Rebecca Saletan.